Lonely Yurt

Smagul Yelubay

The Lonely Yurt • Smagul Yelubay

The book "Lonely Yurt", written by noted Kazakh writer Smagul Yelubay, is the fifth book of the series of books of classic Kazakh writers published in the English language, which the Kazakh PEN-club has decided to publish in the USA. The book collection "We Are Kazakhs" is being published under the supervision of the President of Kazakh PEN-club,

MR. BIGELDY GABDULLIN

Lonely Yurt

Smagul Yelubay

Translated from Russian by

Catherine Fitzpatrick

KAZAKH PEN-CLUB
КАЗАК ПЕН-КЛУБЫ

"We are Kazakhs"

Classic Books of Kazakh writers in English

© 2016, Metropolitan Classics

135 Ocean Pkwy, Suite 1U

Brooklyn, New York 11612

ISBN: 978–157480–007–4

Printed in the United States of America

The Lonely Yurt • Smagul Yelubay

ACKNOWLEDGEMENTS

The Publishers want to thank the Kazakh PEN-club for their permanent support and attention in this project. Initially, it was but an ambitious idea of the Kazakh PEN-club President Mr. Gabdullin – to create an environment in which the best works of Kazakh classic writers could be placed upon the global literary stage, by way of their translation into English. Step by step, due to tireless efforts of Mr. Gabdullin, the project received the financial and logistical support from influential Kazakh state organizations and private companies. The translation of this book became possible due to generous support of the Akimat (Government) of Almaty region of Kazakhstan and The Trust for Support of Cultural Projects Samruk Kazyna.

The Lonely Yurt • Smagul Yelubay

AT THE WELL

1

The deserted steppe grew hushed. The evening twilight thickened and merged with the flood of darkness. Here and there, sparse bushes turned black, but the desert expanse wrapped the cover of night tighter, plunging into a quiet sleep...

But now the evening drowse, already anticipating the hush of the night, was disrupted by the tinkle of little bells. At first their silvery voice carried from somewhere far away, out of the darkness, then fell silent, then arose again, clearly approaching...

From the thickness of the twilight finally the enormous black shadows appeared. It was a caravan, with the *atans*[1] and *nars*.[2] The people accompanying the camels were silent, and the copper bells on the animals' necks rocked rhythmically to the beat of the camels' hooves, tinkling out a simple melody, like an unpretentious *kyuy*[3] of the steppe. It did not disturb the peace spread over the twilight air, and one sensed an ineffable sympathy with it...

The caravan left the path, turning on a flat spot among the sand dunes. The camels knelt down, one after another, and the bags and *khorzhuns*[4] were removed from them.

Finally, the exhausted and weakened travelers – there were seven of them – flung themselves down to sleep just as they were, still dressed, laying their *khorzhuns* under their heads. Broken by the long road, many began to snore.

Azbergen lay without blinking an eye. He was Pakhraddin's youngest brother, the one who was laying nearby, wrapped up in a

---

[1] An *atan* is a gelded camel.
[2] A *nar* is a large one-humped camel.
[3] A *kyuy* is a Kazakh song.
[4] A *khordzhun-vyuk* is a bag made of fabric or skin for traveling.

chapan[5] from head to toe. Pakhraddin was the son of the *baybishe*[6], his father's first wife, and he, Azbergen, had been born of the *tokal*, or second, youngest wife. Azbergen could not fall asleep; he was seriously worried about the conversations he had head yesterday at the bazaar, that supposedly the sun was setting for the *bays*...[7] Sleep would not come...Azbergen raised his head and realized that Pakhraddin was no longer nearby. His brother was standing not far away, off to the side, under the starry sky, which is back to him, his *chapan* flung over his shoulders. Only his silhouette showed dimly black against the background of the sand dunes.

Azbergen had been looking for an excuse for a conversation with his brother alone, and finally the opportunity presented itself. He got up and went to his brother. He coughed and spit. Pakhraddin, looking askance at him, stepped aside slightly. But he did not say a word in anticipation. Azbergen, as ill luck would have it, also kept a gloomy silence for some time. Knitting his brows, he gazed out into the night steppe. He knew that if he opened his mouth, the anger that was suffocating him now would burst out.

Finally, no longer able to hold back, he let out a muffled growl:

"It's you...you're the one to blame! We should have moved on from here long ago! We should have left! And now..."

Azbergen was not a master of words; he was more a man of action. He immediately grew flustered, and choked in mid-sentence. He fell silent. Pakhraddin did not utter a word. He stamped his feet in place and with the same mournful gaze headed toward the bales, growing dark at the camp. He lay down, and covered his head with his *chapan*.

The moon lit the eastern edge of the sky purple. A comet streaked rapidly across the western dome of the sky. The crickets chirped incessantly in the wormwood trees.

---

[5] A *chapan* is a cloak.

[6] The *baybishe* is the senior wife.

[7] The *bays* were wealthy owners of herds.

Stretched out flat on his back on the sand, Azbergen gave himself up to thoughts as endless as the night sky above him. From the leeward side, the pungent scent of sweat wafted from the *atan* with the low-hanging lips, and the dromedaries, tied to one another, chewed their cuds with relish. Pakhraddin lay the same way, his head covered. No, he didn't understand his brother. A *biy*[8] nonetheless, imagine, everyone was in awe of him...To be sure, his brother did not have herds and flocks of thousands like Mazhan had – there he was, over there, asleep – but not without herds, after all! He had sufficient means. And if someone mentioned the Soviet government, he would freeze with a submissive look. Perhaps he thought the Soviet government would do him some good? Damned if he, Azbergen, could understand anything! But how to reconcile himself to the fact that his elder brother ingratiated himself and groveled before the aul[9] boot of Sharip, who obtained the elder's seal last year?

...

And to recoup himself on Shege and that puppy Sharip, who also had begun to show his teeth...Oh, would he like to lash leather whips on his back! Azbergen grew furious just thinking about it. And how could you not grow furious? The bastard didn't understand who and what he was, and was still brazenly expectant of Khansulu! This aul punk had gotten out of hand!

Khansulu was Azbergen's niece. Pakhraddin's only daughter. She was as slender and lithe as a reed. She was a beauty, and a mischievous child. Azbergen would rather die than allow that monster Shege to come near her!

...And once again the caravan with the swaying, stepping dromedaries set off on its way, bells tinkling. Somewhere ahead was the aul, people – families, wives, children, whom the caravaners had not seen for nearly a month...

2

---

[8]A *biy* is an arbitration judge.
[9] An *aul* is a Central Asia village.

Here was the autumn nomad camp. The earth here was barren and ugly. The dusty grass shriveled. The yellow bare spot by the well, where there wasn't a single blade of grass, even a trampled one, looked depressing.

Shege came trotting up bareback to the well on a shabby chestnut horse. There was a racket everywhere – the sheep were bleating, the dogs were barking and the camels were groaning – it was the usual scene in the life of the aul. It was the busy evening time when the yards and outskirts of the aul were full of people and animals. But Shege didn't heed the noise and din, he was lost in his own thoughts. And the more he thought, the heavier his heart grew. He was strange. He had fallen to thinking about Khansulu, without appreciating his opportunities. Day and night he dreamed of her. But was Khansulu enough for all the eager guys? There were a lot of girls in the aul. Why shouldn't Shege look over another? Why Khansulu? Why yearn for the moon in the sky which you couldn't reach, anyway? He didn't know.

"Pull!"
"Back! Baaaaack!"

The voices of people turning the hoist above the well distracted him from his thoughts. Shege raised his head. The sun was already hanging over the horizon.

Approaching the well, Shege noticed his friend Jdakhay in the crowd, watering his camel, and grinned. He and Jdakhay were peers; only with him could he share his most sacred thoughts. They both had the same sorrow. Like Shege, Jdakhay was in love – with Balkiya the young *tokal* of the *bay* Mazhan. No sooner did the friends get together than each of them struck up the same song – about Balkiya and Khansulu.

Seeing Shege, Jdakhay broke into a white-toothed grin. The young man was husky in appearance, solid, with smallpox scars on his face.

"Puullll!" Bulysh, a strong, tall, swarthy fellow cried, grabbing the pail. An enormous black *nar*, harnessed to the *shygyr*[10] was opening its jaws; it was about to step back but once again tipped forward with its whole mass, dragging the rawhide lasso tied to the saddle on its back. A little boy holding the halter threw himself cross-wise.

...

Jdakhay poked Shege in the back.

"Hey, you poor devil, look here! Not over there, back here!"

Shege turned around to where Jdakhay was pointing, to see Khansulu, skirting the well, gracefully trotting on her horse, Karaker. She was wearing a round beaver cap, and the owl down on its crown waved in the breeze. Her red silk camisole was held snugly to her slender waist with a fine clasp; her silver saddle glistened with all the colors of the rainbow in the rays of the setting sun; the three-year-old Karaker fairly danced, easily kicking out his slender legs as if he sensed what a fine beauty he had as a mistress. Shege hungrily drank in the girl's black eyes like currants, her long eyelashes bending upward, her pouty, slightly protruding upper lip. He sighed sorrowfully.

"Don't be sad!" Jdakhay said, clapping him on his shoulder. Let her put on airs! But remember my words – she will be really and truly yours, falcon!

"Jdeke-e[11]...Now look...over here!

As soon as Jdakhay saw Balkiya walking along the path – the dust under her feet twinkled silver in the sunset's rays – he was transformed, poor fellow, before your eyes. The stiff hair on his head stood up even more, it seems. He grew flustered, and didn't know where to put his hands. Let Shege laugh! Jdakhay turned red, a bead of sweat appeared on the tip of his nose.

"You idiot," he said. "Don't blab to anybody, but I'll show you something neat today..." He switched to a whisper, likely in order

---

[10] A *shygyr* is a special device for getting water, a hoist.
[11] A diminutive form of Jdakhay.

to lend his words significance, and at the same time distract his friend's attention.

"What is it...you have there?"

Jdakhay placed a finger to his lips as if to say "hush," and glanced towards Bulysh, who had once again seized the pail. It suddenly dawned on Shege that Jdakhay's secret was connected to Bulysh.

3

After dinner, people in the aul went to bed. It was as dark as pitch. The new moon had not yet risen. Shege, intrigued by Jdakhay's hint, hid himself at the dusty camel spot in Mazhan's aul. Rising up in the darkness like boulders, the camels lay in a circle. The friends settled down on the leeward side of a great old haystack, watching Balkiya's *otau*[12] attentively. It was facing them in the darkness ahead.

Balkiya bustled about her chores for a long while, appearing and disappearing, which they guessed from the tinkling of the *sholps*.[13] Finally, the light went out.

Jdakhay poked Shege in the back.

"Did you see? She went to bed. As if alone. Now you're going to really get an eyeful..."

A little time went by. There wasn't a soul or a sound near the *otau*. A quiet hush fell over the aul. Even the crazy dogs fell silent. Only from beyond the paddock, a commotion could be heard – the sheep were agitated after grazing, and were butting heads with a crack and bellow as was their habit. A goatsucker cried outside the aul as if he were lamenting. If only he wouldn't bring disaster. Nasty bird!

It would good if the friends got lucky. But Bulysh the hunter, who, according to Jdakhay, should have visited the home of the young *tokal,* did not appear.

---

[12] An *otau* is a home for young wives.
[13] The *sholps* are silver pendants.

"He won't delay, he will come. He will come before the moon comes out," Jdakhay promised in a whisper, thrusting up his neck to look between the humps of the nearest camel. The dromedaries loomed up like heavy clouds, chewing their cuds with relish. The sharp stench of the animals' saliva tickled their noses.

"You should tell me in the meantime what you saw. What's the point of sitting here for nothing?" Shege asked.

Jdakhay turned toward him, ready to share his secret.

"I wanted you to see for yourself...with your own eyes...but you see, the hunter is making a fool of us, he isn't coming."

He shrugged his shoulders sadly. "Her old man," said Jdakhay, nodding toward the yurt. "As soon as he leaves for the city with a caravan, I go directly to her. Every evening, I am at her doorway."

"What are you saying?"

"Her husband is an old wreck. But she's nice and young, in the pink of health! When do you think she's going to have fun if not now?"

"Just as the sun goes down, I come straight here, stealing my way... But here's the thing. I get to the door and it's as if I'm deprived of sense, I stand like a pillar. The door might as well be at the end of the earth; I can't reach it. My hands are shaking, I can't breathe, I hear ringing in my ears, and my heart is knocking. So yesterday, there I was, standing at her door like a statue, when all of a sudden I hear someone coming in the dark! It was Bulysh! Frightened, I ran home. I couldn't breathe, my teeth were clenched. When I collected myself, I heard voices. Quiet sort of voices.

"Come here, come here." It was Balkiya's voice. "Watch out, the *kumgan*[14] is there on the floor, don't trip."

---

[14] A *kumgan* is a pitcher with a narrow mouth and spout for washing.

The Lonely Yurt • Smagul Yelubay

And he said:

"Are you alone?"

"Why wouldn't I be," she said. "If I weren't alone, and was with my old crank, then would I be waiting for you?"

And he said:

"Wait, I wonder if the child is nearby?"

"Don't be afraid," Balkiya said. "What a thing to be afraid of!"

And then I heard the bed creaking. I pressed my ear to the wall! She asked him in a whisper if he missed her, and her voice was devilishly sweet, like honey.

Then it grew hard to hear, they began whispering very softly. I tried pressing my ear to the wall different ways – nothing! Somehow, you see, they sensed I was eavesdropping. Balkiya suddenly yelled:

"Get out! Get out, you beast!"

"Well, I ran out of there as fast as my legs could carry me..."

"The moon is already setting," Jdakhay whispered after a remaining silent for a while.

"Now Bulysh will die – he won't come!"

"Well, the heck with it then, let's go home," Shege replied with regret.

"Why go home? Two *jigits*[15] like us.... You idiot, there's a woman over there...young...succulent...alone..." and Jdakhay's voice broke off hoarsely.

"Well, go on then. Maybe she's waiting...for you," Shege snorted.

"Well, what if I do? I'll go!" Jdakhay seemed to egg himself on.

"Go on! Go on, now!"

"Well, if something comes up, let me know!" And with these words, Jdakhay ran after the pack of camels and bending over, set off at

---

[15] A *jigit* is a daring young Kazakh horseman. The word is applied to any young man.

a jog. He looked around him as he ran. Shege waved to him surreptitiously. Jdakhay was careful, so that it seemed from the side he was catching flies. He reached the house. Before the very door, he froze.

Shege grew agitated, his heart burst from his chest as if it were hiding behind the door.

Finally, Jdakhay spoke up. He didn't have long to wait; the door opened. A silhouette disappeared in the black space.

"Wonders!" Shege uttered. He himself didn't know how he managed to lunge forward. Coming to his senses he realized he was racing toward a closed door. He had only one thing in mind: to be at the house, to be a witness to Jdakhay's achievement. But when he had almost reached his goal, he heard a thump, as if a stick was striking a goat skin, and next, the clanging of iron. Jdakhay suddenly burst out of the yurt, then rushed headlong in the other direction.

Shege also sprinted ahead – what was he to think? In the moonlight, both young men ran to the ravine. They kicked up such a racket that the camels were frightened and jumped up from their spots. The dogs broke into hysterical barking.

Running up alongside Jdakhay, Shege asked what happened, trying to catch his breath.

"She hit me, my fellow, run!"

Jdakhay sprinted off again, throwing his head back. Thus they ran to the ravine and slid down to the bottom.

"What happened?" Shege asked, puzzled.

"It was what it was…She did well, that's what happened," Jdakhay let out a nervous laugh, and pressed Shege's hand to his temple – his head had swollen.

"You win! Congratulations! Well, go on, tell me…"

"She opened the door. I went in," Jdakhay began, heaving a sign. "Balkiya was just in her night gown, oh, the scent of her….'What do you want?' she said, and her voice…well it wasn't like when she and Bulysh whispered. A completely different voice. I grew flustered and croaked out, 'Let's play, *jeneshe*,'[16] and I got down on my knees and hugged her legs – she will take pity on me, I thought.

But instead she said, "You little devil, I'll give you something to play with!" and imagine, she hit me with something…right on the crown of my head! It turned out to be a rolling pin. I saw stars. I headed toward the door. Then I tripped over a basin at the threshold, I don't know what it was, but I stepped on something. There was a clatter…And she hit me between the shoulder blades with that rolling pin! "Here's something to play with!" she said. I managed to hit my forehead too on the door lintel. So I really got it…"

Shege lay on the ground, his arms thrown back, his shoulders shaking with laughter.

4

The next morning, Shege awoke to the sounds of an argument. As always, his father and mother were quarreling over the morning tea. Not wishing to hear them, Shege wrapped his head in the warm blanket. The row didn't stop. On the contrary, it was growing worse.

"Gulzha-an!" his father suddenly shouted. "Go to Pakhraddin, bring a piece of sugar from them. Tell him when people get back from the bazaar, we'll return it for sure."

Gulzhan was the youngest of Shege's five sisters.

"She won't go!" his mother said decisively. "Little girl, eh, don't you dare go! Sewing boots became shameful to him, you see since you became an *aulnay*.[17] Well, I'm ashamed to go begging, the wife of an *aulnay*! She won't go."

---

[16] *Jeneshche* – the wife of an older relative.
[17] *Aulnay* – aul elder.

"Oh, you hard-headed one, it's not up to you to send the child." Familiar whining notes began to appear in his father's voice.

"She won't go!" his mother insisted. "Every day you whine and complain – the government is a poor peasant, the government is a poor peasant, but you yourself, as soon as it's dawn, run to the *bay*. Tell me, what's the point in you being the government?!"

Shege's mother was a broad-boned, swarthy woman with an even, calm temper. She would object in her firm, ringing voice, and her reasons would seem convincing.

Shege choked down a laugh. He could visualize his father's face clearly – swollen, red with anger and helplessness, his eyes bugged out, awkwardly twisting the tussock of hair at the crown of his head. Understandably, he couldn't find the right words to reply.

"You brainless idiot! What are you going on about? We're asking because we're poor. Who would have supported us if we weren't poor?"

"Supported…are you going on about the seal, again? You fuss about with it like with an unborn baby! What use is that seal for us? You amuse yourself that you became the leader of the aul. You abandoned your craft. You have a bunch of hungry children living off water alone, just thrilled to pieces that you have the seal! Well, chew on the seal instead of a lump of sugar!"

Shege snorted again under the blanket.

"Stop, you seed of a shameless clan! Don't you dare touch the seal!" he screamed.

The girls simultaneously broke into tears. Shege jumped out of bed. Just as he had supposed, his father was ominously lunging at his mother, the seal in his hand. Shege stood between them.

...

Shege went outside. A cold, piercing wind was blowing. It was the usual dank, autumn morning. The sky to the east was covered with dark grey clouds. The sun could not be seen behind them, although it had long since risen. Women hunched against the wind were driving the camels to pasture. Somebody was drawing water from the well, clanging the bucket. Along the ridge beyond the well, a lone horseman was riding along with a white hound – it was Bulysh heading off on a hunt. Recalling Jdakhay's story yesterday, Shege laughed heartily.

Bulysh was a famous hunter in the region. A *jigit* among *jigits*. He was already 30 years old. Who loved Balkiya as he did?! Moreover, Bulysh was a bachelor; his wife had died two years previously. His house was tucked away forlornly on the far edge of the aul. Bulysh lived there with his old mother.

Bulysh's dark horse and white hound disappeared from view when he crossed over the slope to the south. He was on his way to the sands of Sarybay.

Oh, why wasn't he a *jigit* like Bulysh? Then he would see how Khansulu would boast. Pulling a woolen vest tight over his chest, Shege sighed sadly. This ugly yurt was his dwelling. But in the center of the aul, amazing people with its magnificence was another yurt, a large one, white as the snow. It was Khansulu's yurt. Nearby, Karaker, her three-year old stallion was tied up. It was the purest of thoroughbreds. There wasn't another horse like it in the region. It was a famous Turkmen Akhal-teke breed, which Pakhraddin had driven from Beskala[18] especially for his daughter.

"They're coming! They're coming!" The cries rang out from the direction of the pasture. It turned out it was Kozbagar overstraining himself. The plump Kozbagar, stumping along clumsily, was ecstatically waving around his arms and running as fast as his legs could carry him back to the aul. "Who's coming?" Shege wondered and immediately saw a caravan rounding the northern slope of Karaul Hill. From afar, it seemed as if the steppe was crossed by a long wedge of flying geese. It was the caravan of city-goers who a month ago had headed off to the bazaar in Temir.

---

[18] *Beskala* is the old name for modern Karakalpakstan or Karakalpakia.

"Khansulu! Khansulu! Hey! Father is back from the bazaar! Faaather!"

The overstuffed Kozbagar yelled as if his own father was coming back from the market. Kozbagar was pasturing the cattle on Pakhraddin's land. Good Lord, he was only a shepherd yet they said he had eyes for Khansulu, too...

The whole aul heard Kozbagar and all spilled out of their yurts together. The kids whistled and hurried to meet the caravan. Khansulu also came out of her house. Her outfit accentuated her slender, fine figure: grey *sharovars*[19]; a red plush *kamsol* elegantly hugging her torso; high-heeled boots; atop her head, a fur cap with owl feathers on the crown; and a whip in her hand. She didn't even glance at the happily agitated Kozbagar, and went toward the horse.

Khansulu easily leapt on the stallion who had come to a halt, and was nervously shifting from hoof to another. She bent slightly toward his mane. Karaker's hoofs barely touched the ground – the horse flew. The chilly evening wind beat against her fine, girlish face with a wail, bringing tears to her beautiful slanted eyes. She drew in the nostrils of her small nose, pursed her lips, and sped ahead without a backward glance.

Very soon, Khansulu's steed left behind the whistling kids and intercepted the path of the tired caravan which stretched along the yellow mountain slope. Khansulu's gaze roamed through the crowd, searching among the tired, bearded travelers in dusty clothing, many with red, inflamed eyes, for the face of her father Pakhraddin, but she didn't find him. Her uncle Azbergen walked ahead of the caravan. With the build of a *bogatyr*, he had grown even more coarse; his meaty face had spread and grown round, and there was many-days' growth of gray stubble sprouting from his cheeks.

"Ah, Khansulu! Are you well?" he said, knitting his brows.

"Well. And where is *koke*[20]?" asked Khansulu.

---

[19] *Sharovars* are baggy pants or pantaloons.
[20] *Koke* is an affectionate name for a father.

The Lonely Yurt • Smagul Yelubay

Azbergen gazed red-eyed at the girl with some hostility, his face like a dark cloud threatening a storm.

"He just turned in toward Labak-*akhun.*"

The caravan passed by. Khansulu turned her impatiently prancing horse toward the sun. Karaker, like an arrow released from a bow, flew along the scorched, flat earth. She drifted up the gently rising slope, and saw two travelers ahead, one of them on a camel and the other on a horse. She recognized her father as the man on the raven stallion with a white spot on its forehead. The man next to him on a white camel in a white *chapan* and a white *chalma*[21] was Labak-*akhun*. The *ishan*[22] taught all the children of this district to read and write. Akhun was a learned man, a *jyrau*[23], who had read numerous books and knew about everything on earth.

Pakhraddin, a handsome man with beautiful eyes, prematurely gray, with sunken cheekbones, a large and broad-shouldered frame, slid from his horse and lovingly embraced and kissed his daughter who had hurried toward him, and then, minding the proprieties, had gradually approached her father with reverence.

Before Khansulu, Pakhraddin had had two sons, Ali and Kali. Both had died of smallpox. He loved his only daughter Khansulu, who had been born after them, no less than his sons.

"How are you here, Sulutay[24], are you alive and well?" he asked, worriedly, and his voice was shaking. His large, wide-open eyes glistened moistly.

Khansulu noticed that her father's large, aquiline nose was swollen and red. And he looked as if he had a cold.

"You're not sick, *koke*?" she asked, and her thin girlish brows shook like the wings of a swallow before flight.

---

[21] A *chalma* is a tunic.

[22] An *ishan* is a learned man.

[23] A *jyrau* is a bard or poet.

[24] Sulutay is a nickname for Khansulu.

"No, Sulutay," her father replied.

But it seemed to Khansulu that her father was hiding something from her.

After tying up the horses, they caught up soon with the lean *akhun*, white as the moon, who had managed on his light camel to get ahead. Without turning around, the old man began in his melodious voice.

"Well, my brother Pakhraddin! We spoke together in our day, you likely remember: the rich *bays* will be humiliated, the *batrak*[25] will be elevated; the bold who go up against them will be knocked under a horse's tail. Consider that the rulers have grabbed them by the throat for real. What you heard in Temir is only the beginning of the trouble. Everything is God's will, what is judged for us we will see in the future."

After a silence, the *akhun* continued:

"Everything in the wide world will reach completion from the day of the creation of the world to our days, it is a matter of God's hand, everything is under the power of God's will...

The two-humped white camel he was riding, its hanging fur swaying, moved forward in an even trot...

From her elders' conversation, Khansulu understand that her father was bringing bad news from the market. The authorities had once again started to persecute the *bays*. Akhun let drop another bit of news that intensified the doubts:

"Shoshu was taken in Jayyndi. God knows whose turn is next..."

5

---

[25] A *batrak* is a hired hand or servant.

The Lonely Yurt • Smagul Yelubay

There was a joyful enlivening of the aul as if a holiday. After they had sold their cattle at the market in Temir, the men had brought back textiles, clothing, sugar, and tea. How could people not rejoice?

People gathered at Pakhraddin's open guest yurt. The guests listened carefully to Labak-akhun's melodious recitation. At the center of the yurt, hot coals burned crimson on a cast-iron stand. Small tongues of fire from the hot little embers reflected in Khansulu's black-currant eyes.

"Oh, what words!" Sharip exclaimed now and then, spurring on the story-teller.

The *akhun* had assumed a place on the *tor*[26], his beard and mustache were silver white, his clothing white as snow; he was a man of thin, ascetic build, who looked like a personification of a holy spirit. The *dombra*[27] hummed and groaned under his hand.

Pakhraddin also listened to the *akhun*, his head lowered deep, heavy thoughts tormenting his soul.

"Oh, deceitful, low world, who you haven't outlived!" sang the *akhun*.

The *akhun* repeated this refrain now and again in his weak, vibrating voice.

"How many valiant sons, the worthiest in the human race since the day of the creation of the world, since the day Adam stepped upon the earth, have you accompanied along the way from which there is no return! And tsars like the unforgettable Sultan Suleimen[28], shaker of the Universe, and heroes like the fearless warrior Eskendir[29], you have accompanied... No one, no one has yet attained peace in this

---

[26]The *tor* is the place of honor in the yurt.
[27] The *dombra* is a long-necked Kazakh musical instrument similar to a lute.
[28] Ottoman ruler Suleiman 1, known as Suleiman the Magnificent in the West.
[29]Eskendir is Alexander the Great or Alexander of Macedon.

world, no one has found respite. Oh, deceitful, low world, whom haven't you outlived! Who, tell us, has managed not to leave you without attaining peace, abiding in you?!

"Ay, don't stint! More!" squealed Sharip, pressing toward the *akhun* with his whole body as if he was mounted on a horse. "Oh, ho-ho! What beauty in the wise words of the ancestors!"

Frowning, Azbergen looked gloomily at Sharip. Labakh-*akhun,* inspired by the vigorous support, lay into his *dombra*, and the worlds of the *terme* [30] hailed down on the listeners.

"Oh, you...oh, you...don't spare it!" groaned Sharip, unable to conceal his admiration.

When the *jyr*[31] ended, as the evening twilight descended, a large platter with boiled, smoking meat was placed in the very center among the guests, Khansulu seized the moment to slip out of the yurt. The night was fresh in the steppe, the air was wonderful to breathe. Numerous stars twinkled in the bluish-black sky. The scent of smoke wafted from everywhere, the scent of smoldering dung. Filling the serene night with laughter, the young people were having fun playing "blind goat."[32] Childhood awoke in Khansulu, and she also felt like playing and went toward the voices.

> "Khansulu?" someone said, surprised.
> "Khansulu is coming!"
> "Oh, Khansulu!"
> "Hey, now let Khansulu be the goat!"

Of the young men, Shege, Kozbagar, and Jdakhay were here. Balzhan, Shege's little sister was here – they were a year apart in age. She flew toward Khansulu and bound up her eyes. The handkerchief was black and tied tight – and "blinded" Khansulu completely, she

---

[30] *Terme* – a genre of epic poetry of the Kazakhs, performed in recitative style.
[31] *Jyr* – a heroic song.
[32] *Blind goat* is a version of blind-man's buff.

The Lonely Yurt • Smagul Yelubay

couldn't see anything. Balzhan led her by the hand to the circle, walked around her in place, and then cried:

"Blind goat, butt us, go on!" and jumped nimbly to the side.

Khansulu, laughing, grabbed at the air. With her movements, the owl's down on her beaver cap shone, the fabric of her *shalwah*[33], tucked into her morocco boots rustled, the lithe and well-knit girl instinctively hurled herself at the voices and laughter and grabbed again at thin air, laughing loudly, baring her teeth, which were blindingly white in the light of the stars. Everyone noisily twisted away from her outstretched hands and laughed as well.

The bumpkin Kozbagar was having fun, laughing louder than everyone, deafening everyone with his guffaws. Light in her movements, Khansulu, orienting herself towards his bass voice, was able to catch the youth by his hand. Kozbagar tried to break away, roaring with laughter, but Khansulu would not let him go.

"That's it! That's it!"
"You're caught! Kozbagar, now you're the blind goat!"
"*Oybay*[34], we're doomed! God save us from the rabid camel!"

Kozbagar, stretching out his huge arms, moved forward. Jdakhay got into place behind him. Without breathing, he cleverly imitated Kozbagar's every step, his every movement. Kozbagar didn't suspect that something like this was happening behind his back. Everyone around was convulsed with laughter.

Jdakhay grew bored with playing Kozbagar's shadow, and pinched him in his fat buttock and shrank back to the side.

"*Oybay*!" Kozbagar shouted, outraged. He whirled around, but his hands grabbed at air.

"He's behind you! Behind you!" Shege hinted.

---

[33] The *shalwah* is a type of Central and South Asian pantaloons worn with a tunic.
[34] *Oybay* is an expression of surprise in the Kazakh language.

Blundering about, Kozbagar, suddenly turned smartly. But he missed again. What does youth need? Just give it an excuse for loud fun. The cumbersome Kozbagar didn't catch anyone. He stamped in place like a bear and waved his arms. The young girls and boys, as if they had been waiting for this, twisted away, then leapt toward Kozbagar, poking him in the back and then immediately jumping away. The slow-moving Kozbagar began to grow tired; sweat broke out on his forehead and poured into his eyes. But still, he was laughing to his heart's content himself. His eyes were bound tight, and he couldn't see a thing. He lunged here and there, letting out giggles. Somebody finally got caught. The girls squealed all together. The fingers of the one he caught were thin, soft and even scented with perfume. A girl! Just what Kozbagar needed!

"Ohhh! Oh!" he roared joyfully, embracing the victim nimbly bending away from him.

"Don't lose it, fellow!" Jdakhay urged him. "What you asked of the sky you have found on the earth! Hold on tighter!"

The girl twisted and turned, trying to break away. There was bedlam everywhere. Her girlfriends hammered on Kozbagar's shoulders.

"Let her go!"

And what were these light fists to him? He had a girl in his arms.

"Ohh! Ohh!" he roared. He dug his face into the girl's neck, and intoxicated by the perfume, he part kissed her, part bit her.

"Let me go!" the captive cried and slapped Kozbagar.

Then he came to his senses. It was Khansulu! No one else would dare to behave like that. Frightened, his heart sunk to his heels and growing cold, he released his embrace.

"Good for you, *batrak*!" Jdakhay rejoiced. He leapt in place for joy.

"You insolent fellow!" Khansulu shouted in Kozbagar's face. Tears spurted from her eyes.

Then Azbergen appeared. As if a thunder-cloud from the skies. With his right hand he seized Kozbagar and with his left, Jdakhay. In a blink of an eye, he shook both of them so much that the young men's knees bumped together, and then he knocked their foreheads together like the most common of goats. Everyone nearby turned coward and ran away. Jdakhay, twisting about with all his might, finally freed himself from Azbergen's clutches, then lunged away to the open steppe. In the nearby bushes, he nearly collided with Shege.

"What are you doing?" Shege stopped him.

"I'll beat him, I won't spare him, bad things will come from the *batrak*" – and would have lunged further if Shege had let him.

"You have to help me," he demanded. "Let's go!"

"You idiot, are you mad?"

And off he ran. Racing without a backward glance, like a bull bitten by a gadfly.

"*Agata-ay,*[35] I'm dying!" Kozbagar's crying roar resounded.

"Take that, *agatay*...You piece of shit low-life...take that! Take that!" Azbergen wouldn't let up.

Breaking into a run, Shege butted Azbergen in the back with his head. Not expecting such an attack, Azbergen barely kept his balance, pitching forward from inertia and nearly falling on all fours.

"Oh, I'm dying! Who is that?" he gasped, turning and throwing a glance.

---

[35] *Agata-ay*

The nimble Shege raced forward, looping around like a fox. Azbergen couldn't catch up to him. That evening, Shege had never guessed that such an innocent game would cause a conflagration. If only he knew that not just anyone would burn in that fire, but he himself, along with Khansulu....

The aul broke into a commotion. A piercing woman's shriek broke the silence. That was lame Torka screaming, Kozbagar's mother. Her rage was purer than the most terrible February blizzard.

"The hell with you, Azbergen! Where are you, *oybay*!" the furious Torka wailed, advancing like a storm. Although she was puny, she had a bad temper.

Lame Torka was Sharip's elder sister. She had heard about the beating of Azbergen's son, and immediately jumped out of the house with a poker; crossing the threshold, she knocked her forehead on the lintel, her *jaulyk*[36] flew off her head, but nothing stopped her. Her husband, Uap, a well-known blacksmith in the aul, was withdrawn and unsociable; he liked only tinkering with metal, and everything else was meaningless for this recluse. That was why he wasn't the one jumping out with a poker against the enemy, but desperate, lame Torka.

"Cursed be your tribe, Azbergen! Stop! Who are you humiliating? Come, I will die in your arms, *oybay*!

However, she did not find Azbergen on the way. The bastard, he likely ran away from her. Torka no longer had any doubt: Azbergen had run away like a coward. The lame old woman now gave vent to her unrestrained anger:

"Just you wait, you hateful creature, you! If it is true that there is *Sabetski blasty*,[37] then I'll get you, you bandit!"

---

[36] A *jaulyk* is a kerchief for an adult woman.

[37] *Sobetski blast'* is a corrupted local form of the term *Sovetskaya vlast'* or Soviet government.

The old lady found Kozbagar in the dusty desert. Limping hard with worry, she led away her son, blubbering and limping himself – they had walloped him good in the back.

In Torka's tiny home, the oil lamp shone dimly. Lanky Uap was still sitting up in bed and had crawled half-way out from under his torn blanket and was groaning: his mustache, thin and droopy, trembling like the down-turned corners of his mouth, was a sign that he was angry. Ignoring him, Torka led her son to the fire, peered into his face and then shrieked – Kozbagar's nose was broken, his eyebrows as well, he was covered with bruises. Blood from his nose had stained his chest. Cursing, she wailed:

"Oh, a plague be upon you and your clan, Azbergen! Where are you, *oybay*!" She reached for the hoe at the doorway, which was twice as long as she was tall.

Unable to restrain himself, Uap slid from his bed. He loomed like a staff over his wife.

"That's enough, old woman, that's enough, who do you think to knock off there?"

The corners of his mouth jerked again. He tried to block the way of the ragged, little old woman, but she waved him away in blind rage.
"Get out of my sight!"

She headed straight to Azbergen's home, dragging her son by the hand. Her cries filled the aul.

There was no light on in Azbergen's yurt – they had evidently gone to bed.

"Cursed be your clan, Azbergen, come out, if you are a man! I'll show you how to beat people! Come out!" and with these words lame Torka began to pound with the hoe on the double doors, locked from inside with a hook.

"Why did you kill the boy, eh?! Here, kill him, the cursed one!" and pushed her son forward. He slammed into the door. The lintel squeaked.

"My dear people, eh, could you leave, please, ah? My house is falling down!" Azbergen's bass resounded from the yurt.

"I'm knocking it down? Yes, I'll knock down your *kibitka*[38]!" the old lady shrieked and went crazy, jumping around the yurt like a goat, banging on it with the hoe.

"Look at that, she's already smashing it," Azbergen, already angry, responded from the yurt.

Torka's fury was unrestrained.

"Why, what is she, damn it, a khan's daughter or something that you can't kiss her?! I kissed her. So what? If need be, it could be worse! Your little bitch Kozbagar isn't worth my little finger! And they'll jack the price up there! Come out, *basmach*[39], come out here, so your father will wail in the grave! They'll tie you by the hand and foot and send you to prison! If it's true that the *blasty* exist, I'll fling you so far, look out, you won't hit a *batrak*! *Oyba-ay!* Where are you, Sharip?!"

Torka's heart-rending cries had long ago brought the aul to its feet. The pack of aul dogs barked furiously. The sheep in their sheds grew quiet, the camels, tied up, cocked their ears and stopped chewing their cuds and turned their heads toward the noise. A crowd had gathered outside of Azbergen's yurt, young and old had come. Warmed by the attention, Torka continue to rage, jumping like a goat back and forth, poking the hoe at the yurt.

Two women were able to stop her by force, taking her under the arms.

---

[38] A *kibitka* is a nomad tent.
[39] The *basmachi* were Muslims from Central Asia who led a revolt against the Soviet government.

"Calm down! Calm down, mother!" they reproached her. "Get yourself in hand!"

People were puzzled.

"What is the scandal all about? Explain it to us!"

The ubiquitous kids, jabbering away, reported what had happened. From their contradictory story people understand: Kozbagar, the son of the blacksmith Uap, the *batrak* of the *biy* Pakhraddin, had forcibly kissed Khansulu, the daughter of the *biy*, when they were playing "blind goat." The offended Khansulu slapped the uncouth *jigit*, and then the girl's uncle, Azbergen, threw Kozbagar to the ground, then pounded and bloodied him.

Pakhraddin arrived, and shouldered his way through the crowd of people which had formed. He spoke to Torka, who was publicly wiping away her tears.

"Don't be angry, *jeneshe*," he said. "Do you see how many of us there are? We'll somehow find a harness for one rowdy."

The burly Pakhraddin, straightening his woolen *chapan*, turned toward the yurt and shouted: "Hey, you rogue, what are you laying there for, when people are here? You should come out, ah?"

"Leave me in peace, dear people! Go away!" Azbergen's voice resounded from the yurt.

People were dumbfounded. The women pinched their cheeks from outrage – this was a gesture that indicated that Azbergen had gone beyond the bounds of decency. Ever since the aul had existed, there had never been a case when somebody had opposed the *biy* Pakhraddin, and even publicly.

Pakhraddin grew angry, and left. People did not know that the brothers had returned from the market quarreling.

Sharip was among those in the crowd. He was silent, nibbling the end of his sparse beard. The attention of the aul-dwellers switched to him. As if to say, what would the *aulnay*, the representative of the government, say now?

But Sharip, usually the first to meddle in a scandal, for some reason was silent. Torka, who had been about to calm down in the arms of the women, once again began flailing – she was incensed by the calm behavior of Sharip, the brother, and accordingly, from the government.

"What, have your cheek bones fused, *oybay*? What is it to me that you are the *aulnay*, *oybay*! You can't defend your only sister, you give me up to the reproach of the evil, what do I need your *blasty* for, *oybay*! Let me go, I had better die, off wandering…"

"That's enough, old woman, you had better go home." Lanky Uap hung over the old lady, and his mustache, thin and sharp at the ends, also hung. Grabbing the withered Torka with his sinewy hands, he hoisted her on his shoulder and headed home. Jerking her arms and legs, madly pounding on his shoulder, she cried:

"Let me go, cursed by God! Let me go!"

Everyone broke out laughing. Only the former shoemaker Sharip, recently elected as head of the aul council, didn't feel like laughing. Reflecting on the underlying class reason for this quarrel, he kept beating and pinching his beard.

6

In the morning, after having lain comfortably on soft pillows and blankets, Azbergen was drinking tea when suddenly a policeman came barging in wearing a dagger. Azbergen's young wife – Rash – jumped up from her seat in fright.

Azbergen, crushing the down pillows even more comfortably under his elbow coldly stared at the guest.

The Lonely Yurt • Smagul Yelubay

"Eh, that isn't you, is it Bukhabay?!" he said, concealing his fear under a feigned jollity, exclaiming animatedly as if he had seen a relative.

"End of conversation, Azbergen! Get up! Get dressed!" said the policeman. He was a narrow-eyed dark strongman with prominent cheekbones, and spoke in a bass voice like rolling thunder. His gaze was stern.

Azbergen realized that Sharip had summoned the policeman.

"So, let's drink some tea, *tabarysh*?[40] Sit down! Azbergen offered, indicating the place next to him.

"I told you to get up! In fact, you're going to a place where you'll have time for tea! That's the law."

The butt of a rifle jutted up over the policeman's shoulder; he wore a tightly-pulled rawhide belt with a dagger. His brass buttons sparkled; there was even a steel glint in his eyes.

Bukhabay stared at the master of the yurt. Azbergen grew dejected. With difficulty, stamping the heels, he thrust his feet into his boots. He got up. As if waiting for this, the policeman twisted his arms behind his back and tied them with the rawhide belt. Azbergen didn't resist. He went outside and saw the crowd before Sharip's house. Everyone turned toward him animatedly at once. It was toward Sharip's yurt the policeman drove him. Azbergen seethed with fury. The entire aul riff-raff and even the women had gathered in order to mock him. Oh, the shame! Had he, Azbergen, not at one time driven away this entire rabble with a switch, like cattle?!

The prominent men of the aul, the *aksakals*,[41] sat solemnly in Sharip's yurt. When Azbergen, his hands bound behind his back and his body triply hunched crossed the threshold, the first person he noticed was the master of the house, Sharip, the roosting Sharip, with his owl's eyes unblinking now. Sticking out, like a forefinger, looking

---

[40]*Tabarysh* is a 1920s aul version of the Russian word *tovarishch* or "comrade".

[41] The *aksakals* are the elders of the aul.

rather comical perched on the *tor* of his own home. On his right side was Pakhraddin, his brow gleaming bright and open; on his left side, white as down, was Labak-*akhun,* who was running his fingers through his beard. Among the women who had arranged themselves near to the threshold Azbergen noticed the puny Torka.

"Ah, the cut-throat has appeared?" Sharip laughed, growing animated. "Let him take a seat there...on the door jamb...haha..."

Azbergen perceived Sharip's remark like the blow of a whip on his forehead. But what could he say? Humiliated, sullen from hurt, he could only bite his lip. All eyes were on him. The policeman poked him in the back. Growing even more gloomy, which made his meaty face swell, Azbergen fell heavily on his knees. He barely glanced at his elder brother – he evidently felt so terrible that he didn't have the strength to tear his eyes away from the floor.

"Write!" Sharip uttered solemnly and nervously squirmed in his seat. A pleasant moment had come for him.

Azbergen threw a gloomy eye on the *aulnay*, who slid a piece of paper to his son, Shege, who was lying before him. Shege sat with his pen at the ready. He kept glancing at his father's mouth, it seemed, as was licking his lips from the tension.

"Ah, you puppy, I didn't catch you at night, too bad!" thought Azbergen, choking in rage.

"Write the *prtokol*....[42] ...Did you write it?

"I did!"
People fell silent. Outside, people were talking loudly.

Torka cried, "Hey, shut up out there, the plague take you!"

It immediately grew quiet, as if the *aulnay* had thrown icy water on them. Only the chia on the walls of the yurt fluttered in the wind from the direction of Arka.

---

[42] A local corruption of the Russian word *protokol* or record.

"The reason for the writing of the *prtokol* is the following: write that yesterday in Pakhraddin's aul there was a class confrontation. The *bay* offspring Abergen Musauly, in front of all honest people, beat the *batrak* Kozbagar, Uap-*ugly*[43]... yes write...He beat Kozbagar Uap-*ugly*. But the main reason for the beating was this: the *batrak* Kozbagar, who had fallen in love with Khansulu, the niece of the *bay* offspring Azbergen, had the carelessness yesterday to display this love of his."

Shege grinned.

"Write! This is not the first time when Azbergen scoffed at defenseless poor people. With the coming of *Sabetski blasty*, he has, to be sure, not diminished his arrogance. For he has been an inveterate cut-throat – if you cross him in the slightest and he will thrash you! The aul has grown tired of the unlawful outbursts of this brazen fellow. Who was it during the annual memorial services for Ibray, who ordered to kick me out of the yurt where the *aksakals* were sitting? And it was because I, a shoemaker, you see, should have my place at the hearth, next to the women. That wasn't all, he pounded me as if I were a goatskin. This Azbergen is the greatest *contra*[44] there ever was..."

"Sharip!" Pakhraddin spoke up, straightening his chest. "You and I are peers, you don't have to mince words. This is a matter of the past, and wasn't it resolved by a council of the very same *aksakals*? Why dig up what has been forgotten?"

"Alright. Let it be. Let's move on. Write. The *blasty* are the poor peasants. Who is a poor man? Kozbagar is a poor man. Since Azbergen raised his hand against Kozbagar, that means he raised his hand against the *blasty*! Write!"

Here, many people began to grow agitated and began whispering to each other.

---

[43] *Ugly* means "son of."

[44] A *contra* or "counter-revolutionary" was a person in opposition to the Soviet government during the civil war.

"Write! There is no law that a *batrak* should be beaten! The times of Mekalay,[45] when there was such a law have passed, and will no longer return!

The crowd began to buzz and hum like a disturbed bee's nest.

"Write!" shrieked Sharip's reedy voice. «Let Azbergen as a *bay* be tried for beating a *batrak*. Let him be driven to forced labor where they ride on dogs!

Pakhraddin's face appeared frightened, his eyes grew round, he glanced at the *akhun* sitting next to him who seemed to be dozing off, clutching his beard. But no, apparently the holy man sensed Pakhraddin's gaze begging for help. He raised his head. He combed his beard with his fingers.

'Sharip, come to your senses!" he uttered in the urgent voice of the righteous man.

However, Sharip did not want to heed anyone's pleas. His face expressed decisiveness. He sat erect, immovable, like a pillar dug into the earth. Jaybaskan, his well-mannered wife, was bothered by her husband's cruelty.

"What, there are no other places besides Siberia?," she said. "Write the *prtokol* correctly. Don't make an elephant out of a flea."

"We will not change it! That's it! Bring the seal, Shege!" cried Sharip, triumphant. "Let him tramp along with the cut-throats' prison convoy! That'll teach him whom to tangle with!"

The word "Siberia" seemed to stun the bristling Azbergen. He raised his head, looking around at everyone with surprised eyes, as if to ask, "Are you really serious with this, people, or do you just want to scare me?"

The old woman Torka then jumped in:

---

[45] Mekalay is a corruption of the name of the Emperor of Russia, Nikolai I and Nikolai II.

"Enough shame from him! His way lies to Siberia, cursed by God!"

"Shhh, mother, isn't that enough fire from you that you have thrown between two auls?" some woman reproached her.

The round seal, made of a camel's hoof, was in Sharip's hand. He gathered himself up ominously, setting his sharp shoulders forward. Some frightened women's voices rang out. Pakhraddin, rocking his heavy body, let out a sound like a groan:

"You should think it over first, ah?"

But Sharip remained deaf and mute. He spread the *prtokol* out in front of him, and raised the seal to his mouth and began breathing on it. The crowd held their breath, watching him in fear. But Sharip did not look at anyone, but drew his hand back and with a sweep stamped the seal on to the paper! People jerked and some of the women couldn't hold back and screamed.

"Ay!"

"Oh, God the Creator!"

Holding the paper with the seal out to the policeman, Sharip said:

"Here, take this! You'll give it to Duke!"

Duke was the name the aul-dwellers gave to Dukenbay Ismailov, the chairman of the *volost*[46] council. The policeman Bukhabay had a beefy, hard nape. He slowly rolled up the document and just as slowly stuffed it into his chest pocket, then buttoned the pocket shut. Frowning, he looked at Azbergen, then ordered in Russian:

"March!" and then added in Kazakh, "Go!"

---

[46] The *volost* was the regional division or district in the tsarist era.

Azbergen got up clumsily. His meaty face had turned crimson. Heading toward the door, he threw a glance at Pakhraddin. His older brother sat staring at the ground.

The crowd spilled outdoors in order to see of the *arystybay*[47] Azbergen.

"Hey, people! Where are you going? Don't split up yet. And the host's duty? The meal?" Sharip raised his voice.

"Hey, Shege, get up! Hurry up and serve the little black lamb!"

"I'm stuffed, my peer, I couldn't fit more!" Pakhraddin said through gritted teeth, not concealing his hurt. He got up heavily, intending to leave.

"Don't get angry at me, you yourself say we are peers. It would seem that you should understand me. A government matter is one thing, and our friendship is another. Is that not the case, *akhun-aga*[48]? If you're invited, you don't come, you're terribly distinguished, but since you have found yourself under my roof, then you must try what is due guests!"

Sharip spoke sincerely. Pakhraddin and Labak-akhun exchanged glances. They understood each other – they had to accept the invitation and find a common language with Sharip.

It was noon. Young and old looked at the only dusty highway in the east which climbed to the ridge. A horseman was riding away along it, driving along a man on foot. He was driving him ruthlessly, not allowing him to catch his breath. Dust blew up high from the feet of the man walking. This was the *arystybay* Azbergen.

Clouds stretched a gray swaddling over the sun. A northern wind whistled around the steppe, gathering strength. Taking in one

---

[47]The arrested Azbergen.

[48] *Aga* is a suffix that denotes respect.

　　　　　The Lonely Yurt • Smagul Yelubay

hand a *kumgan*[49] for washing and picking up the edge of his *chapan* with the other, Pakhraddin and the lanky Labak-*akhun*, dry as a stick, disappeared into the overgrown wormwood. Both were unhappy.

Pakhraddin cleared his throat and asked:

"What do you think, *akhun-aga*, how will this end?"

"Allah knows, He is witness to everything…very, very soon the times will change, my brother. If someone doesn't run after to play tricks on him – they'll interrogate him for a while and then let him go."

"It's good if that's how it is. If the case will not take a bad turn. I cannot forget the words of the commissioner at the market. It was if you had seen it in the water, saying "The *bays* will be destroyed, and the slaves, on the contrary, will be raised up. Now the unfortunate is being brought to the *volost* administrator, and once he lands there, consider it prison…"

"Time! Time! Cold winds blow from you, oh little time," Labak-*akhun* signed nearly with a groan. Pakhraddin once again coughed and cleared his throat.

"And Squealer[50], I sense, knows a thing or two, which is why he acts confidently. You know, the times are such that an elephant can be made out of a flea and that is exploited. What is to be done, *akhun-aga*? Azbergen of course is a dog, but he's my brother, my only bulwark, the time is such, you yourself see, the scandal could have been resolved peacefully without taking out dirty laundry…This fire emerged from that innocent children's game…

"From a children's game…Well, yes…God is a witness…"

Labak-*akhun*, placing the *kumgan* on the ground, ran his fingers through his long, silver beard for a long time.

---

[49] A *kumgan* is an Asian pitcher with a narrow neck and spout used for washing.
[50] Sharip was called "Squealer".

"God is my witness, the girl is a bride and the boy is a groom, ah?" he said later.

"That's how it was," Pakhraddin replied sorrowfully. He looked crushed, even exhausted.

"Hmm," the *akhun* muttered and looked thoughtfully at the greying sky.

When they returned to the yurt, white Labakh-*akhun,* having settled upon the *tor*, turned to the host:

"Oh, Sharip!"

"At your service!" Sharip responded readily.

"Bend your knees! Torka-*kelin*[51], you sit down, too! Uap, and you listen! God is my witness; a scandal has occurred in the aul. People! It was said: 'Even if you are bloodied, forgive one another, because you are relatives.' If children quarrel, they must be reconciled. If there is a dispute among people from one clan, then their relationships must be strengthened. Sharip Pakhraddin, Torka-*kelin*, my brother Uap! 'The resolution of a lawsuit is peace; the task is to reach the goal; the goal is for the girl to leave her father's roof with honor.' Young people have an attraction to each other. Torka-kelin's son has grown up; your daughter, Pakhraddin, as God sees, has blossomed. Become in-laws! Return the *azamat*[52] home! If you agree, bless their union! I would like to bring you to consent. I would like to make you relatives."

And here Labak-*akhun* was the first to make the ritual gesture – to unfold his hands in prayer.

The outcome of the matter turned out to be unexpected for both sides; it was like a thunderstorm on their heads. Shocked, people maintained silence. Pakhraddin, without uttering a word, rocked his heavy body, staring at the ground. Sharip, clearing his throat, which

[51]The suffix *kelin* indicates she is a sister-in-law.
[52] An *azamat* is a "dashing young fellow," a Central Asian term which originated from the Arabic word for "greatness."

The Lonely Yurt • Smagul Yelubay

had suddenly grown strangled, coughed and looked confusedly at Pakhraddin, at the *akhun*, squirming in his seat, as if water had rushed under him. Old Torka, at first about to jump up, was now silent as well, not even breathing – waiting for how it would all end, apparently. Uap's face was stretched and the corners of his mouth jerked. Shege was working over the skin of a slaughtered lamb at the door, sprinkling salt on it, and when he heard what was said, cast a wild glance at those sitting inside.

Sharip finally came to his senses. Sparks flashed in his round, owl eyes, and shifting from one foot to another, he laughed with a sort of wooden voice and exclaimed:

"Uap, holy father! A wonderful decision! What question can there be? Uap, let me be a victim for the sake of a noble cause, that's what it means to be a wise man! What advice! Torka! Have you not yet exploded from such joy? Your snot-nose is a fortunate one! Let's have the blessing, what are you waiting for?" He excitedly spread out his hands.

Torka, chuckling, poked her old man in the back and quickly unfolded her palms. Only Pakhraddin was delaying with his answer. The old *akhun* turned toward him:

"Well, brother Pakhraddin, give the blessing! I bless your union!" And jerking up his sickle-like nose, gazing somewhere into the distance over their heads, he threw forward his dry, bony hand. Pakhraddin, rocking heavily backward, spread out his palms in prayer. At that moment Shege ran over the threshold.

"Uap, wild man!" Sharip called after him.

With feeling, Labakh-akhun began to pronounce the solemn words of the blessing:

"*Aguz-zi bil-lakhim*[53]..."

The people in the yurt fell into a respectful silence.

---

[53] A chapter from the Koran.

7

The news that Pakhraddin was giving away his daughter to Kozbagar, and thus saving Azbergen, flew around the aul in a flash. In front of a large white yurt, Khansulu was throwing wood chips into the samovar when she heard about the news in Sharip's house from boys running past. She ran toward the house, getting tangled in her dress with its long hem, crying "Apa!"![54]

Her mother was whipping *kumys*[55] in a *saba*[56]. She had heard the news from the cries of the same boys. Pale, she had frozen in place with the beater in her hand. She hugged her daughter who came running in from the yard.

"Oh, Creator, he didn't seek advice…Let's go, let's go, my little daughter, to your insane father!"

"I won't go!" Khansulu abruptly cut her off. Her eyes smoldered with anger. She stood with her fists clenched.

Her poor mother realized that it was useless to try to persuade her daughter.

"Alright, I'll go myself," her mother said.

She adjusted her white *jaulyk* on her head and set off with her unhurried, soft step. That was the kind of mother Khansulu's mother was – the world around her could be going up in flames, but she would not change: she would remain unperturbed…

Khansulu knew that if her father decided something, that it would likely come to pass. Therefore, now it was if the sky had come crashing down on her, and as if everything around her had turned to ashes.

---

[54] *Apa* is the Kazakh word for mother.
[55] *Kumys* is fermented mare's milk.
[56] A *saba* is a skin bag.

The Lonely Yurt • Smagul Yelubay

The *kamcha* hung from the *kerege.*[57]

Kozbagar, still not healed from the bruises by Azbergen, was in bed. The black-and-blue marks had not faded from his body or face. Shege had just visited him and whipped up fear, the dolt. He hurled himself at him in broad daylight, grabbed him by the collar and then dragged him out of bed! Why, he said, do you need Khansulu, you son of a bitch! And then he tried to strangle him.

And he himself…was nearly crying. Kozbagar was frightened, and shouted, "Oy, Shege, why are you doing this? What's wrong with you?" And Shege – he was outright out of his mind – once again threw him on the bed and that was the last of him. He ran so fast that you would think that Azrail, the angel of death, was chasing him….

Oh, God! While Kozbagar, shaken, was coming to his senses, the boys ran past the house, shouting. Now Kozbagar realized why Shege was going mad. Khansulu, Kozbagar's wife? How could he have believed that? And before his eyes he saw Khansulu, lithe, like a reed. As if she was coming toward him, embracing him, and then herself hiding in his embraces.

Then the door opened with a crack and…Khansulu herself came in! And her bearing was just like a Russian officer! Her currant-black eyes shone. Oh, how beautiful she was! Her eyelashes were turned up, and her lips swollen. He only later noticed the whip in her hand.

Kozbagar immediately darted under the covers, and hid his head under the blanket. But Khansulu flew at the bed and tore off the covers.

"Are you the one who will take me?" she asked.

"Not I, *oybay*, not I!" Kozbagar wailed, not taking his eyes off the *kamcha* raised above him. But Khansulu then lashed his right side with all her might.

---

[57] A *kamcha* is a whip, and the *kereg* is the latticed top frame of the yurt.

"*Oybay-ay-ii!*"

Unassailable, unbending, Khansulu left the yurt, slamming the door behind her loudly.

Meanwhile, behind Sharip's, Pakhraddin and his *baybishe* met.

"My lord and master," she asked, not daring to raise her voice. "What's wrong you you? Are you thinking of what you are doing?'

The wind rustled Pakhraddin's mustache, touched with gray, and his beard, and the wrinkles on his handsome manly face stood out more distinctly; it was clear that he had grown haggard. He kept gloomily silent, thinking about something.

"Understand," he said quietly to his wife. "Today we have to look at the world differently. Nowadays, the worthless *batrak* is one too many for both the *bay* and the *myrza*. You have to see this, you have to feel this...So I thought – your daughter has to have a future...You have to understand that, *baybishe*...

...The echo of this event which occurred in the late autumn of 1927 at Taskudyk reverberated through all the auls of the great Tabyn clan in Ushoymaut and Donyzgau along the south side of the Jem River. Pakhraddin was not famed for his wealth, but people valued him as a *biy* for his intellect, eloquence, and fairness.

NOMAD'S ENCAMPMENT ON THE USTYURT[58]

1

All night, a dry snow fell. People in the aul, who had intended in a week or two to head to the warm, sturdy *zimovkas*[59] on the sands of Sama far from there were alarmed. Snow that fell early made it difficult to break up the nomad camp.

Khansulu was tormented by insomnia. Curled up, she snuggled down in her warm bed, vainly summoning sleep; her thoughts would give her no peace, she tossed and turned from one side to the other. It seemed as if she were alone in the whole world, face to face with the bad weather and the night, and the darkness which had blanketed the universe and would never disperse.

Only toward dawn, exhausted, Khansulu fell asleep. She awoke from the warmth of the oven, from the fire which was crackling loudly at the very center of the yurt. The brightening sky was visible through the *tunduk* [60] which had been thrown back. Her mother with

---

[58] The Ustyurt is a plateau between Kazakhstan and Uzbekistan.

[59] *Zimovkas* are winter homes dug out of the side of a hill.

[60] The *tunduk* is the opening at the top of the yurt which is covered with *koshma* or felt cloth.

her own mother helping her were wrapping up tight the clothing, rugs and other domestic goods into rolls.

"Sulutay, get up! The aul is moving on," she said, giving her warm clothing: a fox *tymak*[61], a squirrel coat and leather pants.

The women themselves were already dressed, their sashes tied tightly. Khansulu went out of the yurt and squinted – she was blinded by total whiteness. All around as far as the eye could see, snow was drifting down. Men crowded around the kitchen yurt; among them was her father, Pakhraddin, her uncle Azbergen, Bulysh, and Sharip the Squealer; they were dividing up a just-slaughtered fat mare. A thick steam went up from the pile of meat with the guts exposed.

"*Oykho*y, what a fat little horse! The fat is five fingers thick, from the palm! Oh, oh, oh!" Sharip groaned.

Azbergen, rolling up his sleeves, chopped the meat with an axe and threw the pieces on to the awaiting trays.

"Take some!" Pakhraddin kept saying, his voice sonorous in the morning air. "Take some! There's enough for everyone! Let your way be fortunate!"

In the kitchen yurt, there was an enormous *kazan*[62] on a tripod. The fire burned furiously underneath it. The father ordered all the rest of the horse meat to be put in this *kazan*. And while the meat was boiling, the men took down the yurts. Things were rolled up into the *tyuki*, and the *tyuki* lashed down with ropes – all so that the household goods could be more easily loaded up on the camels.

Bulysh and Kozbagar were busy gathering up into bundles the fuel left in the sheds -- poles and pieces of boards and logs.

"Bring the lassos here!" ordered Pakhraddin. They brought the lassos, thick and woven from hemp.

---

[61] A *tymak* is a fur hat.
[62] A *kazan* is a large cooking pot.

"Bulysh, bring the *nar* here!"

The lashed poles and logs formed a heap of impressive dimensions.

"Strap it up!"

Bulysh led the haughty, slowly-stepping Shoyynkara to the loads. An enormous black *nar*, huffing noisily through his nostrils, he inspected people from on high. The camel's large grey eyes sparkled from under his heavy lashes. Bulysh brought him to the pile of goods and forced him to kneel to the ground. With a bellow, the camel knelt, grinding his teeth. A saddle was placed on the animal's back, and two *jigits* tightened the girth. The two ends of the lassos were tied as hard as they could to the two sides of the saddle.

"Go on now, raise it up now! *Chu,* Oysylkara![63]!

The giant Shoyynkara rose up, splaying out his legs. Bulysh took him by the reins. The snow had already reached the camel's knees. Only large and strong animals – camels and horses – were capable of travel across deep snow that was still not packed down, but the sheep and goats, for example, wouldn't take a step in it.

"Wait up! Let's see!"

Shoyynkara strained and budged the wood pile from its place. It slid, shaking off the fluffy snow. Behind the camel a path opened up as broad as outstretched arms. Unrestrained, Sharip yelped enthusiastically.

"Oh-hoh! I wouldn't mind dying for you, animal!"

...

It was noon, and the day was overcast. The dull, cheerless sky merged with the remote, white snowy steppe. The colorful nomad's group froze in place amidst the white silence. It could not move. It

---

[63] *Chu* is an expression to goad the camel, and Oysylkara is the patron saint of camels.

couldn't move, because Shoyynkara, who was supposed to plow the way for the caravan with his load of wood, would no longer heed the reins. Bulysh, angry, even lashed him with a whip, but the camel only shook his head.

"Don't beat him! Do it differently!" said Pakhraddin, riding up on a horse, in the camel's defense.

People were driven crazy from the cacophony of the bleating sheep. The flock were complaining because they couldn't walk in the deep snow. Their poor shepherds were tormented trying to force the goat, the leader of the flock, to go forward. On the ridge, like a forsaken spirits the aul *bay* Mazhan bustled about, he also prepared to move the camp. People took down the yurts and took up the *tyuki*.

The black *nar*, who was supposed to break the path, was still stubbornly refusing to move. It would take a step, then another, then gritting its teeth, turn back and freeze in place with its mouth gaping. People were desperate. The old women spinsters, sitting bent between the humps of the camels, angrily reviled Shoyynkara. A motley crew of female riders, young women and girls, stood to the side of the caravan in waiting. Khansulu was among them on her horse Karaker. She wore a fox *tymak*, and a squirrel fur coat with a black plush interior tightly bound with a broad silver belt.

"Damn you!" resounded Pakhraddin's loud voice. "I realize now I need my old nag!" Pakhraddin laughed till his shoulders shook. "Oh, *jigits!* Lead the herd ahead! Over there…everything depends on them."

The *jigits* quickly lead the camel herd, which had been at the tail of the nomad's camp. Shoyynkara, with overgrown clumps of fur even hanging from his mouth, bristled, stared fast at the slender-legged female camel with bare thighs, one-humped and two-humped, young and not so young, flashing before his eyes. This was his herd, over which all summer, he had been the full-fledged leader. His nostrils caught the soft, alluring scent of the *aruana*.[64] In one of the hidden corners of the soul of the enormous *nar*, a plaintive call arose,

---

[64] An *aruyana* is a one-humped camel.

powerful, bowing to none, Shoyynkara gnashed his teeth. Sparks showered from his angry eagle eyes, and he lashed his tail across his powerful buttocks.

Rearing up in a black cloud, he lunged forward toward the female camels. Without particular effort, he dragged forward the wood load, which measured as wide as the body of the largest camel. The fluffy snow parted and fell in waves along both sides of the beaten track. The nomad's caravan now had a broad, convenient path to travel on.

A din went up as people grew cheerful and cracked jokes.

"Well, drop dead, Shoyynkara! That's a good one!"

"Who would think! What a dog!"

"You should be ashamed at your age, eh?"

The last retort was said by women who pinched their cheeks to express their indignation.

The nomads lined up into a column and followed Shoyynkara's trail. Following the nomads were the horses, and herds of noisily bleating sheep followed after them, then the tethered goats, with their moon-shaped horns and bells on their necks. Thus, the aul began its half-month crossing to the other end of the world to far-off, fertile sands, generous and warm, in the Great Sama.

The immense universe was frozen with the endless white shroud, and the nomads slowly crawled across the endless snowy expanse. In a frigid hush, the aul searched for their winter refuge.

2

By noon, the group of riders with the hoes, shovels, and spades tied to the bows of their saddles were scattered across the steppe at a rapid trot. They rode forward, leaving the caravan far behind. Afternoon came. The horsemen, driving their overheated horses to a frothy sweat, kept hurrying along. Shege's dock-tailed chestnut horse was barely keeping up with the stronger stallions, and the gloomy Shege was not driving him very hard. He was silent and withdrawn.

...

The *jigits* reached the designated place before sunset. The southern foothills of the rounded, lone hill on the plain had from time immemorial served as a reliable camp for the nomadic auls. Now it was covered with snow. The *jigits* dismounted from their horses together and without delay got to work. The heaviest job was to chop the ice and clear a place for the yurts and the large animals. Experienced *jigits* like Bulysh and Azbergen took on this task while Shege, Kozbagar and others who were younger began to clear the snow away for the sheep shed. The men sweated profusely. When the sun was already inclined to set behind the north horizon, the tinkling bells of the long nomad's line could be heard. At the head, laying down the path, stepped Shoyynkara, he could be recognized from far off by his shaggy black withers.

Close to sunset, the noisy caravan reached the camp. The remote steppe frozen by the cold came to life. At the very center of the cleared square, exuding steam, rose Shoyynkara. The *jigits* had hastily freed him from the lashes. Exhaling noisily from his black nostrils, the enormous black *nar*, his legs splayed wide, haughtily surveyed the area, white foam hung in clumps from his chest and belly, and sweat poured down his flanks.

Trying to get some use out of the last sunlight, people hurriedly erected their *shalashes*[65] on the cleared areas. They tied up the herds and milked the cows. They lit the dung and firewood they had brought along with them on the trip, fires burned in the hearths, and *kazans* were hung over the flames. In the *shalashes*, which had been erected with the *kereg* of the yurt and some *koshmas*, people ate their hot dinners, without complaining about the cramped quarters.

After tea, the wrinkles on Sharip's forehead had smoothed, he grew more cheerful and contrived even to stretch out on his back and

---

[65] A *shalash* is a hut made of branches and grass; in this case they were huts temporarily made of parts of the yurt.

The Lonely Yurt • Smagul Yelubay

put on his chest the little Gulzhan, and was even murmuring something in satisfaction. Then his gaze fell on Shege, who was sitting with an abstract expression, and he raised his head. His sparse red mustache bristled.

"Hey!" he shouted at his son. "Hey, you bearded dog! Look over here! I'm talking to you!"

Sharip's five daughters, crowded into the *shalash*, were laughing noisily and uncontrollably. Shege turned to his father. He stared at him silently. There was cold in his small, sharp eyes.

"Hey, you bastard! Why are you going around so down in the mouth? What happened? Speak!"

"Nothing happened," Shege snapped back, unperturbed.

"Oh, you dolt! You want to deceive us? Speak! We're listening."

"You should keep to yourself! The boy has yielded to you, why are picking on him?" Jaybaskan said indignantly. She was preoccupied with the *kazan* at the hearth.

"Picking on him! Imagine that! People are saying: Shege is growing up to be a fine *jigit*, he will be a bulwark to his home. So let us hear the *azamat*, let him have his say. Why is he so gloomy?"

Little Gulzhan suddenly interrupted his speech.

"You're bad!" she proclaimed, poking her father's chest with her forefinger. "Why are you giving Khansulu away to Kozbagar? Shege-*aga* loves Khansulu...Don't you see?"

"Shut up!" Shege barked at his little sister.

Gulzhan obediently covered her mouth with her tiny little palm.

Jaybaskan dropped the scraper which she used to scrape the *kazan*. Balzhan, pouring the tea, drew in her head in fright. Sharip widened his round owl's eyes. Pulling his sparse beard, he looked at his wife and jerked his head as if to say, "Have you ever seen such a thing?"

Finding his tongue, he turned toward Shege and said:

"Now that's a bastard! Now we have learned the reason for the trouble," he said, nodding his head again.

With that, Shege's patience snapped. He could no longer restrain his anger.

"What have you learned? You haven't learned anything!" Shege wailed, jumping up from his seat. "You haven't learned anything! You're pandering, you're breaking the law, that's what!"

"Hey, you pig-fed puppy! Sit down, don't shout," Sharip said, about to get angry. However, he said this for some reason in a soft voice. Bristling, Shege glared back at him.

He really is a jigit, Sharip thought to himself.

"Sit down!" he asked quietly.

"I won't! I'm leaving! I don't need such..." and choking on his words, Shege was about to lunge toward the door when his mother blocked his path.

"Sit down! You're getting too overheated. Are you seeing your father for the first time?!" she said.

With the frozen snow squeaking under their feet, the nomads moved on. The heavily-laden but mighty *nars* were unfazed by winter troubles like frost and whistling wind. They continued to step along boldly. The mothers' *jaulyks* gleamed white inside the carriers on their backs as they rocked quietly back and forth, to the rhythmic step of the camels.

And where there were warmly-dressed *jigits* and young women on the spirited horses trotting along, there were jokes and laughter and a happy hubbub. But the goats and sheep were bleating louder and louder since they hadn't had any hay to eat since the previous day.

Ahead of the line of nomads the camel herd trotted along at a gentle pace. Ahead of them the enormous Shoyynkar was dragging his huge load through the snowy expanses. The snow had settled, and apparently the thin crust of ice over it was not yielding, yet Shoyynkara was ripping through it, as before, easily laying a path for the whole nomad village; the snow mounds fell off like boulders on both sides and rolled away in waves. The step of the horse's strong legs was inexorable, the powerful haunches shook, and although the sunken underbelly was already overgrown with icicles, a hot steam blew out of the black nostrils, and fire blazed in his eyes.

After spending three nights in camps, on the fourth day the nomads came out across Koltaban to the Ustyurt Plateau. The weakened sheep and goats, dying of hunger, stayed on the road. With the animals' hooves knocking on the flat surface, moving ceaselessly on the flat plain, the nomads descended to the brackish Okim-Kiyk Lake in a week, and then in a few days, reached the sands of Sama. The snow lay in a thin layer on the sands, but there was thick grass in abundance. The herds, which had starved during the long trip, hurled themselves with wolfish greed at everything that showed dark on the snow, even the bare, dry bushes. The aul wedged themselves deep into the wide saxaul thicket, people settled into the warm winter lodgings at their customary camp, to which they returned every year.

3

For Khansulu, the joyless, gray winter days dragged on. Coddled by her parents' love, the girl had never heard a shout or a harsh word in her whole life, stoically endured the trial that had fallen to her lot without complaint. She didn't say a word to her father, as if to say, "why are you giving me away to a man I don't love," but she ceased to call him with the tender name *koke* as she used to. Pakhraddin, to be sure, meanwhile did not notice her state very much – he was busy with other things. Every evening, he and Azbergen got together for a talk and argued and argued...They often mentioned Afghanistan and Iran....

Her mother also kept quiet. As soon as they settled into the winter camp, she set about preparing her daughter's dowry. Day after day, she spent at the hand sewing machine, enthusiastically stitching the fabric.

...The winter evening fell early. The lamp had not yet been lit in the yurt. The semi-twilight was thick. The *kazan* bubbled on the iron tripod in the very center of the yurt. The aroma of stewing meat filled the home. Burning coals blazed hot under the *kazan*. Without tearing her eyes away from the fire, Khansulu quietly strummed the strings of the *dombra*; it was the only one to empathize with the wounded girl's soul. Like an old, wailing women, the *dombra* groaned and signed.

Syrga the *baybishe* finally gave her sewing machine a rest. She got up quietly, lit the lamp and hung it over the threshold. Attractive, forgiving, she noiselessly, like a shadow, moved around the yurt. She didn't want to disturb her daughter. But then the *dombra* fell silent.

A heavy, twilight silence fell on the yurt. It seemed to crush the whole aul. Outside, somebody's shout disturbed the hush. Syrga the *baybishe* suddenly flinched, listening to the sounds, as Khansulu jumped out the door and saw in the center of the aul there was a bonfire with a pile of saxaul, burning from the leeward side of a great snow drift. People were trampling the clean snow to get water for drinking. The problem wasn't the bonfire – that was an ordinary scene for the winter camp. Near the fire, Jdakhay was circling on a yearling foal, pointlessly racing around the *aulnay*, who had run toward the ridge. Sharip shouted as well. People sitting at the campfire got up and followed Sharip to the edge. Khansulu also ran. At first she saw a woman running away from the Mazhan winter camp, a horseman in a fox *malakhai*[66] was lashing her with a whip and following on her heels. Already on the hill now, the aul-dwellers recognized that the woman was Balkiya, and her pursuer, the *bay* Mazhan. That was why Sharip was shouting!

Poor Balkiya's hair had spilled over her back and shoulders, the hems of her gown dragged through the snow, and she covered her

---

[66] A *malakhai* is a fur hat with flaps.

head with her hands against the blows. She kept throwing up her hands. But Mazhan kept working the whip, he swung and swung...

People made noise.

"Oy, he'll kill her!"

"What, has he gone crazy, the old man?"

"He shouldn't have taken a young woman because he can't bear her spoiling!

Mazhan's horse knocked the woman off her feet with his chest, and she fell down. Jdakhay, on his stallion, and Bulysh followed on foot. Mazhan then lashed Bulysh, who had come to help Balkiya get up.

"Stop it!" Bulysh roared, choking with fury, and tearing the whip from the old man's hand, broke the handle in half and threw it away.

Out of shock, the single hair on a black birthmark on his cheek bristled. He lit into his wife:

"Go, complain now to your government! Oh, sooner you should die, you whore!"

Turning around his sorrel ambler, the *bay* trotted back home. The valley between the two auls was dotted by herds returning from the pasture. The shepherds and horse-wranglers hurried to the place of the incident. Bulysh and Khansulu led Balkiya by the hand; she was barely able to move her legs.

...

The whip had left its mark in two places on Balkiya's beautiful, pale face. Her head lowered, leaning on Bulysh's arm, she was silently shedding tears. The beautiful Balkiya had seemed to Khansulu to be a proud and free woman, but now she saw this same Balkiya humiliated and disgraced. Khansulu shed a tear out of pity herself. Anger at the coarse men like Mozhan burned in her heart.

Bulysh's home was already nearby when the clear, strong voice of *Dau-apa* rang out. A tall, dark old woman, grasping a stick in her hand, stood next to her home, full of holes.

"Sonny, can you hear me? I have enough of my own troubles. But the government – there it is, behind you – she said imperatively, pointing at Sharip. "It resolves disputes. Bring it over here, do you hear?"

"*Apa-au,*" Bulysh protested, but the old woman waved her stick at him.

"Stop contradicting! I know what is in your heart. Do what they say!" the old woman said, ending the conversation.

"Bulysh," Balkiya said, gathering up her strength. "I don't need the government or anything else. Help me, find me a way to get back to my family."

"But it's night-time, Balym[67]!" Bulysh, black as coal, begged her, helplessly looking from side to side.

At that moment, Khansulu began to pity Bulysh. His late wife had been a distant relative's of Pakhraddin's, so he called her "sister"; Khansulu thus treated Bulysh traditionally, as an in-law, calling him *jezde*[68]. Such an address somewhat simplified their relations; a *jezde*, as it was customary, was lenient toward requests, so she dared to say:

"Let Balkiya come to our house and spend the night with us," she said.

The dusk gathered and it grew dark, and there was the usual bustle in the aul: the owners of sheep were locking them into sheds, the camels were tied up to the lassos for the night – it was late. And Pakhraddin, as it turned out, was not home – he had gone to visit the

---

[67] Balym is a diminutive form of the name Balkiya.
[68] *Jezde* is brother-in-law.

grave of the sacred Barak; it was the duty of sons to pay their respects to ancestors.

Bulysh accompanied Balkiya to Pakhraddin's home, and whispered something to her at the door. She nodded her head silently. Khansulu did not hear what they exchanged.

…Without delay, the moon rose over the sea of sand dunes. A northern wind blew up, howling, rocking the thick tops of the saxauls. The shaggy dogs, the guards of the nomads, which had earlier been barking vigilantly, crawled into their warm corners protected from the wind and fell asleep. In the distance, the howling of wolves roving the desert could be heard. It was the dead of night, and the aul slept soundly…

The saxaul thicket was bushy before the winter; if you drove a camel into it you wouldn't find it later. Bulysh stood at the entrance to this virgin forest, in a secluded place between the trunks of the trees. The moon had already risen to its zenith in the night sky. But the door to the large white yurt in the center of the aul opened a crack, a shadow broke off from it and slipped toward the thicket. Bulysh, watching from the bushes, held his breath. The little female silhouette slowly came close. There was a jacket over her shoulders and on her head, a white, silk fringed kerchief. Balkiya moved along, holding the hems of her skirt in her hands.

Bulysh came out of his hiding-place. Balkiya came closer to him along the snowy path, weakly lit by the moon. She smiled at him. It was a smile so close to his heart – nice, light, and bright. In his warm boots, *malakhai* and woolen vest, Bulysh clumsily embraced Balkiya, pressing her tender breast close to him, clinging hungrily to the warm kerchief on her head, and kissing her temple.

"Let's go further away!" she whispered.

The sky was clear. The full moon poured milk-white light through the black branches on the snowy earth. Each step on the snow made a squeak. With each step, they were more concealed in the saxaul thicket. The trees were like beautiful girls, letting down their hair and baring their white shoulders to the moon. Or like silently dancing girls with bared thighs. In the depths of the saxaul grove, there was not a breath. Here was a secluded place. Behind the thick shadow of spreading trees there were little meadows drenched in moonlight. At one of these tiny meadows, blocked on all sides by the saxauls, they stopped.

"Well, now, show me!" asked Bulysh, turning the woman's face to the moon, and peering at her. Balkiya squinted, and obediently held up to the moon her found little face, wet with tears. One mark from the whip went crosswise across her open white forehead, covering the left part of her face, and the second, which had fallen on her beautiful, slightly blunt nose, stretched to the right corner of her mouth, as small as a thimble.

"At least it didn't bleed…it just made a mark. It's nothing…it will go away," Bulysh impatiently began showering Balkiya's eyes and face with kisses, especially the places marked by the whip. Balkiya didn't open her eyes clung to him with a death grip.

"My hero…," she whispered, and her hot breath scorched his face. Their hands and bodies met in a warm embrace; they merged as one, standing under the moon. It was cold, and the dark crowns of the saxaul loomed on all sides, and the snow squeaked under foot.

"Why did he reproach you? Why did he hit you?"

"Oh, don't…forget about him!" Balkiya pleaded.

"Perhaps he will let you go? The *talak*[69] has not been pronounced."

"And what's it to you? Are you marrying? You can't cross the threshold…"

Balysh grew flustered.

"Balym," he said. "Don't judge me severely. I won't let you be humiliated…My heart is with you…"

---

[69]Under sharia law, it is enough for the husband to pronounce the *talak* or word for divorce three times for a divorce.

The Lonely Yurt • Smagul Yelubay

"I don't want it to be with me like that!" Balkiya took his hands away.

"What would you order me to do? You saw my mother. Going against her is like going against God. She has buried four children. No, likely no one has suffered as much as she from the torments of orphanhood and widowhood. And yet, she raised me…"

"Stubborn old woman," said Balkiya, brushing away her tears. "How am I to blame?"

"Balkiya, the most correct thing to do in these circumstances is to be patient…

"You…you are patient…but I'm…unhappy…and before the entire aul…" Balkiya convulsed with sobs. She would have fallen, her legs giving way beneath her, if it were not for the strong arms of Bulysh catching her in time. Holding her entire weight, he began to kiss her beautiful eyes, full of tears.

"My Bulysh!" she signed at some point through her sobs, and with mad desperation hanging on his neck, she tipped him over. They both fell on a snow mound. They came together like two fiery shafts, burning the cold world, indifferent to everything, with their desire.…

4

Khansulu had nodded off. She woke feeling a cold spot next to her and discovered that Balkiya, who had been next to her, was gone. Her place was empty. Sleep fled her immediately, and her heart pounded loudly in her chest. She recalled how Bulysh had whispered about something with Balkiya as he left…The wide world suddenly shrunk in her eyes, and became a fistful. Khansulu had considered Bulysh to be sacred. Gossip was hard to silence, and speculation about the connection between Bulysh and Balkiya had reached her repeatedly. After each such tale, Khansulu grew somewhat chilly to her brother-in-law. But time would pass and seeing Bulysh later acting as if nothing had happened, heading off to hunt accompanied by his white hound, she would settle down and forget about what she had heard, and would once again feast her eyes on his heroic look. It was impossible not to admire him. He seemed to her to be like the legendary *batyr* [70]Kambar on his black horse with the white forelock...

The door noiselessly opened, and Balkiya came in. The ornaments jingled in her braids and fell silent, and stepping quietly, she stole into the bed. In the darkness, her breathing could be heard as she undressed. Khansulu remained motionless, pretending to sleep. Cold crept into the bed under the warm blanket along with Balkiya. There was the scent of the snowy night, the scent of saxaul bark, and finally in Balkiya's even breathing Khansulu caught the scent of Bulysh. As soon as Balkiya's head hit the pillow, she fell asleep. She slept deeply and calmly...

No sooner had the *dastarkhan*[71] been picked up in Bulysh's home than a chubby, mobile man appeared. He smiled artificially, right from the doorway. The guest's voice was ingratiating. He was Jorga Kuren, and had been sent by Mazhan. As was fitting for a guest, he immediately sat on the tor. Kuren was a distant relative's of Mazhan's. And he was also his right-hand man. He understood a little grammar, had lived in the city, and had his view on life. Therefore, he was the first advisor for the *bay*. He also conducted Mazhan's trade in the city. Thanks to him, Mazhan lived well. He was nice to everyone – both friends and enemies; he smiled at all of them alike. His nickname was Ambler Kuren.

"Listen, *jeneshetay*[72], the guest began, settling himself comfortably on the tor, looking at *Dau-apa*. "Consider that our auls are next to each other, but yet we see each other only once a month or even a year. How are you living and prospering? How are your cattle? How are your people?"

"Well, thank God," Bulysh's mother said casually, stirring the milk in the boiling *kazan* with a ladle.

---

[70] A *batyr* is a war hero.

[71] A *dastarkhan* is a table cloth.

[72] *Jeneshchetai* is an affectionate address to the wife of an elder relative.

Seeing no disposition from her side, Jorga, smiling just as artificially, turned toward Bulysh.

"Well, Bulyshzhan,[73] nowadays they say there are plenty of saigas[74] in the sands. We heard that you are an accurate shooter, and that you crack the whip from the horse successfully.

Every word had to be dragged out of Bulysh, but in conversations with Kuren, he simply was lost. *Dau-apa* sensed her son's state, and cut him off on the fly.

"Jorga, don't you beat around the bush, spit out what you came here for."

"Oy, *jeneshe,* and you can be offended, after all, eh? Well, here's what I came to talk to you about. Yesterday my capricious *jenge* left Mazhan's home and they say she is staying in your aul."

"And what do you think it's about? My house is a shelter for crazy women who run away from their husbands, eh?"

"*Oybay, jeneshe,* listen…"

Here is what he told her.

Yesterday in Mazhan's aul a council was held, at which the respectable men headed by Jorga Kuren had a comprehensive discussion with the *bay*: why, so to say, wed a young woman because somebody's evil slanders cannot be forgiven her? Truth be told, the old man didn't want to part with Balkiya. Only egged on by the children of his elder wife had he driven the beautiful *tokal* from his home, but he himself was suffering terribly for what had happened. He could ask that the *tokal* be returned; his pride did not allow him. Therefore, on the whole, he was overjoyed when Jorga Kuren offered him his services, saying he would take upon himself the return of Balkiya. The *tokal* had

---

[73] Bulyshzhan is an affectionate form of the name Bulysh.

[74] The saiga is a type of antelope found in Central Asia; it is now a critically endangered species.

an obstinate nature, so the old man had thought that if something could persuade her, it would only be Kuren's sweet talk…

Mazhan seemed to have seen into the future; somewhere about noon, Jorga Kuren, leading Balkiya, was already descending to his yurt from the sandy ridge between the two auls.

5

Khansulu's parents began to prepare for the wedding in earnest: her mater was consumed with the dowry, day after day, sewing on the machine; her father intended in the second half of winter to go to the bazaar in Beskala – he had decided to sell a half heard of stallions and camels there in order to use the cash to buy from the Karakalpaks everything needed for the wedding, including the *yurta-otau*[75] for the newlyweds.

After the men left for Beskala, yet another incident occurred in the aul. At dawn, Sharip the Squealer went out of is home with the *kumgan* in his hand to answer nature's call. He looked at where Azbergen's home, which abutted Pakhraddin's kitchen yurt, usually stood and saw the spot was empty. Only the black circle from the yurt remained. So yesterday, there was a yurt, and this morning it was gone. It disappeared. The bastard had migrated. Fled. Sharip, who was responsible to the authorities for the aul, froze in place, not believing his eyes. He only came to his senses when he dropped the *kumgan* full of water. He flinched.

"Oh, that cut-throat! Oh, that *contra*! He did his dark deed nonetheless! Well, just you wait!" he vowed and hurried with all his might toward the pasture, wildly looking about. In the pre-dawn shadows of the saxaul bushes, the kept imagining that he saw Azbergen's camp everywhere.

Sharip got the whole aul to its feet and then jumping on to the chestnut horse, he galloped off. In his haste, he had gotten on the horse

---

[75] The *otau* is the new family of husband and wife who separate from the father's house; the *yurta-otau* is the yurt for such newlyweds.

without a saddle and then before he reached the pass, felt pain, since he was thin. He returned, leading the horse by the reins. He poked the sleeping Shege, and sent him to the head of the *volost* government in Koksengir.

After lunch, the fat Bukhabay, the policeman with the dagger, appeared. He also rode around the aul, poked around the edges, and the said:

"You yourselves are to blame, he should have been shot last time, and now he has fled and become a bandit!"

Several more days passed, and a warm wind blew from the south, the sun warmed the earth, the snow receded in places and began to melt.

After May's cold weather, the lambing time began. For the livestock-breeding aul, the appearance of the animals' young was the busiest time of year, since everyone turned out to catch the newborns! As soon as the sheep gave birth and the lambs' legs grew strong, the nomads who had wintered in Sama began gradually to move from the camp, heading toward the summer pastures in the far-off shores of the River Jem. Now the move was not so hurried as at the outset of winner; they didn't move one behind the other in a long, dismal line. Now they moved as free travelers, spreading their wings wide on the steppe. And they didn't hurry in fear, as they had in the winter. The camp was moved slowly, using the natural goods along the way, giving the sheep and lambs a chance to scatter over the grass, and the horses and the camels to pasture in large herds.

The multi-throated bleating of the lambs and sheep, weaving with the songs of the shepherds, gave the nomad's grove a lively and festive feeling as they moved along the green valleys. The *nars* majestically glided along with their loads. The cooper bells clanged to the rhythm of their step. Everyone was cheerful – the old women, the children sitting in the carriers atop the camels, the young men on horses, the *jigits* and girls going ahead, galloping alongside. The nomads' age-old yearning for their free life on the *jaylyau*[76], their

---

[76] The *jaylyau* is a summer pasture for a nomad community.

games and *toys*[77], the furious activity, made itself felt. Ahead the long summer awaited. There was a place to straighten one's shoulders and stroll through the open spaces. The summer promises the fun of games and *toys*, the beauty of moon nights, noisy holidays.

But this summer wasn't awaiting Khansulu, nor calling to her; it was the first in her life to be burdensome for her. Every time she heard the chuckling of the idiot Kozbagar, she grimaced. Poor Kozbagar was prepared to flatten himself into a pancake if only to please Pakhraddin; he was busy only with his jobs. But Khansulu hardly softened toward him; on the contrary, she hated him more and more strongly. Khansulu swore she would die before marrying Kozbagar. Of course she would obey her father's will, but no one could force her to bow her head before that dolt...

A week later the nomads descended into the Balga Valley. All night until very morning the moonlit, white rain was falling. The smooth ground of the valley, overgrown with wormwood and bramble, was washed clean, was turning green, and was like a fluffy rug. It was easy and light to breathe the fresh, aromatic air. The caravan came to life, the sheep and goats began bleating, the lambs and kids rolled around, the camel calves cavorted, their bells tinkling, enjoying the freedom.

There was another unhappy soul who didn't notice all this beauty – Shege. He had grown gaunt and dark, and sat hunched over and sad in his saddle. He and his father were at the very tail end of the caravan, driving 40 head of sheep.

The nomad's group travelled along, the bells clanging, making halts at night, and during the day letting the herds graze. This was the nomad's life, everything was mixed up in it – both joys and sorrows and jokes and pranks. The road was long. It was the life passed on to them by their ancestors. It was the customary path. With each day, the grass grew higher to the joy of animal and people. The lakes flashed bright all around them, grey ducks and goose could be seen. People's faces were bright and joyful.

---

[77] A *toy* is a Kazkh nomad community's feast to mark a wedding or holiday.

The Lonely Yurt • Smagul Yelubay

... Two weeks later the noisy nomad's group halted at the summer *jaylyau* on the south bank of Lake Tugisken. The auls had been on the road with the herds for almost a month, making halts at night, and now people refreshed in soul felt as if the great journey remained behind them forever.

The lake was in the center of a broad plain, its southern, sloping bank was a thick green meadow with wormwood and St. John's wort. The aul decided to spend the night here. After lunch, people unloaded the baggage, raised the frames of the yurts and toward evening, when the sun hid in its nest behind Khantortkil Hill, the aul sprang up on the meadow, and the yurts were arranged in rows. In the center stood the large white yurt of Pakhraddin, like an overturned *piyala.*[78] To the right of it was the white *yurta-otau* for Khansulu, the very one her father had brought for his daughter from Beskala.

The hearths had already been arranged in front of the yurts, the fire was already cheerfully crackling...

...At noon, Jdakhay and Shege, frightening numerous flocks of birds on the lake, were shooting ducks in the tamarisk brush. This was their first meeting eye-to-eye ever since the aul had settled on the *jaylyau*. Shege felt bad when he saw the large bruise on Jdakhay's right temple.

"That's the work of Mazhan's thugs," Jdakhay shrugged his shoulders. "Because of Balkiya...Tell me, Shege, is it true that the *rayon*[79] is coming? They say they will destroy the *bays* at the root."

"The *rayon* doesn't come, it is created," Jdakhay corrected Shege. "It's instead of an *uyezd*.[80] The *uyezd*, they say, couldn't do anything with the *bays* so it's going bye-bye! Instead, there will be the *rayon*. And there's no kidding around with the *rayon*; they will now

---

[78] The *piyala* is a wide Central Asian drinking cup.
[79] The *rayon* or region was the regional government in the early Soviet era.
[80] The *uyezd* or district was the administrative unit in the tsarist era.

take the *bays* by the scruff of the neck and tell them enough living in clover for a whole 10 years, now high-tail it out of here!

"So that's how it is. It's about time! Because my neck was already getting sore craning for it, where was it, that new life? You could die before the new life would come."

"That's just in our parts. They say others have long had the new life," Shege assured him with the look of a knowledgeable person. Jdakhay pressed forward:

"Listen, your father here is the government. Maybe, you know, he knows when the *ayyrplany* and *masheny*[81] will come?

Shege only laughed.

"Oh, get out! Now you want an *ayyrplan*...We should first see a *shaytan-arba*[82]..."

"Oh, now if I were in power!" Jdakhay sighed contritely, and tumbled down on his back on the grass.

Shege broke out laughing maliciously.

"What would you do if you were in power?"

"No kidding. I would shoot these *bays* bang-bang with a rifle! So their fathers...! I wouldn't allow them to idle their time away before the opening of the *rayon*!"

And the friends forgot about the ducks, and got carried away with talk, and didn't notice Khansulu, who approached them from the direction of the aul on her horse Karaker.

---

[81] *Ayyrplan* and *mashine* were corruptions of the Russian words *aeroplan* (airplane) and *mashina* (car) in Kazakhstan in the early 20th century.
[82] *Shaytan-arba* is a bicycle, literally "devil's wagon."

Tears gleamed in the corners of the girl's almond-shaped eyes. Respected people from the aul had just come calling on Pakhraddin. Among them was Sharip the Squealer, lanky Uap, *Dau-apa*, and Bulysh. Labak-*akhun* came riding in on a white camel from Jylybulak. Pakhraddin's guest yurt was filled up.

"Sulutay, " she called to Khansulu. "You should go out and get some air…"

Her mother was sad, and the girl's heart sensed something bad. Karaker, as always was agitating at the post; flying up on him, she galloped away as fast as she could, not knowing where she was going.

And right behind her a little boy on a chestnut stallion hurried after her from the aul. Like a whirlwind she flew past the lake.

"Hey, bad boy, stop!" Jdakhay cried after him, still lying on the ground. "Come here!"

The boy had a hard time stopping his overheated horse.

"What do you want?" he asked unhappily. The chestnut stallion flared its black nostrils wide.

"Where are you flying at full speed, you nut? Tell me about it."

"I'm going to invite people to the wedding! The wedding will be next Wednesday! Pakhraddin is giving away his daughter in marriage!" the boy cried and lashed his horse.

"Well, now that's something, lad!" Jdakhay exclaimed. His eyes wide, he looked confusedly first at Khansulu – she was watering Karaker at the lake – then at Shege, who was turning gray. His friend was staring remotely at the ground.

"What are you silent for, you nut? Will Kozbagar really get Khansulu? That his father…! Let's steal her! Will she agree, eh? Does she love you?" Jdakhay jumped up from his place in consternation.

Gritting his teeth, Shege remained silent. He didn't tear his eyes away from the ground as before. Tears had welled up in his eyes.

The herald on the chestnut stallion, kicking up clouds of dust, hurried to the east along the feather-grass plain...

The Lonely Yurt • Smagul Yelubay

A RESTLESS SUMMER

1

There was just a matter of days before the wedding, when the Muslim holiday of *kurban-ayt*[83] would begin. People got up before dawn; in every shed, an appropriate sacrificial lamb had been selected and tied up.

...

"Let *kurban-ayt* be joyful!" people wished each other, and in reply heard the traditional reply:

"Let your words come to pass!"

In all the homes, the doors were flung open wide, in the yurts the *dastarkhans* were richly laden, they would not be cleared for three days. People were in a joyful mood. All three days would pass in an endless flow of well-wishers. Whoever came in the door would be a guest. People were dressed in their finest. The trunks were open, the *kebezhe*,[84] all the best garments were dragged out into the open air, the fabrics, everything was displayed for general review. People's lives were transformed for several days by the multi-colored decorations of the yurt like the wealthy dowry of the *bay*'s daughter. Young people were in an uplifted mood. No one would stop them all through these days of playing games and having fun, they could go to visit neighboring auls, and visit any home where the smoke rose from the hearth.

Toward noon, a cloud of dust appeared at the Jem river and a horseman emerged. This was the messenger from the chairman of the *volost* council. The lathered horse, wet from foam, stopped before

---

[83] Eid al-Adh is the Muslim "festival of the sacrifice," commemorating Abraham's willingness to sacrifice his son, when God intervened through his angel Gabriel to tell him his sacrifice was already accepted.
[84] A *kebezh* is a felt container.

Sharip's yurt. The aul instantly filled with rumors. "The commission is coming...the very head of the *rayon*..."

No sooner had the messenger galloped away than Sharip, small, on bent legs, ran from yurt to yurt, passing on the order of the head of the *volost* government:

"Respected people, put your houses in order! The head of the *rayon* is coming! He wants to see how we live with his own eyes! Prepare yourselves well!"

"Well, of all things! Good Lord, what more can we do to get ready?" Torka grumbled. "No sooner is it summer than the bosses come out like marmots from their lairs!"

"Hey! Don't you dare talk like that!" shouted Sharip. "The people who are coming aren't to be joked with!"

"Hey, people, get ready! The new boss is coming! He'll open any door he likes! He'll stay wherever he likes! Hey, people!" Sharip shouted, running through the aul and stirring up everyone. He stopped at Pakhraddin's yurt.

"Hey, brother-in-law, you get ready, too! The head of the *rayon* is coming. Who knows, maybe he'll decide to stay at your house...There is no other more decent yurt in the aul, as you know."

"Eh, what of it. Don't worry, brother-in-law," said Pakhraddin, and in order to calm Sharip, slapped him on the back.

Khansulu was not at home. She had galloped off with the young people to Kolkudyk for *kurban-ayt.*

The guests arrived exactly at noon, and hurried to the edge of the aul. Two policemen with rifles on their backs accompanied them. The barking dogs had come running before the people arrived, but Sharip had managed to chase them away with a stick in time. Mincing along, he rolled up to the tall Russian *jigit* in the leather cap and grey tunic, wearily and gloomily surveying the aul, and then fussily stretched out his hand.

"Good day!"

"Good day!" the Russian replied in a thick baritone, once again, rather coldly.

Sharip had heard that the boss – a young Russian *jigit* – was not from these parts. He didn't know Sharip, naturally, and looked on the thin middle-aged man in eyeglasses as if to ask him, "Who is this?" Sharip knew the man in the glasses. This was the well-known Apanas.[85] Sharip knew Apanas. Apanas had been exiled here, to the Kazakh steppe, even during the time of Tsar Mikolay[86]; in Temir, before the Soviet government came to power, he had taught in a school, and now he was the chairman of the district executive committee. Apanas spoke Kazakh like his own native language. Slapping Sharip on the back, he hastened to introduce his boss.

"This is Comrade Kaspakov! In the Kazakh language, this is Sharip-aga."

"Yes, Kaspakov, Kaspakov," sharip said, stuttering and breaking into a smile and nodding his head.

The gloomy face of the boss smoothed, and he also nodded his head. Apanas congratulated Sharip:

"Happy house-warming, Sharip-aga!" He meant the arrival of the aul at the *jaylyau*. "Let your *ayt*[87] be filled with joy!"

"May your words come to pass, Apanas!" Sharip said emotionally.

The chairman of the *volost* council, Dukenbay Ismailov had also accompanied Kaspakov, and Asan Aytzhanov, a member of the *volost* council and two policemen; one of them was the big fellow Bukhabay, the same one who had taken Azbergen away to prison, and

---

[85] Apanas was the Kazakh name for Afanasy Grinin, a former exile in Western Kazakhstan.

[86] Tsar Nikolai II.

[87] The Muslim holiday.

the second was not known to Sharip, a sinewy *jigit* with a dark grey cast to his face.

"Jekey," Apanas introduced him.

People from the aul headed by Pakhraddin had managed to arrive to see the guests. Apanas continued to introduce them.

"Semyon Kharitonovich, this is the man," he said, pointing to Pakhraddin. "The *myrza*. Respected by everyone, Pakhraddin, about whom I told you on the way here. And this is…" he turned his attention of those gathered to the main guest. "This is the first secretary of the rayon committee of the Party, Semyon Kharitonovich Kalashnikov. I beg you to love and pity, as they say. Here we're going around the auls. Semyon Kharitonovich wishes to become acquainted with the auls, with the activity of the Soviets[88] in the regions, particularly in the auls. He is on Kazakh land for the first time…

"Oh, welcome! Get acquainted! Be our guest!" Pakhraddin replied in Russian.

Kalashnikov looked at him not without some curiosity; the *myrza* produced an impression. He was large, proportionately constructed, broad-shouldered; his high forehead was covered at a slant with an expensive *tyubeteyka* [89]with fine embroidery; a handsome round trimmed beard and a mustache touched with gray; reflective deep eyes looking openly.

"Pakhraddin-*myrza*, do you speak Russian?" asked Kalashnikov.

"We can ask for bread in Russian, comrade secretary," said Pakhraddin, twisting his mustache.

"Come to the table! Pakhraddin-*myrza* prepared a treat for you," Sharip said, leaping ahead.

---

[88] A soviet is a local council or government body.
[89] A *tyubeteyka* is a Central Asian skull cap.

Afanasy Vasilyevich translated Sharip's offer to Kalashnikov, but he preferred first to go around the aul. No matter what home the secretary glanced into, everywhere there were displayed for show on the occasion of the holiday – original local crafts, finally sewn sheepskins, wolf and fox skins, women's jewelry. On the floors, he saw patterned felt *tekemets*[90] with *korpeshkas*[91] and pillows piled up in heaps on beds. There were rugs of every color of the rainbow. There were boxes made of bone, with carved work on the faces. Woven ribbons hung from the ceiling. Silk curtains on cords covered part of the yurt. The guests were met with a bow by young women and girls in colorful dresses, in painted kerchiefs and scarves – like flowers of the steppe; the women's hands, fingers and ears were studded with bracelets, rings and earrings...

The area around the hearth was cleared. The dastarkhan was abundant with impressive piles of *baursaks, kurt, irimshchik, maysok* and *jent.*[92]

"So show me the home of a poor fellow," asked Kalashnikov.

"But you were just in the home of a poor fellow!" Sharip replied. They had just come out of Bulysh's home.

"How many animals does he have?"

"*Oybay,* he's a poor man, a total poor man! He has 20 goats, 3 camels, if you count their calves and one horse."

"And how many does the *myrza* have in his herds?"

"Oh, the *myrza* was once prosperous! Now he has less herds. He gave the meat to the government. Now, consider he has almost nothing."

"Alright. How many are left?"

---

[90] A *tekemet* is a kind of felt rug.
[91] A *korpeshka* is a kind of mat.
[92] National desserts and preserves made of milk products.

"There are about 200 sheep, there are about 50 horse heads and about a dozen camels."

Listening to the explanations, Kalashnikov observed the young men and girls passing by, seeing their movements and gestures and noticing how they were dressed.

Pakhraddin himself had opened the doors of his yurt and invited the guests to come in. Bukhabay the policeman remained outside. Kalashnikov, heading to the *tor,* was shocked at what he had seen and did not hide this. The decoration of the yurts he had just been in, compared with the magnificence which opened up before him in the home of the *myrza* looked like the setting of a cheap shack. He was astounded not only by the luxury, but by the taste, guessing that in everything that surrounded him, the taste was subtle, unassuming and yet elegant. "Where does some beauty here come from, in this god-forsaken place?" he wondered. He recalled the words of Filipp Isayevich Goloshchekin[93], the first secretary of the Kazakh *rayon* committee of the government, as he sent him off: "The *rayon* where you are headed is the most backward in the steppe. It's a remote area which the Soviet government has not reached. You'll have to start from scratch…"

The Syrga the *baybishe,* moving softly and daintily, poured the fragrant *kumys*, shimmering yellow. The round low table in the center instantly filled up with several big cups of the aromatic drink. As a final touch, Pakhraddin solemnly set on the table two quarter liters of vodka.

Comfortably sitting on the soft Persian rug, the guests relished the *kumys*.

---

[93] Filipp Isayevich Goloshchekin was a Russian revolutionary, Old Bolshevik, and Soviet party functionary, and member of the Bolshevik Central Committee (1927-1934). He is known for taking part in the shooting of the Tsar's family and for his devastating role in the Sovietization of Kazakhstan ("Small October") which resulted in the deadly famine of 1932–33, which took between 1 and 2 million lives.

"Marvelous!" Kalashnikov pronounced and nodded his head. Sweat had broken out on his forehead. He was trying *kumys* for the first time. Becoming a bit tipsy, he joked: "You have a lot, Pakhraddin-*myrza* – both wealth and refreshments, but for some reason, I don't see women, eh? Why?"

Apanas translated this into Kazakh. Sharip, who was waiting on the guest – handing him *tostagans* [94]with *kumys* – couldn't restrain himself and rolled with light trills of laughter.

"But we're getting ready for a wedding! It's not in vain we call Pakhraddin the 'model *myrza*'?" Sharip interrupted him, and now there was no stopping him.

"He is giving away a daughter, his very own daughter, to his *batrak*, the wedding will be soon. And that's not all, he's giving her away without the *kalyn*[95]. He's that kind of man. Just."

"Really? Your daughter?" Kalashnikov stared at him.

"Yes, my daughter. My only one," Pakhraddin lowered his moistened eyes.

"Interesting," Kalashnikov said, surprised. He shook his head.

Lean Syrga the *baybishe* silently bustling about the household chores, quietly knelt to the right side of the steaming samovar. She brought out of the trunk a brand-new Russian porcelain tea service, wipe it with a silk towel and placed it on the table. And soon the guests were drinking aromatic Indian tea, poured into painted porcelain coups.

The main guest observed all this attentively.

Pakhraddin in his green silk chapan thrown over a white shirt, sitting Turkish-style with his legs crossed, raised his head and looking straight at Kalashnikov, said:

---

[94] A t*ostagan* is a small wooden cup.
[95] The *kalyn* is the bride price, which the groom's father would pay the bride's father.

"We have heard many things here about the policy of the government. We understand. The government will take excess cattle, excess goods. Everything is to go into the common pot. Let it be, we will put into it, thus it will be. I personally have no objections. Let them take it and give it away to poor people. But one thing I still do not understand, no matter how much I think about it. What are the unfortunate *bays* guilty of, that their goods and cattle must all be taken away completely...to ruin them and drive them away with their families?"

Kalashnikov, pushing the pillow a little towards the wall, reflected and raised his head.

"I knew that there would be such a question," he said. "You are not the only one, representatives of the privileged class, the strong of this world, to ask this. Your people have a saying, 'Livestock belongs to him who pastures it and things belong to him who finds them.' This is the word of the people. The policy of the party today is aimed at having people turn this dream into life. The *batrak* pastures the *bay*'s herds. The party believes that the *batrak* himself should be the owner of that herd which he pastures. It's true, the Soviet government does not pat the *bay* on the head that he has *batraks*. Just as the *bay* does not pat the *batrak* which he keeps on the head, although the man is pasturing his herds. After all, we have the poor man's government now.

Pakhraddin realized that he had been beaten.

"No, that's not what I mean, comrade...I am not at all against such a policy by the government. On the contrary, I supported it. I myself, at my own wish, if the government considers it necessary, and prepared to give away the excess. Take it. Please...But I'm interested in something else. Let us say that they take from us what is owed, but what then? Why are some let out into the world like plucked chickens? That's what I would like to know."

"Oh, no...," Apanas reassured him. "It will all be done fairly. According to the law. You have a different case, Pakhraddin-*myrza*. Your services to the government will be taken into account.

"*Bi-aga*[96]!" Dukenbai also reassured him. You aren't considered a large *bay*, after all. Do you have to fear idle rumors?"

"Thank you for the bread and salt![97]" said Kalashnikov graciously, bowing to Syrga the *baybyshe*, and quickly, in military fashion, getting up from his seat. The rest of the men jumped up as well.

The grey-faced policeman Jekey went out first. He looked around and saw Bukhabay was not at his post. "What happened to him?" Sur-Jekey said worriedly, his eyes darting about, and went behind the house. There he saw Bukhabay and two young people arguing about something. One of the young men who was sturdy and solid, was trying to break through to the yurt, but Bukhabay was blocking his way with his powerful body. Jekey immediately came over.

'What's going on?" he asked sternly.

"Some *jigit* acquaintances, before we used to pasture goats together," Bukhabay began to explain, wiping the sweat from his brow. "They insisted, they had to save the *bay*'s daughter, they said, and asked to speak to the bosses. I won't let them, but they wouldn't listen…"

"*Tabarysh milisa*[98]!" Jdakhay couldn't hold back, now appealing to Jekey. His eyes seemed to roll out of orbit. "We are fighting for justice! We have a statement for the boss!"

"Eh, what kind of boss is he! He's the secretary of the *rayon*," Jekey frowned angrily. Now get out of here!" and he added in Russian, "March!"

---

[96] *Bi-aga* is a combination of two respected titles.
[97] A Russian expression referencing the traditional offering by hosts of a plate of bread and salt to guests.
[98] Jdakhay is thus pronouncing the Russian words *tovarishch militsioner,* or "comrade policeman."

"But we have a statement!" Shege demanded, looking straight at the policeman.

"What statement?"

"Pakhraddin is giving away his daughter...forcibly."

"And who are you?"

"We're poor youth."

"Well, get out of here! If it is forcible, let the girl herself complain! March!"

Jekey simply began pushing them away.

"But we can't fight for justice! Where is the *sabetski blasty*[99]?"

"March!" barked Jekey, now beside himself, his face turning ash grey.

Unwillingly, Jdakhay and Shege stepped backward.

Meanwhile the guests had mounted on their horses and had managed to leave. Their route now lay through Mazhan's aul. When Pakhraddin's remained behind, he said, "Really, it's as if nothing has happened here. As if the revolution had passed this territory by...eh, so much to do ahead! Much to do..." he said, sadly shaking his head.

2

Khansulu had seen many weddings. But she was at such a joyless one for the first time. And this was her own. Her father had spent his entire estate, it seemed, on the festivities, and had been excessively extravagant. More than a hundred yurts were placed along

---

[99]He is thus pronouncing the Russian term *sovietskiye vlasti* which means "Soviet authorities" or government.

both wings of the aul; about a hundred sheep were slaughtered; the *jyrshes*[100], who sang the *Toy-bastar*[101] arrived and thus heralded the beginning of the marriage ceremony; he presented a race horse; about 200 horses took part in a *baige,*[102] where the main prize was two thoroughbred *nar* camels with enormous humps. The epic wrestlers competed in fights, and each received a mare.

But nothing touched Khansulu. She sat behind a silk curtain in the yurt set aside for the bride, surrounded by her girlfriends and watching the happy, immersed aul through the bars of the *kerege*; her eyes were sorrowful and full of tears.

The story-tellers attracted her attention. At first, she didn't want to listen to the performance of the poets. However, the *akynay*[103] gathered on a little hill near her, and willy-nilly, she was forced to become a participant in the events. Toward evening, the hill and its foot were covered with rugs. As the moon came out, people began to stream there from all over. And in a little while, like a living spirit, a tall, old man in a white *chapan* and a white *chalma*, withered like a saxaul, his beard and mustache also white, rose before them with a *dombra* in his hands. The old man went to the top of the hill, covered with carpets and soft blankets, and knelt down. The moon poured milky light over the hill.

When the people had taken their seats and no more footsteps were heard, Labak-akhun took the *dombra* into his hands. The roaring crowd instantly fell silent.

The *akhun* shrugged his shoulders, and pushed forward, as if he intended to fly, and that movement only emphasized his resemblance to a swan. Suddenly, a voice poured out from his old man's larynx, heart-rending, as if the *akhun* was not signing but chanting in measured tones. The elder meanwhile turned to

---

[100] A *jyrsh* is a bard.

[101] The *toy bastar* is the ritual commencement of the feast.

[102] A *baige* is a type of long-distance horse race (5 to 50 kilometers) in Central Asia in which the horseman's mastery of the horse is critical.

[103] The *akunay*

enumerating the *dastans*.[104] There were many of them, very many! Name the one that has taken your fancy!

The *akhun* fell silent, listening to the buzz of the people, and drank some tea from the *piyala* in front of him. The hubbub did not let up. Everyone was calling out their requests, and they settled finally for the *dastan* about the 40 girls.[105] Few in the steppe knew it.

…The vast steppe, covered in a soft moonlight, groaned and lamented along with Labak-akhun's *dombra*. The hushed, silver wave rolled across the tops of the grass, dittany and sage…another wave rolled and another…a sea of fragrant steppe herbs stirred up and the chia rustled. The entire world under the moon went into motion, touched by the throaty melodious voice of the story-teller. The ancient rhythm came from the depths of the ages…from the age of grief and lament.

The skies shimmered in the sky. The moon bent down to the very aul. Wrapped in a bright smoke, the Milky Way stretched its cloudy trail across the sky. The steppe turned over and heaved a sigh – of course it remembered everything…

Khansulu found much that was similar between her own fate and the fate of the fighter, the leader of the 4 warrior girls, the fearless Gulyay. Once again the vortex was stirred up, causing a disturbance in her soul. And once again a tear broke away from her eyelash…

Khansulu's white *yurta-otau* was placed alongside the home of Kozbagar. She was brought there. The inside of the yurt was a palanquin with a silk curtain. In the evening, the religious ritual known as *neke-kiyu* was performed. The *kaysh*-mullah "blessed" the water in a chalice with a prayer which the groom and bride were supposed to drink, expressing their consent to the marriage. Khansulu did not take a proper swallow but merely touched her lips to the chalice and muttered to herself: "Not in this world, nor in the next world, do I consent to this marriage…I do not consent…" With that, she returned the chalice. For herself, Khansulu decided that her marriage was not blessed and not

---

[104] A *dastan* is a folk epos in verse form.
[105] "The 40 Girls" was a Karakalpak heroic epos.

legalized. She had heard before that if the bride does not drink from the ritual cup, the marriage has not taken place.

In the evening, when the time came to go to bed, the young girls and young men who had been with her these four days gradually began to disperse, and even her closest girlfriend Balzhan disappeared.

The noise and bustle of the wedding faded away. Khansulu remained alone in her conjugal bed behind the white silk curtain. Was this real or a dream? Strangely, Khansulu perceived what was happening as a joke, a bad joke, which deranged people, headed by her father, had played on her. Khansulu kept having the feeling that a sensible person would come along and put an end to this insane vision, and say, "Stop! Everyone go home! And you, Khansulu, come with me, I will take you to your real betrothed..." Her heart refused to believe what was happening, she believed in a dream, in the power of miracles which would save her. She lived with that expectation. And what was happening? The savior did not come. She was wearing a white *jaulyk* on her head. She was a wife. Whose? Kozbagar's! A spouse fated by God. And she was sitting in a dark yurt waiting for him himself, her husband...

She didn't have to wait long, as it happened. Women's whispers could be heard behind the door, suppressing laughter, and she head:

"What are you standing there for, you dolt?"
"Go on in, darn you!"

Someone was pushed inside. That "someone" froze at the threshold. He stood like a post rooted to the spot. It was dark. His silhouette could barely be made out. Khansulu knew that Kozbagar had come. What an appetite, eh? What, did he consider himself her equal?! Her equal?! Him?! But everything was his fault! Exactly. If he hadn't called himself a groom, the blind-man's buff came would have remained just a game. A game, and nothing else.

"Who invited you here?" Khansulu, boiling with irritation, asked Kozbagar, who was breathing heavily by the door. Kozbagar stepped backward and was about to push open the door but it wouldn't yield – the aunts were all pushing against it, laughing and whispering.

"Where are you going, you dolt? This is your home, you hear? You can't take a step away now!"

The helplessness of the big lug – he was broad-shouldered but his back was to the door infuriated Khansulu.

"Why did you get married then if you are running away?" she snarled.

Kozbagar began to shift from one foot to the other, coughing. Leaning against the door, he begged of the women:

"Well, go away then, for God's sake!"

The women immediately fell silent and then giggling, went away.

"Khansulu!" Kozbagar was barely able to speak out of shyness. "What am I to do? They said to get married...they yelled at me."

Khansulu sniffed angrily, turning toward the wall. What a groom!

The bed curtain at the wall was drawn, everything nearby was clearly visible. The lake twinkled, the frogs croaked. The waves splashed in the tamarisk undergrowth on the shore, the herd had apparently wandered away. Birds rustled in the bushes, and the beating of their wings could be heard. A cold breeze blew from the shore as well. The scent of the damp sand on the shore wafted by.

"Khansulu!"

The girl shuddered. The poor thing had forgotten that Kozbagar was here.

"Ugh, what else do you want?"

"Khansulu...for God's sake...I didn't want to offend you..."

The Lonely Yurt • Smagul Yelubay

"Anything else?"

"I…love…you…"

"It would be better if you didn't! Because I don't love you!"

Kozbagar heaved a sigh.

"Well, what am I to blame for, Khansulu, eh?" He was silent for a moment, then broke out in a sob.

"I knew it would be this way. I knew for a long time. But…everyone yelled at me. What now?"

And Kozbagar began sobbing heavily – there was no holding back! His broad shoulders shook from his sobs.

By that time the moon had risen and peeped into the yurt through the opening of the *kerege* lattice, it was brighter. Khansulu got up from her bed, her earrings and tassles lightly jingling. She had on a long white silk dress. Seeing it, Kozbagar was overjoyed. His mother, Torka, he remembers, grew soft-hearted when he cried, and would come to him and strike his head and speak tenderly to him. Perhaps Khansulu would come and stroke his head as well, he thought. But Khansulu did not approach him. She did not stroke his head. Her tassles just kept monotonously jingling and jingling. She threw him a blanket and pillow on the threshold.

"Make your own bed!"

Her tone was harsh, but for Kozbagar, it was sweeter than honey. He had not expected from Khansulu even these words. He made his bed near the door and lay down. Khansulu had not allowed him next to her – but that was nothing, let her at first grow accustomed to him. Meanwhile, the scent of her perfume was on the pillow and blanket…And after all, her hand had touched both this pillow and this blanket…His heart pounded…poor Kozbagar at that moment was ready to die for Khansulu…

She was next to him, a proud, beautiful wife, with lightly jingling tassles, stepping softly, white as the moon, there she was behind the silk curtain, tossing and turning from the chilly wind, and Kozbagar was grateful for this. If he would not be a groom this night, for God's sake, racing full speed toward the lake like this – naked and unclothed, laughing from an excess of feeling, he would shout at the top of his lungs! He would shout to the whole world of his fortune!

The moon quietly went behind the clouds. The aul was in a deep sleep. The camels, towering above like mountains, were chewing their cud in the dusty desert. The dogs had long since quieted down. Only on the lake, life still made itself heard – the crickets were chirping, the frogs were croaking, birds were sleepily singing, and fish were splashing. Everything was hushed…

…But someone was hiding in the undergrowth of tamarisk on the lake shore, holding the reins of saddled horses. One of the horses was Azbergen's. As soon as the aul was fast asleep, he came out of his hiding place and began to quietly creep toward Pakhraddin's high, white yurt. The enormous dogs, the size of a donkey awakened, but recognizing Azbergen, wagged their tails.

"Eh, who's there?" asked Pakhraddin, hearing the creak of the door.

"Me," Azbergen said in a muffled voice. Throwing on his *chapan*, Pakhraddin opened the door. Syrga the *baybishe* awoke and wanted to light the lamp but Azbergen wouldn't let her.

"What are you doing here?" Pakhraddin asked, trying to peer at his brother who sat on the edge of the *koshma*.

"I came to the wedding, brother, although you didn't invite me. You are engaged to the *Sabety*[106], congratulations! That's why I came, to congratulate you!" Azbergen replied venomously.

"What are you babbling about, you half-wit?" Pakhraddin retorted angrily. "You would have long ago rotted in prison if it were not for this wedding…"

---

[106] *Sabety* is how the Kazakhs say "the Soviets".

The Lonely Yurt • Smagul Yelubay

"Babbling? Alright. But the half-wit between us is not me, brother, but you! You gave your daughter to the *Sabety*, and cattle, one after another, to them as well. You alone are the only one in this territory who has gone so mad. But others are dying in battle. You will die currying favor with them, you know that, don't you? Let us see how tomorrow, these *Sabety* will thank you," Azbergen bristled.

"That's enough! An old tune. I've heard it before. Where are you staying now?"

"I won't say for now. Here's the news, brother: the *Sabety* will fall with a crash! The British are pressing from one side and the Turks from the other. I need horses."

"Eh, I'm afraid you're mistaken, my dear man. And badly. So there won't be any horses."

"Let us be like dogs to one another now, though we came from one womb. Although I could level you with one bullet!" Azbergen jumped up and headed toward the door. As he stepped over the threshold, he stopped for a moment, and wanted to say something, apparently, but then thought better of it, slammed the door and left.

...Kozbagar slept soundly. He didn't sense a thing – neither how someone knocked at the door, or how Khansulu unhooked the latch, nor how Azbergen came into the yurt. Only when someone lumped at him, heavy as lead, and grabbed his throat did he wake up, blinking his eyes in confusion. He could try to jerk away – but where?

"A werewolf," he thought to himself, half asleep. It was dark in the yurt and he couldn't make anything out. But soon he realized the "werewolf" was Azbergen. And he also noticed how Khansulu was rushing about in the back of the yurt, packing things into a bag.

"Recognize me?" Azbergen growled through his overgrown black beard. "One word and here's the knife, I'll cut you on the spot, you puppy! Where are Pakhraddin's horses?" He pressed on Kozbagar's throat so much that he gasped. Then he let up a little: "Well!"

"In Tugisken...on the eastern side," Kozbagar blurted out.

"You're not lying?" Azbergen once again grabbed his throat. Kozbagar's face, round as a cup, turned crimson. Coughing, he shook his head.

"Listen, you puppy! As long as I'm alive, you won't get Khansulu! Get it?"

Azbergen once again twisted the knife before his nose. The sharp blade dazzled Kozbagar, and he jerked his chin.

"Azeke[107], don't kill him! I'll do everything…you say!"

"Give Khansulu a *talak*[108]!"

"What?" Kozbagar didn't understand at first that he was talking about a divorce.

"*Talak*, say it, your father…"

"But how can that be…?

"Say it, you puppy, or I'll…"

"*Talak*, *oybay*, *talak*!" Kozbagar repeated, swallowing back tears.

Azbergen stuffed a towel in his mouth and tied up his arms and legs. Then he gave him a good hearty kick in the butt for the road. While Kozbagar shed silent tears, bent over with his back to them, Azbergen and Khansulu overturned everything in the yurt, knotting bundles together. Then they left. Kozbagar was afraid to move. He lay there like that until dawn.

In the morning people poured out of their homes and began opening the flaps to the yurt. The camels standing at their tethers began

---

[107] Azeke is a nickname for Azbergen.
[108] Under Sharia law, a divorce is made by repeating the word "*talak*" three times.

to bellow softly. But it was quiet at the newlywed's house. Torka decided to wake up the bride.

"*Kelin*, oh, *kelin!*" she called to her daughter-in-law.

There was no answer.

The old lady then peered inside. Her son, blue in the face, with a cloth stuffed in his mouth, tied up hand and foot, was rolling on the floor by the door, and behind the curtain – oh, God! – the newlyweds' marital bed was empty. *Kelin* was gone!

"*Oybay!* An enemy has attacked! They kidnapped her!" exclaimed the little old woman with a heart-rending cry and raced away.
"*Astapyralla!*[109] What else will happen so early this morning!" people asked warily.

"Curse them! Kidnapped! An enemy has attacked, *oybay!*"

"What enemy, mother?"

"*Oybay*, my boy was tied up there! Oybay, is he dead or alive, I don't know! *Oybay*, *kelin* is gone! What, that's not an enemy, you think?"

Everyone hurried to the yurt in fright. Shege was the first to arrive. The curtain was thrown aside. The bedding had been folded up. Khansulu was gone. Kozbagar, bound and gagged, lay on the floor, groaning. It seemed he was alive. As soon as Kozbagar was untied, chocking back his tears, he told them what had happened last night. Not holding back, Torka hugged him.

"Oh, and you're crying! Don't cry! The hell with them…And the hell with that woman! At least you're alive!" And then hugging her son's head, she lamented. "Curse be your kind, you bandit! We are glad

---

[109] *Astapyralla* means "forgive us, oh, Lord!" and is an exclamation of surprise in the Kazakh language based on the Koran prayer.

you have gone from our sight, you enemy! And it turns out you were rooting around nearby here like a hungry wolf. Oh, you spawn!"

Sharip was not in the aul. He had left yesterday for a meeting at the new region. Bulysh could have organized a chase, he alone was capable of this in the aul, but he was gone as well. He had gone hunting. People loitered around the yurt for a while and then went their ways without doing anything.

"Her own uncle kidnapped her," they told Torka, trying to reassure her. "Don't be sad. He'll go wild for a bit and then it will pass. He'll bring his niece back. What else can he do with her?!

3

That summer was hot. No sooner did the sun peep out than the horizon was covered in a mirage. The sand storms whirled to the sky, gathering sand and dust, racing along the flat earth.

On one such day, at high noon, Sharip came into view from the direction of the River Jem on his bob-tailed bay. Underneath his *borik*[110] was an enormous white kerchief covering his head. He sat uncertainly in the saddle like an owl on a bough. The listless nag under him was barely lifting her legs.

"*Alakay*! *Koke*! Papa *Koke*!" Sharip's five girls, seeing their father, shouted for joy and ran to meet him, and tenderly pressed her soft little face to himself. He gave her something. A piece of candy, most likely.

Sharip was quiet for some unknown reason. He hoisted his youngest daughter on to the horse

Pakhraddin, watching him from his own yurt, remarked: "Something apparently happened to the poor fellow."

---

[110] A *borik* is a round hat.

No sooner had Sharip managed to have a bite to eat after his trip than the news flew around the aul: "Sharip the Squealer has been removed!"

"*Oybay*, dear, I heard – they removed my *kaynara*[111]!

"*Kotek*,[112] what do you mean "they removed him"?

"*Oybay*, he is no longer the *aulnay*!"

"Shut up, you stupid thing! What's gotten into you, really?"

The gloomy and non-communicative Sharip immediately tumbled into his bed. He told his family that he had a terrible headache. He got up only towards the evening tea-time.

"Our daughter-in-law, Khansulu, has run away," Jaybaskan recounted, little by little approaching the aul news.

Sharip, holding the cup to his lips, froze, and stared round-eyed at his wife.

"What do you mean, ran away?"

"Well, how do you think? Azbergen kidnapped her."

"Serves her right!" Sharip sighed, and his red mustache bristled. As if to prove true the proverb, "A mischievous woman is a load for 40 asses," Khansulu's wedding had turned into a headache for the head of the aul soviet. At the district, he was summoned for a reprimand over the excessive number of cattle slaughtered for the *toy*.

After two or three swallows of tea, drops of sweat broke out on Sharip's forehead as he semi-reclined on the pillows. Meanwhile the voice of the old lady Torka, coming to her brother's yurt, could be heard, and as usual, she was raging.

---

[111]A *kaynaga* is a brother-in-law, a senior relative of the husband.
[112] *Kotek* is an exclamation of fright by a woman.

"Just you wait, you bandit, cursed by God! I'll make sure you're put away beyond the snowy mountains! Or let my name perish!"

Limping, she stepped over the threshold. The appearance of his elder sister was a nuisance, Sharip didn't like it.

"Eh," she cried, hurling herself at Sharip, reddened and sweaty from the tea. "I've had enough of that bandit! If it's true that you're the *blasty*, bring that bandit to me, with his hands and legs tied!"

With these words, she pounded her boney fists on the ground. Sharip, as if he had gone deaf, didn't tear his eyes from her fists, pounding the animal skin, and continued to gulp his tea. Deciding that Torka had calmed down, he began to feel through his pockets, looking for something. Both women stared at him with unblinking eyes. After a while, he pulled out a completely crushed rag and threw it at his sister. It turned out to be the simple little bag in which he had used to keep the seal, the very round seal made of a camel's hoof.

"*Kotek*, but where's the seal itself?!" the old lady Torka exclaimed.

"Where's the seal?" she asked again.

"Truly, where is the seal?" Sharip repeated her question mockingly.

"Eh, if the owner of the seal himself doesn't know where it is, how can we know?" Jaybaskan put in.

"You should know. It's bad that you don't know," and biting a lump of sugar, Sharip noisily sucked his tea through it. With his entire demeanor, he gave them to know that the conversation was over.

"So, God struck him right on the top of the head," Torka concluded. There was neither malice nor judgement in her voice.

Getting up heavily, she made her way to the door, limping even more heavily. Silently, she closed the door behind her.

Pakhraddin's prediction came to pass – what Sharip had feared the most had happened: he had been relieved of his position as chairman of the aul soviet. They accused him of getting mixed up with a *bay*, entering into familial ties with him, and as *aulnay*, giving rise to the disorders in the aul – he had allowed the slaughtering of many animals for the wedding.

Pakhraddin was finishing his morning prayers when horse hooves knocked along the yurt, almost at the very walls. He cast his eyes toward the noise: who could display such disrespect and barge at a very yurt on a horse?

Syrga quietly slipped outside.

"I need the *biy-aga*!" cried the man outdoors. "There's an order from the district!

Pakhraddin, gathering up his *jaynamaz*,[113] got up, irritated. His customary ritual was disturbed.

"You're wanted," said Syrga, appearing in front of him. "The elder son of Jorga Kuren. Jdakhay."

"Why doesn't he come in the house like normal people?"

"He's a busy man. He has a bag around his neck…"

Throwing his *chapan* over his shoulders, Pakhraddin came out, and there on a chestnut stallion was a plump young fellow with round owlish eyes on his pock-marked face. He devoured, you could say, the *biy* with a superior gaze.

"*Assalaumaleykum, biy-aga*! An order from the district! A tax from you!"

"Speak!"

---

[113] The *jaynamaz* is a prayer rug.

"120 kilograms of wool, 60 of butter, 80 of sheepskin. The deadline..." – here Jdakhay pronounced the word "deadline" in Russia – "is one week from today."

"Tax collector!" the young man said, straightening himself. "Instead of Kilybay. If you don't deliver it by the deadline, remember, your case will be reviewed at the KPU!"

Pakhraddin didn't like the youth's hoarse voice.

"Jorga's son, hey, don't shout!" he reprimanded him. "We're not deaf. We heard. And you should say GPU[114], and not KPU. See that you don't lose your bag!"

"You're getting mad for nothing, *biy-aga*!" Compared to the cases of Jarasbay, Ulman and Mazhan, yours is a cinch! If someone is going to kick the bucket, it'll be them! Ha-hah-hah!"

Jdakhay had scared away all the aul dogs.

5

Pakhraddin was still paying the tax, when the Red Yurt appeared. Mazhan had placed it in the aul, and from that day hence, the partying never ceased: every day there was music and young people having fun. The owner of the yurt was Asan Aytzhanov, a Bolshevik who at one time made Sharip the *aulnay*. At that time, on his first trip, he had ignored Pakhraddin and Mazhan, and only went around to the poor people, as if to show the aul-dwellers what a confirmed Bolshevik he was. He was continuing the same policy now.

At the very first meeting he announced, they say, that the first task of the Soviets on the path to the new life was to "rid the auls of *bays* and mullahs," which, so to speak, were opponents of everything that was new. One of those attending asked then:

---

[114] GPU, the Russian initials for "State Political Directorate," was the name of the Soviet security police in 1922-23. Jdakhay got the acronym wrong.

The Lonely Yurt • Smagul Yelubay

"So we'll destroy the *bays* and mullahs, alright, and then what?"

"And then what? Confiscation of the *bay*'s property and we'll divide it up among the poor people. We will unite in associations. We'll live as one family. We'll plow the earth and sow seeds. We'll build houses, and then we will settle on the land and will no longer be nomads. We'll begin studying, we'll gather knowledge. We will live in the big cities. Thus we will achieve a flourishing new life, a new culture…

Asan Aytzhanov thus built such a life of paradise overnight. The happy and excited young people clapped their hands, but the blacksmith – the lanky Uap, the shepherd Kaukash and the herder Janbyrbay for some reason were left unhappy.

"Listen, brother," they said, standing up together. "Why do you need us old people? Why should we dig around in the earth when there isn't long till the grave? We'll manage to feed ourselves with our grandfathers' crafts, we'll pasture the herds, we'll migrate a bit. Your city isn't for us. We were born in a poor little yurt, let us die there! Don't drag us into your city…"

They say Jdakhay then shouted:

"However wants to, let him languish in a yurt, but we will live in the cities!"

And the young people, they say, enthusiastically supported him. Asan the Bolshevik reprimanded the old men:

"Stop it, *aksakals*[115], get back! The future is with the young people."

At the end of the meeting, he loudly recited some poetry – as if throwing a slogan to the crowd:

> *Batraks and poor guys*
> *Go ahead today!*

---

[115] *Aksakals* are elders.

Whip the mullahs and the bays
Like sheep, chase away!

The young people immediately learned the poem by heart. And from that day hence, every snot-nose kid was droning away, whether the kids were playing bones or another game – they had that poem on their lips. They would go around reciting the verse day and night.

People heard about the little song in the outer auls. Shepherds and *batraks* and even milkmaids would be doing their household chores or toiling in the steppe and they would hum the song under their breath:

Batraks and poor guys
Go ahead today!

The old men and old women grew sad, as if to say, "Oh, Creator, it turns out there is much we have not seen in our lives."

Pakhraddin had heard a lot and had a lot to think about. He had foreseen such a course of events. The major Kazakh *bays* were arrested in 1918. Pakhraddin thought then at the time, *"What can happen to the bull can be expected by the calf."*

Batraks and poor guys
Go ahead today!
Whip the mullahs and the bays
Like sheep, chase away!

The canopy on the yurt was thrown open, and Pakhraddin looked out at the steppe through the lattice of the *kerege*, stretching far, far away, dull and bloodless; tears froze in his eyes. A sand storm whirled up and flew first in one direction, then another and then whisked along the foggy horizon, shimmering from a mirage. Where had this whirlwind come from? Where would it go? Existence was senseless. Was not he, Pakhraddin, like this whirlwind, chased by the wind? What was happening with the land, where he had once felt himself to be master? What was happening with the people upon whom he had once relied? Like the grass of the steppe, a tumbleweed torn from its roots, the wind was blowing him along the steppe. God alone knew what pit he would be thrown into by the storm...

"My falcon," Syrga called quietly behind his back. Lost in thought, he had forgotten about her, his faithful Syrga.

"Oh!" he cried. His voice shook. He didn't turn around. He was ashamed of his tears.

All his life, Syrga, his faithful spouse, guessing his state by just one movement of his brows, as it is said, was displaying her intuition even now – and without bothering him, tactfully, she said, "My falcon…"

Only he, Pakhraddin, could understand her call to him, in which was mixed both love and empathy and fear for him. Syrga understood what Pakhraddin was like now, restlessly alone among numerous people. His priceless friend, Syrga! The joy of his life – Syrga! His elder brothers had left. His younger brother had left. His daughter was gone. Only his love, his spouse – Syrga – had not left. Stepping quietly, almost soundlessly, she approached and sat down next to him and put her head on his shoulder. Her tender fingers, soothing him, stroked his back.

"And looking at you, I am upset, too. Don't, don't upset yourself. We'll get through it somehow, it is destined by fate," she said. Embracing him, she pressed her forehead to his broad back.

The desert solitude in which his soul had blundered disappeared, and Pakhraddin found what he had thirsted most for: the warmth of his sensitive, beloved wife. They embraced each other, and his soul, yearning for the heat of love, melted in his wife's caresses. Pressing his face to the beautiful oval face of his wife, washed with his tears, he suddenly broke out sobbing.

"What's wrong with you? Stop it!" Syrga said, frightened.

Pakhraddin never showed his weakness to anyone. And now his powerful shoulders shook, like a reed on the lake under a wave. Syrga was spare in her words, but if she did start talking she would charm you with her nice, silvery voice, that was how she had been raised. She won over a person with her kindness and tenderness. And now she won her husband over again. Her peaceful face shone with tenderness, she soothed her husband like a little child. Pakhraddin lay on his back, the nostrils of his huge nose flaring. He smiled, as if he had remembered something.

"But people are fools," he said. "They count Pakhraddin's cattle over and over to see if he is a *bay*...or not a *bay*. Oh, they don't get it! They just don't realize that his entire wealth was there in his yurt, it was his *baybishe*.

His wife's face with her regular, fine features lit up with a smile; her black eyes shone archly; her teeth, white as snow, were bared; her cheeks reddened with blush. She leaned over her husband, laughing quietly.

"Look out," she said. "Someone will hear...they are confiscating your *baybishe*..."

6

This summer was different. It was not like those to which people had become accustomed. At one time the summer was long and stretched out like the juice of a milkweed. But now no sooner was it dawn, and you didn't manage to blink before it was evening. There were a lot of conversation, and you didn't notice how the day went by with them. The activists were hurrying hither and yon, raising dust, they were young and desperate. Some of them were calling themselves Komsomols.[116] The people of the steppe did not know what that was, and viewed them warily.

Shege, Jdakhay, Kozbagar, Balzhan and other young people who spent evenings at the Red Yurt, who were always with the Bolshevik Asan Aytzhanov also became Komsomols one fine day. On the occasion when her Kozbagar became a Komsomol, Torka went around all the yurts in the aul, limping, telling the news. Even so, she would keep repeating authoritatively:

"Curse them! There they go! Don't joke around with the *batraks*!"

Thus the young people acquired weight. Now when someone like Kozbagar came along, who was now no longer a *batrak* but a

---

[116] The Komsomol was an acronym for the Russian words for "Young Communist League."

Komsomol, the "shards of the old world," like Pakhraddin, would yield the road to him. And the Komsomols would sing like this:

> *Barefoot batrak all alone*
> *Now the world is yours*
> *If you plow the land you know*
> *Live just like a bay*

"Oh, all-powerful God!" the old women clucked in surprise. "We have lived to hear the prayer of the new times."

The Bolshevik Asan, manager of the Red Yurt, grew close to the young people so they did not take a step without him. He, Asan Aytzhanov had seen it all – in 1916 he had dug trenches, he had taken part in the Russian-German war, he been to unheard of cities – Moscow, Petrograd. Under Asan's influence, Shege himself spoke at a meeting for the first time as it happened. This is how he began his speech:

"The time has come when the old has to be hacked at the root! We cannot take a step forward to the new life without this! The past has entangled our feet!"

"*Kotek*!" a talkative young fellow couldn't help blurting out. "Look here, another Asan has been found!"

What a lot of laughter there was! Then the policeman Bukhabay, dozing off at the meeting, got up and thrusting out his second chin, read out the list of the "comrades" who had guns; he counted them all, and didn't forget any of them. Since the question of guns had come up, people stopped laughing and began looking at each other, but Bukhabay – now without a paper – coldly explained:

"Order from the center – turn in your guns! That's the law!"

He let loose his sternness – apparently he had had a good sleep. The notice that people had to turn in their guns did not elicit any enthusiasm.

...

That same day, sighing and saying they didn't one to war with the government over a gun, people brought their weapons to the Red Yurt. Only Mazhan's three sons and Bulysh did not turn in their guns.

"We can't give up our guns," Bulysh grumbled to Bukhabay when he came to his home. With his huge hands, the hunter smoothed out the skin of a young wolf that had landed in his trap; it was a large skin, one and a half times a span.

"Bulysh-*aga*, the law requires it," Bukhabay began to explain, but Bulysh, his face darkening, interrupted him:

"I don't have anything against the law. But everyone knows I am a hunter. The gun that feeds me, I repeat, I am not going to give up to anyone. Just like the horse I ride and the hound that helps me hunt."

"But Bulysh-aga, the law requires…"

"Eh, son of Igensart," *Dau-apa* boomed from inside the yurt. "Get out of here with your law. What kind of law is it that allows a gun to be taken away from a hunter?! You won't get the gun! You tell them that where you have to – *Dau-apa* will not allow it. Let them cut off my head if they must, but I will not turn over my gun!"

That was the end of the conversation. Bukhabay, without uttering a word, silently mounted his horse and rode from the yard. Not only Bukhabay but everyone around knew what it meant to deal with Bulysha's mother, *Dau-apa.* They say that in her youth, she took part in marches alongside the men. She would tuck her braids under her cap – and attack the enemy! She was from the warrior sub-clan Kunanorys of the Aday clan. She married Bulysh' father – the hunter Arshu – against the will of her brothers, and eloped with him. In 1916, Ashu was taken into the army and then went missing. It fell to the young mother with little children to get through the hunger year of 1921. Two sons died that year of smallpox at the ages of 12 and 13.

Left without a herd after a die-off, *Dau-apa* went away together with her eldest son Bulysh in search of work in the valley of

Oy.[117] Along the way, she met a trade caravan. At the bazaar in Konyrat, she met with a Turkmen *bay* and hired herself out to herd his camels. The *bay* was called Pirimkul. He promised *Dau-apa* a camel per year for her work. For two years, mother and son pastured the *bay*'s camels and then decided to return to their homeland and asked the *bay* to settle up. He selected out of the herd a lousy yearling camel and an old mangy female camel. How a widow and a boy not yet grown supposed to contest the *bay*'s payment? They loaded up their pathetic household goods somehow on the young camel, mounted the female camel themselves and headed out into the wide unknown, cursing the stingy *bay*. After a day's travel they climbed Ustyurt. Beyond Ustyurt was the boundless Kazakh steppe. *Dau-apa* thought of stopping here. She let the camels kneel and order her son to unload their goods. Bulysh was surprised – what did his mother see in this bare, stony plateau? And she told him:

"My son, don't think I will budge from this spot until I get revenge on that miser! It would be better to die here than return on a lousy camel! Go and get revenge on that cursed Pirimkul for what he gave us. Take two select *nars* from the herd and bring them back here if you are my son!"

Without saying a word, Bulysh took his rifle, jumped on the mangy female camel and trotted back. After midnight, as his mother had ordered, the bold *jigit* had driven back two huge *nars* with humps as big as trunks. Then, they say, *Dau-apa*, cheered, said:

"*Barekeldy,*[118] now we can ride, my son!

That story grew into a legend as testimony of one of the many feats of the brave *Dau-apa*. Bukhabay knew that legend as well, which is why he didn't start arguing with her. But at the center of the list of citizens who had refused to turn in their guns to the government, according to the decision of the Khantortkil aul soviet, now the name of Bulysh Arshauly was in big letters.

---

[117]The lowlands of the Amu Darya River.
[118]*Barekeldy* is a ritual exclamation of approval.

Early autumn was marked by yet another great upheaval called "the confiscation" (*konfiskatsiya* in Russian) which was garbled in the language of the steppe-dwellers to "*kampeske.*" It went from Basoymaut, Ortaoymaut, Sarybay, and Donyztau, and soon was going to come to the populous Khantortkil and Tuisken. The rumors came thick and fast; supposedly in one day they confiscated the property of Jarasbay and Teginberdy; on another day they ransacked Baytak, Ulman and Kulman. The details of the rumors were terrifying: people said that the soldiers took everything down to the last thread, and the *bays* were arrested and exiled to the city of Temir.

It was the hour of sunset on one such day when long shadows settled on the earth. Frightened by the alarming news, the people of Pakhradd .5 in's aul were languishing in their homes when they heard the horses' hoofbeats. They uttered the prayer *astapyralla*[119] and people poured outside. A horseman was galloping from Mazhan's aul. What news would he bring? The rider broken into the alarmed aul with a shout – it was Jdakhay.

"Hey, hey, listen to me, people!" he shouted on the run. "Everybody come over there!" he said, waving his arm toward Mazhan's aul. "There's going to be a *kampeske*! Mazhan will have a *kampeske. Kam-pes-ke-e!* Everybody to the meeting!"

"It's enough to set your teeth on edge! What meeting?" Someone asked.

"Is a devil chasing him or something, he's like a crazy man!" the aul women said, and began to curse Jdakhay in their hearts. But the word *kampeske* was so terrible and incomprehensible a word that people inevitably were drawn to Mazhan's aul, everyone wanted to see what was going on. So some went on horseback, some on foot, men and women, old men and old women and even children streamed toward Mazhan's aul which was at the distance of one gallop by a three-year-old stallion. And Pakhraddin, on his raven stallion with the little star on its forehead also went along with everyone else.

---

[119] *Astapyralla* is a distorted form of the Koran prayer, "God save me."

Mazhan's aul was spread over a long, gentle ridge. Here the hustle and bustle of a large bazaar reigned. On the outskirts, at the Red Yurt with the red flag on the top, there was a huge crowd of people, swarming like ants in an anthill. They formed a chain with the reins of the harnessed horses. There were numerous herds of animals in front of the aul; the dust hung black over the herds of sheep, horse and camels. Everywhere were horsemen waving their whips. The barking of dogs, the bleating of the sheep, the neighing of the horses – all of these sounds merged together into a powerful roar. As if he had seen a wall of fire, Pakhraddin instinctively flinched. He had heard that the harsh measures taken by the Soviet government concerned only those *bays* whose number of large horned cattle exceeded three hundred. He himself had sold some, slaughtered some and now had only a dozen camels and a hundred head of sheep in his yard; with such a head count he hoped to avoid the confiscation.

When the people approached, the Bolshevik Asan Aytzhanov climbed up on one of the wagons. He read out the decree of the Kazakh Central Executive Committee on the confiscation of the bay's property. While Asan read the decree, a group of people climbed up on the wagon. Among them was the new chair of the aul soviet, Jorga Kuren. Smiling, he stepped forward. Of course, he wasn't Sharip, and was quite suited to the job of *aulnay* – and his speech was succinct and his voice soft.

"Comrades!" he said. "We are giving the floor today to *Tovarishch* [Comrade] Kaukash Koshekbayev, a *batrak* who spent his entire life in the home of the bay Mazhan Uteshev, our class enemy!"

"*Tabarysh* Koshekbayev? Who is that?" people in the crowd at first didn't understand. Someone chuckled.

"Kaukash?!"

And immediately, the comments started:

"Yoo-ho, *Tabarysh* Koshekbayev, where are you?"

"Curse you, come out here!"

"Speak up, since they're asking! Your hour has come!"

A dark-skinned, unprepossessing little man in the crowd handed the reins of his camel to his neighbor and made his way to the wagon, crushing an old *borik* on his head from which tufts of cotton poked out. The laughter wouldn't let up. Coming up to the wagon, Kaukash stopped and turned toward the crowd. Once again, he clamped his cap to his head and grinned.

"*Tovarishch,* get on the wagon! On the wagon! Let the people see you!" they suggested.

Kaukash struggled to clamber up on the wagon but couldn't manage. Asan helped him. Finding himself at the same level as the bosses. Kaukash grew shy and withdrawn, like an old, dry skin. But glancing at the crowd, which had frozen in expectation, he grinned in a familiar way. The wags wouldn't let up.

"Oh-oh, it's Kaukash time..."

"Oh, don't joke with Kaukash!"

Asan glanced sympathetically at the tongue-tied orator:

"Well, *tovarishch*! Your word is the word of the people. How do you view the Kazakh Central Committee's decree? Talk about that."

"Come on, Kaukash, say your piece! Don't spare anything," Sharip took up the cry. Kaukash rubbed his shoulder, confusedly shifted from one foot to the other, holding his cap to his head, then to his shoulder.

"Oh, leave the old cap alone! It's already in rags," lanky Uap cried from the back rows.

"Oh, go one with you, Kaukash! Take off your cap?" Sharip squealed.

"Ahem!" Kaukash cleared his throat hoarsely. "They said you will give a speech...ahem...I wanted to patch up my cap yesterday...ahem...I went to Mazhan's *baybishe*...

"The heck with your hat and you along with it! You don't have to say anything more, it's all clear!" Sharip burst out.

"No! No! Let him talk!"

"Speak, *Tovarishch* Koshekpayev," Asan Atzhanov urged him.

"...So I went, and Jamal the *baybishe*..ahem...was digging around in a trunk. I told her why I needed some thread...ahem...I asked for some thread, see, and the *baybishe* said, 'give me your cap,' she said. So I gave it to her. And she took the cap and threw it across the doorway."

"The hell with your cap! Curse you, Kaukash. Don't beat around the bush, tell us about the *kampeske*. Tell us whether you support the government's policy or not!" Sharip wailed.

"I agree...with the *kampeske*...what can I say. Only...only...ahem... tomorrow the *bay* Mazhan might come back, after all...ahem...He might then...Oh, the hell with the *bay*'s herd, I've had enough trouble with it. Now I'd like 10...of my own...ahem!"

"*Tovarishch* Koshekbayev, just a minute!" the *batrak* Aytzhanov interrupted him. "You're being afraid for nothing. You shouldn't scare people. If the meeting decides that we have to chase the bay and his family out of here in three shakes – we'll chase them! And you'll never see him again! You, Tovarishch Koshekbayev, say it exactly and clearly. Should the *bay* Mazhan be subject to confiscation and exile, or not?"

Kaukash the shepherd felt as if he were on pins and needles, he mumbled and hemmed and hawed in search of words, looking around on all sides, as if he was looking for a place to hide from the hundreds of pairs of eyes which were expectantly watching him from all sides. He was driven into a dead end. Mazhan and his *baybishe* were sitting at a prominent place, in front of the wagon. They were also waiting what he would say, and were outright staring at him.

"Go on, speak!" Jorga Kuren said, pushing him from behind.

"Eh…let them exile them," poor Kaukash mumbled. "The government is right. The government likely…ahem…doesn't do anything without a reason…"

The crowd roared. Some supported Kaukash, some cursed him roundly. Jamal-*baybyshe* began lamenting bitterly. Plump as an inflated skin, she got up with difficulty and holding her back, turned toward Kaukash:

"You should speak well of my bread, Kaukash! Let it backfire! What have I ever done to you, oh!"

Kaukash turned into a pathetic, speechless lump of flesh; he had not expected such from the *baybishe*. He looked with fear at the bosses.

"Good man!" Asan smiled with his long and lean face, and clapped him on the back in approval.

Only then did poor Kaukash calm down.

Jorga Kuren, looking over the crowd with a cunning smile, asked:

"Who else wants to speak?"

"I!" Jdakhay exclaimed, energetically making his way through the rows. "I'll speak!"

"Good. Jdakhay, son of Kuren has the floor. Ever since he was a boy he has shepherded the lambs for our class enemy, the *bay* Mazhan. He is a member of the confiscation commission."

The broad-shouldered, husky Jdakhay easily, like a panther, jumped on to the wagon from a distance. His eyes shone, the hair on the top of his head stood up like a hedgehog. His fists were clenched. He fervently got to work:

"*Da zdrabstbit rebolyusiya!*[120] Long live the revolution!" he cried in Russian, raising both arms above his head.

"Long live the revolution!" he repeated again and continued in Kazakh.

"It defends us, the laborers, who have nothing to lose...such people as Kaukash, from the *bays*!"

Those standing on the wagon clapped vigorously. The crowd grew agitated, troubled by the attack of the young orator, and people began exchanging glances. Shege cried from the back rows:

"*Da zdrabstbit rebolyusiya!*"

Some old man grumbled:

"Oh, Creator, save us!"

Another sighed:

"God let everything end well!"

Jdakhay, meanwhile didn't shut up.

"It's not enough to take away their goods! And exiling them is too soft as well. They will get settled there and live the good life. Kaukash is right – if you let them remain alive, then, God forbid, they will come after us, unhappy, seeking to get even. Oh, don't you laugh! Let me be damned on the spot if they will not seek revenge. So these black kites have to be wiped from our earth completely. Bound their hands and legs and put them in an iron cage for the eternal ages! These are my words!"

"Oh, that your foul mouth end up on the back of your head!" Mazhan's *baybyshe* swore. "That you perish, that you dry up forever,

---

[120] A distorted form of the Russian phrase *Da zdravstvuyet revolyutsiya*" ["Long Live the Revolution!"].

you monster!" The woman pounded her hands on the earth in desperation.

"Stop the noise! We will read the edict!" Jorga Kuren announced her, and grinning, unfolded a large sheet of paper in front of himself.

"Read it, read it! We're listening!" the crowd shouted.

Jorga Kuren began to read:

"At a general meeting of the poor people and *batraks* of the aul no. 5 at the Khantortkil aul soviet it was decreed…First. At our meeting, we reviewed the case of the largest *bay* in our aul, our class enemy Mazhan Uteshev. Mazhan is a large *bay*. An inherent exploiter, a vulture, like all seven generations of his ancestors, sucking the blood of the working people. For that reason, all of his property and herds are to be confiscated, he and his family are exiled under the condition that they are not to return here alive. Second. At the start of the local aul soviet, yet another of our class enemies arrived. This is Pakhraddin the *bay*, who in the tsar's time was a bay and ruled the district. The number of herds he possesses now no longer enables him to be considered a *bay,* therefore he must be numbered among the kulaks. His cattle and property are also subject to confiscation. But taking into account that he helped the Soviet government of his own volition with horses and meat, that is, was a harmless *kulak*, then he must be relieved of exile in a foreign land. Thus is the edict, comrades!" concluded Jorga Kuren, raising his head from his paper.

"Yes, comrades, there is one more matter which must be discussed! Among us is a man who is not a *bay* and not a kulak and not a poor man as the Soviet government defines it. This person is a hanger-on. And who do we call "hangers-on," comrades? Those who to this day serve our class enemies in secret…"

"Who is that? Name him, don't be shy! Well!" Sharip squealed, coming up.

"But you are the hanger-on! You, Sharip! Didn't you try to become an in-law of Pakhraddin's, you are a hanger-on!"

"What? What? Eh?" Sharip, said, not understanding immediately. "Repeat that!"

The crowd was about to buzz like a bee hive, but quieted down, sensing that a scandal was brewing. Jorga Kuren, smirking nastily, said:

"And isn't it true that you were a relation of Pakhraddin's by marriage, and sucking up to him, and trying to get in good with him? And after that, you beat your chest that you are a poor man's activist..."

"Eh, eh, Jorga! What...what are you going on about?!" Sharip broke into a screech. Running forward, he tore his hat from his head and threw it on the ground, in the style of the aul orators. A cloud of dust flew up.

Jorga Kuren shuddered. People held their breaths.

"So I'm a hanger-on, am I?! In your grandfather's grave! You are Mazhan's mare, on which the bay rode to the bazaar. Aren't you the one who managed all of Mazhan's affairs at the bazaar, and deceived people? That's where you and Jorga got your amblers. Why are you, of all people, going on in the name of the downtrodden, you sell-out, you kopeck huckster?! Yes, I was Pakhraddin's in-law. That's true. But he is not a *bay*, you mediocrity. Why are you hiding that, you bitch tit?!"

"Calm down, calm down, Sharip-*aga*!" Atzhanov, the former *aulnay* called him to order.

Jorga Kuren, as if nothing had happened, smirking, remarked:

"Well, you tell people the truth, and you can't please them."

Two policemen, Bukhabay and Jekey, grabbed Sharip under the arms and dragged him away by force.

"Let me go," Sharip cried, struggling. "I'll punch him in his brazen mug, the villain! Let me go!"

"*Tabarysh*, don't interfere with the meeting!"

The nimble Sharip, despite the fact that he was being dragged away, still managed to pull off a boot from his foot and hurl it over the policeman's head at Kuren.

"Take that for the 'hanger on'!"

The boot flew past Kuren's temple, almost grazing him. Suddenly Kuren and Asan fell, one to the left and one to the right. A cheerful hubbub arose, and Sharip was locked up in the Red Yurt. His wails would not subside, and he swore furiously at Jorga Kuren.

The crimson sun began setting, flooding the entire aul with a velvet red color. The crowd that had been at the meeting poured toward Mazhan's large, brown yurt. The horse reins tugged in the same direction. No one remained on the open square where the gathering had just taken place; no one was left except Mazhan's *baybishe*, who had let her hair down and sat facing the sunset, weeping.

Jdakhay had reached the yurt before the others, shouting out something enthusiastically. He galloped by at top speed, and managed to cut the ties to the *koshmas*, and ripped off the *koshmas* himself. The best *yyki* were laid bare[121], yellowing, untouched by the sun and wind, they were like the ribs of a living being. Shege, galloping behind him, threw the *koshmas* open even wider. Now an entire wing of the yurt was exposed. Jumping from his horse, Jdakhay was the first to slip inside. The *bay* Mazhan was in the corner with his back to him, feverishly sticking things into his pockets. Like a panther, Jdakhay lunged at him and grabbed his arm.

"Hey, you swine!" Mazhan yelled, and from Jdakhay's unexpected lunge, he carelessly jerked his elbow and the banknotes tumbled out. The knotted kerchief fell open, revealing a mass of red 30-ruble notes.

"You see, sabotage!" cried Jdakhay. This he screamed to the crowd which was gathering, once again as before, on a wagon, and

---

[121]*Uyki* are bent crossbars of the yurt's frame.

threw up both hands. He jumped in place, happy that he had caught the *bay*.

"Do you see what a bastard?! How well he was hiding! There's your cash, there!" And with these words he seized a handful of the bills, threw them up in the air under the *shanyrak*, and then caught them himself, capering around.

"Let God punish you, perjurer!" the *bay* snapped, sitting back on his haunches and counting his money.

Now the policemen had arrived and grabbed the *bay* under both arms and led him to the wagon. With difficulty, in tears, Mazhan crawled on to it and drew himself into a ball. His *baybishe* was led to the wagon. The reckless young *jigits* then caused a ruckus, overturning and flinging things around. They began dragging out and gutting the contents of the yurt – the trunks and the boxes, the *tyuks* and the bundles. They threw things out without discrimination; rugs were ripped roughly from their hinges, and lay in the general pile. In an instant, the *bay*'s large yurt gaped open. Mice ran along the walls, frightened by the abundance of light.

"And what should be done with the home? Is this also *kampeske*?" Jdakhay remarked, laughing. He was strongly aroused; the angry poor people in the aul were no less agitated. Someone started singing:

> *Batraks and poor guys*
> *Go ahead today!*
> *Whip the mullahs and the bays*
> *Like sheep, chase them away!*

Singing the song, the young people piled on and swept the *uyks* into one heap – and the *shanyrak* of the yurt tipped over; they didn't manage to prop it up in time and it collapsed with a crash. There was nothing left of the *kulreush* or cross-pieces in the cupola of the yurt – they had shattered into bits.

"Let God turn away from you! Let my tears pour out on you!" sobbed the *baybishe*.

The spectacle of the shattered *shanyrak*, broken into numerous pieces, had a depressing effect on people.[122]

"An enemy will seize your *jaylyau,* fire will burn your winter dwelling," someone recalled the proverb. An old woman in an outsized *jaulyk* hurried her grandson home.

"Let's go, little one, let's get far away from the sin and trouble."

Pakhraddin's hair stood on end when he saw how Mazhan's *shanyrak* splintered and fell. He felt as if what had happened was like the ruination of his own hearth, his own welfare. Everything was horrible – both Mazhan frantically stuffing his pockets with money at the moment his fate was being decided, and how the callow youth Jdakhay rudely grabbed the arm of this middle-aged man.

"The people have gone off the path, nothing good can be expected. If our life has come to children going against their fathers, then it means everything is over for us. Everything is over!" thought Pakhraddin. Unable to bear the depressing scene, he nodded goodbye to Mazhan, and went back home to the aul.

Asan Aytzhanov, seeing the broken *shanyrak*, cursed Jdakhay. Jdakhay in turn sputtered, trying to justify himself.

"Asan-*aga*, you curse me for the broken *shanyrak* of enemies, but look, what have they done?" Lifting his shirt, he showed his back, striped with a whip. "They also broke my rib."

"Stop this insubordination! Do what they tell you!" Asan said sharply. Dark, thin, weak in appearance, Asan was terrifying when angry. Jdakhay immediately retreated.

"That's it, *aga*! You don't have to repeat it twice for Jdakhay!" he twisted away, like a snake.

---

[122] The shanyrak or roof of the yurt holds it up, and is also a symbol of hearth and home for Kazakhs. It is part of the national symbol of modern Kazakhstan.

The Lonely Yurt • Smagul Yelubay

The semi-twilight grew thicker. A commission headed by Jorga Kuren distributed part of the *bay*'s livestock among the *batraks*, then headed to the *bay*'s yurt, where people were gathering. Passions were boiling over here. After driving Mazhan away to the back of the beyond,[123] no one noticed another man in the twilight – an eyewitness to the event – a horseman who had quietly frozen still in his saddle. This was Bulysh, returning from hunting with his hound, with a rifle over his shoulder. Even from far away he heard the long, hysterical cry of Mazhan's *baybishe* and hurried toward it. While Jdakhay, Kozbagar, and Shege headed off with the bay's household goods on a cart, piercing cries could be heard from Mazhan's second yurt, where his young *tokal* lived. "Get out! Get out!" cried Balkiya. The door opened with a crack, and the hem of the *tokal*'s white dress could be seen.

Bare-headed, disheveled, she was resolutely dragging out of the yurt some hulk of a fellow who had grabbed on to her for dear life. He had seized her waist and would not let go; the blouse on her high breast was unbuttoned. The hulk turned out to be Bukhabay.

"Look, look at that!" men and women, youth and children cried, rushing toward the *tokal*'s yurt.

"Let me in!" Balkiya cried, breaking through.

"What, you're against the *kampeske*?" the narrow-eyed, obese Bukhabay snuffled, his second chin shaking, refusing to let go of the woman's waist. "Oh, how you have decked yourself out in gold, you *bay* whore! Take it off!"

Balkiya's white hand, showered with bracelets and rings shot out and landed on Bukhabay's face as he spread his arms out for an embrace. The beauty's blow was perfect. The policeman, gasping, bent over, his hands clutching his nose.

"Take that, you deserve it!" Balkiya cried, lowering her head and straightening her hair, which had fallen over her shoulders. She buttoned up her blouse.

---

[123]Literally "Barsakelmes," a former island of the Aral Sea; used in folk expressions to signify places from whence no one returns.

"What's going on here?" Jdakhay demanded to know, pushing his way through the crowd.

"Well, that bitch of Mazhan's...he wanted to confiscate her property and she picked a fight! Sabotage!" Bukhabay set about explaining to the boss what had happened.

"*Kampeske*, look at him! And who caused an uproar, going into the yurt; saying, undress now, comrade! And who attacked a woman?"

"Eh, what else would I say besides undress? Here she put on all kinds of valuables on herself! That belongs to the *kampeske*. It's the law."

"Bukhabay is telling the truth!" Sur Jekey shouted at Balkiya. "Go on now, give up the things yourself. Otherwise, we can use force, we have that right."

"If you need something, take the *bay*'s livestock! What business of yours are my bracelets? Or did I borrow from your father?" Balkiya said, refusing to surrender. She caught sight of Bulysh in the crowd, on the very edge, hidden in the darkness, and grew bolder. Jdakhay, who had long ago become sympathetic toward Balkiya, squirmed, not knowing how to help her. Seeing that the matter was taking a serious turn, he raced to the Red Yurt, to Asan Aytzhanov:

"Asan-*aga*! Asan-*aga*!" he cried.

Asan himself came out to meet him.

"Asan-*aga*! Bukhabay is...how should I put it...Mazhan's *tokal*...there... Asan-*aga*! A riot has broken out!"

When they reached Balkiya's white yurt, there really was a fight going on outside it. In the dark, the woman's white dress flashed as she desperately fought with the man.

"Damned bitches! Who's there! Sto-ooo-p!" Asan the Bolshevik said, outraged, heading toward the fighting pair.

"*Oybay*!" a woman screamed in fright.

"What blasphemy!"

"Outrage!"

Unable to restrain himself, Shege leapt toward Sur Jekey, ready to grab him by the throat.

"Jekey, what has gotten into you!"

"Stop the sabotage!" Sur Jekey shouted in Russian, unlatching his holster.

"Beast!" cried Balkiya then and broke into tears.

Bukhabay had by that time already crushed the rebellious woman beneath him, baring her white hip. He stripped her of everything: beads, necklace and bracelets.

There was an unimaginable uproar. The young men jostled each other, gripped by the incredible spectacle.

"*Oybay*!" some woman wailed, leaping aside. A horseman with a whip pushed his way into the crowd and lashed the bear-like back of Bukhabay with all his might. It was Bulysh. Bukhabay leapt up, but Bulysh grabbed him with his iron-like fingers and before he could come to his senses, dragged him away like a goat to *kokpar*. [124]

"*Oybay*, don't touch him!" cried Shege after Bulysh. "It will be no end of trouble!"

A lot of people ran after Bulysh. Someone wailed after him:

"Sabotage! Sabotage!" and suddenly a rifle shot rang out.

---

[124]*Kokpar*, a Central Asian form of polo; a game on horseback using a goat's carcass; the object is to drag the goat's carcass on to one's horse.

The bullet flew right over Bulysh's head. But he didn't let Bukhabay go. The dogs were still tagging along, and the horse, spooked by them, galloped away, far from the aul. Bukhabay grunted, twisting in the hunter's iron grip; only now did he realized who had taken him captive. He begged pathetically:

"What have I done wrong, Bulysh-*aga*?" and broke into tears.

"What have I done wrong? You're one of the locals, you punk! You're a puppy, did you forget about that? Your eyes have grown fat; I'll get rid of some of that fat for you, eh?"

"Bu-bu-Bulyah-*aga*...The b-b-ay's *tokal*...what could I do?"

"I'll gut you like a goat, you asshole! I'll gut you, you piece of shit!"

When the aul was behind them, Bulysh halted the horse and pushed Bukhabay in front; until then the poor thing had hung like a goat's carcass in a game of *kokpar*, helplessly dangling from the flank of the horse. His face, already bloated, swelled up and turned crimson.

"*Kyr...kyr...*" he gasped helplessly.

"You bastard, you hear me? If you so much as lay a finger on Balkiya, I will gut you with my own hands! You understand?

Bukhabay nodded his head.

"*Kyrr...kyrr...*"

"If you understood, then don't forget it!"

Bukhabay's strength was waning; his face was turning blue. Bulysh, relaxing his fingers, threw him out of the saddle with disgust. Bukhabey flopped on the ground like a sack. Voices were heard coming closer. Bulysh melted into the night.

Finally, the confiscation of Mazhan's possessions in the aul was over. That same time, Mazhan and his *baybishe* were taken to Temir. God knows where they were then to be sent after that by convoy. With Asan Aytzhanov's help, Balkiya obtained her freedom, but then did not follow the *bay*. Asan accused Sur Jekey of leftism, and Sur Jekey caught him aiding the *bays*. Mazhan's livestock were driven to the district.

The next day a commission headed by Asan Aytzhanov, traveling in several wagons, went to visit Pakhraddin's aul.

Pakhraddin and Syrga the *baybishe* did not sleep that night – they took their goods out of their home. Pakhraddin, coming back from Mazhan's aul completely depressed and gloomy, said to his wife:

"Let's take out everything, except the bed and dishes! As long as they don't tear our *shanyrak* to bits, we'll give up our goods ourselves, hang it all!"

Syrga the *baybishe* considered her husband's suggestion to be smart.

"Hang it all, you're right. The main thing is that we ourselves are alive and well…"

The commission reached the aul at dawn – the herds hadn't left for the pasture yet – and were surprised at the scene before their eyes: in front of Pakhraddin's house were rugs, heaps of fabric, expensive fur coats and fur skins, and gem stones, all laid out in neat piles.
"Here, *jigits*," he said. "Here's everything except a change of underwear and clothes and also bedding and what is needed for house-keeping which we've left for ourselves. You can come in and see," he said, inviting Aytzhanov in with a sweep of his hand.

The members of the commission followed Aytzhanov: Jorga Kuren, Shege, Jdakhay, Kozbagar. Two policemen accompanied the commission. Syrga the *baybishe*, frightened by the stern look of the crowd coming in the door, stepped back to the threshold; the members of the commission greeted her respectfully. They looked over the yurt. In fact, nothing excessive remained. The commission was shocked by this. Only the horse bridle with the silver saddle hung at the door, so Bukhabay took it and clutched it under his arm.

"You want the master to walk on foot?" Aytzhanov reproached him.

"It's nothing," Sur Jekey replied instead of Bukhabay, in Russia. "He'll walk."

"Let him take it!" Pakhraddin said, not objecting.

A small black *kebezh* stood under the blankets. It was the only one left. Syrga the *baybishe* put away the remaining clothing in it. They didn't look into the trunk. First they inventoried in detail all the items that had been placed by the door, then loaded them on to carts. The commission left the aul at noon.

THE REFUGEES' AUL

1

The aul was hidden in the thick saxaul, surrounded on all sides by dunes. It was made up of modest, brown yurts, numbering about 60. Refugees from various places found safe haven in them; these were people who had fled from the confiscations. It was a settlement far from human habitation, in the sands; even a bird from Ustyurt would not fly to this waterless desert, so the "government personages" didn't show themselves here, either.

Khansulu was brought here by the wind of fate like a butterfly as well. She had spent a year in this aul already. Urging on her horse Karaker, Khansulu scrambled up the next sandy ridge, overgrown with grass. She was wearing her black plush *kamsol*, cinched at the waist with a red belt and on her head was a *tyubeteyka* embroidered with braid made from the down of an owl. The shadow of prolonged grief was on her windblown face. She gazed with sad eyes at the dusty, brown horizon. Who she was waiting for, or what, she didn't know, but she was still waiting. That night when she had run away with her uncle Azbergen who had freed her from Kozbagar, she was so happy that it seemed her heart would burst from her chest. She was free! But that joy was short-lived. She awoke in that saxaul cover among people depressed by fear, in whose eyes was only one question: what will happen tomorrow?" Even the aul dogs refrained from barking. And children didn't play noisy games.

...

Since early in the morning it had been windy. It looked like a sandstorm was starting. On Karaker, climbing up yet another grassy crest, Khansulu tried to peer into the distance, but the gusts of dusty wind wouldn't let her open her eyes. Among the distant, dusty whirlwinds, hurling slantwise along the dunes, something dark blinked, it looked like a nomad's camp. Khansulu felt a chill.

She immediately turned the horse around toward the aul. The aul was in a valley surrounded by saxaul and high dunes, in a secluded place.

Many women and children were out in the yards when Khansulu came galloping in at top speed.

"*Jeneshe!*" shouted Khansulu upon seeing Rash, Azbergen's wife.
"*Jeneshe*...They're riding this way...with rifles. I think they are soldiers..."
"What are you saying? ...What should we do?"

Meanwhile, on the other side of the ridge, a nomad's group of five-six laden camels accompanied by Red Army soldiers on horseback came into view.

"*Oybay!* We're done for!" shouted the people. Women scattered, wailing, hiding in their yurts. In the confusion, many ended up in Azbergen's yurt. They froze in fear. Balkiya and Khansulu were also there. A voice was heard outside.

"Hey, people! Why have you run away from us? We are not enemies. We are representatives of the government. Come out! We will talk," said the soldiers.

The women trembled.

"It's Asan!" whispered Balkiya, running her finger across her cheek in surprise.

"Asan-*balshebek*[125]!"

A woman with a blinding, white-toothed smile in a nicely-pressed white dress peeked out of the brown yurt in the very center of the yard. The horsemen – Shege, Jdakhay, the policemen Sur Jekey and Bukhabay, led by Asan – froze, their eyes bugging out.

"Here's our runaway," said Asan, thin, dark, in a Russian leather cap, shaking with laughter. His face fell into folds from his grin.

"Well, where are the men, Balkiya?"

"I said, they're coming."

"W-e-e-l-l, where did they all get to?"

"Ask them when they get back. Come inside!" said Balkiya.

Asan and Sur Jekey, covering their faces from the gusts of wind, exchanged glances. *"What should we do?"* their expressions said. Asan made a decision, and burst out laughing.

"We'll come in, we'll come in, just a minute," he said, nodding politely to Balkiya.

As soon as the woman retreated into the yurt, Asan and Sur Jekey went into a huddle.

"That wench isn't inviting us for tea by accident. There's a trap here," said Sur Jekey. "Maybe, this is where the men are hiding, and they will fire on us as soon as we come in."

Shege and Jdakhay were assigned to survey the area. The narrow-eyed Bukhabay remained with the horses, and the others went

---

[125] *Balshebek* is how the Kazakhs pronounce the Russian word "Bolshevik".

into the yurt. It turned out there was nothing but women – old and young – who stood up in unison, stepping back in fright, giving the guests the opportunity to go to the *tor*. Balkiya hung the tea kettle on the tripod.

"What are you afraid of? Or you haven't seen a man in a cap before?" Asan joked, lowering himself down to sit on the blanket on the floor. He leaned his rifle up against the wall.

Sur Jekey, who had sat down next to him, notice at the doorway the tall Khansulu, wearing *sharovars*, and jerked his chin toward her.

"Oh, yet another runaway has been found!"

Asan's attention lingered on the beautiful girl with neat facial features, her eyes, as large a deer's, twinkling in the semi-darkness. Finally, he had managed to see this bold girl who was the talk of the whole world for leaving her husband!

"Don't be afraid. We will not cause anybody harm…we just want to take you back. That's all."

The old women exchanged fearful glances. The women remained coldly silent. The black tea kettle on the tripod whistled, coming to a boil. The wind howled outside. The clatter of horse hooves rang out suddenly.

"Asan-*aga*!" Shege's desperate shout resounded.

Sur Jekey was first to rush out of the yurt. Asan jumped out after him. The women began to stir noisily, but not a single one of them left the yurt – they were afraid. Only Khansulu sprang to life when she heard the voice of Shege: "Is that really him?"

The old women prayed, calling the spirits of their ancestors:

"Oh, Barak-*ata*! Oh, Beket-*ata*!
"Oh Lord, preserve us!"

Khansulu, pressing against the doorway, stared out warily. First she saw the men who had been in the yurt – they had run toward the horses – and then made out Shege as well on a ginger stallion which was bucking wildly underneath him. The *jigit* was pointing somewhere to the east with his whip. And upon his head perched a Russian leather cap, just as Asan had, but he wasn't in a Red Army uniform. Instead, he wore a belted, woolen *chapan*, with a rifle slung over his shoulder. He was no longer the Shege he had once been, a bare-foot, long-legged terror, who once played *aksiyek*.[126] They used to fight over the bones. This Shege was a *jigit*, who had drawn himself up straight, his profile as if carved from stone. His face was now unfamiliar to her; it was more stern, adult, and as for his gaze...He had a cold gaze. Now Jdakhay the troublemaker was galloping toward Asan. The wind was howling. You couldn't hear what they were saying. Snatches were carried on the wind.

"There's a lot...Asan-*aga*...A whole...troops..."

"It's our guys, I think, coming back," said Khansulu loudly so everyone could hear.

"Oh, save us! Oh, spirits of our ancestors, help us!" the old women shouted loudly.

The horsemen emerged from the thick saxaul – it was the men of the aul. Among them was the *akhun* on a hairy white camel taking long, broad steps.

One of the horseman in the first rank noticed the Red Army soldiers and shouted, turning his horse back. The men, reining in their horses, were about to race backwards, but stopped, taking up their arms in readiness. The *akhun* continued his way, unperturbed.

"*Askers* are in the aul!" they warned him, but the *akhun*, murmuring a prayer, turned his camel toward the group of *askers* who were waiting on the edge of the aul. The whistling wind kicked up clouds of dust under the camel's feet. Urging his horse along, Asan went out to meet the elder.

---

[126] *Aksiyek* is an ancient game of aul children called which involves being the first to find a bone thrown in the dark.

"*Assalaumagaleykum, akhun-aga*!" he cried.

"*Uagalekumassalam*[127], sonny! Success to you!" replied the *akhun*."

"May your words come to pass! Here, we must unite, as it is said."

"As God sees it, sonny, unification is sought without arms."

"That is true, *akhun-aga*.

"Let us try to speak in peace."

The old man, hair as white as the moon, fell into thought, leaning on his camel, stroking his beard. Finally, the *akhun* turned his camel around, waved his hand to the others who had huddled into a bunch in the distance. The others stumbled, not understanding what was wanted.

"Go on, you cowards!" the *akhun* called, nodding his head. "Fifty men are standing here, and you're afraid of five…"

The women began to make their way out of the yurt. The men, heeding the *akhun*'s will, went toward him, reluctantly, seeing the policemen Sur Jekhey and Bukhabay among the policemen. The aul-dwellers reared back like cats who had seen dogs.

Bulysh was riding ahead. The hunter was angrily tense – his teeth were clenched, the veins on his temples stood out. He stopped alongside Labak-*akhun* and Asanov. His fellow travelers froze a little way away.

"*Assalaumagaleykum, Aseke*!" Bulysh declared, pretending that he didn't notice Sur Jekey and Bukhabay.

"How are you, alive and well, *azamats*[128]?" Asan replied briskly, turning at the same time to Bulysh and his fellow travelers.

"Thank God!" one of the *jigits* let out, and another one added, not without some venom,

---

[127] The Arabic greetings used by Muslims, "Peace be unto you!" "And may peace be unto you, too."

[128] *Azamat* means "great one" and is used as a term of respect.

"Well, if the government is alive and well, what can we do?"

A few of them, unable to restrain themselves, snorted in laughter.

"Well, *jigits*! We haven't come to you with war, but have come to seek agreement. Who's in charge here?"

"Bulysh is our leader! And the *akhun* is our mentor!" cried a full-cheeked young *jigit* in a red cap from out of a group of horsemen.

"Hey, Asan-sonny, aren't talks conducted in a home" Labakh-*akhun*, sitting atop his camel, let drop softly, stroking his beard.

"*Akhun-aga*, we'd all like to listen!"

"Then God help you, let it be as you wish, sonny! Hey, come together everyone! Come closer, closer!"

Labakh-*akhun*, stretching his slender neck, looked from side to side. People approached. Azbergen kicked his horse's flank and rode right up to Bulysh.

"Let us get away!" he thundered. Both of the men headed off on their horses into the dusty steppe.

"I'm listening to you!" said Bulysh, unhappy with Azbergen's behavior. He didn't get along with him. He didn't like him because Azbergen couldn't get through a single day without offending some poor man or widow. Every time he saw him, Bulysh clenched up inside. He was even waiting for Azbergen to turn his anger toward him. Then Bulysh, thanking his good luck, would let him get acquainted with the power of real men's fists. However, Azbergen always tried to keep his distance from him.

Now Azbergen grumbled in a gloomy, deep bass:
"Let's say the old man is out of his mind, and what do you want? Will you listen to a baptized communist? His old tune is already known. Don't let him talk: take the head away and all the conversations!"

Bulysh stared at the dark hulk. Azbergen's meaty face, his beard overgrown, loomed before him.

"What are you going on about?" he burst out. "You want our band to go up against the whole government?"

"Ah, so you don't want to take off a communist's head," Azbergen's hairy face flushed. His horse, galvanized by a kick to his flank, whirled like a top in place.

"Mark my words – tomorrow he will knock your head off!"
"Don't fight – they came seeking agreement!"
"There is no sacred trust!" Azbergen barked, his eyes now red.

The sight of this *kafir*[129] alarmed him.

"Let us suppose. There is no trust," he said, reducing his tone.
"But what can they do with just five of them?"
"Don't let them babble! Imagine, they'll even babble here! Let them get out of here quicker, while their heads are on their shoulders!"

"Wait, Azbergen!" Bulysh was barely restraining himself to keep from shouting. "You're only thinking of yourself. But we have women, old men and old women, and children over there. What will become of them?"

Having said this, Bulysh turned his horse around. Azbergen followed him with wild eyes. The three sons of the *bay* Mazhan – Motan, Shotan and Kapan – surrounded him.

Waiting for Bulysh, Asan kicked his horse with the heel of his boots and came out to the center of the circle. The people grew quiet, all eyes were on Asan.

"Hey, people! I have a question for you," Asan spoke up.
"We're listening!"
"People! Here you've run away from the auls, you've run

---

[129] A *kafir* is an infidel or unbeliever.

away from the authorities. But what are you doing? Perhaps you're preparing a revolution, eh?"

People's voiced all resounded at once.

"Wait a minute! One at a time!" Asan requested.

All gazes turned toward the white-haired *akhun* who was seated on the large white camel.

"Sonny," he began. "Our ancestors said: 'There is no way of the *tulpar*[130] that it would stray from home forever; the falcon does not fly away so far that he leaves his master. We can't say that we will find peace and harmony together with the authorities. It is worse than death for the Kazakh if the government takes away his livestock, forbids him to pray, and deprives him of the custom to freely travel at his will, as a nomad along the age-old paths. For that reason, we ran away. What awaits us ahead? We don't know. It is covered in darkness."

"The *akhun* speaks the truth!"

"*Barakeldy*…you could not put it better!"

"Akhun-aga!" Asan hastened to shout above the other voices. "You have expressed three complaints the aul-dwellers have toward the government. Let us clarify whether they are appropriate. Attention! I beg your attention! You say they took away your livestock? That's true. They took away your livestock. But only from the *bays*. They took them away, and gave them to the poor, those who had nothing. The rest went to the government. Consider that this is good for the people. That's one point. You say they have deprived you of your prayers? I personally haven't seen such a law that would forbid people from praying. That's the second point. The third. They have deprived us people of our freedom to be nomads? I have an objection to that. Yes, we are a nomadic people. But the times are different. There is a fire wagon, our neighbors have airplanes, but the nomad continues to hold on to the horse's mane, he can't keep up with his neighbors. He is not thinking of the future of his little children, his women…"

---

[130] The *tulpar* is a winged horse in Central Asian myths similar to the Greek Pegasus.

Suddenly, Azbergen broke ahead on his overheated horse, making a path for himself through the crowd, and struck Asan the Bolshevik over the head with his whip as he rode by. His cap flew off, and blood seeped from the orator's forehead. Everyone around him broke into action. People on foot scattered in all directions. The horsemen hurled themselves at each other. The crack of rifle shots rang out. Khansulu saw how someone out of the crowd, evidently Shotan, dragged Shege off his horse. The *jigits* threw themselves on Sur Jekey and Bukhabay, knocking them off their horses, confiscated their weapons and bound their hands behind their backs. Someone at the side kicked Jdakhay, who was roaring in pain, the poor fellow's mouth was covered in sand. Azbergen wanted to tear Asan out of the saddle, and was preparing to grab him, in order to drag him away like a goat in *kokpar*, but Bulysh sat on him from behind.

Labak-*akhun*'s camel, frightened by the fighting ran off to the side. No one heeded the *akhun* any longer. The women, who included Khansulu, ran off further away and bunched together in a pathetic huddle like sheep. They watched the clash from the side.

Asan the Bolshevik, Shege, Jdakhay, the policemen Sur Jekey and Bukhabay rolled around tied up on the ground, in the mud and blood. The clash now before the eyes of the cautious *jigits* was between their own people – Azbergen and Bulysh. There was an incredible ruckus, it was hard to understand who was for whom. The hefty Azbergen in both height and weight exceeded Bulysh; both friends and enemies followed the fierce fight, as if seized by the zeal of a competition. It seemed as if it was the brutal clash of two beasts, natural enemies, who had accumulated anger for a long time, who couldn't stand each other, and who had run into each other on a narrow path. It seemed that the destiny of the leader of the aul was in fact being decided here. Ragged, they fought to the death. The clothes on both of them were torn into rags. The nimble Bulysh, with the grip of a leopard squeezed the massive, immobile Azbergen in his clenches so that he couldn't breathe, and an instant later, he threw him on the ground before the *jigits* like a poplar tree ripped from its roots. A hue and cry went up from the people. Bulysh twisted his opponent's arms around almost to his elbows, dumped him on his back and shouted to the amazed young fellows:

"Give me a rope!"

Someone threw some horse reins at him. Tying up Azbergen, Bulysh dragged him to the five men, and threw him down next to Asan.

"God bless you!" cried Labak-*akhun,* returning, in satisfaction.

"Untie him!" Bulysh ordered, pointing to the Red Army soldiers. He himself began to untie Asan the Bolshevik's arm.

"Why?" Motan, Shotan, Kapan and several other *jigits* protested.

"To the horse's tail with him!"

"Destroy him!"

"Beat the enemy!"

The majority supported Bulysh:

"Let them go!"

"Why should we quarrel with the authorities? We are not bandits."

"We need peace!"

Labak-*akhun,* frowning, concluded:

"What is done with reason is correct, Bulysh is right."

Coming to himself after his recent shake-up, the expression on the elder's face as always was bright and blissful. Free from the shackles of the representatives of the authorities, pale from what he had suffered, he got to his feet and put himself in order. The *jigits* led in their horses.

"And return our weapons!" Bulysh ordered, gazing sternly at Mazhan's sons. Without a word, they returned the rifles and pistols they had collected. They were frightened likely not so much by Bulysh as the decisive expression of the people in solidarity with their leader.

Neither Asan, nor Sur Jekey, nor Bukhabay, nor Shege, nor Jdakhay uttered a word. They picked up their weapons, looked all around them, and mounted their horses. The wind was howling and wailing as before. Bulysh mounted his raven *argamak* as well.

"Aseke," he said, glancing at Asan. "One sheep pellet, they say, can spoil the *burdyuk* of cream. That's how it was with us here today. There's one fool, and due to that one, we all sullied ourselves. Our paths, it seems, are going their separate ways…

"What is true, is true," said Asan, struggling to wipe the blood from his face. "We now must make our way back!" and kicked his horse's flanks with his heels.

With a rustle, the five horsemen separated from the crowd where Khansulu was standing as well. She didn't take her eyes off Shege, who sat like a statue on his ginger stallion, his fluffy mane and tail rustling in the wind. Today she had seen how Shege had grown up and changed drastically. He was no longer the adolescent she had known. The *jigit* galloping on the stallion suddenly turned back. His eyes fell on Khansulu. The girl did not avert her gaze...

But Shege galloped on.

2

As soon as the "people of power" were out of sight, the aul-dwellers began to hurriedly dismantle their housing. There was a hub-bub with children crying, dogs barking and camels moaning. The elders of the aul, headed by the *akhun*, decided Azbergen's fate. They untied his hands, and summoned Shotan, Motan and Kapan. Labakh-*akhun,* gathering all the men together, stroked his beard, and before their eyes, pronounced a decision:

"My son Azbergen, we have chosen the head of the aul as Bulysh, and sworn to obey him. You have violated the oath. You started troubles among us. Our word to you is: live like everybody else or go away to the four corners of the earth! That is the common will."

Azbergen was silent, breathing heavily, and then said:
"The fault is ours, forgive us, *akhun-aga*."

They forgave Azbergen.

The aul quickly prepared for their journey: no sooner had they boiled some tea than the entire load was already on the camels.

Labak-*akhun* said a blessing for the road:

"Oh, Lord of worlds, protect us! Oh, Kydyr-ata[131], be our protector on an unknown path!". Then turning to Bulysh, he concluded: "Let's head off, sonny!"

Bulysh let his raven stallion into a gallop. The long line of nomads followed behind him slowly.

The dust kicked up, not letting them open their eyes. The road went across a thick growth of saxaul, with sand dunes spilling across it from time to time. People tried to move in such a way that the sun was on the right side of the nomads. Toward sundown, they found themselves at the wall of an old cemetery. Shrines with little towers were dotted heavily over the inclines and gentle slopes. Some of the shrines were built of black stone rubble and others out of adobe clay.

"The grave of Barak-*ata*," the rumor ran through the nomad community.

Khansulu, her head bound up in a red kerchief, stood in a crowd of other young men and women. Following the example of Labak-*akhun*, the men had moved quickly. According to knowledgeable people, the shrine of the ancestors was at the very peak of the hill, the old saxaul tree had grown at the headstone of the grave. The stone shrine of Asau, son of Barak, towered a little below. For the first time, Khansulu saw the graves of the legendary *batyrs*, father and son, whose names had gone down in songs and sayings. Her heart beat strong.

The people, who had turned toward the place of eternal rest of the blessed ancestors, knelt down and bowed their head. Labakh-*akhun,* sitting ahead of everyone, closer to the cemetery, recited from the Koran in a sing-song voice, the wind fluttering his white beard. There was something new in the way the way the *akhun* sang the Koran verses. In the drawn-out melody, there seemed to be the heart-rending lamentation of the camel separated from its native habitat. The howling of the wind, the creaking of the dry saxaul increased the impression from the cracking voice of the old *akhun*, it was as if they were spoken about the unreliability of this dangerous world. The *akhun* did not

---

[131] *Kydyr-ata* is a saint and protector of travelers.

finish reading the surah,[132] his shaking voice broke. He wiped his eye with a handkerchief. This was sufficient for the men and women to begin exclaiming!

"Farewell, father! Farewell!" the *akhun* pronounced with great effort, finishing his prayer.

The people, upset and subdued by grief, did not move; all of them remained motionless in place. Then, with tears in their eyes and with a funereal prayer, they bid farewell to the grave of their ancestors on the earth, never forgotten, who had accepted their blood and sweat, and who were their fatherland…

…The nomads continued on their way, keeping the direction toward the setting sun now. The women were no longer able to restrain their sobs and gave voice to them and they could be understood: a long road, and what would it end with? Ahead was a cloudy future. Soon, even these voices fell silent; gradually the wailing was replaced by sighs, heavy and long. The women calmed down, the men calmed down; both the old and the young had reconciled to their lot. Ahead they knew were still many trials, and they had to preserve their strength. The slow, monotonous camel step rocked the travelers back and forth…

The aul sought shelter in the thick saxaul grove for the night, and as soon as dawn appeared, they once again set on their way. With the rise of the sun, the striped brown dunes of Sama were left behind, and the nomad group came out upon the Usyurt plateau, polished flat by time. The wind, which had exhausted everyone, quieted by the will of God and immediately the horizon was cleared and the view widened into the distance.

The aul moved along without stopping, only making short halts at lunch and dinner times, and even then, largely so as to give the animals a chance to rest. The danger had not yet passed. They feared pursuers following on their heels. On the third day of travel, danger finally overtook them, but not from behind as they had expected.

---

[132] A surah is a chapter in the Koran.

Trouble came straight at them. The Ustyurt plateau ended, and crumbling sands began with a different type of plants, larger and bush-like: St. John's wort, thyme and feather grass. People stumbled on to the old caravan route. The path, beaten down into the sands went a whole span into the earth. The red sun lowered itself into a faraway dune. The men were riding ahead of the caravan, intending to go around a barrier which was blocking their path; the outlines of the long hillock reminded them of a camel that had knelt down.

Suddenly, out from behind the hillock turned a group of galloping horsemen. These were Turkmens in their *papakha* fur hats, with rifles over their shoulders.

Khansulu's heart contracted. *"We ran away from the government, now we've trekked to the* basmaches,*"* the thought came to her. "Now there will be shooting, shouting, carnage."

"Oh, *Barak*-ata! *Beket*-ata!" the prayer raced through the nomad community.

And Khansulu, too, began to pray to all the saints…

The Turkmens, seeing the caravan, reined in their horses. The nomad group came to a halt. For the first time, Khansulu saw the famous *basmachi* who, it was told, ruthlessly rob travelers and kidnap girls. But the Turkmens, coming off the road, peacefully continued their way, talking about something among themselves. Khansulu felt a chill go up her spine.

The men in the caravan – and Bulysh along with them – fell silent. They were in a turmoil, not knowing what their sworn enemy would do. All of them carefully looked at the Turkmen. Heedless, the Turkmen rode on their beautiful *argamak* horses with swan-like necks, the horses bucking under them. They wore *shekpens*,[133], sashes stretched tight in several rows, and *khorzhuns* strapped to the saddles. They rode along, looking askance at the nomads. All was quiet. Only the camels were smacking their lips and snorting a little. Even the women bit their tongues.

---

[133] A *shekpen* is a camel-hair robe.

A small man with a broad, bushy beard rode ahead on a bay stallion with black-and-white legs; he wore a *papakha* on his head that seemed bigger than he was. His proud stance said without words that he was the leader of the group.

"Will they really pass by without a single shot?" thought Khansulu, relaxing her palm with the reins clenched in it, looking around. People were riding along pale with fear. Suddenly, noise rolled through the nomad caravan. Khansulu once again looked behind her at the Turkmen. Broad-bearded, letting the *nukers* ahead, they stood across the path. They were waving their hands and shouting something. Bulysh quickly set his horse trotting toward them. One of them rode up.

"*Oybo-oy!* What will happen!" some woman whispered.
"What do they want?" a quiet hum swept through the women.

Bulysh did not tarry. The negotiations were brief. The broad-bearded man galloped after his comrades, and Bulysh turned back. Everyone's attention, including that of Labakh-*akhun*, was fastened like iron on Bulysh, hurrying back to them on his raven argamak. His expression was hard. Even from a distance, he waved his whip and shouted:

"Move out!"

It resounded like an order. The girls and young men following alongside the caravan were left in the dark about their leader's negotiations with the Turkmens. Bulysh only informed the men, and then later the conversation reached the women. These were their words:

"Where is the caravan coming from and where is it going?" asked the Turkmen.
"From the current government, we are going away to Afghanistan," Bulysh answered.

"You shouldn't skedaddle, you should fight!" the Turkmen reproached him.

"We don't have the strength to oppose them!" said Bulysh.

"You don't have it, but I do. Turn the nomads' caravan to Shagyl's well! Not much time will go by, and we will bury the government at that well."

"Don't order us around, traveler! We are still a free aul!"

"Oh, you Kazakh! If you ran away from the government, don't think you'll run away from Khan Joneyt[134]!"

That was the entire conversation. Something was concealed within it, which added to people's fears. "Now, not only the government is taking up arms against us, but even more seasoned wolves, the *basmachi* of Khan Joneyt!" the old people, who had seen everything, commented, shaking their heads.

… The caravan went further into the sands. The dunes stretched many kilometers all around, rolling against each other like waves. The clean, granulated sand stretched along both sides of the path. Here and there were clumps of feather grass, their stalks yellowing in the sun. Century plant, camel thorn and agave were also growing. A wild desert, without signs of life, completely devoid of people, without even hoof prints of animals….

The sun baked down. The dunes seared their faces with heat. Their mouths were dry and they were tormented with thirst. They found two wells along the way, but there was little water in them, not enough for everyone; finally, at the third, called Sarsheyt, they got lucky. There was also a lot of camel thorn growing around that well. People took the cargo off the camels, watered them, and then let them out to pasture. They decided to spend the night at the well.

3

An armed group of 50 men led by Afanasy Grinin and Asan Aytzhanov – among them volunteers and representatives of the people's militia – pursued the fleeing aul along the old caravan route. By the evening of the third day, when the detachment was deep in the

---

[134] Khan Joneyt was the head of the Turkmen resistance to the Soviet government.

The Lonely Yurt • Smagul Yelubay

Turkmen Karakum,[135] Asan's sharp eye noticed a camel's head flashing among the sand dunes. Were *jigits* flying out from the ravine?

At Asan's sign, they retreated.

"If the livestock has been detected, then the aul is there," he said to Apanas, who was already pressing his binoculars to his eyes.

Apanas summoned Jdakay and Shege.

"Over there is the watchman, you see? He is alone there," he told them. "You are the most, shall we say, aware fellows in the detachment. I order you in the name of the revolution to remove the watchman, only without any noise. Is that clear? And if possible, try to take him alive. We must seize the moment before dawn when they will still be asleep. You yourselves realize that if they manage to get on their horses, the shooting will start and blood will be shed…Have you understood me?"

"We have understood, Comrade Commander!" said Shege and Jdakhay, straightening themselves up, military-style, and vying with each other to reply. Their eyes burned with zeal.

"This is your first battle assignment, fellas. I trust you will do as required. Soon the moon will rise, everything will be as visible as your hand. Take the watchman – and let us know. Wave from the hill," said Apanas.

Having received the commander's order, Shege and Jdakhay crept up to the hill through gullies and ravines, reaching a large dune. Darkness surrounded them. Every bush ahead of them was like an enemy hiding out. The young men's hearts knocked as if they would burst from their chests. After a while, Jdakhay whispered:

"Fellow, we've in for it…"

"What, are you scared?" Shege hissed.

---

[135] The Karakum, literally "black sand," is the desert in Turkmenistan.

"How could you not be scared…what will you do if somebody falls on us from behind, like a bear?"

"Don't be afraid! Besides the watchman, everyone is asleep."

It was quiet – only the dry grasses rustled under their feet.

"Quiet!" Shege reproached Shege in a whisper. Neither of them took their eyes off the watchman, whose lonely silhouette stood out darkly against the peak, reminiscent of a camel hump, a triangle etched against the starry sky. Both had a knife and a Berdan rifle. Hunched over, they ran in short spurts. But before the moon came out, all that they had managed to was to reach the foot of the dune. They hid in the birdweed bushes under dry branches. They lay prostrate, not breathing.

The watchman was still in the same place, his rifle slung over his shoulder. Now and then he would turn around and look at the sleeping world, half in moonlight.

"His father's soul is in him," Jdakhay grumbled. "If he is going to go on being so vigilant, we won't be able to creep up to him."

"Let's wait, it's a long way until morning," Shege whispered.

Ahead, a little corner of the dense darkness began to light up, and soon the moon had risen, rather the half-moon, reddish like a *lepyoshka-kulshe*.[136]

Jdakhay poked Shege in the side, nodding toward the summit. Shege carefully extracted himself from the dry branches and saw how the watchman was sitting down, tucking his legs underneath him, holding his rifle in his hands.

"God willing," whispered Jdakhay. "He will get tired. It's good he sat down, he will fall asleep quicker."

Shege turned his eyes to the sky, to the moon, transiting to the center of the sky's cupola, lighting everything around. It lured toward

---

[136] A *lepyoshka-kulshe* is a flat roll baked on a skillet over hot coals.

itself the smooth, white shoulders of the dune. It all seemed like a wonderful dream. Oh, to run barefoot over those slopes, crumbling under your feet! And why not run to the moonlit distances? Especially with Khansulu...

...

Glancing at the watchman, Jdakhay was dreaming about his own desires as he lay under the bushes. He had his own pain, Balkiya. The bright-faced beauty Balkiya with the eyes of a wild cat....

At about midnight, the moon was at its zenith. A cool wind blew from somewhere, rustling the heads of the feather grass. The watchman had hung his head, poor thing. It looked like he was dozing off.

"Jdakhay," Shege whispered. Jdakhay, lost in his dreams, jerked up.

"It looks like he fell asleep."

The moon reached its very zenith. The tops of the feather grass rustled drily from the cool night wind. For a little while, they concentrated on the watchman who was sitting with his head hanging over his chest. It seemed as if he really had nodded off.

The friends began to circle the hillock. It was good that you couldn't see its foot from its top. They climbed up the dune on the windward side, behind the watchman's back. They crawled along like lizards. From the slope, the hidden aul was visible, lit by the moon. It was at the distance of a stallion's gallop. There were no yurts, and instead there were tents and *shalashes* with the *kerege* as a window. The horses stood nearby, saddled.

The friends clambered up the hill, the soil crumbling under their hands and feet. They had agreed that if the watchman woke up, Jdakhay would throw his knife. If he were close, Shege, like a leopard, would attack and muffle the watchman's mouth. They would not shoot. The watchman appeared to be young. He wore a *shekpen* made of camel hair. He wore a wide belt with round of ammunition. On his head was a round *borik*[137]. He was sleeping, his forehead leaning against his rifle. Jdakhay crawled toward him and leaned toward Shege's ear:

"It's Rysbek, I'm going to fail!"

"Stop it!" Shege said, frightened.

Frowning, Jdakhay nodded his head in confirmation. Both of them look at the watchman's back for a while, scared. Before Shege's eyes was Mazhan's red-haired, snub-nosed shepherd, Rysbek the Orphan, who had once pastured the *bays*' horse herds.

He had a strong body, but he was shy and cowardly. It seemed only yesterday that in the summer sun at the edge of the aul, he had spent hours with the aul's children, gambling with the *asyki*. If boys who were a little bolder like Jdakhay, kicked up a fuss, demanding that the *asyki* they lost be returned, Rysbek would timidly return them immediately. His father and mother, who were Mazhan's *batraks*, had died at an early age. Rysbek was left a total orphan. He slept and spent his days in the sheds with Mazhan's herds.

"We're taking him alive, you hear?" said Shege, not tearing his eyes off the watchman.

"Obviously, if we can manage," replied Jdakhay.

They crawled along, almost not breathing. The distance between them and the sleeping Rysbek grew shorter; he was quite near. Rysbek snored. The friends exchanged glances, then kept crawling. Their hands and knees sunk softly into the crumbling sand. Something rustled in the grasses. The night desert was letting its hidden life be known. They crept right up to the watchman.

And suddenly something happened which they hadn't expected at all. Something cracked in the feather grass and a desperate rabbit's shriek sliced the night.

It turned out that rabbits lived in the dunes; they were frightened and then frightened everyone else around them.

---

[137] A *borik* is a warm men's fur hat.

"Huh? Huh?" Rysbek waved his arms and jumped up. But he didn't see the danger creeping up behind his back.

Right at that moment, Jdakhay and Shege lunged at him like wolves. Shege's rifle remained back at the place from which he had leapt, stretching both hands forward. The humped nose and mouth of the tall Rysbek was under Shege's hand. The lad thrashed about, trying to break free, and wanted to shout out, but he couldn't: the two sat on him, crushing him underneath and not letting him breathe. Shege's grip was like iron. He looked at Jdakhay. The other hung on to the belt of the tall Rysbek who was desperately trying to get away. And then Jdakhay with a sweep of his arm stabbed Ryzbek in the stomach. Shege tried to shout something but his dry throat would not give out a sound. However, Jdakhay still heard something. He once again swung his knife, but the second time he couldn't strike a blow. Both Jdakhay and Shege looked at the bloody knife.

Rysbek crouched underneath them both, shakily jerking his body, then stretched out to his full length. But his soul did not yet leave his body...

Shege jerked his hand back and jumped to the side. The rabbit's shrieks continued, but now their bleating was coming from somewhere far away. Shege didn't want to be seen by the dying Rysbek. He was in shock by what had happened. Even if the sky crashed to the earth, he wouldn't have found in himself the strength to react to this. He became indifferent to everything, even if the aul woke up and surrounded them from all sides and shot at them.

"He's dead," Jdakhay said after a little while, coming up to him and falling to his knees. He said it with a sigh.

"Why did you do that?" asked Shege softly, without looking at him. He was shaking with anger at his friend, but also exhausted by a feeling of complete powerless.

"I don't know myself how it happened...Jdakhay looked down gloomily.

In the east, the light was appearing, barely noticeable. He was shivering.

Shege got up, swaying from side to side. All his muscles were trembling. He looked at the dead body. Rysbek had fallen face down, with his head toward the east. His cap was missing. It had slipped down the dune; a dark spot was visible below where it lay. Jdakhay fished a handkerchief out of his chest pocket and waved it in the pre-dawn air.

4

The aul slept heedlessly, only Labak-*akhun* was away under the moonlit sky, his white *chapan* and white *chalma* gleamed in the darkness. From time to time, his fingers picked up the hems. The *akhun*'s eyes were shut, his consciousness was in another world. He didn't know how long he sat there; only when he came to his senses, the thickness of the short summer night was already dispersing. He got up, his joints creaking, and collected his *jaynamaz*[138]. Turning back, he glanced at the summit where the watchman was supposed to be standing and froze. The summit was empty. The old man at first did not believe his eyes. He peered more closely. No, his eyes had not betrayed him. There was no one standing at the top of the hill.

"Bulysh! Hey, Bulysh!" he shouted desperately. The old man's yell pierced the sleepy quiet. Men who had been sleeping in their clothing with their guns under their heads instantly jumped out of their *shalashes*.

"*Attan-an!*"[139] – Bulysh let loose the traditional battle cry, jumping on his *argamak*. "To your horses!"

The jigits moved out with warrior sentiment, deafening the area with the drubbing of horse hooves. A shot rang out up ahead. The horsemen froze before the opening of the dunes. They realized they were heading into an ambush.   "Stop! Put down your arms if you do not want bloodshed! Drop your weapon!"

---

[138] A *jaynamaz* is a prayer rug.
[139] *Attan-an* is a Kazakh battle cry which means "to your horses!"

The old ears of Labakh-*akhun* heard the warning; he ran toward the people shooting, the hems of his chapan flying in the wind. Upset, the women knocked down the *shalashes* and hurriedly loaded up the camels.

"Oh, Beket-*ata*![140]" the akhun sobbed as he walked.

"Oh, Barak-ata![141] the pitiful voices of the women replied. Goose bumps sprang up from their lamentations.

From the other side, an authoritative voice rang out:

"Whoever surrenders voluntarily will be forgiven!"

"You take us for fools!" a voice rang out.

"Take cover!" shouted Bulysh.

The men galloped away on the horses, and lay down behind a round sand hill overgrown with feather grass. They heard return fire.

"Bulysh! Hey, Bulysh! It's Apanas!" a voice rang out in the silence. "Listen to me. Remember yourself! Don't get your people killed for nothing. Surrender! Give up voluntarily. I swear to you – we will not punish anyone! We will return you to your homeland, that's the whole of the punishment."

Three shots rang out from various sides in reply to Afanasy Vasilyevich's proposal. The detachment did not reply to these shots, however. This totally surprised the *jigit* nomads. There continued to be calls to surrender by the Red Army soldiers. And this angered the *jigits* all the more.

"Drop your weapons! Surrender!"

---

[140] Beket-ata was a prominent 18th century Sufi scholar who built a madrassah and several underground mosques in the Mangistau region of Kazakhstan.
[141] Barak-ata was a legendary *batyr* or warrior. Kazakhs have a tradition of worshipping their ancestors.

The *akhun* stood to the side, helplessly tugging his beard and chanting:

"Oh, my children! Oh, my children!"

"*Akhun-aga*, take cover from the bullets!" people cried from all sides, but he didn't pay them any mind. He had a prayer on his lips and tears in his eyes. The detachment apparently was not waging fire with good reason. The voices of the Red Army soldiers could be heard on the left and right, and from behind the slope of the large dune.

"You're surrounded! There are machine guns on both sides of you!"

"Drop your weapons!"

Shege's voice piped up.

"Bulysh-*aga*! Don't resist! Bulysha-*aga*! You're getting people killed for no reason! For no reason!"

"To your horses! To your horses!" Bulysh cried hoarsely. He didn't think to surrender easily.

But the Red Army soldiers appeared from the rear as well. Without aiming, Bulysh pressed the trigger. The first Red Army soldier fell from his horse and flopped on the ground like a pike out of water, then stretched out flat.

A second one also fell; one of Bulysh's *jigits* shot him.

"Fire!" the command rang out sternly.

The machine guns thundered. Four *jigits* were instantly torn from their horses. The horses, wounded, neighed and reared up straight; soon there were more and more of them that had lost their riders. The machine guns continued to fire. Bullets showered like hail, who could withstand them? The time came when everyone man began to think to save himself. Bulysh's *jigits* began to retreat into the dunes. The scattered nomads' community also began to retreat there.

In the very center of the field of battle, on a hillock behind which the *jigits* had just sought cover, the akhun remained, illuminated by the morning light. In his hand was his staff and his white *chapan* fluttered like a flag. He had seen how young people died today, with his own eyes; he had heard how the bullets whistled and carried away young lives. It was better that he had not seen and heard this!

The old man begged God for death.

"Send me the bullet of death! Send it to an old fool who has gone out of his mind! Let me perish! Why am I still alive until now? Why haven't my bones collapsed? Why haven't I fallen? In my heart, I sensed trouble, and could not get to sleep last night. Why didn't you immediately understand what was going on, you old fool?! Why didn't you rouse the nomads last night and move out on the trail?! Oh, you crazy old man! You are guilty of people's deaths! You are guilty of bloodshed!" Tears streamed down his face.

The old man pounded his staff on the ground. Fifty horsemen flew out of the ravine and lunged after the fleeing nomads. No one looked at the old man shouting on the hill; no one paid any attention to him. The horsemen raced by him, whooping. When the village elder came to his senses and looked around, he saw there wasn't a soul left by the well. Greedy crows and gyrfalcons had already landed screeching on the dead horses. Nearby, horses without their masters wandered, munching the grass.

The *akhun*'s keen old ear caught someone's prolonged groaning somewhere. He peered down into the ravine. There – oh, Creator! – he saw two people leaning over a body; for some reason they were supporting the body's head. It turned out not all were dead, there were some living and wounded! The old man began to descend down the hill, taking big steps. One of the two people turned out to be an elderly Russian man and the second – a young Kazakh – was winding a bandage around the wounded person's chest.

"Oh, *aksakal, salam!"* the Russian man greeted the *akhun* when he saw him.

The *akhun* nodded his head. He recognized the wounded man. It was Asan the Bolshevik! He was evidently severely wounded. He was groaning.

"Water…water…" he begged.

A young *jigit*, who was helping the Russian doctor, poured some drops of water into the wounded man's mouth from a canvas *burdyuk*. Asan's eyes, wandering, fell on the *akhun*. The old man nodded his head. Asan didn't say anything. He couldn't. Unable to look at the dying man, the *akhun* kept nodding his head.

"Ah, sonny…ah, sonny…" he mumbled. And went forward, not seeing anything in front of him.

The poor man was now going to wander until his incomprehensible life ended, hidden from the eyes of the world.

"Oh, Creator! Oh, Creator!" he prayed.

The *akhun* left to go wandering. What did he, an old babbler, have left? To wander. And he would die, a wanderer. A punishment he deserved…

From the West, beyond the dunes, the nomads could be seen. A long, ragged line of nomads. The people tiredly stepped alongside the camels. Wailing women's voices could be heard. The caravan and the remnants of the livestock that remained had stumbled into the ravine where the well was located. The *akhun*, as it happened, was walking to meet his own caravan…

On Apanas' orders, the nomads stopped at the well until evening. Someone discovered that among the dead was his son; another, his father, someone else, his brother, and the aul, already hurting, was filled with mournful lamentations and hot tears. For the detachment, that day was a sad one as well: they turned over to the earth three of their dead, including the Bolshevik, Asan Aytzhanov. They gave them a triple rifle salute… When the heat of the day had passed, the nomads once again set off on the road. They were retracing their own steps. A large part of the nomad group was made up of women, children and old people. There were men who had surrendered willingly – they accompanied their families without any weapons.

...When the aul had fled into the desert, one lone nomad's group had gone off to the side, between the dunes. Hiding, they made their way through the ravines and the gullies, going further and further away. This was Balkiya's group. A courageous woman, seasoned from the bitter experience of past flights, she realized that if Bulysh fled from the Red Army soldiers, he would inevitably go looking for her, and therefore she decided to leave.

Bulysh's *jigits,* distracting the attention of the detachment from the fleeing aul, headed into flight, fending off the enemy as they went. But the commander of the detachment turned out to be cleverer. He threw his main forces on Bulysh's fighters, and the remaining ones at the aul. It was obvious that soon, the fugitives were in the hands of their pursuers, which is what essentially they demanded of them, and then the main forces ceased their gunfire.

Bulysh's *jigits* realized that resistance was futile, that the Red Army were superior in number and arms; then the troubles began among them – shouts, arguments, clashes. If it were not for Bulysh, they might possibly have ended up killing each other in their fever. Having become the witness of the death of innocent people, Bulysh came to a firm decision that no one yet guessed. Now was the right time to announce it.

"Listen to me!" he urged.

The *jigits*, ceasing their noise, turned to listen to him.

"I have committed a sin by sending you against an enemy who is stronger than you are. If we go on resisting, our wives and children will have to mourn us. I don't want your wives to become widows and your children to become orphans. Turn back from this place! That is my word to you. I will go on alone," said Bulysh.

He spoke from the saddle. Already dark, he had grown completely haggard, his bloodshot eyes were sunken in his face. His rifle lay across his saddle. The *jigits* had expected anything from

Bulysh, but not this. There was a stirring among the ranks of the horsemen.

"For me, the way back is mandated. What is ordained, I will accept myself. But to you, my order is to go to your families! Consider that this is my blessing. Who comes with me will meet my bullet." With this words, he began to turn his horse around.

"What do you know!" somebody uttered.

"And now...who are we with...Bulysh-*aga*?"

"With Apanas! He isn't a bad Russian. He's honest. He will keep his word. He will forgive us.

And he turned the raven horse toward where Balkiya's camp was hidden.

The *jigits* were crestfallen and silent. Then once again they began arguing. Half of them wanted to return with the aul, and the other half was waiting for what Azbergen would say, as he was a fierce enemy of the Soviet government. The men divided into two camps. Bulysh and Balkiya were in the part that separated from the rest. Many looked despondently after Bulysh until he disappeared over the hill. What he was thinking and where he would go, no one knew.

5

The detachment accompanying the nomads' group was unable to break out of the endless sea of sands even by the second day. The travelers once again spent the night in the desert. It was a chilly, moonless autumn night. People hid under the dry bushes of dwarf acacia, and went to sleep.

The detachment posted watchmen. Among them was Shege. No sooner did he close his eyes for a second than the image of Rysbek arose before him. Shege could not forget what happened in the dunes. He grew haggard from insomnia, his cheeks were sunken and he looked as if he had suffered a disease. He just couldn't forget about the night incident on the hill. Ever since that night, he couldn't stand to see Jdakhay, he would grow wary in his presence, like a cat when seeing a dog. And he kept remembering about Asan who had died. For the first time in his life, the youth reflected on life and death and grieved.

Recently, at Apanas's request, Labakh-*akhun* had given an exhortative speech for the people. And the cold, black clouds that had accumulated in people's souls began to soften and tears flowed from their eyes. For a time, people were preoccupied with remembering the recent tragedy; they heeded the sincere voice of the old man with all their hearts. Shege went deep into the dunes and there could no longer keep himself from breaking into tears. He felt endlessly alone. Only Khansulu could share his heartfelt grief...He began to look for an occasion to talk with her alone. And soon there was an occasion. At dinner, when people were busy with chores and not paying attention, he found himself next to the girl and whispered to her:

"I will be on the watch tonight. I will wait for you."

The moon would soon appear, and everything around was softly illuminated. Everyone had long ago gone to sleep. But Khansulu had still not come...This journey had opened his eyes to people. For example, he was shocked by Apanas' behavior. No sooner did Labak-*akhun* stop his camel and spread out his prayer rug (and he did this mornings and evenings) and begin praying, then Afanasy Vasilyevich gave the signal to both the nomads' group and the detachment to stop. Everyone, except for those who were praying along with the *akhun*, waited for when the elder would fold up his prayer rug. Such was the procedure established along the way by the commander of the detachment. The aul-dweller's attitude toward Apanas also changed; "he's a good man," they said, "with a conscience, although not a Muslim," the old people said. Jdakhay and several of the *jigits*, however, grumbled, not understanding why the commander was nannying the mullah, so to speak, and Sur Jekey asked outright: "Why such respect for a bandit, Afanasy Vasilyevich?" And the commander had one answer: "Every people's customs should be respected."

Shege started. In the darkness, he could hear the rustling of a person quietly walking along. A slender silhouette came into view. Shege peered into the darkness. Khansulu! It was she...Shege's mouth grew dry. What was he to do now?

The soft steps fell silent; she was already next to him. Oh, God, it was she! A slender, nimble silhouette. The Berdan rifle over his shoulder suddenly seemed incredibly heavy. Was it suddenly starting to bother him?! Almost tripping, he awkwardly made a step toward her. The thought swam through his head detachedly that the starry sky was above and the sand below their feet, and all of this boundless abode was as if in a dream…

"Khansulu!" he cried, his voice cracking. It was a quiet call. But Khansulu heard it.

"It's me," she replied.

The tenderness seeped through her soft voice. Shege went up to her. Then he stopped. There was a thin *chapan* on her girlish shoulders. She was gazing at him from under her long, turned-up eyelashes. And although it was night, he could see her large, beautiful eyes well, and guessed their expression. She stood near, he could have reached her with his hand. Just like a night star, here she was. The girl smiled. And Shege realized that he had been silent an indecently long time. Trying to calm his beating heart, he suggested to her:

"Let's go to the dunes! And take a walk…"

The smile still played on her girlish lips. She silently went along with him. Shege's heart was pounding, his chest was bursting with feeling. The dry autumn grass crunched under foot. Listening to the quiet, he tried to get control over his contradictory thoughts. What would he say to her whom he loved, for whom he had waited so long?! What would he reply if she asked, "Why did you summon me?" The starry night was overhead…The Milky Way dusted its light across the sky. All around was a realm of sand. From here, from the dunes, there was a clear view. Khansulu was stepping along as if reluctant, her forehead shiny; she seemed like a fairy.

On the dune, they were once again silent, unable to come out of the awkward state they were experiencing. They fastened their gazes on the weakly-lit waves of sand as if they were expecting something.

"Let's sit down!" Shege offered, and sighing sadly, was the first to lower himself down on the crumbling sand. He took off his Berdan rifle and lay it down beside him.

The sky in the east had noticeably lightened. The moon had already risen markedly over the horizon. Khansulu arranged herself with her face to the east.

"The moon is being born," she said softly and sadly.

"Now the moon will come out and the sands will be beautiful," Shege continued. "Have you ever wandered among the dunes under the moon?"

Khansulu clicked her tongue which apparently meant "no."

"That's too bad, because you know, it's beautiful…In our lands, the moonlit night is one kind, and here it is different…"

The girl sat side by side, tracing something on the sand and now and then glancing at the *jigit* with a smile: sparks were just barely lighting in his eyes, and it seems he had even grown more handsome when he was talking about something with a smile.

"Shege," she said, turning to him. "You should better tell what will happen to us when we return?"

"Hasn't Apanas told you? Nothing will happen. We will work in an artel and live a new life."

"That's it? Somehow, it's not believable. If everything Apanas says is true…"

"Apanas is a real *rebelsener*[142]! Shege assured her fervently, as if to show to the girl how politically literate he was. "What Apanas says will be."

"Are you a…*rebelsener*, too?" she asked.

---

[142] *Rebelsener* is how Shege pronounces the Russian word *revolyutsioner* or "revolutionary."

"All those who fight for the Soviet *blasty* are *rebelsenery!*" Shege exclaimed. And then withdrew. What was he going on about? He seemed to be trying to listen to what was on her heart, what was causing her anguish. Her heart was yearning for something. But it wasn't a conversation about the revolution. No. Her heart wanted to open. But how to open it?

Khansulu looked at him sideways. The moon lit his simple, half-childish face and his sparse mustache. Shege signed and turned toward her head. And he saw the eyes of the girl radiating warmth. He looked away. For the first time in his life he was seeing that Khansulu was looking at him like that – softly and trustingly…

The Milky Way dusted light over their head; the sand dunes, like a wave surrounding them, flowed under their feet. He felt as if he and Khansulu were sitting together at the very center of the universe, bathed by the animated light of the moon. It seemed to him that his tormented heart no longer ached, possibly from the joy that was miraculously flowing into his heart, drop by drop. Shege didn't move, afraid to frighten the girl's trust. He didn't want to interfere with the dawning that had overtaken him. There was brightness in his head and his chest. And it became easy to breathe, and his heart beat hard with a new strength.   "Sulu!" he burst out, calling her by a nickname.

The girl swept her gaze over the sandy hillocks which really were amazing under the moon – they were drenched in all the shades of silver, as in the fairy tale. Shege stretched out his hand to her. It was a mute gesture, it was as if he were begging, "Take me out of the darkness…" His hand touched her braid. His heart completely burst from his chest…A soft barely sensed aroma of perfume came from her hair. If he were up to him, he would have gone on breathing in that fragrance until morning, so desirable, so familiar…Both of them were silent.

Shege took Khansulu by the hand, and was amazed at his own boldness. Her slender fingers – oh, what a miracle! – ended up in his palm. But Khansulu, trembling, withdrew. Gazing at him with her radiant eyes, she quietly extricated her fingers. The warmth of her hand remained in his fingers.

"I have to go," she said and threw her *chapan* over her shoulder.

"Sit for a while," asked Shege, although he felt that she would leave. He couldn't believe that this was all happening for real...

"No," she replied, smiling and shaking her head. Shege idolized her at that moment. He got to his feet, and could barely stand. The tall girl with the light *chapan* over her shoulders disappeared into the night like a shadow. And that silhouette, disappearing into the night, seemed to say to him, "I am yours."

It was night, and the moon slipped through the sky. Shege sat on a dune. He was utterly stunned with happiness...

THE NEW LIFE

1

The caravan began to encounter populated areas, and it came time for Khansulu to be surprised. In the year of their wandering through the sands, life had changed. There were fewer small auls of five or six households, which were usually bunched together near a hill, like beans in the hand of a fortune-teller. Now the settlements were concentrated around wells and springs, and there were more homes and people in them. Permanent homes were built, people made bricks, raised walls; a red flag waved over some buildings. Most likely these were the auls that had quickly come toward the "new life" about which Khansulu and her fellow travelers had heard so much.

...

According to Shege, their old aul had settled at the Jylybulak spring, and now this association was called Janazhol.[143]

In the first minute, it seemed to her that a whole town had spread out from the base of the rocky hill. The yellow foothills seemed animated; it was as if people were at a festival. My, how the world had changed in just a single year!

---

[143] The Kazakh words "*jana zhol*" mean "new path".

Khansulu very much wanted to see her mother and father as soon as possible. All her attention was fastened on the white yurt which stood at a certain distance from the aul. Khansulu recognized her yurt. Her mother stood before her home. Tears sprang to her eyes.

"Oh, you bastard, what a *kallektep*!" Jdakhay enthused.

"No, you look, Shege, what a school they built! Kozbagar's great!" Jdakhay, jumping for joy, nearly flew off his horse. Khansulu recalled what Shege had told her. Kozbagar was the chairman in the new aul! The aul, it turned out, was now being governed by that dolt Kozbagar, from whom she had fled. Just try to believe all this!

People stopped their work and stared at the caravan which had alarmed the aul dogs. Some woman began to vehemently egg on Torka:

"Mother, look who's coming! Your runaway daughter-in-law is back, what a joy!" she cried deliberately for everyone to hear. The old woman Torka immediately went into a rage:

"Damn that daughter-in-law! What use is a fugitive kulak daughter to my son! Let her keep far away from my sonny!"

Some of the nomads stopped at the edge of the aul. From habit, the children ran toward it, but the adults were not in a hurry. Shege, seeing Kozbagar, asked in a deliberately loud voice:

"And where is the chairman? Where is the chairman?"

Kozbagar was working – he was digging in the earth with a hoe. Hearing Shege, he wiped the sweat from his brow.

"Hey, comrade! Come meet your people!" Shege said, stinging his heart. Kozbagar, feeling awkward, stumbled awkwardly toward the nomads.

"Go back!" Torka cried instantly.

"*Apa-a*, it's my duty…"

"The hell with your duty! Go back, I'm telling you! Ba-a-ck!! *Oybay,* let my eyes bug out if I have ever seen such a dolt! Damn your gang of kulaks!" cried Torka.

In righteous anger, Torka flopped to the ground and beat the dry clay of the hillside with her bony fists. Shege, leaning down to the very ear of the crazed old woman said softly:

"*Apa,* be careful with words like "gang" and "kulak." These people have been sent to us by order of the GPU. How can you say such things? You're the mother of the chairman! Comrade Stalin himself ordered to stop the *otkoshyobki*[144]! Shege said in Russian. "That's the policy!"

"*Oybay!*" Torka stared at him, and without a word, hurried toward the camels. Shege speaking Russian was the last straw. "*Oybay!*, the devil take it, I let the calf nurse and didn't milk her...ay! Listen, here!"

Everybody had a good laugh. Even Khansulu chuckled. She liked Shege's resourcefulness. With just one phrase, he had managed to chase away the scandalous old woman. So she graced him with a long gaze.

2

The little nomads' group wove its way through the sands for a long while. At first, fearing pursuit, it had kept going without stops, just to get as far away as possible. But there was no pursuit. And then the fugitives decided to head south – once again, hurriedly, heedless of day or night. The dunes continued. Only on the third day of travel did they find a resting place, overgrown with camel-thorn and morning-glory. There they stopped and unloaded their goods. They let two camels and one calf out to pasture, hobbling their legs. They then removed the saddles from two horses – there were only two people in the nomad's group, a man and a woman. While the man busied himself with the livestock, the woman started a fire and got the water boiling. Both were

---

[144]Shege is pronouncing in this way the Russian word *otkochyovki,* which means the nomadic wanderings.

silent. They quickly raised a *shalash* using two walls of a yurt. They sat in it, hunched over, and drank tea. The hot tea soon caused him to sweat; wiping his wet forehead, the man said:

"Put up the yurt, I'll raise the *shanyrak,* and you do the rest. I'll start digging a well..."

The woman sighed happily.

"Oh, bliss! Finally, we've managed to sip a bit of tea in peace...

The bright-faced, nimble woman, stretching like a cat, flopped down on the spread-out blanket. The tea had made her drowsy, and she kept lazily opening and closing her large, pretty eyes, full of light. It was Balkiya. And the man next to her was Bulysh, her Bulysh, that she had managed still and all to "hook" with a noisy scandal. Waking and sleeping, Bulysh was always before her eyes. Black as iron, Bulysh. As coarse as he was on the exterior as tender was he at heart. Bulysh, her Bulysh, rejecting all the joys of the world for her alone, the only chosen one on this earth. And Balkiya essentially didn't need any other life. Just as long as Bulysh was near, just as long as Bulysh was alive and unharmed.

"Stir yourself, my dear, it's not the time for lying around, the horses over there want a drink...Get up, now," Bulysh commanded although it was pleasant for him to look at her, sweetly stretching herself. Balkiya smiled, seemingly forever in slumber, and opened her eyes slightly. Her eyes gleamed like a wild cat's.

Bulysh's heart knocked. His gaze slid along the rounded female hip and then to the endless sea of dunes visible from the *shalash.* There were the yellow humps like freshly-baked loafs of bread, and then a little higher, the flatness of the sky, boundless as far as the eye could see. The bottomless sky was clear. An age-old, settled quiet reigned. Peace penetrated deeply into his soul, pleasant to the heart and long forgotten. The crickets chirped. The horses snorted.

Balkiya lay barefoot. The hem of her dress sewn along the edge was pushed up, revealing taut, white calves... Her heels seemed fine and clean like flour or sand. Bulysh's heart was pounding; taking off his *shekpen*, his gaze fell on Balkiya's face. Her lips were slightly parted, as if burning with thirst, her eyes were overcast with bliss. Under her tender chin, the pulsating vein of her neck was barely visible... Bulysh forgot about everything. He reached for her and she, too, rushed to meet him. Balkiya's strong embrace was like a grip and Bulysh was barely able to breathe...The *shalash* was cramped for them and they rolled out on to the sand.

The autumn sky was high and clear. The silence cast its wings over the endless expanses.

In the afternoon, Bulysh and Balkiya set about doing the chores. Balkiya picked up the yurt and Bulysh dug a well. The water appeared only toward evening at a depth of three fathoms.

When he was finished with the household chores, taking a trap and his gun, he sent off on the occupation to which he had been accustomed since childhood.

3

Once again, there was a hubbub in the aul. Not an evening went by without a meeting. Every evening, people argued heatedly until they were hoarse. They attacked one another, divided into groups: someone was a "kulak," someone else was a "henchman" and yet another was a "ragamuffin." Commissars of all ranks combed through the auls front and back. The uneducated people gaped at them, open-mouthed, because they didn't whom to listen to.

The last commissar with whom the aul at Zhylybulak had to deal in the absence of Shege – he was then involved in an operation to catch the fugitives – was none other than Bukhabay. Now everyone called him respectfully by the name Bukha.[145] He had left police service and become a commissar, a person who was supposed to show people the path to the future...

---

[145]*Buka* on the one hand is a respectful short form of a Kazakh name, but on the other hand the meaning of the word in common speech is "bull" and his name "Bukha" sounded similar.

It was an ordinary day. As always, the work was in full swing, people were making bricks, their trowels clanging. During the evening prayer, a lonely horseman appeared over the Khan-tortkil hill, seemingly out of place. Judging from everything, he was in no hurry, and even seemed to be drowsing in the saddle.

"Well, my lad, come quickly! Go and meet him! It's Bukha!!" Sharip ordered Kozbagar.

Kozbagar's face changed. He grew flustered and began bustling about. But where could he go? Stumbling, he jogged toward the horseman. Bukhabay was in fact riding on the old ginger mare with her belly sagging like a sack. His greasy neck was in folds, his narrow eyes swam, seeing nothing. It seemed as if Bukha really was sleeping. He didn't reply to the greetings of poor, breathless Kozbagar, but the latter had grown accustomed to putting up with everything. He was prepared to do everything to please the important guest, he got underfoot, trailing Bukha and repeating, "*aga, aga!*"

Bukhabay uttered a guttural sound, stretched, and made a long yawn. Dragging his fat backside from the horse with difficulty, he muttered:

"We need a meeting, on the go…"

He said the expression "on the go" in Russian. For Kozbagar, this only emphasized the importance of the moment and he nodded his head. Was this Bukhabay the same as the old Bukhabay? Ever since he had become a commissar, he had changed drastically. Talking with Kozbagar, whom he had known since childhood, it was if he were seeing him for the first time, he only moved his lips lazily. Mumbling something incoherent, sparing words, he managed Kozbagar with just one movement of his eyebrows.

"Alright, Bukha, right away…"

Out of breath, Kozbagar raced off to call the people together… With his stomach thrust out, the badger-legged Bukha stood blowing rings of *papiros*[146] smoke from his mouth.

"So, comrades!" the commissioner began when the people had gathered. "The private property owner is on the agenda today. Our sworn enemy is the private property owner, comrades! However, has a lot of private property is a *bay*, a kulak! Whoever has less private property is a *serednyak*[147]! And whoever has no property is a real

batrak… So there! Who is building *satchilism*?[148] The *batrak* is building it. Do you understand? So there! That's the way."

"Ay, golden words! Ay, a long-awaited speech! *Pay*[149]! *Pay*! Here is the wisdom of the new age! Go on! Harder! Don't let up!" Sharip cried, egging him on. He was sitting in the first row.

"So…," Bukhabay continued, inspired. "If we don't destroy the goddamn private property owner, if we don't destroy him at the root…we will not move forward. We can't. That's how it is! Kalashnikov has said so. Down with private property! Down, dammit! Long live the *kallektep*!" he cried, and began clapping.

People supported him and began clapping enthusiastically themselves. Bukhabay caught his breath and wiped his sweaty nape with an enormous handkerchief. He bent down towards Kozbagar's ear and whispered, "Where could I get some tea to drink, eh?" Kozbagar understood – they had to wrap things up. Jumping up from his seat, he shook the commissioner's hand on behalf of the entire aul. Janazhol, embarking on the course toward a new life, was grateful for a substantive speech and assured him in conclusion that the members of his *kallektep* would fulfill the tasks set to them with honor.

---

[146] A *papiros* is a type of filter-less cigarette.
[147] *Serednyak* is from the Russian root *sredniy* which means "average" or "middling". It means a mid-size farmer.
[148] "*Satchilism*" is how Bukhabay pronounces the word *sotsialism* (socialism) in Russian.
[149] *Pay* is a Kazakh expression of approval.

When they were left alone, Bukhabay poked Kozbagar in the side and said

"Take me now to a good *dastarkhan*!"

Kozbagar pondered a bit, his eyes darting back and forth.

"And so there's a girl in the house, you hear!" Bukhabay's double chin shook with his lascivious laugh. Kozbagar scratched his head. There was a *seredynak* in the aul named Zhumash. And he had a girl who was marriageable in fact – Narkyz. How fortunate that Kozbagar recalled Zhumash!

"Let's go, Bukha…"

Zhumash's home was suitable for such guests. Kozbagar led the commissioner through the aul.

The tall, thin host, seeing the guests, hastily got up, a half-naked bay under his arm. Narkyz, as was proper, laid a blanket down at the guest's place. She had been making bricks in the yard, and was still in her work garments when the guests arrived. Boots and *sharovars* didn't become her. On the contrary, they made her already ample figure seem coarse. The commissioner, cautiously following the movements of the girl, knit his brows. Then he glanced at the chairman unhappily as if to say, what, you couldn't find a better home? Feeling awkward, Kozbagar was clumsily stamping his feet in place. Narkyz meanwhile returned from taking out the samovar. Now she was wearing a red chintz dress with a dark brown plush vest and had put on a necklace and bracelets on her arm. Naturally she had washed and combed her head. She was a girl, after all. Bukha, forgetting about his host, immediately turned his attention toward her. His eyes flamed and he began to chuckle. His mood had clearly improved. So like Bukha! Kozbagar relaxed.

After a little while, they said goodbye, after agreeing that Bukhabay would spend the night at the hosts and Kozbagar would come for him early in the morning to see him off.

Their host Zhumash turned out to be an extraordinarily garrulous complainer, and all even fretted about things that were wrong, which finally exhausted Bukhabay. He was the guest, what was left for him to do? He listened to the host, although it annoyed him. The time was different – everyone complained. You couldn't find a home where the master wasn't crying – everyone had been driven mad by the taxes. Bukhabay had long grown accustomed to such outpourings. When Karkyz, with the bangles jingling in her braids, set about making up his bed, Bukhabay cheered up. A guest was supposed to go outside for a stroll while the hosts made the bed. Finding himself in the yard, he drew a breath with satisfaction, hungrily inhaling the chilled air. The night was dark with dense clouds. Before his eyes was a girl with a cinched vest, a bit plump for his taste, but young, well-built, with pretty arms and legs. And how well-brought up! She hadn't uttered a word the entire evening! She just whispered about something with her mother. She had not looked him in the eye for the entire evening. And thus in fact ignored his soul. And remained a mystery to him. He had to have a word with her. It seemed she didn't oppose it.

They had snuffed out the lamp and it was pitch dark. Narkyz had gone out somewhere but would soon return. She had closed the door. With her beads jingling, she went to the bed in the right part of the home. She was to lie down with her little brother, apparently. Her parents were on the left half of the house. Bukhabay was in the center, in the place of respect. The home was blanketed in darkness. But for Bukhabay, the world was lit up, he could make out the attractive silhouette of the girl undressing in bed. His heart grew constricted in his chest as he caught the scent of her perfume, and his head spun. The girl slipped under the blanket. Not a sound, not a motion, even her breathing could not be heard. Oh, what torture for Bukhabay!

The aul dogs barked. But even they quickly settled down as if someone had sprinkled sand in their throats. The hosts snored. The girl lay without making a sound. She could only be waiting for Bukhabay. A genius! The next two to three hours crawled by like years.

The girl's parents slept soundly, now and then mumbling something in their sleep. Even if he stamped his foot, they wouldn't awaken. It was time to act! A bit of sky could be glimpsed through a hole in the *koshma*; the clouds had apparently parted. The sky put Bukhabay into a lyrical mood; if he didn't get close to her now – now, immediately! – life would lose its meaning for him! Sliding off the bed, he crawled on all fours to the girl. The girl who had taken control of his thoughts lay sprawled on the bed on her back, her face toward him. One braid hung from the pillow. Her left hand – in bracelets and rings – was over the blanket and her feminine breast rose slightly as she breathed. Not knowing what to do, Bukhabay frozen on the back of his heels at the girl's bed. Narkyz, to his disappointment, was sleeping and apparently not expecting him. After thinking a moment, he took her by the hand. Her hand was hot. He squeezed it slightly, so that she would awaken. The girl woke up and raised her head. Then she jerked her hand away. Bukhabay saw fear in her eyes.

"What do you want?" she asked harshly.

Bukhabay was taken aback. What did she mean, what did he want?! Was she that arrogant? It was as if she had poured a tub of cold water on his fervent feelings.

"I was just...Don't be afraid," he explained, trembling. What indignity! He, Bukhabay, a representative of the government, was trembling?!

"Well, just what are you doing? Go back to your bed!"

"Narkyz! I have a word to say to you. I have not seen you since your childhood years. And I saw you... Understand, I am not fooling around...I am serious. If you are not opposed, I would like you to become my wife...

"And when did you get that idea into your head?"

"When? Well, now...Well, today, I saw you, and I decided..."

"Don't be in a hurry. Think about it.... Be patient... So that you do not regret it later."

There was sarcasm in her voice, but the inflamed Bukhabay thought she had warmed to him, once he had promised to marry her.

Now that promise ought to be reinforced with embraces or at least a kiss.

"I'm serious, dear," he whispered fervently. "At least one girl I can manage to make happy. Just don't refuse me…"

"Well, what do you think I should do if I don't refuse?" she asked.

"Oh, nothing. Exactly nothing at all, dear," and with these words, he began to paw her.

The girl helplessly turned her heard, trying to tear herself from his embrace.

"My little dove, my love, my soul," Bukhabay kept repeating. He pressed her to him, showering her face with kisses. The poor fellow's mouth was dry, as if from a great thirst.

"Let m-me go," she hissed.

That only made inflamed Bukhabay even more.

"Don't be afraid, I will marry you," he choked from impatience, falling upon her with his heavy body, knocking her back on the pillow.

Surprisingly, she didn't cry out. She resisted him silently, pressing her strong hands against his chest, and tore him off her in that way. What strong hands she had! Holding his chin in her right hand, she kept pushing and pushing Bukhabay away. And no matter how he tried to touch her high breasts, his head landed on her elbow and slipped to the side…For some time, both fought in silence. Elbows and shoulders clashed…Gradually, little by little, Narkyz began to free herself. Bukhabay's vanity rose up. What was this? He didn't have the strength to overcome this wench?! Anger reared its head – the girl's hand slipped from his chin but by that time the girl herself was no longer in the bed – she had managed to slide out.

Out of inertia, he rocked forward, grabbed her shirt, pulled her to himself but her leg – let it be dammed! – landed somewhere. The baby began squealing – Narkyz' little brother. Bukhabay dragged the girl back into the bed – he couldn't retreat now, could he? But something struck his forehead, sparks flew from his eyes and he retreated and dove back under his own blanket.

With his wails, the little boy brought everyone to their feet. Narkyz set about calming her brother.

"What happened, Narkyz?" her mother asked.

"Nothing," the daughter replied briefly.

…Kozbagar, the poor thing, did not shut his eyes until morning, fearing to sleep through the dawn. While it was still dark, impatient, he went out into the yard and looked at Zhumash's home. The ginger mare with the bent spine had been tied up outside the day before. But he had disappeared. Kozbagar grew alarmed. "He's gone!" he thought. "I missed him." He was about to run into Zhumash's house, but just in time he noticed that someone, heading toward the ravine, was drawing away from the aul, whipping the horse. It was the commissar…Zhumash told Kozbagar that day:

"I don't have anything against guests, brother, but…but…you brought me a goat yesterday!"

Kozbagar almost fell through the ground from shame.

4

Lately, Shege had begun to come home late. Sharip lay near the wall, already falling asleep when some grumbling would wake him up. Jaybaskan, it turned out, was awake.

"What are you thinking about, honey?" she asked. "Your son is now engaged."

And it was if sleep was wiped away. Sharip grabbed his scraggly beard and gazed out at the starry sky through a hole in the *koshma*.

"Eh, he's now a Komsomol member, and independent. What do I know…He must think for himself…

"For himself," Jaybaskan signed. "That's just it, he's thinking for himself. He will ruin everything if he thinks for himself…"

Sharip got up abruptly and stared at his wife. And she said to him: "He's getting mixed up with that bitch. Torka-*apa* came running today, yelling and making noise again.

"What a dunce! What a lout!" Sharip exploded and shook his head dejectedly.

"I was surprised for some reason that that lout was going around so quietly, and look what he's cooked up! Where is he? Oh, that lout!"

"He isn't here. Do you know what time it is? And he's still not here."

…The aul slept. The dogs didn't bark at their own people. No one interrupted the quiet. The sparse stars in the sky shrank from the cold.

…And at that time, two horsemen trotted through the deserted plateau. Their path was guided by the North Star. Both were silent. In her whole life, Khansulu had not gone on such a pleasant trip. The feeling she was experiencing washed her soul like the milky-white dawn that was already washing over the steppe. She hungrily swept her gaze over the waking steppe. So wide, so wonderful was the world! The deer, seeing them, break away from the whitish *takyrs*.[150] Grouse flew up from under the horses' legs.

With the rise of the sun, the frost covering the grass melted, dampening the horses' hooves. Toward midday, Khansulu, tired from the monotonous ride, began to get drowsy.

"Let's take a rest, if you are sleepy," Shege proposed. "And the horses can rest as well."

---

[150] A *takyr* is a type of cracked, dry desert from the bottom of a former lake.

Khansulu agreed. They stopped at the south side of the shale cliff. The horses were put to pasture in a grassy meadow, their legs hobbled. And themselves lay down as they were in their clothes under the caragana bush, placing a *korzhun* under their heads. But they couldn't shut their eyes, as if they hadn't been sleepy moments before. Shege hugged his wife hard. Khansulu, in a cinched red vest wound with a sash, in leather *sharovars*, lay motionless, stretched to her full height. She wouldn't accept the *jigit*'s affections, and pushed herself away. Her long lashes fluttered and she knit her brows unhappily.

"Sulu!" Shege laughed. "Sulu!"

Sulu remained silent, glaring at him.

"We're a married couple now."

"Who said?" A note of mockery could be heard in her voice.

"I said," replied Shege.

"You can only become a married couple after the *neke*[151] ritual. Remember that," she told him seriously.

Shege felt he had been beaten. They were no longer sleepy, and both of them mounted their horses once again.

5

At Narkamys, Khansulu and Shege rented a room from a single old woman whose house was on the banks of the River Jem. During the day, Shege pastured the horses belonging to government institutions. In the evening, he and his wife attended literacy courses. In the evening, after driving the horses out to a grazing area on the river bank, Shege stood looking at the evening aul, plunged into the twilight to the drone of the radio loudspeaker.

...Shege and Khansulu's married life had begun happily. Their love now that they were together flared up with new energy. Both of them began to die of yearning if they didn't see each other at least

---

[151] The *neke* ritual is a Kazakh Muslim wedding ceremony.

every half day. Khansulu seemed to discover Shege for herself for the first time. It was as if the best male traits were embodied in Shege.

Shege was beside himself with happiness. And no wonder, given that the brightest star glowing among the numerous other stars had ended up in his hands. And he reveled in this. And no wonder – Khansulu, a beauty with a great name famed throughout the whole territory, was his wife. As soon as he began thinking about the fact that they didn't have their own home and belongings, he lost his calm. He was also fearful that Khansulu would fall into the view of some city rogue, fashionably coiffed, with a home and a good job. Thus, as soon as Shege drove the horses out to pasture, he would keep thinking only of how to get home faster and once again see his beloved.

Today, he left for the village from the river side. The sky was cloudy and it had grown dark early. The herds were returning from pasture, and in every yard there was the usual bustle. Shege did not see Khansulu in front of the house. Tying up the horses in the shed, he went inside. The boots were heavy on his feet, and the cotton jacket, belted with a simple twine, was no lighter. His wind-blown, sub-burnt face was gloomy. The wattle and daub hut of the deaf old woman was on the very edge of the aul on the river. Shege walked past the house from the side of the shed. The street was behind the house. Suddenly he saw smoke from a car on the street in front of the house. He saw Khansulu as well, she was standing, leaning, at the door of the car. Shege froze as if rooted to the ground. No sooner did he get a hold of himself than a male head thrust out of the car, and drew Khansulu by the hand into the car.

Shege stood frozen where he was. For a moment, it was as if he had been struck dumb. His cheeks burned, and the toxin of jealousy blotted out his consciousness. By that time, the car had already started off. Rrrrr – and it was gone. Poisoned by jealousy, to Shege, Khansulu now seemed the most stupid, the most thoughtless woman on earth! It turned out he was the greatest of fools if he had married such a flirt! The sky turned a somersault and the earth fell away from his feet…Unusually sluggish, he went into the little kitchen, then to his room…Hunched over, he froze in place at the stove. He looked at the red-striped chintz curtain which separated their corner, where only the bed fit, and their former paradise. There was their marital bed, where they had been united in embraces, whispering especially sweet words, dizzy from happiness. It was as if that bed was on fire. His pure feeling had been betrayed. He had been deceived…brutally deceived.

Shege groaned, unable to bear this torment of the heart. He collapsed on the rug as if knocked over. Once again he groaned, angrily, hysterically, like a wounded beast.

Suddenly someone flew rapidly into the pantry. Next, the door opened. Khansulu appeared, glowing with burning cheeks.

"Shege!" she exclaimed joyfully. "You're home?"

Khansulu was happy. Of course, someone had been courting her, and who but some educated *jigit*! And why shouldn't she be happy? Shege fell silent. He was ready to burst from anger.

"Shege! It was so interesting! I took a ride in the car!" she announced, laughing melodically.

The room was dark. Khansulu didn't notice Shege's state.

"It started off, and I was so scared I grabbed some piece of metal! Ibragim shouted, 'Don't touch that!' It turns out I grabbed that very piece of metal which makes the car move. How should I know? And Ibragim laughed so hard, so hard…"

Ibragim was a young Tatar, Kalashnikov's personal driver, who combed his hair in the urban style. He knew everything, he could do everything and was a jack of all trades. Never a dull moment with such people. It was clear why his wife was so happy. She probably admired Ibragim as much as the car. Why did she need Shege, a simple horse-herder, trudging behind horse-tails?

"Shege? What's wrong with you? Why are you silent?" Khansulu asked, and crouching down next to him on the backs of her heels, she peered into her face. She was laughing. Was she laughing at him?

The slap was very hard. Shege had a strong hand. Khansulu was thrown back on the rug. It was dark, but Shege saw how her eyes gleamed. She had instinctively balled up and pressed her hand to her cheek.

"Why-y-y?" she cried, blazing with indignation. Her flaming eyes were just about to burn Shege up.

"As if you didn't know?!" Shege cried even harder.

"I don't know! I don't know!" Choking on her tears, Khansulu flung herself from the room. From the threshold she shouted:

"You fool!"

And slammed the door. The old woman returned, she and Khansulu collided in the cramped pantry.

"What's going on?" the landlady cried in alarm, stopping at the doorway. Khansulu hurried away, saying nothing. The old woman came into the house. It was dark and quiet.

"*Oybay*! God help me! What are you doing? And you haven't lit the lamp…"

No reply followed.

"What happened, sonny?"

The old woman began bustling about the stove, looking for the matches, evidently.

Shege remained silent. The dark room seemed to him to be a closed trap. It became suffocating. He rushed out into the fresh air. Twilight was gathering over the aul. The cool of the night brought alarm with it. The hour was late, people, having locked their livestock into the shed, were gathering around the hearth, in the warmth and light. Shege was utterly alone. A motley pup, as if in sympathy with him, wriggled around him, wagging its tail and looking him in the eyes. There was no one beyond the fence surrounding the house. He looked for Khansulu. But she was gone. The world, coming apart at the seams, collapsed before his eyes….

Dazed, he couldn't concentrate on a single thought. He didn't know how he managed to climb the fence and head to the river. He walked along dejected, his shoulders sunken. The motley pup, as if it understood what was happening to him, followed him, whining pathetically under foot. The fire in his head gradually began to extinguish and Shege tried to put together in his memory what had happened.

He stopped and looked up at the sky. It was covered with clouds. A gloomy, heavy sky. It stopped his thinking, and terrified him.

"Who am I? Nobody! I'm not a revolutionary at heart. I'm not a Komsomol. I'm just a sorry henchman, a weapon in other people's hands. A henchman!" And he began to feel painfully sorry for Khansulu who had trusted him as a conscious person, as an activist. The fire of remorse burnt him.

"Khansulu!" he called. Stepping heavily, he began to run. He sat down for a bit, peering into the already encroaching darkness. There was no one. Maybe she went to a woman acquaintance's house? She had already been working for 10 days at the warehouse, on a shift brigade. Oh, hardly. Khansulu was too proud, she would not go looking for reassurances. Shege returned at a run, went around the shed again, the house, and look over the fence.

"Khansulu!" he cried, his voice falling away in the darkness. He was ashamed to shout louder. What would people say? He poked around near the house then ran to the river. The puppy ran behind him, barking softly. This time, he reached the bank of the river itself. Who knows, perhaps the pampered, willful daughter of Pakhraddin had thrown herself in the water in the heat of her indignation?

He peered into the water. The surface was quiet.

"Khansulu!" he cried.

The night was still. The river was still. The impenetrable darkness seemed to have swallowed up Khansulu. But perhaps she crossed the river and ran directly home?

The puppy, circling nearby, had disappeared. He no longer heard its whining. Then he heard the dog's bark from upstream. Then the pup appeared himself, his tongue hanging from his jaws from excitement. He rubbed against Shege's legs and thumped his tail on the ground as if he wanted to call him somewhere. Shege ran after him. In the distance, on a sandy hill, in the very center, he could make out a human silhouette. He went closer. Khansulu was sitting in a white dress with her back towards him. She had tucked her legs beneath her like a mullah praying in the direction of Kybyla.[152]

Shege was overjoyed to find his wife, and sat down quietly beside her. The waves splashed against the banks of the River Jem. Both were silent. Only the pup could be heard barking as it rubbed against them.

"Sulu!" cried Shege. Khansulu didn't move a muscle. She gazed into the night as if Shege was not beside her.

"Alright, I'm to blame…"

Khansulu was mute.

"Let's go home. No doubt you're frozen…"

Khansulu regained her speech.

"You don't have to worry about me!" she said, cutting him off.

"What, we're going to sit here like this?"

"I'm going away! I won't live with you anymore!"

"Tonight? Let's wait until tomorrow, when the dawn breaks." Khansulu pouted.

"You got into a car…You took off your *jaulyk*[153]. How can that be understood?" asked Shege.

---

[152] Kybla is in the direction of Mecca.
[153] The *jaulyk* is the white kerchief of the married woman.

Khansulu interrupted him.

"You yourself cried: men and women are equal! Freedom! And what if I had slapped you for getting into a car?"

Shege was embarrassed. Khansulu was right. Yes, he had shouted about equality, but he had never thought back then that the equality that he so fervently advocated would someday come back to haunt him! Khansulu had given him a puzzle, he didn't know how to reply. He began to get angry.

"Why aren't you talking?" Khansulu asked, totally irritated.

Shege exploded:

"And you...you...whose wife are you? Mine? Or...freedom's?"

"Yours, of course," said Khansulu, flustered.

"So that's enough chatter!"

Khansulu fell silent. They both sat for a while in total silence. The pup lay down between them, placing his muzzle on the sand, and looked at them expectantly, as if he were asking, when will your quarrel end?

The old woman's cry was heard from the direction of the aul.

"Khansulu! Shege!"

Reluctantly, they got up. They wended their way back home in silence. The puppy, overjoyed, hurried toward home.

THE TIME OF TROUBLES

1

A strong, howling wind dogged their heels, chasing ahead, and forcing them to shrink from the cold. The travelers – some on horseback, some on camel-back – were rattling along the road from Narkamys to Khantortkil. They were advancing toward the south. Last in line, lagging behind the others, trudged Jorga Kuren on a five-year-old Igren horse.

Jorga Kuren had definitely not liked today's meeting. Kalashnikov had stood up and announced:

"We will destroy the kulaks as a class!"

As if they had destroyed little until that time. And what a slogan he threw out:

"In a week, we will transfer nomad auls to settlements! Full and universal collectivization, comrades! There is no place among us for independent farmers! Even if we are a nomadic region, we will end this campaign earlier than Russia!"

A certain Suranyshev jumped up from his seat and shouted at the top of his lungs:

"Semyon Kharitonovich, you're right! We will overtake Russia in collectivization!

Would-be activists like Sharip began clapping and shouting:

"True! Golden words!"

"We must speed up collectivization!"

"Why drag it out three years?"

Jorga Kuren, sitting in the back row, chuckled to himself. What a people! Well, what of it, do as you think best...

The laggard Kozbagar was removed from his position as chairman of the artel and sent for training. Jorga Kuren wanted to put in Kozbagar's place his own son, Jdakhay.

...

Jorga Kuren, rolling up his sleeves, set about realizing his plan, and began to try to convince his acquaintances. And here he saw sitting next to the chairman of the regional executive committee...Shege himself. His suspicion was confirmed: when the conference was over, Afanasy Grinin announced that the chairman of the Janazhol artel would be Komsomol member Shege Kaspakov. Moreover, this witless fellow sitting next to Apanas immediately wrote a statement about acceptance into the Party. It became clear who was behind all this...

The whistling wind drove against his back. The sky was burdened with heavy clouds. An excited Sharip was trotting along, rocking back and forth on a grumpy camel, the wind ruffling the ends of his *treukh*[154]. His mood was carefree, after all his son and his daughter-in-law were alongside him. He was singing something. Hearing his voice, Jorga Kuren gathered himself up internally, and on his lips, as always, was a sarcastic grin.

2

The wedding took place in Sharip's home. Khansulu was happy. But no sooner did a day go by after the wedding of Khansulu and Shege than the peaceful life of the aul once again was disturbed by turmoil. Once again the commissars came. The aul activists mounted their horses and the galloping to and fro began. All of them had one word on their lips, as if they had coordinated it:

"Down with the kulaks!"
"Let's have 100% collectivization!"
"A week's deadline! That's the plan!"
"Who obeys is ours! Who isn't with us we'll force to be with us!"

People hid in fright. Who wanted to end up being a kulak? Old men and old women prayed: "Oh, Allah! Carry us through! Oh, Allah, save us!"

As twilight gathered, toward evening, a heavy, dark man with swimming eyes and a bumpy nose came galloping into Janazhol on a bay stallion. He was as gloomy as a winter storm. Jorga Kuren fussed with the stirrups of his horse, wanting to help the guest to dismount. The commissar who had arrived was his old acquaintance Bukhabay. In the old days, he usually dozed in his saddle and here he looked to be a

---

[154] A *treukh* is a round fur hat, usually made of sheepskin, with a broad flap at the back that covers the neck all the way to the shoulders, and two smaller earflaps.

new man fur sure! He was unhabitually business-like. Energetic. But his face was very dark, as if he had put out a fire somewhere.

"Go on, comrade aul-leader, get the people together! On the double!" he barked, mixing Russian and Kazakh words together as was his habit, which once again indicated the significance of his visit.

"Oh, Bukha, you should first, as they say, come and have a bite to eat at the house," said Jorga Kurgen, as always trying to lure the important guest to the table.

"What bite?! What are you going on about, comrade?!" the commissar barked, flashing his eyes angrily. "I don't have time to sit and gab with you!"

The ominous expression of the government representative frightened Kuren, and he fell to currying favor.

"Oh, Bukha, you're right, you're right. I'll be right back," he said, and ran to his home, shouting on the way, "Zhdakha-ay! Come out!

People were heading toward the brick building with the sign "Asan Aytzhanov School." Bukhabay sat with both hands on top of a desk covered with red cloth. He looked gloomily at the people pouring into the building. The commissar was extremely irritated: he could barely contain his anger at these ignorant, undisciplined people who kept drawing toward the school...Bukhabay was tired. For two days he had sat in the saddle without sleep or rest. Did people understand that? Where was he to go? Not only didn't they understand, they were still sending informers' reports after him, claiming that he guzzled vodka and molested their daughters.

"If you don't eat and don't drink, what's the point of rushing around day after day? Molesting the daughters? But what young Kazakh doesn't chase after girls?" thought Bukhabay.

The school was full to the point of overflowing. Bukhabay's eye immediately picked out a beautiful young girl in the hall, lithe and slender. She had red cheeks and long lashes and when she raised them, her eyes glistened like stars in the night. This was the infamous Khansulu. And he saw Narkys as well. Whenever he remembered that nightmarish night, he felt so terrible that he wanted to fall through the ground, not from shame, no, but from frustration. His face grew even darker from anger, turning mottled.

"Open the meeting, open the meeting!" he urged Jorga Kuren. He would never forget Narkyz's strong fist nailing his nose. Bukhabay Igensartov had never seen such a humiliation in his life!

"Comrades! Quiet!" Kuren said, flustered. "Restrain yourselves. So, I propose opening the general meeting of the Janazhol aul. Comrades, we must choose a chairman of the meeting."

"Suggestion!" Jdakhay said, getting up from his seat; he was sitting in the first row.

"Go ahead!"

"I propose electing the *aulnay* as the chairman of the meeting and as his assistant, the chairman of our association, Shege Kaspakov, and the poor man's activist Kaukash!"

"Hey, Kaukash, go on up! It's your moment!"

"Fire up the meeting!" some voices could be heard joking.
"There should be someone from among the women...Let's have a woman in the *prezdyom*[155]!

"Comrades!" Jorga Kuren hastened to correct the mistake over the *aulnay*. There is a suggestion. We are forgetting about the main issue, about our comrade women. Let Shege wait. Propose a woman instead of him, alright?"

"Khansulu instead of him!" Jdakhay cried, once again jumping up from his seat.
"Ah, well, why not! Let it be her," the *aulnay* conceded.
"*Oybay*, she's too young still," some old lady exclaimed.

---

[155] The Kazakh is pronouncing the unfamiliar Russian word *prezidium* (presidium) as *prezdyom*.

"The young people have to be raised up!" Bukhabay cut her off. "That's the policy."

Jorga Kuren hastened to ask:

"Who is for the comrades named to be elected? Raise your hand!"

They all raised their hands together. Only Torka, glowering, did not raise her hand.

Bukhabay jerked his chin at her.

"They're not raising their hand over there."

"*Jeneshe*, aren't you making a mountain out of a molehill? Explain yourself, *jeneshe*," Jorga Kuren sang out, very happy that someone had been opposed.

Torka, rocking back and forth, stood up. People who had been about to make noise quieted down, and turned toward the tiny, sallow-faced old woman.

"Damn her! I'm against it! That's how it is!" Torka said, and waved her hand.

"*Oybay, jeneshe*," Zhorka Kuren said, bursting into a chuckle. "You can't be more coherent?"

"How more coherent? That one, Khansulu, she'll be sitting there?'

"Yes, Khansulu."

Her eyes bright, Torka stood with her arms akimbo.

"Do we have *Sobiet guberment* in this aul or not?"[156]

"*Oybay*, we do, *jeneshe*, God bless you! Who said we didn't?"

"Don't you laugh! If we have *Sobiet guberment* here, then tell me the *low*, [157] how is it that a *bay* kulak's daughter should sit in

---

[156] Torka says the unfamiliar Russian phrase *Sovyetskaya vlast'* (Soviet government) as _Sabetski blasty._

[157] Torka says the Russian word *zakon* or "law" as *zakun*. Hence "low" for "law".

a…what is it…a *prezdyom*? You, Kuren, explain it, and don't go smirking at me…"

Bukhabay carefully raised his head.

"Who is this *tabarysh* Khansulu? Show yourself," he spoke nasally, pretending that he didn't know whom they were talking about.

Everyone exchanged glances. In the backs rows, there were all women and girls. Embarrassed, hiding her face with a corner of her kerchief, Khansulu was among them. Sharip the Grump couldn't help squirming in his seat.

"Get up, *kelin,* show yourself to people," he asked.

Slowly, embarrassed, Khansulu got up. Her cheeks were burning from shame and from offense by Torka. Bukhabay, looking her over, leaned down toward Kuren's ear. Kuren immediately stood up and said in a deliberately loud voice.

"Then I ask the comrades who have been named to come up! And you, kelin, go on up!" he said, turning toward Khansulu. "We take into account the opinion of the majority, and not individual people. That's the procedure."

Khansulu was glad that she had got the best of Torka, but was afraid to go up to the presidium. She was shy. Looking at her father-in-law and mother-in-law in the first rows, as if asking them permission. Sharip, startled, nodded his head:

"Go on, dear, go on. The majority has decided," he said.

Jaybaskan, too, nodded her head in approval.

Embarrassed, Khansulu went up. Her *sholpy* jangled and sang as she walked. She walked along and felt the hard stare of the commissar on her. That bothered her. She wanted to sit further away, but Zhora Kuren, groveling, sat her down next to him.

The portly Bukhabay melted, seeing the proud beauty nearby – it was as if a bird of paradise had landed on his palm, his heart thumped hard in his chest. The scent of her perfumes intoxicated him. He forgot about the people all around, and the meeting that he had called, and all his thoughts were obsessed with Khansulu...

"Comrade Igensartov, you have the floor!"

Bukhabay shivered as if ice water had been poured on him. He got up. He looked at people coldly, his double chin hanging.

"So...," he began, somewhat flustered. "All of you of course have heard the latest news in the district. I think Comrade *aulnay* and the new chair of the association Shege Kaspakov have told you. So, I will just tell you the crux of the matter. I'll tell you the main thing. Soooo. This campaign, it's a *surious*[158] campaign."

Then Bukhabay began saying not just a word, but a whole phrase in Russia. "It has *a wery stong palitikal meaning*," he said, pronouncing the unfamiliar words with a Kazakh accent. "Today we will cut down at the roots the bourgeoisie who like leeches suck the blood of the working people. We will destroy the kulaks and other contras forever! We must inform them in this way: gather up your belongings, get out of here while the going's good, that's the way. Am I right? This is how we will free the people of the contras. Understood?"

They all knew what the Russian word "bourgeois" meant. No one wanted to end up belonging to the bourgeoisie.

"And who are the bourgeoisie?" they asked.
"Oh-ho!" exclaimed Bukhabay. He had apparently been waiting for just such a question. "That's where the problem is! Who are the bourgeoisie, you ask? What precisely is a bourgeois person?" and he stared at them all so hard that people averted their eyes. "We all should find who the bourgeoisie are. Find them – and cut them down at the root! That's the way! For that reason, we are gathering here today. That's the way."

---

[158] Bukhabay pronounces the Russian word *seryozny* (serious) as *suryozna*.

The Lonely Yurt • Smagul Yelubay

"Allah save us!" the old men whispered. "Who else could they be looking for?"

"Save us, oh Creator!"

The frightened voices multiplied. There was a hum in the hall. People were alarmed.

"Didn't we chase out...those bourgeoisie...last year?" one man asked.

That was the tall Uap. The folds of his downturned mouth quivered.

"Who is that? Stand up, I urge you!" Jorga Kuren scolded. Hunched over like a shadow, Uap stood up.

"I wasn't asking you, but I wanted to ask the comrade," he said, nodding toward the commissar. "There was a *kampeske* last year, and we turned in Mazhan. The *bay*. Then we were told that we had no more bourgeoisie, that the bourgeoisie had ended. So what happened? We're supposed to destroy someone again? What, the bourgeois grows every year?

"Who is that?" asked Bukhabay, nodding at Uap suspiciously, his nose wrinkling.

"What are you going on about?" Kuren exploded. "You say what you are supposed to!"

"No, I'm not joking!" Uap shouted back, rolling his eyes as well, like a goat. "What, now you can't ask anything? And if I want to find out? Why send a representative to the district? In order to explain things to us uneducated ones, isn't that the case? But if you want me to be quiet, fine, I'm done."

"What is your last name, comrade?" the commissar asked him sternly.

"Zhartybasov."

"Comrade Zhartybasov! So...wait. How many hearths in the aul?" Bukhabay threatened with his finger.

"Well, more than forty."

"How many are not in the artel?"

"Well, about five or so all together."

"So...so...Comrade Zhartybasov!" the commissar drawled. "The master of one such hearth that is not yet in the artel is Pakhraddin. Right, comrade?"

Pakhraddin, sitting in the back rows, squirmed. Almost the entire hall turned to look at him. The commissar continued:

"During the times of Tsar Mekalay, Pakhraddin was a *biy* – that's one thing! Perhaps not so large as Mazhan, but he was also a *bay* – that's another thing! He had three *batraks* – that's a third thing! No, you say?"

No one answered the question.

"If Pakhraddin was for the *Sobiet guberment,* he would have long ago signed up for the artel. Isn't that so?"

"Comrade Commissar!" Pakhraddin stood up. He had on a beaver cap, and a baggy lambskin coat. "I urge you not to distort the Party's policy. There isn't such a policy of the Party!"

"Soooo…Explain it, in that case," said Bukhabay, sullenly leaning forward like a boar caught in a trap. His dull little eyes sparkled with anger.

"It's true that I am not a member of the collective. But that is not due to my own wish. You don't take me. But I read the newspapers, Mr. Commissar. Stalin himself said that joining the collectives is a voluntary matter. So it would appear that it is not my fault that I am not in the collective.

"Look, a law professor, imagine…" Bukhabay mumbled under his nose, growing more anger. "Alright, Comrade Pakhraddin, let us say you aren't to *bame*[159], that's you're not in the *kallektep*" – he had switched to the familiar "you" in speaking to Pakhraddin. "But before the *kampeske* you had more than 300 heads of small and more than 100 heads of large livestock, isn't that true? And you kept *batraks*. Isn't that also true?"

"By *batrak*, I must assume you mean a shepherd," Pakhraddin raised his voice. "And by shepherd, you mean Kozbagar. It is a sin to lie in the courtyard at night; I didn't ask him to be a shepherd. And all the more so, I didn't force him. His parents here, Uap and Torka, let them say that is not the truth. They almost went begging. It was '21, you know, there was a famine. We said, "It is a sin to grow fat in solitude, it is better to share our food with everyone." We gave it out –

---

[159] Bukhabay pronounces the Russian word *vinovat* (to blame) as *vinaut*.

to some a horse, to some clothing, to some food, not a single hearth in the aul was snuffed out. Glory to Allah, thanks to this, everyone survived...

"Pakhraddin is telling the truth!" some supported him.

"The *biy-aga* has told the truth!"

"Kozbagar shepherded the flock for about three y ears. But likely on the other hand he was able to feed and clothe himself. And now I'm to blame?! My respected fellows, let God be my witness, what have you seen bad from me, tell me? There must be justice," Pakhraddin finished with difficulty.

"Oh, these are correct words!" Sharip couldn't help putting in.

"True!"

"Quiet! Don't make noise!" Jorga Kuren called people to order. Everyone looked at the commissar. He was muttering something angrily to Kuren.

"You, *Tabarysh* Pakhraddin, just wait a minute," the commissar said in the end. "Do you understand what you are doing, *Tabarysh* Pakhraddin?" The district representative's forefinger hung in the air. "You're getting in the way of work! You are disrupting the meeting! That's sabotage! That is just in the bourgeois way. You are disorganizing work. That's how it is. The main thing in our campaign is to expose such bourgeoisie in time. They are the ones preventing us from building a new life. That's why we must get rid of them. We must cleanse our environment of such *bay*-kulaks, *mullah-khodjais*, and other such devil satans! Down with them! That's how it is!"

People grew alarmed and began to worry.

"That's how it is!" Bukhabay said, getting into a rage and throwing his hand up. "The district headed by *Tabarysh* Kalashnikov has taken on greater obligations. 'Even though our district is backward as it is so remote, we will finish the work of cleansing our environment of the kulaks within a week, and the general collectivization within three months,' said *Tabarysh* Kalashnikov. Not in three years as is said in the plan, but in three, I repeat, months! That, *tabaryshy* is a big revolution! In three months we will transfer to a settled form of life, we will be one *kallektep*! That is how we cut our old life down at the root. That's how it is, *tabaryshy*!"

Jdakhay, red-faced, excited, thrust himself forward, clapping furiously. But only a few people supported him, including Sharip.

"Oh, what words! Go on! Don't stint!" he wailed in a falsetto.

"*Satsalizm, tobaryshi,* is flying forward on a fiery chariot toward a happy life! We have to hurry; we cannot keep up with the fiery chariot on camels!"

"We can't keep up! We have to strive forward!" Jdakhay picked up from Bukhabay, shaking his fist.

"I'm done," said Bukhabay, sitting down. He looked at Kuren. "Let us give the floor to the poor men tabaryshy!"

Jdakhay spoke, and as always, was incendiary.

"*Tabarysh* Commissar speaks truly here. It has been twelve years already since the Tsar fell and *Sabetski blasty* was established Everything is changing all around. In the cities, railroads are built. And why in our cursed area nothing changes? We built a school. We dug *zemlyanki*[160]. Hah! It's only a joke! Let everything go to the devil, in three months we will have a *kalletep*, not three years! Who doesn't want to do this, we will push them by force!"

"Tabarysh, wait! Bukhabay stuck his hand in his pocket. "Sooo. I have a question. It is a list of kulaks. I drew it up myself. Using your old list, by the way. Sooo. Pakhraddin is the first, then Kulatay, he is in Khantortkil, then there's Zhumash.

People stirred and began making noise. Zhumash, the father of Narkyz, was sitting in the back. He sprang up from his chair.

"What?! Zhumash is a kulak?! Are you mistaken?"

"Is your *pamiliya*[161] Koybasov?" Bukhabay inquired.

"Yes, it's Koybasov, and what of it? This is slander, brother, slander. If you don't believe me, count the livestock in the shed. What kind of kulak am I?"

"So…you have thirty sheep, six goats, six camels, if, of course, you count the camel baby, and one horse, is that right?" Bukhabay fixed his eye slits on Zhumash.

---

[160] *Zemlyanki* are earthen dugout homes for the winter.

[161] This is how he is pronouncing the Russian word *familiya* or «last name.»

"But we ate one goat. Five are left," Zhumash said in self-defense.

"Wait. Your sister in Donyztau has a female camel and a camel baby. Isn't it so? You hid it from people, you said it wasn't yours, supposedly," said Bukhabay. The harder Zhumash shouted, the more stubbornly Bukhabay stared at him.

"Bu I didn't hide anything! I gave them myself. They're without milk!" Zhumash desperately tried to prove.

"We don't believe that, *tabarysh*! So I'm sorry, we counted everything: you are, so to say, on the level of a kulak, if you count everything."

"It's not fair! It's a lie! You shouldn't have registered the female camel to me! It's deception! Slander! Then count up everybody's. Both what livestock they have in the shed, and what they have at their relatives!" said Zhumash, pale and thin, waving his arms around.

"Zhumash, *oybay*, what have the others to do with it?" somebody berated him.

"Don't drag the others in," people began murmuring.

"But what are you talking about, I'm a kulak now?!" Poor, limp Zhumash began to look like a plucked chicken. Narkyz, his daughter, sitting next to him, was pale – she cursed the commissar to the high heavens and that fateful night when he had tried to molest her. No one in the hall dared to speak. Then Jorga Kuren turned toward Bukhabay and in a mannered, drawling voice, said to him:

"Isn't Shege, the fresh chairman of the artel, sitting among us? Why is he silent? The question is relevant, even urgent. Or is he not the chairman?"

Having said this, Kuren grinned smugly.

"Eh, that's true. Let him speak. Let's listen," the majority in the hall agreed. The smile that had frozen on Jorga Kuren's lips infuriated Sharip. He of all people understood the meaning of that smile. *So you're digging underneath me, you bastard, oh, what a devil, you're throwing your nets? Oh, you, beast!*

When Shege stood up, the hall grew quiet. Khansulu started to worry. Something was about to happen, it seemed to her. It was horrible. She wanted to run away from here, from all these people gnawing at each other. Here her father, lost, beaten down was sitting.

There was Shege, caught between two flames. *Shege, dear Shege, don't be silent! The only hope, the only bulwark, Shege, please speak!*

"As the *tabarysh* commissar said," Shege began, straightening himself, fire in his eyes, "the political significant of the campaign is great. I, as the chairman, support the policy of destroying the kulaks as a class."

Jorga Kuren broken into a smile.

"You tell me, Shege," he asked, leaning forward. "You tell me, Shege, is Pakhraddin a kulak or not a kulak?"

Chuckling in satisfaction, the *aulnay* leaned back in his chair. Shege sighed with a wheeze.

"Kulak!" he shouted angrily. "Kulak! Is that what you wanted to hear from me?"

That was it! Next the world fell into bedlam, as if the wind had rocked the meeting – passions flamed in the hall. Some were already lunging at others and a fight was about to break out. Khansulu squeezed her eyes shut.

Then she heard the voice of her father-in-law:

"What the devil have you done, Jorga! Why are you bringing trouble?"

Khansulu opened her eyes, and Sharip, grumbling, was pushing people aside and making his way to the table. He threw a kick at a few people on the way, and crushed a few people's hats down on their heads. He broke through to the presidium, he took his big *treukh* from his head and threw it on the floor. Dust flew up to the ceiling. The commissar was startled. Jorga Kuren turned dark. Sharip gave them what for:

"You are stirring up evil…You are a traitor! You hide behind the campaign in order to suck the people! What, that isn't true? You made a *serednyak* into a kulak. But now I'll open up your class face! You are Mazahan's fox, you, a trader, did all the *bays'* business for them at the bazaars. I have spoken and will go on speaking about your affairs! That's how it is! He fed you, and you, Kuren, you gobbled him up! That's the whole truth for you!"

Bareheaded, Sharip was yelling, the veins of his temple throbbing. He stared right into Jorga Kuren's eyes.

"That's the true! He's speaking the truth," people started yelling.

"Pure truth!"

"The *aulnay* is unjust!"

"Stop, Kaspakov!" Bukhabay shouted, striking his fist on the table. "This is sabotage! Outright sabotage! You will answer for this before the law!"

The people kept shouting.

"Let the *aulnay* not fool everybody!"

"....your father! We don't fear blood!" some of the dare-devils like Kisykbay, rolling up their sleeves, got up from their seats.

"Kaspakov, you will answer for this sabotage!" Bukhabay roared. Sharip bent over and lunged at him. Though Sharip was puny, in anger he looked terrifying. His eyes, bloodshot, bugged out, the veins of his temples bulged like knots. It seemed he would grab on and not let go until he had drunk his enemy's blood.

"Me? I don't think so!" squealed Sharip, thrusting himself up nearly to commissar's very chin. "You, son of Igensart, what are you making yourself out to be? I know you, and your shitty father, too! What are you shaking your jowls here for, who are you scaring with the law? You're no one to scare me. What, are we blind? All you know how to do is to roam around the girls and guzzle vodka. And you're going to teach me the law?! Look, the crowd will take you! You think a court can't be found to try you? You'll learn how to deal with Sharip!

"Oh, Shake!" [162]!

"Long live the power of the poor!"

"Now there's an activist! He sure told him off!"

"Hang in there, poor man!" people whistled and yelled.

---

[162] Shake was Sharip's nickname.

Sharip picked his *treukh* from the floor, shook it out, and smashed it back down on his head. With a sense of a duty discharged, he headed toward the doors without turning back.

"Oh, Shake! Where are you going? The meeting isn't over, sit awhile," Jorga Kuren cried after him unctuously. And after that display of flattery, Sharip's authority only rose in people's eyes.

He only waved his hand. He slammed the door loudly.

"That's how it is!" somebody said.

"What does a meeting matter to him? He was a man at a congress…"

After Sharip's exit, the meeting didn't last much longer. It was decided that Pakhraddin and Kulatay were kulaks, and Zhumash was left among the *serednyaks*.

3

Outside it was pitch dark. It was a windy night. Khansulu saw how her father left the meeting and now, stumbling, she ran to the yurt on the edge of the aul. All of her thoughts were about her father. She wanted to reach him faster, confounded, humiliated in the eyes of the majority. How was he now?

The wailing, freezing wind burnt her face, fluttering her fur coat open and trying to push her out into the frozen steppe. The word rang in her ears: "Kulak! Kulak!" And who had said that, after all? Shege. Her faith, her bulwark – Shege…He was the one who had said it! Then what could be expected of the others? Khansulu and her father had one hope – Shege. That hope was now snuffed out. Her one bastion was Shege. Now that bastion was cracked. The sky crashed down on her head. The earth shook under hear feet. What was happening with the world, what…?

The dogs whined and the wind wailed plaintively. Khansulu didn't hear either the dogs or the wind. She only heard her own voice repeating worriedly, "Of course that's all…Everything has perished."

Sparks from the fire flew out from the *tundik* of the lonely yurt on the outskirts of the aul. Khansulu, fighting the wind which kept pushing her backwards made her way by touch toward the door. The home was bright. The heath burned hot in the very center. Her father sat hunched over, his face toward the fire. To the right of him was her mother. Both had apparently talked everything over. They were silently dejected. They jerked up in fright when their daughter appeared, staring at her, surprised at this unexpected appearance. Khansulu's white shawl slid down to her neck, and she stood bare-headed, fear in her eyes. She looked back and forth at her mother and father. The fire crackled on the hearth. The wind wailed outside, tearing the *koshma* on the yurt. But inside it was quiet; three adults listened to the wail of the wind – and were silent. They were hushed, like children fathoming the secrets of the night after a horror story. Her mother grabbed the poker and began stirring the coals on the hearth. The flame grew hotter.

"Come in, Suluzhan," said her mother.

Her father glanced listlessly at his daughter and once again sunk down. Khansulu threw herself at her mother and hugged her, breaking into sobs. Pakhraddin frowned. But he didn't move a muscle. Armed with the poker, which was in her left hand, the *baybishe* stroked her daughter's head with her right hand. Neither father nor mother uttered a single word while Khansulu sobbed. Someone was scratching at the door outside. Since Kutzhol, their dog, didn't start barking, it must be someone they knew. Someone entered. Those inside grew wary. It was Shege. Searching for Khansulu with his eyes, he froze at the doorstep. Not knowing what to say, he stamped his feet on the threshold.

"I was looking for you," he mumbled, shifting from foot to foot.

"You shouldn't have!" Khansulu cut him off with a burning glare.

Unable to raise his eyes, torn by contradictory feelings, Shege mumbled something under his nose and lunged toward the door. The wide, heavy door flung open and he disappeared.

A painful silence blanketed them once again. Pakhraddin kept staring at the fire, bitter thoughts whirling in his heavy head. The *baybishe*, knitting her fine, pretty, brows, was also thinking of something, keeping silent. Khansulu glanced after the departing Shege... The fire in the hearth crackled and roared. The wind outside tore at the *koshma*. The wind's moaning was like a foreshadowing of an impending calamity. She felt terrible from this wailing; her soul was troubled.

"Suluzhan!" her mother stirred and rose to her feet. "Go home!"

She began making up the nickel bed.
"I won't go! I don't want to," Khansulu replied, hurt.

Pakhraddin, about to squeeze his eyes shut, opened them and straightened himself up. He rolled his eyes angrily at his daughter. But he restrained himself, and didn't say anything, although his gaze said a lot. Khansulu was flustered from his look, and shrunk fearfully into herself.

"Don't do that, daughter," her mother begged her. "No one forced you to marry. Don't quarrel over us. What of Shege? It's not his fault, it's apparently the times. It's our fate, obviously. Go on, be smart!"

Khansulu, her gaze drilling the floor, continued to sit there. Syrga the *baybishe*, wise, having seen a lot in her day, went to her daughter and stroked her. Her mother's hands tenderly touched her hair, her cheeks, her back. They took away the pain in her soul and her heart melted. Khansulu got up and went home. Her mother saw her out the door.

... Shege was lying with his face turned toward the wall. The dung on the hearth had gone out; a weak, barely smoldering flame flickered through the coals and disappeared. There was no other bed in the house, so Khansulu could not lay down by herself. She was forced to settle down next to him with her face toward the hearth. Shege was not asleep, and was sighing. And Khansulu couldn't sleep. She was thinking. Once again, the meeting rose before her eyes. Everything could be forgiven, but how to forgive that? To fling the word "kulak" in her father's face! To be affectionate to her, when they were alone, to say "I love you, I yearn for you," but when it came down to business...Eh! He couldn't say a word in defense, look what an incorrigible Komsomol he had become! Not a word, not a single word could he say; worse than not defending him, he shouted publicly, "Kulak!" That was her father who was a kulak?! Khansulu had never thought of Shege so poorly as she did in that hour. He was worse than an enemy...

The Lonely Yurt • Smagul Yelubay

Shege, signing, turned over on his back. He opened his eyes. The coals on the hearth had gone out. It was pitch dark. The chilly wind continued to blow outdoors, not letting up at all. And there was an icy wind in his head as well, wailing over a dark desert. Anger burned in his chest, inexplicable, incomprehensible even to him himself. On whom could he unleash it? On no one. But why, why because he said the truth – and he had said the truth, after all – was he to blame as well?! Maybe he was to blame that he took the daughter of a kulak as his wife? And perhaps he wasn't to blame, but Jorga Kuren, because he had provoked him into such a speech? Or Pakhraddin, because he had once been wealthy. Or Khansulu, because she had not stood up for truth, but for her father? Who was to blame for everything that was happening? Who was to blame for the troubles for which there were explanation? Who, who was to blame?!

4

All week, the auls on the Ustyurt plateau raged. Day and night there were meetings. There was no respite from the commissars on their foaming horses.

Pakhraddin hurried along the only path leading from Janazhol to Narkamys at a trot. Behind Pakhraddin trotted Sur Jekey on a horse. The day was clear, there wasn't the slightest breath of wind. Everything around was clearly visible as if in the palms of their hands.

The evening before, they had drunk tea. The morning was already coming to an end when Sur Jekey appeared as if he had fallen from the sky. Apparently he had come from the district center, from Narkamys itself. His face was dark, almost black. Without any greeting or anything, he cried:

"You go to the district!"

Syrga was frightened. But Pakhraddin stared at the policeman, not understanding why he had to go to the district. Sur Jekey, pursing his lips, hurried him to go faster.

"Can't I learn, brother, what this is for?" Pakhraddin asked. But the policeman replied:

"You'll find out when you go there. Let's go!"

That was the conversation. Pakhraddin got up, throwing on his *chapan*, and silently started off. Syrga said something. Pakhraddin didn't hear it.

"I'm going after the horse," he told her.

The policeman instantly roared:

"You don't need a horse! You'll go on foot...you'll take a stroll on foot!"

Pakhraddin ran off at a trot. No sooner did he slow his pace that he would hear a stern cry from Sur Jekey:

"March!"

Sur Jekey commanded him in Russian. He had to suppose for the sake of intimidation. In his hand was a whip. And for what? He could strike him. That would be like the policeman.

In 1918, in the area of Oyyl in the desert, they had shot dead the large *bays*. Large drops of sweat rolled down Pakhraddin. On his shoulders was a *korzhun*. It was not heavy. Poor Syrga had stuffed something into it, folded into a towel – either bread or a change of underwear. Pakhraddin was overweight, it was hard for him to run, he kept gasping for breath, groaning as he went.

Sur Jekey was silent. He saw how Pakhraddin was, but he didn't feel sorry for him. On the contrary, the more he gasped, the greater satisfaction he experienced.

"Huff and puff," he thought. *"It's good for you; once I, an orphan, huffed and puffed when I took the sheep from the bay Yesenkul to pasture. I shed tears, running barefoot over the thorns, pasturing the goats. And you then, arms akimbo, rode on horses. You didn't even look out of the corner of your eye at the crying boy. So huff and puff, racing ahead of the orphan Sur Jekey."*

Looking at Pakhraddin's broad back with its damp spots, Sur Jekey for some reason grew furious. He kicked the horse's flank. The stallion neighed and reared up, bumping Pakhraddin with its chest. He fell face down. Sur Jekey tugged the reins, halting the furious stallion. Turning him around, he glanced at Pakhraddin. He was sitting up on his hands, spitting out the sand that had filled his mouth, wiping his wet brow with his sleeve. He then tried to get up.

Sur Jekey waited patiently until he got up. The horse stood across the path, blocking the way. He strained all his attention and hearing, waiting for what Pakhraddin would say.

Pakhraddin rose slowly. He took the *korzhun* off his back and threw it on the ground. Shaking himself, he looked away from Sur Jekey. The policeman's face grew ashen and he stared at him sternly, devouring him with his eyes.

Pakhraddin finally spoke up, putting himself a little in order.

"Brother," he began. "I wonder why you are tormenting me? Consider that death is all the same. Instead of humiliating me like a dog, and then rotting away in a stinking prison, let me remain here, in the wide steppe. Shoot me and leave me here, that is my request, my kin!"

Sur Jekey's face was like a stone. He silently dismounted from his horse, and hobbled his legs. He took his Nagan pistol in his hand, looked all around him, and cocked back the safety clip on the gun.

"That's the way, do a kindness, respect your elder brother," Pakhraddin repeated, and stepped about six paces back, drinking in the tiny meadow, thick with withered grass. He stood sideways.

The policeman's heavy lips gathered into a grey bunch, his roach-like mustache quivered. He raised his outstretched hand with the Nagan, and aimed at Pakhraddin's temple.

It grew quiet. For a moment, a great silence fell. Even the policeman's horse frozen, pricking up his ears, staring at the humans.

Pakhraddin felt no fear in his heart. As Abay said, "what of the torments of life and the humiliations, when there is quiet and peace in the grave?" He had decided to rest from life. He had grown tired of living. The low slope of Karazhon in the distance like a humped chain cut through the steppe. Beyond it was the aul, and in the aul was Syrga and Khansulu. Poor Syrga, he felt sorry for her most of all. He could even hear her lamenting voice. His betrothed...His only love...She would be the one to suffer grief without him! What was he? He was nothing. He would die and disappear. He once was, and then was no more.

Somewhere above a lark began singing. Crickets chirped in the wormwood. And Pakhraddin stood and awaited the sound, the one and only, which would cut off everything that he was hearing once and forever. Pakhraddin would disappear into nothingness. There he would not hear anything…But the shot strangely did not follow, and Pakhraddin turned toward his enemy.

Sur Jekey, his mouth still crooked, was carefully rolling a cigarette from *makhorka*.[163] The Nagan was in his holster. It was if he had forgotten about Pakhraddin. He was even serene.

That was when Pakhraddin sensed how his heart was knocking and how piercing was the ringing in his ears. His body shook, the tense as if stretched on a string released, and his muscles grew weak. Pakhraddin collapsed on the ground like a sack, He landed next to an ant hill. The little ants, running back and forth, oh Creator, continued their endless motion as if nothing, literally nothing had happened. Their vain movement, it turns out, would have continued, as it did yesterday, and the day before that, and always – and several minutes ago, when he, Pakhraddin would have been no more?! Oh, fleeting world!

5

Pakhraddin was lucky; on one of the streets of Narkamys, the chair of the district executive committee happened to notice him, or else, who knows, he might have disappeared without a trace, as many did in those days. Afanasy Grinin was riding by on a horse when among the arrested men mixing clay on the street he saw Pakhraddin. He immediately summoned Sur Jekey to his office and asked him to bring Pakhraddin to the district executive committee (DEC).

Pakhraddin had severely deteriorated in two days of prison. When the policeman took him, dirty, spattered with clay, to the DEC, he couldn't understand where he was taken and why. Only when he saw Apanas, as the Kazakhs called him, through the open door, leaning over his desk, his eyes lit up. The skinny, elderly Russian man was now as close to him as a brother. They embraced. Tears sprang to Pakhraddin's eyes.   Afanasy Grinin, sent to the Kazakh steppes at one

---

[163] *Makhorka* is a cheap kind of tobacco grown in Russia and Ukraine.

time in the Tsarist era, had worked as a rural teacher, and knew the life of the Kazakhs well. Pakhraddin sensed that now, when Apanas had intervened himself, his affairs would improve.

...

Afanasy Vasilyevich began to ponder, and pondered hard. He paced back and forth in his office.

"Eh, my friend Pakhraddin," he said. "If the matter was only in Bukhabay and Sur Jekey, that would only be half the trouble. The problem isn't in them..."

Pakhraddin, turning in his chair, fixed his gaze inquiringly on the chairman of the district executive committee.

"The problem isn't in them," Apanas repeated. "Not in them. Understand, there are enemies all around. The government has no power. In order for them to have power, they need factories, they need technology. And in order to build factories, bread is needed, meat for the working man who will build them. The kulak has the bread and meat. The government doesn't have any money to buy them. What to do? Liquidate the kulak as a class and confiscated everything from him – products, livestock."

"But then what is the kulak to do? Die from hunger after handing over everything to the government?" asked Pakhraddin.

"That's just it...The Soviet government doesn't want to die. Nobody wants to die of hunger. Do you understand me?"

Pakhraddin was hearing such things for the first time. His face changed and grew pale. Afanasy Vasilyevich continued pacing up and down in his office.

"Although it is bitter, that is the truth, my friend Pakhraddin. What I can do for you, is I can give you written permission to travel in any direction of your choice. That is unfortunately all that is within my powers," Afanasy Vasilyevich concluded and sighed sadly.

Pakhraddin returned with this document, devastated, to Janazhol. Jorga Kuren, seeing the signature of the chairman of the district executive committee, scratched the back of his head. He did not return his camel, Shoyynkar, which had ended up in the possession of the collective. Thus, late on the evening of November 29, Pakhraddin's rump nomad's group, looking like a widow's, set off from the aul. Bulysh's mother, Dau-*apa*, left the aul along with Pakhraddin.

"You don't have permission to travel," Jorga Kuren tried to stop them. "Dau-apa needs a paper just like Pakhraddin has."

The old woman cut him off, speaking in her strong, clear voice:

"Maybe you need a paper, but I don't need one! I have lived until now without one, without a paper, and now that I have as long to live as a goat, God will receive me without one. That's how it is!"

Jorga Kuren knew, that the enough dark old woman, who was like a man, would reply in this way. She needed to have the people hear her words.

Many aul-dwellers came to see off Pakhraddin. When the camels laden with belongings rose on their feet, the women broke out in tears.

The nomad's group was read to set off on its journey. Winter was already at full strength, low, dark clouds scudded across the sky. The grey clouds were silent, as if listening closely to the wailing voices. Khansulul sobbed, hugging her mother. Warmly dressed for winter, the tightly-belted Pakhraddin was quiet. He was leaving his land, his people.

Khansulu ran up and hugged her father:
"*Koke*!"

Pakhraddin's shoulders shook. It was good that Sharip intervened in time. "what are you all so mesmerized?" he said. "Enough! There's our neighbors, the Karakalpaks. They're right nearby. Oh, oh! We'll see each other again, God willing. Oh, these women, they only know how to whine…

Thus Janazhol bid farewell to Pakhraddin's nomad group…The sun rolled out from the horizon, far, far away, cold, without warmth. The petrified, slumbering slopes stretched ahead like dead carcasses. The nomads moved in that direction, toward the sun. Slowly but surely they disappeared beyond the horizon.

HARD TIMES

1

Lately Sharip was experiencing enormous satisfaction with life. Everything made him happy. And why shouldn't he be happy? Nobody was dragging him by the hems, nobody was humiliating him, calling him a dirty shoemaker. *Satsilism* needed even shoemakers. There was another joy – his only son Shege. Ugh-ugh, so as not to jinx it! His offspring was known in the community. He had grown especially mature and more serious ever since he had become a *Komones*[164].

And who did he take after, the poor fellow? And what had he dreamed up? "Let's block the Tenteksay River," he said. "We'll release the water into the Saryzhazyk Valley and farm there."

---

[164] This was how Sharip pronounced the Russian word *kommunist* or communist.

The collective broke into two brigades. One was headed by Jorga Kuren and the other by Shege.

People began to do battle with what Nature had created – with an enormous sandy ridge. The hoes clanged as they penetrated the hard soil.

"Hey, lean into it, poor man! Crush it, poor man!" Sharip would urge people on with slogans from time to time. Meanwhile, a girl in a red dress was racing as fast as she could from the aul to the working people. The hem of her dress fluttered so much that it billowed in the wind.

Sharip decided to take a break and leaned on his hoe, wiping the sweat from his brow. People went on working. Noticing the girl, Sharip couldn't help but totter off to meet his daughter.

"Isn't that our Gulzhan? Uh-oh, what's going on there?"

"The *Mili*sa[165] have come! There are two of them!" Gulzhan cried even from a distance. Her braids danced on her back.
"*Milisa*?" Sharip asked.

"*Milisa*! Two of them," the girl repeated. "One is Kozbagar-*aga*, he has a sabre. He asked for his older brother to get here quick."

...

All the way back home, Shege thought hard, trying to understand what he had done wrong in the government's eyes, and he couldn't think of anything. Even so, he could sense his heart beating in his chest. He kicked away a black dog who was affectionately scampering underfoot and fearfully opened his own door. His eyes immediately fell on Sur Jekey, the head of the district police department. He lay in the guest's place with a pillow under his elbow. The boss was leisurely slurping *ayran*[166] from a painted *tostagan*[167], clearly relishing it. Of course he noticed Shege but didn't change his pose. A gloomy Kozbagar was already sitting there as well. He had just

---

[165] *Milisa* is how Gulzhan pronounces the word *militsiya* in Russian, or police.
[166] *Ayran* is a kind of Central Asian buttermilk.
[167] A *tostagan* is a wooden cup.

gone away this past winter to take courses and had evidently graduated. His police uniform was ill-fitting and didn't suit him.

"*As-salamualeykum*! Shege greeted him.

Kozbagar jumped up to shake his hand. Jaybaskan, ladling out the *shubat*,[168] shyly glanced at both of them. Sur Jekey stretched out the tips of his fingers to Shege. They were icy. His gray face was angry, and he exuded chilliness, just as did his rifle and saber leaning against the wall.

Shege lowered himself down next to Kozbagar. There was silence. Only Sur Jekey could break it. Everyone waited for what he would say. And deliberately aggravating the situation with his silence, he took his time drinking the ayran, until he finally drank it up and put the *tostagan* down on the *dastarkhan*. He wiped his lips with a towel.

Only then, glancing at Shege, he said: "Comrade Kaspakov! You are going to the district. Pack your bag!"

Even as he had stepped over the threshold, Shege had sensed that this is approximately how the conversation would end, but just in case, he inquired:

"To the district, you say? Alright…"

Sur Jekey turned toward Kozbagar. He immediately grew flustered like a little rabbit mesmerized by a snake. He looked first at the boss, then at Shege. Beads of sweat glistened on his temples.

"Shege," he said, his voice falling. "Here's the thing…"

Jaybaskan and Shege froze tensely in expectation of bad news.

"Here's the thing… There's this fact. The gold and silver of the kulak Pakhraddin are being stored in your home. A statement came in that he left his goods at your place, since you're his son-in-law. So we've come…to make an inspection.

---

[168] *Shubat* is fermented camel's milk, popular in Central Asia especially in the summer.

"What gold and silver, my God?!" Jaybaskan exclaimed.

"Well, go ahead and inspect, inspect away!" Shege uttered, growing pale.

"*Apa*, then in that case, open the trunks, untie the *tyuks*!" asked Kozbagar, scratching the back of his head.

"Oh, God," Jaybaksan muttered, throwing the blankets off the trunks and *tyuks*.

First, she opened a large black chest. Nothing was found in it but bolts of fabric and clothing. She untied the *tyuk*. It was a *tekemet*[169] rug, Balzhan's dowry, Jaybaskan herself had made it. The gold and silver demanded by the policemen didn't turn out to be there. An iron trunk with ornaments, covered with white *koshma,* remained still to be opened.

"And why don't you open this trunk?" Zhur Jekey asked, his roach-like mustache quivering.

"Oh, that's my daughter-in-law's trunk, I don't have the key!" said Jaybaskan.

"Where's your daughter-in-law?"

"She's at work. They are damming the Tenteksay River."

"Bring her here!" Sur Jekey ordered Kozbagar. Kozbagar hurried toward the door, but suddenly the door opened on its own, and a noticeably heavier Khansulu appeared. She lingered at the threshold, shocked by the disorder in the house.

"Here, she's come herself!" Jaybaskan exclaimed agitatedly. "Open up the trunk, dear! Here, they're inspecting us, they're looking for something!"

Khansulu took two steps and then stopped. She didn't understand anything. "Give me the key to the trunk!" Shege demanded angrily.

Only then did Khansulu come to her senses. Throwing one braid over her chest with a shrug of her shoulder, she stretched it out to the *sholpi* on the end, unwound the key and gave it to her mother-in-law. But Jaybaskan couldn't seem to get the key to work in the keyhole.

---

[169] *Tekhemet* is a traditional Kazakh textile made by pressing felt of various colours (often naturally different, and not dyed) together

"Dog-gone it!" Jaybaskan grumbled and banged on the trunk with her fist.

"Look, since you're the one who needs it!" she exclaimed, moving aside.

"Let's look!" Sur Jekey ordered Kozbagar who seemed not to want to do this very much.

The poor fellow turned red, he was embarrassed to go digging in women's things. But an order was an order. He began to throw out on the *koshma* Khansulu's summer clothing – dresses, *beshmets*[170], a vest, and then her underwear followed. Sur Jekey, exhaling *makhorka*, sat on the *tyuk* not taking his eyes off the trunk. The last thing Kozbagar took out from the bottom was a small gilded box.

"Don't touch that!" Khansulu screamed.

Sur Jekey stood up here, determinedly squaring his shoulders. His hand-rolled cigarette stuck out of the corner of his mouth.

"Give it here!" he ordered. He took the box, hefting it.

"Hmm...Where's the key?" he asked, his roach-like mustache jerking.

"There isn't a key to it! Why do you need it?" Khansulu said sharply. "Oh!" she exclaimed, covering her face.

Her mother Syrga had left the box with her when she had departed on her nomad's journey, giving her an order: "Keep this. It is not known what lies ahead for us. It will come in handy if it gets difficult. Don't show it to anyone." Khansulu had not shown it to anyone, even Shege. But what was in that box were precious stones and gold and silver jewelry.

The box was smashed to bits. Necklaces with precious stones, gold and silver bracelets, rings, beads, finger rings, and silver coins with the image of Tsar Nikolai I scattered across the *koshma*. Sur Jekey, smoking his hand-rolled cigarette, sat down in business-like fashion. He picked up a heavy gold bracelet and weighed it on his palm. He shook his head.

---

[170] The *beshmet* is a tunic common to Turkic peoples.

"And you call yourself a communist," he snorted angrily.

"He is not to blame, *aga*!" Khansulu cried desperately, and sat down, covering her face with her palms. "He didn't know. It's me! Me!"

On orders from his boss, Kozbagar gathered up the valuables lying on the *koshma*. Shege stood as if he had been hit by lightning. He said nothing, his face like a stone.

"Kaspakov! Let's go!" said Sur Jekey, still smoking the *makhorka*.

Shege changed his shirt. He put on a woolen jacket which he had bought when he had become chairman. His mother bustled about, drink some *ayran*, she said, but *ayran* was the last thing on his mind. He put his identification in his pocket and went out of the house. Without uttering a word, he moodily got into the policemen's carriage.

His mother jumped up after him, and thrust something wrapped up in a towel into his shirt; it was bread.

"Giddy-up!" Kozbagar cried, tugging the reins.

The stallions, which had been impatiently chewing their cuds, took off. The old people and children of Janazhol watched what was happening. Even out at the Tenteksay River, people stopped their work. Sharp trudged heavily toward the aul, shouting something as he went. Only Jaybaskan heard what he was shouting. But the policemen, carried away by the strong, neighing stallions, weren't interested. The horses raced away like a whirlwind, leaving behind a cloud of dust.

"Oh, God! What have we done to you!" the sorrowful Jaybaskan lamented. The woman didn't yet know that for the gold discovered in the secret hiding place, many had paid with their heads. Such were the times...

Thus, quite unexpectedly, Sharip occupied himself with the fire at his family hearth.

2

Shege and the policemen reached the district center after lunch. Grinin, the chairman of the district executive committee, was waiting for Shege in his office.

"Well, how is this to be understood?" asked Afanasy Vasilyevich right away, placing a piece of paper before him on the table, covered with writing in Latin letters.[171] Shege picked up the piece of paper. «Statement," it said. The letter was addressed to Kalashnikov.

"Read it! Read it!" said Afanasy Vasilyevich, getting up. He set about rolling a cigarette.

Shege put his hat down on the table and peered at the lines. Whoever had written the statement knew Shege's life well. The writer began from long ago, even back to the moment he had married Khansulu. "Due to the uncertainty of his class worldview, due to his softness," said the statement, "he, that is, Shege, married the daughter of the kulak Pakhraddin, the direct enemy of the Soviet government, and thus became a relative of a 'bourgeois," as did his brother-in-law Bulysh, who recently hid his class face." (The letter explained that Bulysh's first wife was the youngest sister of Pakhraddin.)

"Everyone knew that he was a bandit, and became convinced of this during the confiscation of the *bay* Mazhan's property. In 1928, during the confiscation of Pakhraddin, he hid the gold and silver he possessed from the government. Rumors are going around that he gave the valuables to Shege, his brother-in-law, to keep. Comrade district secretary! The time has come when leftists such as Kaspakov who, as has been indicated above, have consorted with our class enemies and have turned the Party's path to the path of Trotsky, to be resolutely exposed!" It was signed, "Group of Poor People's Activists."

After reading the letter, Shege raised his head. He looked at Afanasy Vasilyevich.

"Who wrote this?" he asked, turning to him. "Kuren…Kuren likely," said Shege.

"I think so, too."

"But the handwriting isn't his, Afanasy Vasilyevich!"

Afanasy merely waved his hand.

---

[171] In the early 20th century, the Kazakhs used the Latin script.

"Scribblers can be found! You had better think what answer you will provide at the meeting. One of the items on the agenda is your case. Think carefully, alright?" And with those words, he left the room, carrying the anonymous letter.

Shege started at the back of the thin, hunched Apanas. He didn't comprehend anything, so crushed was he by what had happened.

"I will return. I'm just going to look in on Semyon Kharitonovich!" said Apanas, hesitating for a moment at the doorway.

Nothing came to mind. Shege knew one thing: he was honest and clean before the party. "Leftist," "bourgeois tendencies" – it was slander! If he respected Bulysh, it was for his humaneness.

"Let's go," Afanasy Vasilyevich said after a little while, opening the door. "Speak reasonably, don't get flustered! Collect your thoughts!"

Several people had reached Kalashnikov's office before Shege. Among them he recognized the secretary of the district committee of the Komsomol, the scrawny, dark Nurilya, and district prosecutor Suranyshev and Sur Jekey. He didn't know the others. The door closed right in his face.

Then Sur Jekey stuck out his head and called him.
"Come in!"

The people sitting on both sides of the long table looked at him with interest. There were openly hostile looks. Kalashnikov, seated under the portrait of Stalin, held his tired gaze on Shege. With a gesture, he indicated a chair against the wall. "Have a seat!"
Shege sat down. He crushed his hat on his knees.
"Read this!" Kalashnikov asked Nurilya, handing the statement to her.
Nurilya jumped up and in a distinct voice, read out the statement. "The time has come when leftists of the Kaspakov type must be exposed!" she finished.
A heavy silence hung in the spacious office. Kalashnikov nodded to Sur Jekey.

"Well, well!"

Sur Jekey placed a rolled-up newspaper on the table, then unrolled it. Shege's cheeks turned red. The gold and silver jewelry blinded those sitting there. From shame and confusion, Shege was prepared to fall through the ground.

"This is, of course, an anonymous letter," said Kalashnikov, indicating the letter, "but this is a fact!"

Shege, weak in Russian, didn't understand everything that Kalashnikov was saying. But the tone and gesticulation of the secretary indicated to him: he would not spare Shege. Suddenly, the grey squint of Kalashnikov's eyes under his thick brows bored into Shege. He grew chilled from fear, and his heart contracted in his chest.

"Get up," Nurliya said, translating the secretary's words.

Shege stood up. Everyone once again fixed their eyes on him.

"Semyon Kharitonovich asks, what do you think regarding this statement?"

Shege had not expected that he would be given the floor so soon. He looked out the window. It was a foggy day outside. Evening was approaching. In far-off Janazhol, Khansulu was likely looking out the window in the same way, waiting for him...

"Everything in the letter is a lie!" he said. And it was not written by poor people activists. It was written by a person hiding behind the name of the activists. They say I defended Bulysh. If I defended him, it was when he was not yet a bandit, and I didn't want him to embark on an erroneous path."

"And that you married a kulak's daughter, is that a lie, too?" Suranyshev intoned in his soft voice, continuing to show him the red back of his head.

"It is true, not a lie," Shege mumbled.

Nurilya translated the dialogue between Suranyshev and Shege word for word.

"So what is that, then, if not consorting with our class enemy?" the womanish voice resounded again.

"Excuse me!" Afanasy Vasilyevich interrupted Suranyshev. "Will you allow me?" he glanced at Kalashnikov, who gestured to him to be quiet.

"I didn't consort with anyone!" Shege burst out. "I took a kulak's daughter as a wife. That is true. But I didn't consort with a kulak because of that. Don't make false accusations against me!"

Kalashnikov stopped Apanas, who was squirming in his seat, with a look.

"Eh, what are you shouting for?" Suranyshev squealed, finally turning toward him with his whole body. "But that gold and silver was found in your home, after all! Or will you say that's not true, either?"

"Now, then," Kalashnikov said, picking up the theme, his chair creaking. "What will you say to that? That is a fact, Comrade Kaspakov!"

It was here Shege became lost. He decided that now no one would believe him, no matter what he said. He mumbled in a hollow voice:
"I didn't know about all those things, for God's sake. I hadn't seen them, either. I only saw them today…along with the police. My wife, it turns out, hid them…"
Suranyshev grinned, shaking his head. Kalashnikov looked at Grinin, the chairman:
"Please!"
Afanasy Vasilyevich readily stood up.

"Semyon Kharitonovich! Dear comrades!" he began, glancing sympathetically at Shege. He spoke in Russian.

Although he couldn't understand everything, Shege guessed what Apanas might say. "Yes, I know Shege," he said. "Last year, in a clash with bandits, he displayed himself to be a real warrior, fearless, resourceful, and loyal to the Soviet government…"

"Afansy Vasilyevich!" Kalashnikov put in again. "We know about that. You had better tell us…"

And it was incomprehensible what Kalashnikov was saying. Nurilya, damn her, also kept silent and didn't translate anything. But Shege felt insurmountable pressure from Kalashnikov. Grinin had faltered from his initial tone. He looked at the precious stones on the table and didn't know what to say about them evidently. Shege began to feel sorry for kind Apanas, who had rushed into battle for him but had suffered defeat – once again because of him! He felt sorry for himself as well because he couldn't understand more than half of the words said here.

"I understand you. This is your cadre. You were the one to give him a recommendation to join the Party. You are obliged to defend him. But comrades!" here the secretary stood up. He was tall, with long legs, with a strong, speaker's voice. Kalashnikov knew how to make a catching speech. He re-emphasized everything that had been spoken before him. Even Apanas, who personified might in the eyes of Shege was pale compared to the secretary. Everyone, mouths agape, listened to Kalashnikov, drinking in every word of his, nodding in agreement with his gestures. He spoke feverishly, and emotionally.

"Where is our Party integrity, comrades?" Kalashnikov thundered, shaking his fist and stopping near Afanasy Vasilyevich. Afanasy shifted in his chair, coughing, but Kalashnikov raised his hand as if to say "be quiet." Covering the distance to the table in two or three steps, Kalashnikov sat back down in his seat and continued just as zealously:

"Comrades! You know full well that a purge of the Party from such weeds is underway throughout the country," he said, pointing at Shege. "It is good that he is for the time being only a candidate member with us. Otherwise, dear Afanasy Vasilyevich" – and once again there was a flood of words that were incomprehensible to Shege. Shege heard the word "disgraced." He began to feel uncomfortable. Kalashnikov articulated his phrases, and under the influence of his speech, Shege felt more and more that he had become something unclear in the eyes of the people sitting in the room. And he already became tormented with remorse.

"I really did overdo it," he thought. *"I really made a mess of things... Otherwise the secretary would not be so angry."*

He lifted his head and saw that another man, Suranyshev, had the floor.

Finally, it penetrated through to Shege that the issue of his possible stay in the Party was being decided. Everyone who spoke had proposed expelling him from candidate membership in the Party.

Hearing his name, Shege stood up. He had not understood Kalashnikov's last words. The lean Nurilya readily explained to him:

"You have been expelled from the Party, and have been relieved of your job. Now your case is being sent to the investigative agencies, and there they will decide how clean you are before the law…"

Shege drew himself up to his full height before them, crushing his hat in his hands, the sweat rolling down his hot, wind-blown temples. He felt as if his face was on fire.

"Let's go!" barked Sur Jekey from the doorway.

His voice returned Shege to reality. Hunching over, he went along the hallway in front of the policeman. He trudged leadenly in his heavy boots. So this is what *arystybay* meant. They had arrested Shege, it turned out, just as they had once arrested Azbergen. When he had been led away in this way, chased ahead, the entire aul had watched him…

Outside, Shege prayed to fate that he wouldn't meet anyone he knew. Sur Jekey only gave him commands: go here, go there…They walked along the only street of the village. The police department, or the *milisakhan*[172] as the locals called it, was at the end of the street: this is where apparently they were taking him, to lock him up in a cell. Everywhere you looked, there were signs of an early spring all around, spring scents already wafted over the air, the slopes of ravines and hills darkened, and succulent green appeared on the banks of the River Jem. Somewhere, a gentle wind blew. The sun, crimson red, slowly receded behind the horizon; the sunset hour was coming.

There was the old woman's house, the very one where he and Khansulu had rented a room last year. The familiar shed and yard. A settled mud and daub hut. His heart contracted. Whatever you might say, those were happy days! That day they quarreled, that day they made up – it turns out this was wonderful, too!

---

[172] *Milisakhan* is how the Kazakhs pronounced the word *militsia* or police.

The *milisakhan* turned out to be a long barracks with a rusty roof. There, Sur Jekey turned over the *"arrestybay"*[173] to Kozbagar. The poor fellow didn't take his eyes off Shege, feeling extremely uncomfortable. He trudged heavily along the barracks with a ring of keys on his belt, and ordered Shege to follow him.

"They will hold you here until the trial," he said, letting him understand that he did not find it entirely pleasant to be taking this role.

They had grown up together since childhood, Kozbagar and Shege. Kozbagar even now was a dolt, even though he was a policeman. His nature had not changed a bit. Just as in childhood, he was afraid to look Shege in the eye. What could be said about everything else, if Kozbagar had remained Kozbagar even when his wife Khansulu had run away from him and become Shege's wife?! That was how it had always been, since their early years, Kozbagar had loved Shege, valuing his directness, his honesty, his boldness. And Shege knew that Kozbagar was not ill-willed and was simple in nature. Therefore, he understood his embarrassment now, when he had to treat his long-time friend as an *arystybay*.

"The investigator is a fellow I know...I'll have a word with him," Kozbagar promised.

Shege said nothing. But he sensed at that moment just how pathetic his situation was, if even Kozbagar felt sorry for him. Drooping his shoulders, he simply kept quiet. Kozbagar opened the heavy iron doors at the other end of the barracks with two keys. The cold struck his face. It was semi-dark, with hay on the floor. In the dark corner, figures of people laying side by side could be made out.

"This is where you'll be," said Kozbagar in embarrassment.
"Well, alright," Shege replied curtly and stepped across the threshold.

A small, barred window in the wall to the right let in light. Kozbagar closed the creaking iron doors. Shege felt as if he was in a

---

[173] *Arrestybay* is how the Kazakhs say *arrestovany* or arrested man in Russian.

cave. The total silence crushed him. Some sort of people began raising their heads in the corner; apparently they had been asleep. Like beasts in their lairs, they fixed their stares on him. Shege felt terrible. He set about finding a little place for himself on the thick straw mat. He found a spot next to the window and plopped down helplessly, but began to feel calmer. Let everyone look at him, he didn't care. He had to rest, and collect himself. The straw rustled suddenly right next to him.

"Hey!" a dark, broad-faced man called to him, squatting down on the backs of his heels. Laughing, he rocked back and force, his little eyes shut. Why, it was the former policeman, then commissar – the infamous Bukhabay! He clapped Shege on the shoulder with his meaty palm.

"Shege! *Tabarysh* Kaspakov! What are you doing here?"
Shege smirked.
"And what do people usually do here?"
"For going to extremes?"
"No, for consorting with the enemy."
"Oh, yes, you married a kulak daughter and so on and so forth."
"Yes, yes, that's what they said."

Bukhabay slapped him on the shoulder again, chuckling, clearly satisfied over something, all the folds on his fat body shaking. He had on a quilt jacket, but his hanging belly stuck out.

"*Neshaya*[174]! Don't give up," he said, cutting his laughter short. "What isn't a real man supposed to experience! Damn them, they threw me in here three days ago. I went to extremes, they said…Chatterboxes, I tell you, our bosses. They themselves don't know what they're doing. First they say let's do the plan, 100 percent. Kalashnikov himself went on about this. So we went galloping around. An order is an order. We did the plan. Then they said, make the *kallektep* – 100 percent. And what of the people? Do they really understand politics? What does he need the *kallektep* for! So they fled.

---

[174] This is how Bukhabay is pronouncing the Russian word *nichego,* or «it's nothing».

Some to Iran, some to Afghanistan, some to the Karakalpaks. Who is *binayat*?[175] Bukhabay is *binayat*. There's a *kebenemat* for you![176]

In his anger, Bukhabay stirred up the straw under him, he wasn't able to sit still, and glanced here and there with a fiery look.

"There's a *kebenemat* for you! Bukhabay *binayat*! I will complain upstairs about them!" he said, jumping up heavily and pointing upwards. Suddenly, Bukhabay's face changed, he looked around and made a sign to Shege, nodding toward the window.

"Your father has come!"

Shege turned toward the window, and his father was standing right there. His *malakhay* was smashed down crookedly on his head. He peered into the darkness of the barracks, searching for his son. Meanwhile Shege stood up and ran out somewhere.

Kozbagar opened the door. He led out Shege for a meeting with his father. The evening twilight had thickened, but Sharip could make out how thin his father had grown in one day. He threw himself at him, hugged him, his heart melting in his chest out of pity for his own kin. Huge tear-drops fell from his eyelashes. He couldn't say anything at first, and turned away.

"Let's go here!" he said and brought his son to a corner to be alone. "I heard everything from Apanas..."

"There will be an investigation. The court will decide what will happen," Shege explained.

His father was silent for a while, staring at the ground. Then he raised his head, and suddenly smiled.

"*Syuinshi*[177]! he cried, laughing. Our daughter-in-law gave birth. Tugelkhan – a daring lad appeared on the earth, the devil take him, that's the addition we've had! She gave birth yesterday...

---

[175] Here Bukhabay is pronouncing the Russian word *vinovat* (guilty) as *binayat*.
[176] Here Bukhabay is distorting Russian swear words.

Shege blushed, and a broad smile lit up his face.

"In honor of the hope that we will once again all be...together...we named him Tugelkhan[178]," Sharip murmured.

'*Koke*, they don't want to release me...Apparently they will prosecute Khansulu as well." Despite his joy, Shege had to speak of the fact that he had heard the threats directed at Khansulu. Sharip's happiness vanished. He grabbed his goatee and fell to thinking.

"*Koke*! Take Khansulu to her parents. There is no other way."

"But the trial is tomorrow...I have to..."

"No, *koke*," Shege objected. "Go home! But here...you can't escape fate...we will see."

And Sharip, mounting his grumpy camel, unwilling trotted back to the aul.

...The time of day had come when the night darkness was waning and the area was just barely visible. The steppe's horizon could be seen, the old caravan road appeared, beckoning on a long journey. A large morning star glowed in the west on the yellowing sky.

Three travelers – two on a camel, another on a horse – rode through the steppe, keeping to a path where Venus was always over their left shoulder. Khansulu sat high on the camel's hump. A long road lay ahead. A hard road through the great Ustyurt, a path that would later take her to Beskala, to the lands of the Karakalpaks and the Turkmens.

Thus began Khansulu's long journey, full of dangers, left without Shege, and a baby in her arms, along the paths of the muddled, changing times.

---

[177]*Syuinsh* is a kind of sweet, and it is the custom of the Kazakhs to demand a reward such as sweets for good news.

[178] The name means "together".

IN THE SANDS

1

The moon poured down milky white light. It was the deep of night. In the sands of Aytu a little aul hid among the dunes, it was this place that the night light was caressing. A figure lone in the night looked out on these amazing moonlit expanses from the sandy ridge. He stood, high on the hill, like the watchman of the aul, which was fast asleep, like the watchman of the endless world plunged in sleep. This man, who had thrown a silk *chapan* over his broad shoulders, was Pakhraddin.

...

"In the land of the Karakalpaks, people still live freely," the nomadic Kazakhs had heard. Dreaming of once again acquiring freedom on the land of a neighboring people, they made their way there; however, here, too, they soon ran into persistent calls to join the kolkhozes.[179]

The steppe-dwellers who had sought refuge in the sands of the Aytu – there were about 50 families here – grew alarmed. What should they do now? And that spring a group of activists from Konyrat descended on them. One introduced himself as an agent for piece-work, a second a member of the aul soviet, and the third as the *milis*. Once again, "excess" livestock were confiscated.

While the *aksakals* of the aul racked their brains in search of a way out, Labak-*akhun* was hurrying on his white camel, going all around the coast of the Amu-Darya in search of land for the aul. Not finding land appropriate for livestock-raising on the shores of the great river, in Khorezm, he finally ended up in the Turkmen auls, who had fled from the Russian revolution to the very Afghan border. They lived

---

[179] A kolkhoz is a Soviet collective farm.

in the old way, pastured their herds, collected fuel in the desert, and apparently were not repressed in any way...

When the elder talked about them – and as always he spoke eloquently, as if re-telling an old tale – everyone who listened to him salivated...

Pakhraddin – an intelligent, educated man, a *biy* in the past, a real leader – had open eyes and a feeling heart, so people turned their gazes on him. What would he say? But Pakhraddin couldn't say anything, he was listening to the people himself. In recent years, he had been occupied with making ancestral trees of the nomads. He collected and worked over his notes, and became totally preoccupied with them. At that time, Khansulu and her father-in-law Sharip appeared, having travelled from far-away Oymaut. It turned out they had travelled for half a month. Khansulu had grown thin, and was wind-blown and tanned. Pakhraddin had heard that Shege was arrested through the steppe *uzunkulak*,[180] but he did not know that he had a grandson. He didn't know anything of the fact that Shege had been put in jail for two years. But the most difficult news for him was the state of his daughter. Caressed by the son and wind, Khansulu, his daughter whom he had raised like a son, in pride and love for himself, had changed drastically, as if she had been broken, and her life shortened. Poor child!

After long arguments and explanations, people turned to Pakhraddin, tearing him away from his writings. Bulysh and the other *jigits* urged him on.

"Let the *biy-aga* have his say!"
"Let us listen to the *biy-aga*!"

Bulysh and Balkiya had come to this re-assembled, hidden aul at the end of the winter. Here Bulysh had also met his mother – Dau-apa.

Pakhraddin, stroking his mustache, thought over his reply.

---

[180]The *uzunkulak* is the grapevine, i.e. rumors.

The Lonely Yurt • Smagul Yelubay

"Well," he began, looking over the men who had gathered on the hill. "So that our way be blessed, let us make a sacrifice of a white and red sheep at dawn!"

"Amen!" the white-bearded Labak-*akhun* blessed his decision and ran his palms over his cheeks.
"Amen!" people echoed through the rows. The rubbed their palms across their faces in the same manner.

Many days of meetings finally ended with an agreement suitable to all – in the morning, the aul would move from this place. With that, people began to disperse to their homes, climbing down from the top of the hill.

Only Pakhraddin remained on the hill. If it were his will, he would not take a step from his native land. Azbergen had tempted him with Iran, Ermagambet had tempted him with Turkey, but Pakhraddin had not budged, and now he himself thought to flee to Afghanistan itself. That was life! A harsh lot! Fate was a cheat!

2

The moonlight poured into the opening of the creaking doors flung open wide, the curtain parted fluttered in the breeze. The couple resting in their common place on the wooden bed couldn't sleep. Pakhraddin and Syrga didn't sleep that night.

"If the government has now gone after our daughter, consider that they won't leave us in peace," Pakhraddin said. "They must throw the noose around our neck as well."

"Damn them all...Let us pick up and move, it will be better than prison, anyway. Except it will be a foreign people," Syrga supported her husband.

The baby started crying. Khansulu woke up. Leaning over the crib, she began to nurse her son.

"Suluzhan!" Syrga cried, folding back a corner of the curtain.
"Yes, *apa!*"
"Did you hear, we are moving."

"To Afghanistan?" Khansulu exclaimed. "And me? What am I to do?" There was despair in her voice. It had become stuffy for some reason, as if a fire had engulfed the home.

"Calm down, daughter!" cried Syrga with a voice shaking from worry, sliding off the bed.

Khansulu managed to break out in tears, her head leaning on the crib. Soon the little boy joined her. "Waa…waa…waaa…" It was if the yurt had never been quiet.

"Oh, Creator," Pakhraddin said sadly, and went out of the yurt.

The moon was rolling over the western part of the sky, its light had noticeably dulled. The east glimmered, and the approach of dawn was felt. The dark outlines of several figures could be made out, old men with metal pitchers in their hands going out to morning prayer. Someone stood on the hill closest to the aul. It was Labak-*akhun*! In a white *chalma*. Apparently he was praying, gazing at the dawn.

Syrga's voice rang out.

"Well, what do you order me to do? Wh-a-a-at?" The pain of helplessness could be heard in her voice.

Pakhraddin could hold out no more. He went closer, coughing and clearing his throat.

"Eh!" he said to his wife. "What do you mean, 'what do you order me to do?' You had better say: let us travel on further, so as to wait quietly for how it will all end there. I don't think that Afghanistan is the worst place on the earth. God grant that our people will come to their senses – and we will return. At least, we will do everything so as to return you to your homeland. That's how you should speak, *baybishe*!"

Who would not heed the weight words of the father! The women in the house seemed to calm down and grow quiet. The ringing voice of Labakh-akun intoning prayers carried down from the hill.

"Ash-shadan, la, illakhul, il-alla! Ash-shadan, la-il-lakhul, il-al-la-au!"

The drawn-out chant carried far in the pure, clear air. When the sun rolled out from the horizon, the nomad's group, bells ringing, crawled out from the ravine. Keeping the sun to the left side of the road, the nomads moved toward the south. The men trotted ahead, led by Labak-*akhun* and Pakhraddin.

The loaded *nar* camels went along in their usual even, measured step. Old women in white *jaulyks* sat in the seats on top of them, rocking back and forth. At the end of the first day of travel, people bedded down for the night in a hollow, thickly overgrown with yarrow, camel-thorn and hop. They unloaded the camels and threw the *tyuks* next to them in disarray; they were awfully tired, and after a light supper they all fell asleep wherever they could. The camels lay further from the sleeping aul, crunching their cuds. In the hollow, on the north side of their camp, where there was feather grass and rana, the hobbled horses whinnied. Even the dogs were tired from the long journey and flopped down on the crumbling sand.

Only Bulysh was awake, quietly contemplating the sleeping aul. For two years, he and Balkiya had wandered through the desert. Living the nomad's life as a couple in the unpopulated wild territories, what adversities had they not endured? They had suffered hunger, and cold, and heat, and deprivations. Then they recalled the proverb, "It is better to wander together with other people than go on the highway alone." They then descended from the hills to look for the aul in the sands of Autu, where they had heard the refugees from all over were gathering.

They had seemed to find a wise advisor in the person of Pakhraddin, and his old mother, and they restored their previous unity. Bulysh thought that whatever trials fate sent him now, it would be better to meet them with such an *azamat* as Pakhraddin, such a wise elder as Labak-*akhun*, and next to his mother. The decision of the elders suited him, to have the nomads travel to Afghanistan in search of a free life and land to live in the old ways.

With these thoughts, he drowsed after midnight. The barking of the dogs soon awoke him. He jumped up in what he had lain in – his clothes. He grabbed his hunting rifle. The pre-dawn darkness was dense, and he could barely make anything out. To the dog's barking was added women's voices, full of horror.

"*Oybay*, trouble!"
"*Oybay*, they're attacking!"

Three strangers were driving away their camels, the ones that had lain tied up further away from the aul.

"On your horses!" cried Pakhraddin.

And here at the dunes, where the dogs were barking on the foothills, shots rang out.

"*Oybay*!" wailed the women, hurtling back to the ravine in a bunch.

"*Oybay! Oyba-a-y!*"

"To the ravine! To the ravine!" Pakhraddin ordered curtly.

"Buly-y-sh!" Balkiya's penetrating wail rose above the noise.

Bulysh had no time to look around. Bare-headed, in a light *chekpen*, he dove into the darkness, crawled under the rough brush and began shooting. He took down one of the three men in high *boriks* who were driving away the herd of camels. There was noise, yells, and confusion... Among the women running to the ravine could be seen men as well, wrapped in blankets. They were shooting from the grassy knoll opposite: blam-blam, blam-blam... Pakhraddin ran breathless up to Bulysh.

"Bulysh! Go back! To the ravine!" he shouted. "Everyone is there. We're the only ones left!"

"Where are the horses, *biy-aga*? Run to the horses! We need horses!" Bulysh took aim at the second thief. His rifle thundered. Pakhraddin, struggling toward the ravine, turned around and saw that the second horseman had fallen on his horse's mane.

"Oh, Allah!" he uttered, descending into the ravine. "Oh, creator!"

On the way, like a living spirit, Labakh-*akhun* emerged. Loudly, at the top of his lungs, he called on the spirits of their ancestors.

"Oh, Barak! Oh, Barak!"

His white *chapan* was on his shoulders, his white chalma was on his head, his white staff was in his hand, and prayers on his lips. The old man was like a white flag among the bullets. The cowardly men sliding into the gully turned back. They lay down, and opened fire on the enemies, and the air was sour with gunpowder. The world was once again upside down. The dogs whined, the sheep bleated, along with the goats.

"To the ravine! To the ravine!" Pakhraddin yelled, his voice breaking, as he reached the elder.

Labakh-*akhun* merely briefly waved his staff. That apparently meant, don't stop! When Pakhraddin slid into the ravine, managing his heavy body with difficulty, and grew accustomed to the dark, the first person he saw was Kikymbay, who was wending his way toward him through the crowd of people.

"There are no horses! *Oybay*, there are no horses!" he yelled. "*Biy-aga*, they took the horses, too, *oybay*!"

"A raid! A raid! Why, oh, Lord?!" groaned Pakhraddin, who was usually stonily unperturbable. This time his restraint betrayed even him. What were they to do? Panicked, Pakhraddin shuffled in place. He didn't even have a gun. And what sort of shooter could come of Pakhraddin?

Remembering Bulysh, he staggered back – he was all alone there, poor fellow. The thought that they could kill him, too, didn't enter his head.

...Bulysh didn't see the hulk creeping up to him from the rear under cover of the bushes; he was still kneeling, aiming at someone. The bullet whistled past his very ear and instantly he felt a terrible blow to his right shoulder. His *berdanka* flew from his hands. Bulysh lunged after it, hunching over, and saw Azbergen next to him.

"Oh...your father!" he roared, waving the rifle butt. Bulysh managed to duck his head, but the heavy blow of the butt landed on his left shoulder. Bulysh recoiled. No matter which way he looked, Mazhan's Motan rose before him. The blade flashed. Bulysh dodged, but it was too late – the saber struck him in the back of the head. A terrible fire blazed before his eyes. The world collapsed at once into a bottomless abyss.

Seeing how the enemies were crowding around Bulysh's prone body, Pakhraddin jumped up. Then he realized: Bulysh had gotten it. Pakhraddin immediately sat down behind a bush – he wanted to live. And here the air was pierced with a woman's voice, shaking the soul:

"Bulysh! Bulysh!"

Pakhraddin turned around and saw Balkiya, flying out of the ravine, breaking through the blue smoke of the gunpowder. Barefoot, in rags, a handkerchief in her hand, her hair trailing in the wind, she was racing toward them.

"The enemy has departed! He has fled!" men with rifles shouted out, jumping up from the ravine. The dawn darkness parted, the east grew light, the sandy steppe began to appear. About 30 horsemen, looping through the dunes, were fleeing from them; they disappeared beyond the ridge – bullets wouldn't reach them. Balkiya flew like a bird past Pakhraddin.

"Bulysh! *Oybay*, Bulysh!" her sobs rang out.

Pakhraddin got up, feeling his joints tremor, and awkwardly stumbled after Balkiya, muttering,

"Oh, how unfortunate we are! Oh, what trouble!"

Reaching Bulysh, Balkiya let out a piercing scream.

"*Oybay*! *Oyba-a-a-y*!"

Pakhraddin's eyes closed, and tears sprang from them. His legs, tremoring, bent under him. Try to run faster!

"O-h-h, Bulysh! O-h-h, my Bulysh!" he repeatedly bitterly.

The morning shook from the desperate "*oybays*" of Balkiya. Dau-*apa* ran up from the ravine. And then she began wailing.

Pakhraddin, out of breath from the run, reached the place where Bulysh lay face down, hugging the earth. The first thing he saw: a huge pool of blood had spread all around the *jigit*. Balkiya lay embracing Bulysh, convulsed with sobs. With effort, Pakhraddin pulled her up, pushed her to the side and peered at the defeated man's wounds: the back of his head was smashed, his left shoulder was cut off, his right shoulder blade was torn away by bullets, but on the gloomy face of the *batyr* was frozen a look of fearlessness.

"Oh, light of my eyes...Oh, my bulwark! My *batyr*!" Pakhraddin once again began sobbing.

Wiping away his tears, he turned Bulysh over on his back and covered him with his *chapan*. Only then did he notice that Bulysh's right arm was missing; either it had been cut off along with his shoulder, or he had held on to his rifle so hard that the cursed attackers had cut off his arm to grab his weapon.

Dau-*apa* now had reached her son, and wailed and lamented brokenly. And the other women wept. The entire aul gathered around the corpse.

Suddenly, the aul-dwellers were surprised to see Balkiya hurling away into the dawn's blue light, lit by the sun. She sobbed quietly, piercingly, like a foal that had been accidentally wounded, running headlong, barefoot, bare-headed...

"My little foal! *Oy-ba-ay*! Why should I go on living? Dau-*apa* lamented in a low voice.

Khansulu was barely alive. Pale, shaking, she looked out over the defeated nomad's camp. Once it had existed – now it was gone. People were weeping and wailing. The lambs and calves, the sheep and goats scampered in disarray around the outpost that had served as their stall the previous night. They were all the livestock that was left from the ransacked aul. The disturbed dogs whined. The *nar* camels, the strength and beauty of the aul, were no more. And the horses had disappeared as well. The aul had been diminished, and people now faced poverty.

The bandits had lost two of their own people. One of those laying on the ground turned out to be Kapan, Mazhan's son; a bullet caught him at the foot of the dunes; the second was a young Turkmen in a *papakha*.

They buried Bulysh the following day after lunch on the hill overgrown with agave. His death had shaken the entire aul, making an impression on both young and old. There wasn't a single person who didn't shed a tear for him.

...Poor Balkiya kept fainting now and then. Dau-*apa*, holding her sides with her hands, rocked from side to side and lamented and lamented; in one day her hair turned grey, and his mother, whose courage was known to everyone, bent like a blade of grass.

The brutally destroyed aul, having lost its livestock, was forced to change its plans for the future. While some of the nomads dug Bulysh's grave, others began to dig a well at the bottom of the ravine. A child could see that the journey to far-away Afghanistan now had to be put off. The traveling life-style of the steppe-dwellers dictated: "A grave for a dead man, life for the living." A council of elders decided: after Bulysh was buried, they had to put up their yurts. For a time, the aul had to be based here. Tears and moans were forgotten. People began unrolling and opening the *tyuks,* raising the *kereg,* putting together the *uyks* and *shanyraks* of the yurt.

Only Balkiya could not get back to normal. She lay under the fluffy crown of the dwarf acacia and called out in delirium:

"Bulysh! Bulysh!"

Khansulu held her head, and gave her water to drink. Dau-*apa*, dark-faced from grief, set about righting her tiny little poor yurt. Neighbors and relatives helped the old mother – they raised up the *shanyrak* and tied together the *uyks.*

Toward evening in the shadow of the white yurt, Pakhraddin spread out a large felt *tekemet,* and the aul a*ksakal*y held a council. The unanimously decided that the bandits' raid they had suffered was nothing but a sign from God; the Almighty did not want to let the people go in that direction. But how were they to go on living, what were they to do? They kept coming back to the same question. Some of them proposed pooling the money they had left, the gold and the silver, and trading it for livestock at the bazaar, and little by little, continue their way to Afghanistan. To which the majority angrily objected. How could they, so to speak, go to the promised land without their pants; after all, that attitude toward them, as hicks, would be contemptuous.

Labak-*akhun* sat with his eyes closed and mumbled something to himself softly, fingering his beads; his face was abstracted.

When the moon rose, the council was finished. Five men went with Pakhraddin the very next day to the Turkmen city of Kone-

Urgench, which was closer to the aul than Konyrat. They needed to find some temporary cart work, who as not to have to go into a kolkhoz or artel.

Mirages disappeared and reappeared, whirlwinds raced over the red and white straw. Once a week, the aul's camel, heavy with saxaul, moved in a change toward the horizon to disappear into the haze. Once a week, a caravan sailed back from that haze, in order to sale along the yellow expanse back to the aul, like a flock of cranes. News from the far-away wide world came back with the caravan.

...The aul elders headed by Labak-akhun stood on the edge of the aul, observing the slowly-approaching caravan. Khansulu with a baby in her arms stood near the yurt.

The travelers sat high on the camels, the road had been hard and they looked tired and exhausted. Pakhraddin rode on a brown *nar* with a reddish tint.

"*Oybay*, look here, who is that on the last camel? Not Grumpy?" one of the women exclaimed.
"Is that a howler under him?
"Oh, Creator! Is that really Sharip riding there?"

Khansulu could not believe her eyes. The last one in line, completing the change of the "city-goers," and in fact on his howler, was her father-in-law – little, wizened Sharip, looking like an owl, somehow. You almost couldn't see him because of the camel's hump.

The caravaners, settling the camels, were ringed about closely by the women, children and old men. Labak-*akhun* led Sharip to Dau-*apa*'s home. She lamented for a long time there. The old men chanted from the Koran, passing their palms over their faces in the traditional manner. Balkiya was not at home. The women explained that she had taken a sack and gone to fetch dung. Khansulu went outside and put on the samovar; throwing kindling into the fire, she listened in on the conversations in the yurt, and the old men wanted to know about how life was, and each only asked Sharip a question of his own. Finally, the voice of Syrga, her mother, rang out:

"Well, brother, is there any news from Shege?"

Khansulu ran and pressed herself to the yurt. But her father-in-law called her himself.

"*Kelin*, oh, *kelin*, where are you?"

Shy, Khansulu squeezed sideways into the yurt packed with old men. Her father-in-law was at the place of honor, his legs tucked under him, hungrily sniffing the crown of the head of Tugelkhan, who was sitting on his knees; clearly he had missed him.

"Have a seat, dear. How are you here?"

Sharip's voice shook, he couldn't hide his agitation, and he took a handkerchief out of his pocket and wiped his eyes.

"Shege is alive and well...A letter here has come. The city of Orsk, that's where he is, Shege... And he held out to Khansulu a crumpled, soiled envelope. He couldn't speak any more, and broke into a sob, the tears dripping down on his grandson's head. Looking at him, even Khansulu grew emotional.

Over tea, the restless Kikymbay asked Sharip:

"And how is your *kallektep* doing, *guduldugutpan*?

Guduldugutpan was Kikymbay's favorite expression, the meaning of which he himself didn't know. Drowsy from the tea, the sweaty Sharip jerked his head up sharply. He knew that the cursed hump-nosed Kikymbay had an itchy tongue. He looked around at the people sitting in the yurt, who were expectantly looking at him. The scandal-monger Kikymbay had asked a tricky question, and it was as if he had stepped on a corn. Sharip wiped his forehead with his handkerchief and knit his brows.

"What are you asking? The *kallektep* is the death of us! Damned Jorga has finished us off."

"The death of you? How so? What, Janazhol doesn't exist anymore? It was broken up, or what?"

"It would be better if they broke it up; the *kallektep* has almost breathed its last... The government confiscated the livestock. The commissars threatened people with their shouts: "So that not one bare

hoof remains! Who is against Goloshchekin's policy – get out[181]!"
Kuren thinks up new taxes every day. He took the livestock, then went
after the skins and wool, and then the other day ordered us to turn in the
hooves, that's how it is. If you turn in it, nothing seems to happen. If
you don't, there is no one worse than you. You are an enemy, and a
contra. The slightest thing, and you are threatened with prison. Only
sixteen households are left at Janazhol. People are fleeing the *kallektep.*

"*Oybay!*"

"Allah, save us!"

"For you it is gossip, for me it is bitter life. Believe it or not,"
Sharip continued. "Did you see my grumbler? He's the only one left
out of all my livestock. Once they grab him, consider it's all over for
my family.

"Oh, Shake[182]," Kikymbay said, coming to life, scratching his
chin, which was as bare as a knee. "So what is it, *guduldugutpan*, the
policy of the government or arbitrariness by such fugitives as Jorga?"

"How should I know… The *low* was established, after all: the
higher-ups say cut your hair, and the lower-downs take it along with
your head. It turns out that all the same, we are robbed," said Sharip,
once again wiping away a tear.

«Ohhhhh…."

People grew sad. Exhausted by the long road and thirstiness,
Sharip lay down to have some tea. A fragile quiet settled in. There was
only the sound of dishes clattering.

"Hey, Shake, you told us about what is near and dear to us,
guduldugutpan. But I was waiting for you to inform us about anything
that was important, and governmental…"

---

[181] Flipp Isayevich Goloshchykin, a Russian revolutionary who was
among those who organized the execution of the Tsar and his family.
He was the first secretary of the Kazakhstan Territorial Committee of
the Communist Party, and with his ruthless confiscation policy, is
considered one of the main leaders responsible for the famine in
Kazakhstan in 1932-1933.
[182] Shake is a nickname for Shege.

Sharip didn't understand Kikymbay again, and once again rolled his eyes. Kikymbay raised his voice, pushing forward, and began enthusiastically to tell him a tale:

"I'll tell you a funny story, Shake. Listen. They say Goloshchekin went to visit Stalin and complained, *guduldugutpan*: I can't force the rebellious nomad people into the *kallektep*, he said, they all ran off…Stalin ordered a chicken to be brought to him, then let it run around the room, and said, 'Catch it!' Goloshchekin scurried hither and yon but couldn't catch the chicken. It was cold out. Stalin grabbed the chicken, quickly plucked it, then let it go run around again. And then the shivering chicken ran straight into Goloshchekin's hands on its own.

'Do you understand now how you have to catch a Kazakh?' said Stalin.

'Yes, I understand,' they say Goloshchekin replied. "Our Kikymbay is quite the cheeky bastard, he knows how to approach a topic from far away!" the old men buzzed.

"In the holy book it is said that when the Last Days are approaching, not a single hoof will be left for the litter," Labak-*akhun* suddenly put in. People immediately began murmuring and fixed their gazes on the elder.

"Everything living – the bird flying and the beast growling and the fish swimming – everything turns to ashes and dust and is forgotten. As God is my witness, it is said: the son of a Muslim, when he sees a tuft of wool on a bitch, he will wish to grab it, and after burning it, will enjoy the smell of smoke and remember the days when he herded numerous livestock."

Labak-akhun, having terrified people to death, began describing the details of the Day of Judgement for the sons and daughters of Adam, so eloquently, that it was as if he himself had been an eye witness of the Last Days.

Dau-apa placed some meat on the *dastarkhan*. The guests washed it down with some camel *shubat* and toward evening, when the stars began to shine, went their separate ways.

"Son! Is there any news of Shoyynkar?" Pakhraddin asked cautiously in a restrained voice about his old camel.

"Have you not heard? As soon as Shoyynkar landed in the *kallektip*, he was immediately handed around from person to person, everybody rode him. In the end, that fox Jdakay finished him off."

"How?" Pakhraddin asked in a hoarse voice, his throat suddenly dry.

"Well, this is how…In the winter, under the pretext that the herders needed fuel, he decided to chop down the sacred saxaul which grew at the shrine of Barak-*ata*. He tied a lasso around a tree, and then forced Shoyynikar to pull on it…So the *nar* died of that."

Pakhraddin shook his head without a word.

"Poor Shoyynkar," he sighed sadly. "He was a camel to beat all camels. Eh!"

On the next day, early in the morning, Sharip mounted his grumbler and headed back. It was early in the summer of 1931.

3

The real trouble began in the spring of the following year. Several men headed by Pakhraddin had gone to produce salt at the Karymbet. They hauled the salt from the saline lake on donkeys to the city of Konyrat.

It had already been a month since any news of them had been heard.

The first to leave an aul, as it turned out, are the hungry dogs. They ran away to the desert, preferring to hunt for mice. The aul women gathered together, and headed by *Dau-apa,* went to see Labak-*akhun*. The elder was seated at the top of the hill and was beating his withered head in prostrations, spending day after day in prayer. The exhausted *akhun*, looking like a living ghost, stroked his beard and listened to the people. Without even taking her sleeping grandson from her back, *Dau-apa* bowed slightly, then began to speak.

"*Kaynaga*, what are you thinking of? We have to do something. Of course, we can't speak ahead of time of something bad, but if our men have not returned, what are we to do? Are we to die here?"

"Let us wait one more night. Inshallah, there will be news," the seer-*akhun* replied, rubbing his beard.

The night was windy and moonless. You could not see your hand in front of your face. The aul fell sleep, the restless wind fluttering the *koshmas* on the yurts. From time to time, the wind's gusts were so strong that the *shanyraks* and *uyk*s creaked mercilessly and it seemed as if a yurt would not withstand the pressure from the weather and would collapse.

Khansulu was scared. Swaddling the sleeping Tugelkhan, she listened to the outside world – wailing, whistling, and moaning, as if some strange monsters were scouring the helpless, abandoned aul. Sleep fled Khansulu, and nightmarish visions would not leave her. Something was making noise at the very wall.

"*Apa*!" screamed Khansulu, jumping up.

"*Bismallah*! *Bismillah*! What is it!" Syrga raised her head. "There's somebody at the wall…"

"It's only mice, Lord, what else could it be?"

Her mother lit the kerosene lamp, and went around the yurt, looking over the wall.

"Sleep, mice!" she said, yawning.

Khansulu's eyes lingered on her son, and her heart melted. Oh, that such a little boy would be born – his nose, eyebrows, forehead – oh, Lord! – were his father's! This made her smile, and bending down, she lovingly kissed the little toes of the little feet stretched out from under the blanket. The boy wriggled his feet in his sleep. The wind was unceasing, splitting the ties on the *tyyrlyk*.[183]

Outside, it was if a flood was roaring, washing away the whole world. But reassured, Khansulu hugged her little boy to her breast and drowsed off.

But soon she woke up suddenly from the noise. Her mother was lighting the kerosene lantern.

"What are you doing, *apa*?"

"Your father has come!" she announced, and opened the door.

Her father came in wearing a long down vest. His head was wound up in a handkerchief under his hat as if his tooth ached. His face was dark and swollen. His boots were covered in dust.

"You're back home finally, my falcon?" her mother bustled about, taken the *korzhun* from his arms.

"Back home," her father replied reluctantly, barely able to move his tongue.

"You were delayed for some reason…"

Her father grimaced; apparently his head ached. Syrga sat down and began to pull off his boots. Wincing, he recounted everything that had happened to them.

"They didn't take the salt, or if they did take it, then for nearly nothing, so we spun our wheels. Not to mention the grain – we couldn't even afford the millet. A kilogram was more than two *soms*[184]. And since the salt didn't sell at the bazaar, we had to sell our small livestock to the Uzbeks. For 3 kilograms of millet. It is in the *khordzhun*," Pakhraddin's voice shook and he clutched his head.

Syrga immediately rose and set about massaging his head.

---

[183] The *tuyrlyk* are ties made of *koshma* which cover the yurt.
[184] *Som* is a Turkic word for currency meaning "pure," as in gold. It was used to describe currency in the Soviet era in Central Asia.

"Steppe-dwellers have poured into the city…They're hunger and barefoot, and plague broke out, people are dying…"

Khansulu was about to pour water into the tea kettle, but her father refused tea and went to lay down. Syrga made up his bed. Unbuttoning his ragged jacket, Pakhraddin said:

"At dawn, it looks like we're going to head off to the coast. Bad times have set in."

Syrga, holding her husband's head, helped him to lay down. She snuffed out the lamp.

Khansulu was surprised at her father's "we're going to head off."

…In the morning, her father ordered that the hearth be lit and he himself, wrapped in a fur coat, sat down nearby, his face to the fire. For a long time, he drank tea, until he had sweated seven times. Labakh-*akhun* arrived. Seated in the guest's place, he rapidly mumbled a blessing and closing his eyes, ran his palms over his face. He sat for a little while in silence, rubbing his white beard with his fingers. Mentally, it seemed as if he had looked over all of creation, so abstracted was his expression. Pakhraddin did not speak. Wrapped up in his fur coat, he kept sipping on the strong boiling tea his wife poured for him.

"Ehh," the *akhun* drawled. There is no other way expect going back?"

"There is no other way," Pakhraddin replied.

"Eh," the *akhun* let out a long sigh and nodded his head. He nodded for a long time. Then, just as he had come, so he went – upright, unbent, invincible, in white, dragging the hems of his *chapan* along the ground, in a white *chalma,* with a white staff in his hand.

By that time, the neighbors as well had apparently got up. The sharp wailing cries of the women and the weeping children's voices could be heard.

The Lonely Yurt • Smagul Yelubay

"I don't know what kind of day God will give us, whether there will be rain or not," said Syrga, glancing through the *tunduk* of the yurt to the sky – it was streaked with muddy grey.

Pakhraddin, turning the *piyala* upside down, wiping his face with a towel, said.

"Take only what is necessary. Bedding, dishes, clothing. What an ass can carry – the rest we will leave." And pointing to the *kerege*, he asked his daughter, "Give it here."

The black, plush *torba*[185] hung on the crossbars. In it were old notebooks, those with the genealogy of the Kazakhs which he had been writing for many years. What was written in them? Even people close to Pakhraddin didn't know. If someone was curious, he brushed them off curtly – it's a history, he would say…

Khansulu passed the *torba* to her father. Pakhraddin turned the yellowed pages slowly, silently reading, for a long while. Daughter and mother, busy with preparations for the journey, packed things in *khordzhuns,* exchanging curious glances, and wondered what father was doing. A fine time he had found for reading…

But without paying them any mind, he turned over the whitish yellowing pages, peering at the beautifully penned Arabic lettering of the text.

And suddenly with a crack, he tore one of the notebooks in half. Then he ripped them into bits and threw the pieces into the fire. The paper flared up.

Khansulu and Syrga froze in their tracks.

Pakhraddin went out of the yurt. The wind had not died down; it chased around the aul over the ground, lifting sand up from under yurts, making even more ugly the sad picture of existence turning to ash. Women and children raced around stupidly. There was a bustling with bundles, and other household junk pouring out of the yurts. This

---

[185] A *torba* is a hard, oval-shaped knapsack without compartments.

was a completely different nomadic journey, not like the past ones. This was not even like a nomadic journey, but rather a flight into vagrancy – whatever could be carried in your hands you could take with you, and what you couldn't hold, you would drop and leave behind.

...The drawn old men and women, the worn-out people and children in rags – the starving people had an awful look. The men of the aul who had returned with Pakhraddin from the city had recounted to their families, who had despaired of seeing them, what path was in store for them. As they had had heard in Konyrat, representatives from Almaty had come to the banks of the Amu Darya. Their purpose was to gather together all the hungry auls scattered over the sands, who had fled into the desert because they didn't wish to go into collectives, who were now vagrants. The gathering point was set on the banks of the Amu Darya, along which the refugees were to be taken back to their homeland. And they had also heard that Stalin had supposedly harshly criticized Goloshchekin:

"The nomadic people fled their native land due to the excesses of the local activists and the leadership, which goes against the policy of the Party," he said.

After that, supposedly messengers from the Republic galloped to various locations, and to neighbors of course – to Russians, Uzbeks, Kyrgyz, Turkmen, and Karakalpaks – into whose lands the frightened Kazakhs had at first flooded, in order to make their way to China, Iran and Afghanistan.

When it came time to leave even the yurts in the deserted area, and everything that they had grown used to living with for years, a spontaneous revolt sprang up – a women's revolt.

"How stupid our men are!" Katira, the wife of Kikymbay began as usual, angry that the bundles that she was putting on the ass could not fit on his back. "They knew that we'd be coming back, what the devil did we leave the *kallektep* for?"

"Keep quiet, thrice-damned, shut up!" Kikymbay yelled at her, lunging forward toward her.

Pakhraddin perceived Katira's shrieks as a curse on him alone. They pierced his soul just like arrows, penetrating to his very bones. He closed his ears, he didn't want to hear the woman's cries. His face burned in shame from Katira's baseless attack; the words of the vile woman lashed him like a whip...

Syrga and Khansulu dragged two sacks with the bedding out of the house and loaded it on to the ass. Then they placed the *korzhun* with the dishware and other goods on the ass. The ass was loaded and there was no more room. Pakhraddin's wife and daughter saw this, but still kept fussing. If it were up to them, they wouldn't leave anything behind. Pakhraddin felt bile rise in this throat. He didn't know whom he should get mad at. Either at fate, which had extracted him from many labyrinths but had led him to this dead end and left him stuck, or at himself, always too late and now falling into this brutal noose. Or should he be mad at such stupid women as Katira, out of irritation? Or angry at his helplessness? Pakhraddin's face swelled and grew covered with dark spots, and his brows and beard seemed to be covered with frost. His wife and daughter didn't notice his state. They hurried back and forth, first grabbing at one thing, then another.

And here Syrga the *baybishe* said:

"*Oy-bay-y*! Oh, my falcon! We forgot about the *kazan*!" And she hurried to get the black kettle from the hearth. It was big. Her daughter ran up and grabbed one of the handles. They barely managed to drag it outside. Pakhraddin didn't have the heart to tell them to drop it. Gritting his teeth, he watched as his wife and daughter dragged the large, cast-iron *kazan*. How many years the old patched-up kazan had fed them but it was impossible to take it with them now – the ass' back could not bear it.

"It won't fit," he said, tactfully as usual, but his wife and daughter wouldn't listen. They grunted and groaned, dragging the *kazan* to the ass. Finally, Pakhraddin flew off the handle:

"It won't fit! Where are you going to put it? Where?"

It was likely the first time he had ever raised his voice against his wife and daughter. Frightened, they dropped the *kazan*, their faces fallen. Pakhraddin darkened and turned away from them. "Oh, God the tempter! Do you think this is just what I have not known in my life? This?" he grumbled, looking at the troubled horizon. Sobs welled up in his throat, but his eyes were dry, without tears. His soul was empty – just like everything around him. The whistling and wailing of the wind filled his ears.

"Stop it," he snapped at them, passing by tiredly.

Many people then came out in a crowd to the road, driving their asses. *Dau-apa* seemed tied to the yurt, unable to leave it. Pakhraddin heard her honoring someone with her last words. And the old woman had no ass.

"Bring her things!" he ordered Khansulu.

Dau-apa had two bundles, and somehow they loaded them on to the ass. It was time to move out. *Dau-apa* returned to her yurt, and from there could be heard her loud lamentation:

"Almighty God, you have caused trouble to my ill daughter-in-law! What can be done now?!"

Dau-apa came out of the house and her grandson ran after her crying.

"Oh, Pakhraddin, what am I to do? My crazy daughter-in-law doesn't want to go. If you talk to her quietly, she doesn't understand. If you talk loudly, she cries. What am I to do, eh?"

Pakhraddin turned toward Khansulu and Syrga.

"Even if you have to deceive her, get her out of there somehow!"

Balkiya, her hair undone, sat with her back to the door, clinging hard to the bars of the *kerege*. She clung even harder when she saw Khansulu and Syrga. The old dress she was wearing had a torn shoulder.

"Let me try!" Khansulu urged *Dau-apa* and her mother. "Balkiya!"

Balkiya trembled, turning toward her. Her eyes were mad. She didn't recognize Khansulu.

"It's me, Khansulu!"

Balkiya now stared at the door lintel. Khansulu retrieved a little mirror and comb and placed them before her. It was a tried-and-true method. In the past, she had managed to take care of the sick woman in this way – she washed her head and combed her hair.

"Look, I'll comb your hair!" Khansulu offered, and sensed now that Balkiya was beginning to listen to her.

Soon, Khansulu took her by the hand out of the yurt. No one was left in the aul by that time, it stood empty, as if gutted. A dusty, dry wind wended its way among the abandoned homes, lifting up garbage and driving along pieces of paper.

The aul-dwellers walked on foot, dragging themselves along the ridge in a crowd, ringing round the disorderly bunch of Pakhraddin, *Dau-apa,* Syrga, Balkiya and Khansulu. The abandoned dogs ran underfoot between the departing people and the aul, the very same who had run off to the desert to hunt mice but had now for some reason returned. The poor things couldn't understand where these people were going without their former livestock. The hounds would trot after the people leaving for a while, and then stop, and look around at the lifeless aul, and then whine and howl.

Pakhraddin tried to walk with his back to the wind. To the voice of the great dry wind, rocking the bushes, a certain howl had mixed in, as if the world around was sighing heavily and groaning. It was as if there were a terrible calamity, capable of destroying the universe, which was raising its head. The dusty curtain blocked out the sun and it seemed the whole wide world. The sky was clouded over with a reddish, howling haze. It seemed to be a forecast of the Last Times. Pakhraddin no longer had the strength to look back at the empty homes left behind, at the abandoned aul, without care, orphaned. Now, no matter what happened, they had to only go forward…. At the place where the road, rising to the top of the dunes, then descended below, Pakhraddin, stopped, and wiped the sweat from his brow – the climb was difficult for him as he was overweight. But he didn't start turning back. He was gloomily collected within himself. And it was as if he had frozen in that state. Then his wife, daughter, children, and *Dau-apa* turned around.

At the center of the endless realm of dunes, on a tiny, flat square, a little aul perched timidly. Cute brown yurts with doors and *tunduks* closed tightly, unexpectedly emptied homes pressed forlornly against one another. A dust storm covered the aul.

Except for Balkiya, the women began to weep. Syrga the *baybishe* peered at the white yurt until her eyes hurt; the black *kazan* she had to abandon stood black against the doorway. Tears ran down her face; fearing her husband, she grasped the edge of her *jaulyk* in her teeth and soundlessly broke into tears.

The wail of the wind, tirelessly beating the heads of the agave and the Siberian pea shrub, seemed suddenly to Pakhraddin like a woman's weeping, suspended between the sky and earth. He shook himself, not daring to look at the women, showered with tears. Angrily, he lashed the grey ass' rump with a dry stick; the animal had taken advantage of the stop to doze, his long ears hanging.

"*Chu!*" he said, driving the ass.

THE STEPPE APOCALYPSE

1

It was as if an eclipse of the sun had occurred. It was as if doomsday had arrived, the very one that Labak-*akhun* had predicted...

Depressed, with tears in her eyes, Khansulu wandered along the soft path crumbling beneath her feet. Her child was on her back. Ahead, beyond the pass, was the aul, abandoned, inhospitable, like a cemetery. The sad howling of the dogs left behind carried from there. They howled sorrowfully, predicting something bad. Khansulu was afraid to look behind her, she didn't dare for some reason. The crowd of dejected people, wandering through the sand. Ahead was the grey horizon, covered with billowing dust, promising the unknown. Ahead was an uncertain fate.

The sun was already high, but it was invisible in the dull sky. The dust whirled up here and there on both sides of the path and the bushes, rocking in the wind, sung their protracted, hollow song. Flecks of sand dashed in their eyes. The endless world contracted to a small slit before their eyes. Khansulu had a foreboding of something strange, and her heart knocked in her chest in fear.

The crowd trudged along the path, snaking its way among the dunes. There was someone's wooden trunk, left by the edge of the tamarisk shrubs with the top swung open like the yawn of a devil. Coming closer, Khansulu recognized it: it was Kulzipa's trunk, her pride; she had always placed it in a prominent place in the yurt. Everyone saw it, of course – black, encrusted with bone – but they passed by in silence. Neither her father, or her mother, or *Dau-apa* uttered even a word. Only Tugelkhan on her back stretched out his forefinger toward the truck and said:

"*Ap! Ap!*"

Khansulu later found that that Kulzipa's father, an old, toothless man with a sunken mouth, had grown ill. The old man could not walk, so Kulzipa left behind the trunk, and put her father on the ass.

There was no strength to walk for the whole day. The straggling column made camp at noon in a tamarisk grove. People threw off their loads and gathered firewood, and soon campfires were smoking here and there and tea kettles with water hung over them. Khansulu's family, bringing up the rear, reached the camp. They spread their belongings out under a bush where there was no wind, and made up the *alash* on the ground. A family was situated under every bush. From old habit, people gathered to have supper. Khansulu, when they had been still in the sands of Aytu, had seen a gypsy camp. And now the people scattered under the bushes reminded her vividly of that camp.

Many campfires were smoking all about, tea kettles were on the boil, but her nose couldn't pick up the familiar small of meat, the aroma of fresh, steeped bouillon. Therefore, the women were screaming at their kids louder than usual, and their irritated voices hurt her ears. Katira was exceling more than all:

"Where're you going, you, greedy mug! You'll get into the fire, stupid!"

That was how she yelled at her own children who were drawn to the fire.

Some woman was groaning and cursing as if in delirium:

"Oh, stingy God!"

At Khansulu's *dastarkhan* – two families per *dastarkhan* – there was friend corn, a little bread, and some boiling water. They had just set upon the feast when *Dau-apa* exclaimed in a trembling voice:

"*Oyy-bay*, what a fate we have!"

A ragamuffin with a wooden *tostagan* in his hand, a boy, went around to people's *dastarkhans* one after another. There was one pauper in the aul – Maylybay. He was the quietest of fellows – he wouldn't hurt a flea, as they say – but he had a whole bunch of children, either nine or ten. When the pauper ran out of stores, his son went around to beg. People broke off a bit from their own stores and put it in his cup. Some people evidently were irritated at seeing him, therefore he didn't stay long at some homes. The *tostagan* in his hand was all dented, the boy was barefoot and his faded pants were torn, he was perhaps ten or eleven years old. The boy didn't look anyone in the eye, he kept his head down and didn't raise it.

The Lonely Yurt • Smagul Yelubay

"Oh, come closer!" said Pakhraddin, handing him a handful of fried corn kernels from the *dastarkhan.*

Stepping timidly, the boy came closer. Pakhraddin looked into the tostagan. Khansulu as well. Not even a handful of millet and corn had been made up from all the *dastarkhans.*

"That's all you gathered?!" Pakhraddin asked incredulously, sighing from amazement. He couldn't believe his eyes. The boy nodded. Pakhraddin sprinkled him another handful from a rag bag under Syrga's knee. Fearing for sure now that they would stop him, the boy ran away home. Syrga, raising tired eyes to her husband, knitted her brows. Pakhraddin understood the *baybishe.* He understood, and muttered somehow helplessly:

"Ehhh!"

He was seized by grief, and his shoulders slumped even more. Syrga pointed somewhere to the side:

"Look...there's another one out there...give him everything that's left..." And really, like lost lambs, the ragamuffins were coming from all sides.

The children stopped fearfully.

"Come her! Come here!" Pakhraddin called them. His tone was harsh.

"My falcon," Syrga was about to begin, but he cut her off.

"Stop it! If we're to die, we'll die together! My soul is no better than their souls."

With that, the conversation was over. Pakhraddin sprinkled out a handful of corn into each outstretched palm.

Kulzipa's father died. Without weeping or excessive words, people buried him. No one shed a tear. Only Kulzipa wept...

After lunch, the trek continued.

All the way, Khansulu followed Balkiya, afraid for her. The sick woman had a bad habit – to dash away aimlessly! But Balkiya had not run away yet. She went along obediently and glumly like a camel calf on a leash. Neither *Dau-apa* nor Syrga saw anything suspicious in her and gradually they left her alone and stopped watching her. Only as darkness gathered, Balkiya would show what she was capable of…

After lunch, the travelers overcame three more big climbs. With the onset of evening, people chose a dune overgrown with feather grass for their bed. Hobbling the asses, they let them out to pasture, and themselves gathered some dry wood to build a shelter from the wind. In the dense, moonless night, the dune was lit up by campfires. Human silhouettes darted among them from the side of the dunes, possibly reminiscent of a devil's revelry.

"*Oybay*! She's lost!" exclaimed *Dau-apa*, who had been serenely warming herself at the campfire. "Where is my *kelin,* oh Lord!" *Dau-apa* had suddenly recalled her daughter-in-law. "Balkiya!" she called. "Balkiya-a-a!"

There was silence. Everyone jumped up, Pakhraddin as well. Stepping away from the fire, they all cried into the night:

"Balkiya! Balkiya!"

The darkness was impenetrable. Squatting down, Khansulu peered into the night. The dark humps of the bushes loomed up from all sides. Musical female laughter suddenly could be heard. Khansulu trembled in horror.

"She's there!" her father shouted and clumsily stumped toward the sound in the darkness.

After that laugh, Khansulu was afraid to go very far from the camp. Other men raced to run after Pakhraddin. The voices calling for Balkiya grew further away and soon faded completely. Khansulu and Syrga stood for a little while at the edge of the dunes and then returned.

No matter how much they called or shouted, deafening the desert with shouts, they didn't find Balkiya that night.

In the morning darkness, Pakhraddin mounted an ass and once again headed out to search for her. Labak-*akhun* he ordered to continue the journey; people were starving, he said, and it wasn't right to hold them up. *Dau-apa,* Khansulu, and Syrga the *baybishe* remained at the dunes to wait for Pakhraddin.

...Pakhraddin did not have to work very hard finding Balkiya's tracks. He immediately found the path which she had taken yesterday and headed toward the previous camp. It was bright out, the sun had risen. A little rain had drizzled before sunrise, so the scent of the wet sand and the young grass just barely growing hit his nostrils. Pakhraddin greedily breathed in the earth's aromas. Soon he found Balkiya's footprints on the path. Her barefoot heels were printed clearly on the sand. It seemed she never stopped, but the poor thing ran straight back to the aul. Pakhraddin didn't spare his ass now. He drove and drove him. Only in the afternoon did he reach the ridge where they had camped the day before.

The ass struggled to get a purchase on the crumbling hillside under his hoofs. Then the aul appeared. Pakhraddin had a strange feeling. An unexpected feeling. It was an inexplicable and involuntary fear of seeing his aul and his yurt. He shouldn't have returned to their previous camp; he shouldn't have seen his abandoned home.

Meanwhile, the ass was already at the top of the dunes. The ass -- being an ass – began hee-hawing as soon as he saw the deserted aul.

The brown yurts were bunched together among the dunes in a pit, like bright eggs. Pakhraddin instinctively peered at the yurts as if subconsciously he expected that someone was going to run out of the aul upon hearing the ass's cry. But not even a shadow appeared. Not a single closed door open. Only a lone whirlwind circled around the homes, lifting into the air the ashes of the ruined hearths.

Pakhraddin turned the ass toward Bulysh's grave, standing dark and lonely against the small hill. The grave was not fenced in, only a twig had been stuck at the head; a mound of earth instead of Bulysh. Unforgettable Bulysh!

"Ohhh, Bulysh...my dear Bulysh!" Pakhraddin exclaimed, dropping tears from the ass. "Are you here, my Bulysh? How are you lying, my dear?"

Squatting on his heels next to the grave, he began reciting the memorial prayer. The ass peeled back his long hanging ears, puzzled why he had lost his master on this empty rise.

After a while, Pakhraddin got up, wiped his eyes and shook the sand from his knees. He looked and saw Balkiya's bare footprints all around the grave. "This is where the miserable creature is!" he cried. Looking around, he saw her at last. She was peeking at him from behind an agave bush. She recoiled as soon as he noticed her and raced off.

"Balkiya! Hey! Stop!" Pakhraddin cried, struggling after her.

Balkiya wasn't running, she was flying across the clean sand, only her heels flashing; her crown of hair had fallen loose around her. His eyes were dazzled by her full, white calves flashing ahead.

"Stop, you! Stop, I say! Hey! Hi!" Pakhraddin yelled, not able to catch up with the fugitive.

But Balkiya, dressed in a grey, torn nightshirt looked back and took to her heels even faster!

"Balkiya! Wait! Balkiya!" cried Pakhraddin.

The crazy woman didn't hear him, and disappeared behind the ridge. Pakhraddin, who had on boots and a *chapan*, and didn't have the breath to keep running – he was staggering from one leg to the other. He stopped to catch his breath. Then he climbed up the ridge. He forced himself to climb. Balkiya's trail was cold, and he no longer saw her.

"What a lot of bother with that unfortunate woman!" he sighed angrily, gazing over the endless, sandy world ahead of him. "Goddammed woman, she has gone wild, racing along like a saiga!" Where should he look for her? No matter where you looked, there were heaps of sand dunes. "Where has she gone?"

The donkey suddenly brayed. Pakhraddin whirled around and the ass accompanying him ran off with awkward leaps. The shadows behind it grew sharper – either dogs or wolves. While Pakhraddin was still trying to figure where they were coming from, the ass, bucking its hind legs, disappeared into the hollow.

Pakhraddin froze in shock. "Wolves!" He grew chilled immediately from fear. "Where are they?" He remembered how the ass had brayed back at the ridge when they saw the aul; it seemed it was predicting trouble. Curses! Now here was punishment – all he needed were wolves! It seemed Balkiya had disappeared, as if she had melted into the sands. He himself was standing with his arms dangling helplessly, while the wolves were likely ripping the stupid ass to bits. Once they were through with him, they would leap in a gray pack to the top of the dunes and spot him – what was he to do?

Pakhraddin ran at a heavy trot toward the aul. Gasping, out of breath, he was covered with hot sweat. He sensed that he wouldn't reach the aul. He saw dark before his eyes, possibly because he hadn't eaten for a long while. His legs were heavy and would no longer obey him.

There was the ravine with the aul. Orphaned, abandoned homes. Everything was motionless. A deathly stillness. There was only the dull echo of his steps.

He had reached the outermost yurt, Kikymayev's, gasping as he walked, when he spotted a little creature the size of a lamb which scampered off with a yelp. Ugh, God's monster, it was a sand rat! Pakhraddin had never been so frightened. He felt goose-bumps up his spine, he was so scared. Two more rats raced by, squealing. His legs failed him, overcome with weakness. The yurt taken over by the rats seemed to him to be more terrifying than wolves. His eyes flooded with sweat. Swaying from dizziness as he stood, he was about to head into the nearest yurt – *Dau-apa's*, full of holes – and was already on the way when he tripped into the pit of the hearth, and fell down heavily, hurting himself badly. Leaning on his arms, he somehow got up, and thought to himself: "This is where alone, I will meet my end..."

Brushing the ash off his pants, he straightened himself on trembling legs, and with difficulty, went into *Dau-apa's* yurt.

Beyond *Dau-apa's* yurt, in fact, was his own. The door and *tunduk* were closed tight, the large black *kazan* lay turned over in front of the threshold, the earth had been dug up by mice. No, he wasn't going to go inside his own home, even under fear of death!

It turned out *Dau-apa's* yurt wasn't locked, it was just that the door had been slammed shut. But getting into it cost him quite a bit of effort; it turned out it was packed with sand rats. Nasty, vile creatures! He had no choice but to stuck his head into the yurt. It was half dark, and he couldn't make out anything…He stood for a bit, shrinking, with the sense that he had ended up in a grave, alive. And really, what warmth could there be in a house from which a person had left?! It was the emptiness of the crypt… An old, patched rug lay at the place for guests. He gathered up his strength. Opening up the creaking door, he shook it, slammed it again, then opened the door on the latch. He sat down on the rug. His tired, weakened body begged for rest. *"I'll get some sleep; the sun is going down. Curse it all, I'll move out with the dawn," he thought.*

Listening to the noises all around, he didn't notice how his eyes closed.

…He awoke in the middle of the night, it seemed he had become terribly chilled. He saw the bright stars though a hole in the *tunduk.* Darkness reigned inside the home. His heart knocked in alarm, he didn't know from what. *Thud..thud…*

An unaccountable fear possessed him. He was getting old, no doubt – he was starting to be afraid of everything. No sooner did he think this than his eyes froze on the door, hidden in the thick shadows. It was as if someone were hiding there, watching him. Pakhraddin even heard someone breathing. He began to grope around himself. He turned over a boot that he had removed for the night. Somebody's bugged-out eye was staring at him; he could make it out clearly.

"Ay!" he screamed angrily and threw the boot. The door thundered.

Whoever had come to watch him – whether a devil or fairy[186] – took to their heels.

"*Ayt!*" Pakhraddin roared, jumping up. The rustling of the invisible creature's legs went silent in the distance.

"*Astafiralla*! Oh, my spirits!" Pakhraddin began reciting his *al-ayat*[187] prayers.

There was one after another. How could he think of any sleep now? He paced back and forced in the cramped yurt until dawn. At sunrise, he went out of the yurt, made his *daret*[188], and recited the *namaz*.

The dawn's darkness was still around when he took his stick up in his hand and left the abandoned aul.

2

Khansulu, *Dau-apa,* and Syrga the *baybishe* had not slept for two nights, waiting for Pakhraddin. They lit a campfire on the dunes. They shouted, thinking Pakhraddin had lost his way.

"Curses! It's all over that bitch! Why did he go looking for her? If she freezes to death, let the earth swallow her," *Dau-apa* swore loudly.

Syrga was silent. She covered herself with a sleeveless shirt and sat near the fire and kept looking into the flames. From the day that they had left their home and the aul and gone off on the journey, it was as if she had renounced everything, and had fallen into some kind of listless torpor. She had been a tactful and mild mother, few in words, and now she ceased speaking at all, moving around like a shadow.

---

[186] *Peri* – a fairy-tale creature.
[187] *Al-ayat,* the sign prayer, said by Muslims during an eclipse or other omen.
[188] The *daret* is performing natural functions and washing according to ritual.

With the sunrise, Khansulu went around the nearby dunes, pulling up wild carrots and gathering onions. Without these roots, which at least quelled their hunger a bit, they would use up the remainder of the grain in the *torba*.

Khansulu put one onion in her mouth. At least it was some reinforcement for her weakening organism. As for the carrots, well, carrots were the most real food there was. She wandered quite a way from the camp unnoticed, in search of carrots. *Dau-apa's* shout rang from somewhere below. Since the dawn twilight, the old woman had apparently headed back to the abandoned aul. Had she returned? Khansulu broke into a run, tripped over her long hem, toward the camp. From the top of the hill she could see *Dau-apa* waving her *jaulyk*. She stood at the very foot of the dunes, calling her. Khansulu hurried toward her. Apparently she had news of her father. A man lay at the eastern foothills of the dune, stretched out to his full height. *Dau-apa* sat next to him. From his *chapan* – dark grey – Khansulu recognized her father.

When his daughter approached, he lifted his head. He has apparently fallen ill, his face was swollen, he coughed uncontrollably, growing hoarse, and tears streamed from his eyes. It was good that he had managed to reach the dunes.

Together, holding him from two ends, *Dau-apa* and Khansulu dragged him to the ridge with difficulty.

"Fire! Fire!" he demanded. They lit a campfire, boiled some water, and stretched out a rug as shelter from the wind, placing the *dastarkhan* under the canopy. Pakhraddin's lips were cracked. He swallowed some boiled water with salt added. He pinched off a little corn bread, and tried the fried grain and corn with it.

"Oof!" he uttered each time he took a swallow.

"Oh, Allah! Oh, Barak-ata! Oh, Beketa-ata!" *Dau-apa* wailed loudly to the spirits of their ancestors.

Pakhraddin kept silent. He was wrapped up to his neck in a warm blanket and kept gulping down the boiled water. He wanted to sweat properly and drive the unclean spirits out of himself

Toward noon, the sun began to bake down. The spring sun was bright. A lark sang very high up in the sky, and the midges buzzed and sang. Green usually grows in the sands with the first warm weather. No matter where you looked grew succulent rana, beloved by the animals, along with camel-thorn, licorice, burdock, and feather grass. In the near and far valleys, between the hills, the transparent, blue sky flowed. The desert expanse was blooming and growing more beautiful. Drinking in the lush growth, Khansulu's breathe caught in her throat from the beauty.

…Pakhraddin kept sitting by the fire for a long time, crunching the fried grain, drinking it down with boiled water, and sweating. Then he lay down, and Syrga the *baybishe* tucked a blanket around him on all sides.

"Hey!" he called after a little while.

"What?" Syrga responded, worried.

"What do we have left to munch?"

Syrga didn't answer him. She took the small black *torba* out of the *korzhun* and threw it down in front of him. This was a reproach of sorts to her husband for his inopportune hospitality.

"That's all?" he asked.

Syrga didn't reply. She turned away.

"Hmmm," Pakhraddin hummed. He closed his eyes. The women grew quiet in expectation of what he, keeper of the hearth, would say.

"How much water is there left?"

"A half *burlyuk*."

"*Dau-apa!*" Pakhraddin burrowed deeper into his blanket.

"I'm listening," she replied.

"*Dau-apa,* today it looks like I can't walk. Well, you and Khansulu go ahead, you shouldn't be held back. Syrga will stay with me…We'll live – and we'll catch up with you. Divide up the water. Leave…two handfuls…of the corn behind. Take the rest, and the bedding…However much you can carry. Pack up!"

"*Koke,* perhaps we should stay together?" Khansulu asked timidly. "Perhaps…"

"That's enough!" Pakhraddin barked, cutting her short. "Get a move on!"

Syrga the *baybishe,* having kept silent, wiped away a tear furtively.

"My brother speaks the truth, my dears," *Dau-apa* concluded and sighed sorrowfully. The wrinkles were etched into her face.

Khansulu and *Dau-apa* set off on the journey with the children. *Dau-apa* had the *korzhun* on her back, and Khansulu carried the *torsyk*[189] with water in her arms, along with a bundle of clothing.

The vast landscape was deserted. Khansulu walked away, glancing backward at the dunes covered with feather grass where her father and mother were standing. It was as if the world had melted in her hot tears, the grey horizon swam heavily in this fog, sinking like lead. It was as if everything under the sky and on the earth had stopped dead in surprise, staring at her, unfortunate thing, ready to die from her own helplessness. It was as if life had lost its meaning. If it weren't for her heart beating in her chest, Khansulu could be taken for mute and lifeless. She was not in a state to understand anything, she dragged herself over the sands in grief. The world before her eyes was covered with a reddish haze. Not a single thought came to her head. The only thing in her consciousness was her little boy, trotting alongside her. She only knew one thing: she could not part from him. Knowing that, she held tighter to his little hand.

---

[189]A *torsyk* is a goatskin bag.

Her eyes did not dry for a long time, nor did her child's.

Dau-apa went ahead with a long stick in her hand and a heavy *korzhun* on her back, bent under the load. She stayed quiet, gritting her teeth. Waiting for the right moment, she uttered with sympathy:

"Eh, my little daughter, no matter what happens, stay strong. If only Allah will not leave us without help. What hasn't your poor *apa* seen, who is walking ahead of you..."

The old woman's coarse voice sounded sad and hollow. The path wove between the dunes, sometimes stretching across the smooth salt-marsh. The further they went away, the more frequently they would see camel-thorn, agave, tamarisk, and chia. Even torangyl appeared – a high, strong, thick palisade stretching above. All of these signs reminded them that the desert was little by little being left behind.

Toward evening, the children began whining, asking for bread. The path through the salt marsh went past tamarisk bushes and chia grasses. The tamarisk was as tall as a man, you could rest underneath it. And there was no wind. Throwing the *korzhun* off her shoulders, *Dau-apa* straightened up, flexing her stiff upper back.

"Well, now, little daughter, what do you have there, untie your bundle!" she ordered.

The night before, when her mother Syrga and packed the water and food, *Dau-apa* had not interfered, busy with her own affairs. In the bundle were *lepyoshki* made of corn and a handful or two of fried grain. That was their entire provisions. Khansulu handed it to the old woman. The children, seeing the bread, twitched and were about to reach out their hands but *Dau-apa* barked at them:

"Stop! Be patient!"

She carefully unfolded the kerchief with the provisions; her hands were dark and dry, her fingers crooked and knotty.

"Be patient just a bit longer, children!"

At first she divided the grain into four parts, then eight, and then into twelve. From the side, it seemed as if the old woman was telling a fortune with beans. Neither Khansulu nor the children could understand why she was doing this – the reserves were modest, and would not last long.

"The longest it will be to Konyrat is two more nights, hmmm…" the old woman mumbled, not paying attention to her fellow travelers. "So-o-o…," she said as she broke the bread in half as well. The scent of the *lepyoshki* tickled their noses. Khansulu even salivated. *Dau-apa* took the two halves of the *lepyoshki* and divided them into half again. In the end, the children each got a tiny piece, as big as their palms.

"The road is long, my dears, be patient. When we get there, we'll eat," she said.

Khansulu put the pinch of grain in her mouth. It was as if it weren't grain, but hard and crunchy, and the bits of butter melted right in her mouth. Only just now she had felt as if she had starved to death, her entire insides were coiled like a beast's. Oh, how good the bread smelled! She couldn't tear her eyes off it.

Dau-apa folded up the kerchief into a knot. All eyes were fastened on her as before. She then stuffed the kerchief into the *korzhun*. Then they all stood up.

The tamarisk grove was soon left behind them. The path once again wove began to weave around the sparse, sandy hillocks with agave and caragana.

3

Pakhraddin had a dream…

It was as if it were the old days, before the time of troubles for the people. There were numerous white yurts along the lake shore, like seagulls, and a throng of people in the aul. It was either a holiday of some sort, or simply a nice, joyful day. Everyone was waiting for what Pakhraddin would say. He had universal honor and respect. As the *biy*, he must have his say. He must give a speech. Lord, had Pakhraddin ever avoided an occasion to give a speech to the whole people? He cast his gaze over the crowd in order to begin to orate. Today he had a special speech to give, he would start the conversation from the depth of the ages: where the people had gone with the *uran*[190] of Alasha, who their direct ancestors were. The people, not knowing their origins were giving birth to rootless descendants. Was it not for today's speech that he had leafed through so many *shchezhire* [191]books? And he had so much accumulated in his soul, that it was as if he were ready to speak, to sing until dawn, like the nightingale. It was if he were to open his mouth, his words of discovery would pour from his throat by themselves. At the peak of his inspiration, clearing his throat, he turned toward the people. He had only begun to speak when he…awoke.

Pakhraddin was laying on his back. Lifting up his head slightly, he looked all around. A strange feeling overtook him, he didn't know whether to believe it or not that he, Pakhraddin, was here in the desert, under the open sky. Believe it or not, but under his back was the ground, and under his head was the sky, dark blue, with twinkling stars beginning to appear; he was flying toward it, and it would cover him head to foot any moment. Pakhraddin frowned. Oh, it was too bad it was all a dream. On the one hand, he didn't wish to part with the languor of sleep, but on the other hand, he wasn't in a condition to reconcile himself to the fact of stark reality; his soul was troubled.

"Ohh!" he signed sorrowfully, letting his head back down on the pillow.

It was if the dream had never been. Instead, something else came to life: before his eyes ran the events of the recent days: how they had abandoned their native homes, their aul, and went in search of salvation to the city, and what had happened to them on that long, difficult transition. Fate had played a cruel trick on them, forcing them to wander back and forth through the unpopulated desert, wandering to and fro and finally thrown upon this sandy ridge. Oh, Almighty! Not

---

[190] An *uran* is a *nom de guerre*.

[191] The *shchezhire* is a Kazakh genealogy or family tree.

just any time, but six decades his existence had lasted in this transitory world; would he really complete his life's path on this unknown dune?! Why was he lying down? But where could he go if he got up? Where was his refuge? In what mountains, in what steppes were they waiting for him?

He looked at the dark blue endless sky with the sparse, remote stars lighting it weakly like candles. The very same sky – high, endless, familiar to him from time immemorial; God's same stars, familiar to him. They had been the same when as a boy, Pakhraddin had run around, and they were still the same. They hadn't changed. What an expanse! Unspeakable expanse! Oh, Almighty! Under this sky, human paths and roads swarmed like ant trails, fates crossed, clashed, and flew apart to pieces. A man was broken into smithereens, in order to bring together the affairs of his fate. How many human faces had withered, how many heads had turned gray! Man is in illusion that on him alone the world depends, that eternally, he must wander through the transitory earth. What difficulties he doesn't endure to satisfy his endlessly desires? There was no end to his struggling and insatiability. How many people had become slaves to their passions and burned up in the same fire! They race hither and yon, striving to achieve their sometimes base goals. They lie, they flatter, they cringe, they ingratiate themselves. They pray for empathy but often they themselves know no pity.

Thus Pakhraddin reflected, looking at the starry dark blue sky in the silence. A rustling distracted him. He had forgotten, poor man, that he was not alone, that next to him was another living soul. He turned toward the rustling, tensing up and overcoming his trembling. Someone was coming towards him, shuffling leather *kebises.*

"Syrga, is that you?" he asked, his voice changed.

"It's me," Syrga replied weakly, barely audible.

"Where are you going, my dear?" he swallowed the hot bile rising in his throat.

"I was picking onions. I wanted you to sleep."

"My God!" tenderness overwhelmed Pakhraddin. His eyes lingered on the *baybishe*. He gazed at her for a long time. Syrga had tied a *jaulyk* under her chin. She slid the canvas *torba* from her shoulders and let it down on the ground. Silent, she moved inaudibly, like a shadow. Pakhraddin's heart contracted, everything turned over in his soul. "Oh time, time, turn back," he yearned. Was this really the same Syrga who had once become his partner?! Oh time, time, they had managed to see everything, and even what they had never imagined! Sweet Syrga, dear to his heart! Incomparable among women, Syrga!

In your youth, you were compared with the paradise flowers, they said you had come down from the skies. Whoever saw your beauty or heard your melodic laughter could not forget that blessing, that delight to the soul. To possess you meant to rip a star from the heavens. He, Pakhraddin, had torn it down, and ever since believed himself to be the only happy *jigit* on earth. Since then, they had had many wonderful years together, days radiated by the light of love and the kindness of her heart, the shining of her eyes. Kind, unforgettable Syrga! Sensitive, like a doe, Syrga! It would be better to wash out his eyes than see that canvas *torba* on your shoulders!

Pakhraddin groaned like a wounded lion, sighing in doom.

"My falcon, what's wrong?" Syrga sat down next to him.

How tenderly she looked at him, what loyalty in her moist eyes! She herself, like a shadow, was barely moving, but she pitied him, Pakhraddin. Oh, Syrga, priceless life companion! Syrga! Who gave you your husband? What force revealed him to you?

And how was your betrothed, whom you revered like God, honored? With a canvas sack which you gather onions in, like a vagrant!

"Ugh!" Pakhraddin sighed, letting out a long breath as if venting his spirit.

Syrga grew frightened.

"*Bismillah*! *Bismillah*!" she whispered, nearly crying, leaning over him. "What's wrong with you?"

"Ugh, Allah! What have I done to anger you? Ugh!" Pakhraddin moaned heavily, tearing his head from the ground. His shoulders were shaking and there was trembling throughout his whole body. Tears rolled from his eyes like hailstones. "How have I not pleased you, Allah? What evil have I done to anyone? Where is my guilt?"

"*Bismillah*! *Bismillah*!" Syrga whispered. Then breaking into tears herself, she hugged her husband.

"Quiet, my falcon, quiet!"

"Why, why don't you curse me?! I am sinful, after all, sinful! I am guilty before the people…because of me they became wanderers, I am guilty before you, before the children, I am to blame. I have ruined you, people…"

"Don't, my falcon. It is God's affair…"

Syrga's quiet voice was soothing. Pakhraddin quieted down. Syrga hugged him to herself, hugged him hard.

"Did you think something bad? Well, what if you took us away, you did it for them, you did it for the people's sake! Those who didn't come with us, it's not as if they're living so hot…"

"I don't know, ugh! If trouble surrounds us, soon they will not let us go, they say. You and I are stuck, there is no end or limit. And now we are poor vagrants…"

Both of them then, covered by the night, plunged into thoughts. They were heavy thoughts.

"People, you say…Where are they, these people? Why aren't they looking for you now, when you are here, without strength? There should have been someone to come. But there's no one."

Syrga uttered this clearly, with grief in her voice. Pakhraddin was surprised. He had never seen the quiet Syrga, sparing in words, so vulnerable. It was from a great hurt, apparently. Pakhraddin saw her like this for the same time. She had spoken truly about people. But like her, he no longer expected help from those who had left and perhaps had already reached the Amu Darya. What help could come from them? Those unfortunates themselves could only hope to reach their homeland themselves. There, God willing, soon the government would take them in and help them avoid death by starvation.

"*Baybishe*!" Pakhraddin called.

"Yes?" Syrga replied.

"Shall we get moving?"

"But…can you…?" said Syrga, not containing her joy.

4

If a person is hungry, and without strength, every extra step is a burden. By lunchtime of the following day, Khansulu felt she was close to delirium. No matter how carefully she and *Dau-apa* had rationed the bread, it was now gone. When her son, asking for bread, then broke out crying, she thought she couldn't bear it, that she would lose her mind. Then she grew used to it little by little, and became tolerant of the child's crying. And the boys, thank God, gradually grew quiet – no one had given them anything no matter how much they whined. She carried her son herself, sometimes putting him on her back, sometimes leading him by the hand. Along the way, she would feed him something at times, putting a grain of wheat in his little mouth, like a mother hen with a chick. The child, satisfied with the kernel of grain, fell asleep on her back. Her vision went dark due to hunger, and she was barely able to stumble along, she was on her last legs.

Ahead, knocking with her stick on the ground, a little hunched over, *Dau-apa* was waddling along. *Dau-apa*…a person with amazing will! Khansulu's knees were bending from exhaustion and she wanted to sit down. And she would have sat down but she didn't, because she was ashamed to do so in front of *Dau-apa*. *Dau-apa* was stern, and unsmiling. Her face was darkly closed as if scorched by fire. She walked along with the stubbornness and resolution of a warrior. She wanted to reach their destination, so she was walking along. That was why Khansulu didn't dare utter a word that she was tired. And why? Because *Dau-apa* would up and reproach her – you're young, she would say, and you're more sour than an old woman, well, now, get a move on! No one had ever raised their voice with Khansulu, so Khansulu kept going, reinforced by her own vanity – she didn't want to look weaker than a 70-year-old woman. And on the other hand, as soon as she thought about the little boy stuck to her back, she understood that she simply had to keep going. She had not right to do otherwise. And Shege, in a letter which her father-in-law had brought to her, ordered: "Don't think about me. Take care of our son."

From time to time, *Dau-apa* would ask her:

"Are you tired, child?"

But Khansulu didn't have the strength to reply. She would remain silent. *Dau-apa* wouldn't wait for an answer:
"Be patient, dear," she would say. "Soon we will take a rest! Soon!"
She would cheer Khansulu.

Toward afternoon, they reached a long, wide hollow, totally overgrown with tamarisk, toronjil and willow, and here they stopped. *Dau-apa* placed the *khordzhun* on the edge of the cliff. Khansulu lowered the sleeping child to the ground. The poor little boy was speechless. Apparently, he was exhausted. They spread out blankets and put the children down on them. On a kerchief before them was some grain. It was all there was. *Dau-apa* and Khansulu also chewed on the kernels. Oh, how aromatic fried grain was! The little kernels melted in their mouths like honey. The starving children picked up everything, grabbing everything they could from the kerchief.

The children were still hungry and their little eyes burned, poor things. But *Dau-apa* announced: "That's enough! You're finished!"

And she folded up the kerchief, as if it had never been. The children licked their lips and sighed tiredly, exchanging glances. Khansulu didn't have the strength to bear their hungry, begging eyes – she turned away, shedding tears.

The desert looked scorching. The sky was pure and clear. The sun was unsparingly hot, pouring its bounty on the hills, valleys and hollows. The earth was all in grasses and flowers and the horizon stretched ahead in a shimmering haze.

An unusual heaviness fell upon Khansulu, and she lay down, placing the *korzhun* under her head. She immediately plunged into sleep, unable to think of anything, but only able to sigh sorrowfully.

"Ohh!"

5

Pakhraddin and Syrga did not get very far after several hours. The sky was covered with clouds, the road under their feet could be guessed only with difficulty. Toward midnight, they ran into a dried lake bed and the path disappeared as if it had never existed. They had lost their way, obviously. They didn't stop, but continued their way in the same direction they had come. When the dawn broke, ahead they saw a miniature meadow, thickly overgrown with bushes with small, narrow leaves that ended in spirals. Spreading out their blankets, they rested on the grass, and when the sun rose over the lands to the length of a horse hobble, they threw the *korzhuns* over their shoulders and moved on.

Toward noon, they wandered into a low dune with caragana and agave. Pakhraddin spotted a stand of wild onion under the bushes. Exhausted, they stopped to rest.

"What, my falcon?" Syrga asked, totally out of strength.

Pakhraddin looked at the far-off horizon, wrapped in haze.

"Oh," signed Syrga, collapsing on the fine sand.

"Hmm, Creator," Pakhraddin stroked his mustache. "According to my calculations, we should have passed Esek-olgen and should be next to the Jideli ravine. But where is the gorge? There shouldn't be such a dune in those places. How can this be? *Astafiralla*!

Syrga didn't have the strength to respond, and leaned her head against the *korzhun* and closed her eyes. Pakhraddin, not believing his eyes, climbed up on the hill and looked all around the area, which was plunged in a mirage. How frustrating! In vain had they travelled at night. During the day, would Pakhraddin ever have gone off the path? Even going along the trackless areas, he shouldn't have so sharply diverged off course. Or had he predicted that he would blunder so? Perhaps when they had dozed before dawn, in confusion, he had set off in the wrong direction? Pakhraddin couldn't understand anything. What would he tell Syrga? With what expression should he look at her when he had to reveal that they were lost? That's all they needed…

6

Khansulu had already begun to lose faith in their ever finding a human settlement. The road never ended; it had exhausted her soul.

"Child, are you coming?" asked *Dau-apa*. She was, as always, walking ahead. The sun was moving across the western half of the sky, everywhere there were palisades of willow trees, tamarisk and chia. The trail wound through them and ran ahead.

"Child, do you see, eh? We seem to be not far from people."

Khansulu raised her head and caught her breath. Ahead, along the right side of the road, far, far away, stood a house, its walls half collapsed. And to the side of it, the walls had caved in.

"Listen!" cried *Dau-apa.*

Khansulu listened. Somewhere far, far away, a donkey was braying. This cry seemed like a miraculous melody to her.

When the sun inclined toward the horizon, the city emerged – the distance to it was the flight of a flock of birds. There was smoke streaming from numerous pipes. This was Konyrat. They looked upon it from a high hill, surrounded by tamarisk. To Khansulu, weak from hunger and travel, Konyrat, stretched out in the distance, seemed unimaginably huge. She couldn't take it in with one look. One large building next to another, how many of them there were! Her eyes swam from the unusual collection of rooves. For Khansulu, who was seeing a city for the first time, Konyrat seemed a foreign, unknown world to her.

"It's great there's a city, but no one is waiting for us with outstretched arms there," said *Dau-apa,* and for some reason began to rock Yedige, who was sleeping on her back, to and fro.

That's for sure," thought Khansulu. *If only someone was waiting for us…I knew it…But then why did we struggle to get to a foreign city, then?*

"It's a foreign city…We will not wander around there at time… I heard there were a lot of thieves nowadays, and just as hungry as we are…Over there…" *Dau-apa* nodded her head somewhere to the west. "There's Mazar, do you see? Daut-*ata* is buried there. There's a place to spend the night. Let's go there."

The cemetery was on one of the nearby promontories of Ustyurt. The square structures with stone ovals at the corners was swimming in the crimson rays of the setting sun.

"Child, I don't know whether you had heard, but the crypt to which we are going also belongs to our famous ancestor, the holy *batyr* Daut," *Dau-apa* said along the way. "First there was Barak. Barak begot Asau; Asau begot Daut. Do you see? The people say: the spirit of the *batyr* Barak settled in his son Asau, and then in his grandson Daut. So we will pray to the spirits of our ancestors. Perhaps they will help…

Dau-apa's voice, interrupted by a spasm, began to shake.

Khansulu liked *Dau-apa's* proposal. If there were spirits prepared to listen to her, she would tell them everything, a great deal of grief had accumulated in her heart…

The crypt was on a low, sloping ridge. They approached the crypt as the twilight gathered. There were numerous square tombs with four loops at the corners, fenced in by large boulders, with various patterns and inscriptions. A dark silence reigned at the cemetery, penetrating to your soul and frightening you; it was invisibly hovering in the darkness.

On the western slope of the hill there was a wattle and daub mud hut with a sod covering instead of a roof. *Dau-apa* had been right, the home was empty and they could spend the night in it. The door was propped open with a shovel. It was likely a home for parishioners, for the pious who came to worship the spirits of their ancestors.

They set the children down on the ground, sighing as they relieved themselves of the burden. The children looked around the unfamiliar place. *Dau-apa* grew noticeably more animated.

"Look, children," she said. "We're home!"

She picked up the shovel propping open the door but suddenly something fluttered along the roof, right above the door jamb. It was a bird, flapping its wing, which dove into the shadows and disappeared.

"Foo! Foo! God's creature! Spit, my dears, if you were frightened, out of sight out of mind."
The door swung open with a creak and whine, a yawning black space opened up before her; and Dau-apa did not dare to step in.

"Eh, I guess I'm to be the victim!" she exclaimed. "Sacred birds abide in these places, they say. I suppose that's what they are. *Bismillah*! she cried, and stepped across the threshold.

Dau-apa was a bold woman, after all! Khansulu stood to the side, holding on tight to the children's hands, fear and hope battling in her soul. The win gradually picked up, clouds began to veil the sky, and it seemed as if it might rain...

Dau-apa lit the building for a moment with a spark from a flint and exclaimed joyfully:

"Oh, thank God, it's here, it's here! We'll live! Khansulu! Come here, child, come here!"

Khansulu's heart began pounding. *Dau-apa's* voice sounded as if she had found a *dastarkhan* full of food. Khansulu hurried toward her call, dragging the children behind her. But besides *Dau-apa,* who had lit the kerosene lamp at the doorway, she couldn't see anything that would gladden her eye in the half-dark home. Khansulu looked for the *dastarkhan,* and some bread.

"Did you see the lamp?" *Dau-apa* rejoiced meanwhile, nodding to the kerosene lamp.

On the floor was an old reed mat with *two tekemets* [192], and closer to the door, a *kazan* and *kumgan.*

"*Bismillah!*" *Dau-apa* and raised the lid of the *kazan.* She peered inside. "Eh, there's water in there, child!" she rejoiced.

But Khansulu was expecting something different. Was there bread in that house? That's what she wanted to know. She was looking for bread – and only bread. The only miraculous word she wanted to hear was "*Nan*"[193].

Dau-apa understood what Khansulu wanted, her eyes wandering over the room and the children who didn't take their hungry eyes off her. Near a house, people's hunger would become even more acute, even more unbearable. The old woman understood that and therefore was searching through all the corners – at any rate, her enormous shadow was trailing along with her from wall to wall.

The children began to lose patience.
"What are you looking for, *azhe? Nan?*" asked Yedyge.
"Patience, patience, children!" *Dau-apa* replied. "We'll set the fire now...Oh-ho! We'll boil some tea, oh-ho! We'll drink some hot tea!"
With a cheerful voice, *Dau-apa* encouraged her family and instilled hope in them. After looking around, she emerged with the *kumgan* in her hand and headed toward the hearth in the courtyard. She had a small bundle with friend grain with her. She had never told them how much was left there. *Dau-apa* was scrupulous, but by Khansulu's calculations, the grain should have run out today. What would they drink tea with? It was a mystery. Still, *Dau-apa*'s expression

---

[192] A *tekemet* is a *koshma* or felt mat with applique.
[193] *Nan* is a type of flat bread.

nevertheless instilled hope. She was conjuring something up at the hearth, as if there would definitely be something edible for dinner.

The black *kumgan* began hissing on the fire.

"It's boiling!" Khansulu said, going up to the old woman.

"It's boiling!" *Dau-apa* confirmed. "Take it into the house, child!"

Khansulu picked up the *kumgan* with a rag and carried it away. But it wasn't the black *kumgan* that Khansulu needed. What had *Dau-apa* gathered to regale the hungry children? That's what she wanted to know. Carrying away the steaming, smoked *kumgan*, she turned all the way around, looking for something. In the darkness, near the heath fire, *Dau-apa* was stirring about and turning something over.

"*Nan!*"

"*Nan!*" the children started squealing, seeing Khansulu with the *kumgan*.

"Patience! Patience" *Dau-apa* interrupted them with a harsh tone.

Khansulu glanced at the hearth. If *Dau-apa* didn't work some sort of miracle now, those urchins would tear her to bits and eat her guts. In order to occupy them somehow, she got out a *piyala*, put it on the *dastarkhan*, got out another, and a third. She threw a pinch of salt into the *kumgan*. From outside, blows could be heard:

Thud...thud.

Entranced, the children looked at the door. Besides the *piyalas*, there was nothing to put on the *dastarkhan*. Khansulu was upset, and unable to bear looking at the hungry children, turned away from them. A gust of wind swept the dust up in front of the very threshold. And next *Dau-apa* appeared with a soiled *jaulyk* bristling on her head and a bundle in her hand. Not the one they had grown used to, another one.

"Oh, Allah!" Khansulu said to herself, and she closed her eyes in exhaustion, the earth seeming to rock under her feet. The children stretched their necks and stared with big eyes at the bundle – they were about to fly at it.

The Lonely Yurt • Smagul Yelubay

"*Bismallah*! Well, here," said *Dau-apa*, sitting down at the edge of the *dastarkhan*, and unfolding the old kerchief. It was *kurt*,[194] white as could be, broken up into pieces.

"Put it on your tongue, suck it, there is no better food. Just don't hurry," she said.

Everyone got a piece the size of a finger nail. The children hurled themselves at the *kurt*. They didn't forget to drink it down with some "tea," nearly choking.

"What did I tell you! Don't hurry! Suck it and take a sip!"

The boiled water flavored with salt gave a special taste to the piece of hard *kurt* slowly melting on their tongues. Oh, what was this drink of hot tea, seasoned with a pinch of salt, the kurt sweetly melting on their tongues; the refreshing taste dissolved in their throats, gradually nourishing the entire body, reaching to the depths of the sinews and cells of the organism. Their foreheads moistened and broke out in sweat. Their eyes cleared somewhat and their heads began to brighten. Khansulu felt as if she had never eaten such tasty *kurt* in her life. It was as if thick, steaming milk was poured down her throat, as if she was eating the food of paradise.

After eating the food, they felt an irresistible fatigue: their eyes closed, their hands and legs grew heavy, and their overworked joints ached. The earth drew them downwards. Khansulu, hugging her little boy who was sucking his thumb, fell down on the reed mat where she was sitting. Her eyes closed on their own. As if crushed by lead, she slowly plunged into a dark state, where there was no strength to be aware of anything anymore, let alone think about where to go, where they were, where they should point their feet tomorrow...*Dau-apa* got up and closed the door.

7

Khansulu opened her eyes and saw that she was lying in an old, abandoned hut with the walls and ceiling smoked through. It was cold in the house from the morning dew. Skinny Tugelkhan had scrunched up in his sleep, the clothing on him was an unthinkable color, it was that dirty. Yedyge, also filthy, snuggled closed to him. It

---

[194]*Kurt* is dried cheese.

was painful to look at the little boys; they were so unkempt. *Dau-apa* was gone.

Khansulu went out and *Dau-apa* was on her knees before the grave of Daut-*batyr*, reading a surah from the Koran. Khansulu sat down next to her. Both of them, gazing to the east, toward the coming morning, performed the ritual of worship to the spirits of their ancestors. Wiping their hands over their faces, they stood up.

They looked at Konyrat which from here, from the hill could be seen like the palm of their hand. The city was still sleeping, but everywhere the roosters were vying to crow. The space before their eyes was filled with countless, crowded adobe buildings, with mulberry trees growing between them like green islands. Between the city and the hill there was a small plain, criss-crossed with numerous paths. The *takyrs* lay like white bald spots.

"Well, daughter, let us embrace the one God within. Let's move!" said *Dau-apa*, not tearing her eyes from the pre-dawn city. "While we get moving, the dawn will come and the sun will rise…"

Hoisting the half-asleep children on their backs, and picking up their bundles, the women moved out through the morning dawn toward the city. While they made their way toward it, the sun floated out from behind the horizon, generous and full of rays. Here and there people appeared on the streets, pedestrians were moving along, the city began its bustling life. The dogs barked, the cows mooed and the asses brayed. An emaciated old man in a *papakha* was hauling hay in a creaking wagon; the ass hitched to the wagon was as dead as his master. Noisy young women in the Karakalpak-style *oripek*[195] kerchiefs were going outside the city, *ketmens* on their shoulders. Likely it was a brigade going to work.

"Well, children, we are in Konyrat!" *Dau-apa* exclaimed. "Let's go to the bazaar. Well, let's move our little legs ourselves!" she cried, encouraging the children and putting Yedyge down on the ground. Khansulu put down Tutelkhan to walk as well. The children,

---

[195] The Karakalpak women's *oripek* was a high helmet-like headdress with hanging fabric decorated by beads.

goggling at the wildness of the city were entranced by its look, and gradually began to walk on their own. The earth was damp from the rain that had fallen last night and gave off the warm scent of soil.

They went into a narrow street, with long, adobe *duvals*[196] crowding its sides. It was as if Khansulu had landed in some fairy-tale world. All of the homes hid behind the adobe walls. Smoke rose over the hearths. *"So this is what a city is like!"* she thought, looking around fearfully. *Dau-apa* had been at the bazaar in Konyrat before, but only one time, and was a long time ago. Khansulu's head spun. If *Dau-apa* had not been there, she would have gotten lost in this pandemonium! So many people! Those women in the *oripeks* must be Karakalpaks, and these other women covered with a *chapan* so that not even their faces were visible must be Uzbek women.

Thus they walked along, noticing everything all around them, when suddenly the long-awaited scent of baked bread struck their noses. Oh, Creator! The smell of hot bread, just out of the oven filling their nostrils!

"*Nan*?!"

"*Apa, nan?*" the little children shouted over each other. Smoke came out from under the *duval* across the street. The boys went mad. They hurried to the wall like sheep who had starved during the winter and not were rushing to the hay. *Dau-apa* didn't manage to stop the boys, she lagged behind. Yedyge reached the gates first, and peeped through a crack. Khansulu peeped inside as well. They weren't mistaken. A young Karakalpak woman in an *oripek* was taking a reddish *lepyoshka* out of the round *tandyr*[197] oven, and placing it on a wooden plate.
"*Nan*!"
"*Apa, nan*!" the children squealed again.

Dau-apa reached the gate.

---

[196] A Central Asian fence made of mud and clay.
[197] The *tandyr* is a type of round oven on the ground in Central Asia and the Caucasus. Flatbreads are cooked by slapping dough on the sides of the oven.

"Step back!" she ordered, and banged on the gate with her fist. "Do they bake bread here, or what?'

"Here, here," said Khansulu.

"Over there," Yedyge indicated, sticking his finger in the hole.

The gate opened. A tall, dark Karakalpak woman, halfway sticking out of the door, looked them over cautiously.

"Daughter, I see you are a Muslim woman, with respect...Sell us some bread!" said *Dau-apa,* and thrust into her hand a soiled, crumpled banknote.

Confused by the unexpected request, she looked back and forth at the money and the children, blinking her eyes.

"For God's sake, daughter! Sell us some bread!" *Dau-apa* begged.

"*Yakhshy!*" the woman said in her own language, which mean "Alright!". She took the towel from the plate and handed them the *lepyoshka.*

"Well, children, let's go! We'll go off to the side," *Dau-apa* announced. The children hurled themselves after her as fast as they good. All four of them settled down by the *duval. Dau-apa* divided the *lepyoshka* in two, and then in four parts.

"Me!"

"Me!" cried the little boys. They could have cared less about the people passing by.

Cheeks full, they munched the still-hot, fragrant bread.

Khansulu didn't think at that moment that the taste of the hot bread which she ate by a stranger's fence would be something she would remember forever. She had never tasted anything tastier, it seemed. The soft, pliant bread melted in her mouth. Khansulu was surprised that she had not learned a single great truth for herself before: if such a red *lepyoshka* is on your *dastarkhan*, all the vicissitudes of fate don't mean anything. Oh, Creator, why had she not understood this before!

The children, of course, were not sated by the little pieces they had received and licking their lips, whined for more. Khansulu and *Dau-apa,* exchanging glances, gave them what they themselves had not finished eating.

"Come now, children, let's move on!" *Dau-apa* said with a sigh.

Shaking the dust from their things, the women hoisted the children on their backs and went further along the same street. They asked people they met where the bazaar was. The street was narrow and winding. There were lots of people; most of them rode on asses. They all had to get to the bazaar – some were driving sheep, some driving goats. The closer they got to town, the more there were all sorts of smells…

They began to see the steppe Kazakhs, as emaciated as they were; some weakened adults were sitting on the ground, their backs against the duvals, and their children begged from passers-by. They also saw some people lying on the ground, not breathing. *Dau-apa* whispered something reverently.

They merged into the large crowd and reached the bazaar. All around was noise and tumult, conversations, gossip, somebody selling something and somebody buying something. The women held the little boys' hands tightly and headed into the very thick of the crowd. The different voices crying all around them were deafening:

"Have to *tushpara!* Hot *tushpara!* Take it!
"Aryan! Who wants *ayran*! Come here!
"Have some *samsa*[198]! Hot *samsa*!
"Corn bread! Corn bread! Come get it!

Yedyge and Tugelkhan stopped near the woman who was selling *samsa,* and wouldn't budge.

"*Azha, nan!*" they clamored.
"Well, here's the thing, my dears," *Dau-apa* then announced. "I don't have any more money. Understand? It's gone. If only…."

---

[198] *Samsa* is a triangular meat pie

Khansulu understood what *Dau-apa* was hinting – how was the time to put out any money she had, but Khansulu didn't have anything except her gold earrings in her ears and a massive silver bracelet on her arm. She took the old woman to the side, took off her earrings and placed them in her palm.

"Sell these, *apa*! We'll buy bread and something else."

"You don't have any money?" *Dau-apa* looked worriedly at the earrings in her great palm. "Well, let's go! Let's see what the price is first."

And they headed off to the goods stalls.

"We're lucky it's bazaar day," said *Dau-apa*. "Look around, maybe we'll see someone we know.

The Kazakhs in camel *chekmens* and lambskin hats, trading firewood, were unfamiliar to them. Their camels lay nearby. *Dau-apa* asked a red-eyed, yellow-face fat Kazakh about this and that. Holding his *nasybay*[199] under his tongue, he whispered, muffling his words:

"*Oybay*, my ancestors! What aul did you say you were from? *Oybay*, the *bashmachi* attacked you in the desert? Oh, that's why you're starving, you say… Oh, God forbid! You, mother, go to the coast, to Ashylbekov there, from Kazakhstan.. That's what you should do, mother!"

"And how should I get there, to the coast?"

"*Oybay*, my ancestors, over there, there! Go straight ahead, straight…"

Suddenly somebody's wail rang out:

"*Milisa*! *Milisa*! Oh, no!"
"*Milisa*! *Milisa*!"

The whole bazaar then broken out in many voices with the word "*milisa*" – police.

Khansulu, staring at the lisping Kazakh, didn't notice how Yedyge slipped away – the sneaky fellow had just been standing next

---

[199] A type of Central Asian chewing tobacco.

to them. In the crowd from where the wails had come, a woman who sold *samsa* was hold the little boy by the hand.

Dau-apa cried:
"*Oybay-ay*! That's mine! Daughter, did you lose him?"

With these words, she hurled herself into the crowd. Khansulu hurried after her. The merchant woman was holding tight to Yedyge. A crowd was gathering.

"He should be turned in!"
"Send the hooligan to the police" people said in the local jargon.
"So many thieves nowadays!" a fat merchant yelled, his mustache protruding, waving his arms.

Yedyge was squealing like a rabbit.

The tall *Dau-apa*, pushing aside everyone hung over the merchant woman ominously.

"Go to hell, bitch, let the boy go!"

The fat-bellied merchant with the mustache sticking out in different directions blocked her path, crying:

"No! No! You can't! To the *milisa,* with the likes of you, the *milisa*!"
"Damn you, get out of the way!"
"No! You can't! *Milisa*!" the fat-bellied man continued to yelp and pushed the old woman in the stomach with all his might. That was enough for *Dau-apa* to slam him over his red, stuck-out ear with her huge fist.

"Take that, with your *milisa*!"

The fat man felt to the ground, hunched over. The *chalma* flew from his head. Everyone watching was rolling with laughter. The merchant woman, frightened by the furious old woman, let Yedyge go. Sobbing at the top of his lungs, he hid himself in his grandmother's wide embrace.

"Don't cry, my little one, don't cry!" she soothed him, pressing him to her chest. "Don't cry, you'll have enough to cry about in time!"

The fat merchant who had been toppled to the ground picked himself up. He shook out his *chalma*.

"Hey, she kills like that, eh?" he uttered, red from shame.

"Hey, where's the *milisa*?" the female merchant took up after him.

"Here's the *milisa*! I'm the *milisa*," someone's voice could be heard and a fair-faced man in a black leather cap of average height stepped out of the crowd. He wrote a black leather raincoat. Seeing the strong man coming toward her, the woman merchant grew flustered.

"How many patties of yours did he eat?" he asked, and reached into his pocket.

"Well, he ate a small one. It was a very…tiny one," she stuttered in fright.

"Here's some money. And give me eight more."

After she got the cash, the woman bustled about trying to please this important government official. He was accompanied by two Red Army men who had just come up. The man put all the rest of the *samsa* into a newspaper funnel and gave it to the little boy, who was resting in his grandmother's arms, still whimpering.

The bazaar crowd were stunned. *Dau-apa* and Khansulu were no less surprised.

"Come with me, *apa*!" the man in the leather cap and raincoat called and started away from the bazaar himself first.

The two Red Army men took the bundles from *Dau-apa* and Khansulu.

"Where are you from, *apa*?" asked the fair-faced man with brown eyes in the raincoat.

264   *The Lonely Yurt* • Smagul Yelubay

"Eh, sonny, it's hard to say where we are from," she began. "We ran away from the *kallektep*. Then the *bashmachi* raided us. And now we are vagrants, sonny, wandering about..."

"That's what we thought, *apa*. These *jigits* will take you now to the coast. There's food and firewood there. Do you object?"

"What are you saying, my dove, why would we object? If there is food, if there is a home, why object?"

There were two carriages standing on the street. The women and children were seated in one, and the very young Red Army man climbed up on the coach box; his mustache was just barely starting to come in. Once they were in the carriage, the women no worse than the boys jumped on the package of food. Only when the package was empty did *Dau-apa* asked the Red Army soldier:

"Sonny, what's that gentleman's name?"
The Red Army soldier laughed.

"Mother, that 'gentleman' is Abdolla Asylbekov. Secretary of the Kazakh Central Executive Committee. He's from Almaty."

The carriage had already reached the salt marsh on the north edge of town.
"Whoever he is," *Dau-apa* concluded, "he was won me over, he is a kind man, heartfelt..."
The *jigit* explained:
"Recently, during the excesses, many people fled the Kazakh territory, like you. And today they continue to flee from hunger. We have come here specially to gather up and return the refugees to their motherland."

"Ehh, that's right, sonny," said *Dau-apa,* nodding her head.

Khansulu was already peacefully looking at the world flooded with sunshine: the tamarisk groves, the expanse of manicured fields, the adobe huts amidst the mulberry trees. And just now at the bazaar, when Yedyge got in trouble, she was in another state: it was as if the world had perished forever, and with withered souls, they had ended up in a *zindan* from which they could never escape, as if they were no longer human. And suddenly a miraculous force picked them up and tore them from the abyss in which they had fallen…dragging them out to broad daylight, to the sun.

From the habit of old people, *Dau-apa* began to inquire of the coachman about the people on the coast, naming some names, asking him if he had met this one or that one, but the Red Army soldier only nodded his head.

Ahead was a grey expanse of water, pouring from the horizon.

"Is that the sacred Amu Darya?" asked *Dau-apa*, looking ahead. Both she and Khansulu were seeing the river for the first time.

"What's that?" the children grew agitated, sticking their heads over the side of the carriage.

Khansulu explained.

"It's the river." And then she herself was surprised. "Why is it so grey?
"It doesn't fit into its own banks, the clay is washed away, that's why it's cloudy," *Dau-apa* suggested.

Leading away in a broad channel to the very horizon, the powerful river amazed them with its severe look. The cloudy, foamy waves rolled one after another, they were squeezed out on to the clay banks; it seemed as if they were sighing for this reason, like living beings. The size of the watery expanse was terrifying, and even just gazing on the river was frightening, somehow.

"*Apa*," Khansulu said, shivering. "There, at the bazaar, when you clashed with the merchant, I saw a certain person in the crowd."
Dau-apa peered into her eyes.
"I saw Labak-*akhun,* with his staff in his hand, well, looking just like a dervish."
"Oh, child, don't be surprised. If a raven is now a falcon, then the *akhun* is a dervish…Why be surprised?" *Dau-apa* sighed. The wrinkles on her face grew deeper. "You speak of him. But I saw something horrible. At the bazaar, oh Lord, parents, a father and

mother, were selling their young daughter. Steppe Kazakhs, eh, just as we are..."

Dau-apa fell silent. And Khansulu kept quiet, as if she had swallowed her tongue.

A colorful settlement could be seen on the coast, one camp after another, with campfires smoking. Women in white *jaulyks* flashed, and barefoot children were racing about. Their carriage stopped at a plateau on the coast, in a dense thicket of willow and toadflax. Three tattered yurts stood here, to be sure, made of a dozen canvas tents. There were tea kettles and pails on the fire, people were preparing food – it was lunch time; the women were cutting and crushing something and the men were chopping firewood.

Their children surrounded them first. Then, leaving their work, the women hurried up, showing them with exclamations.

"*Oybay*, it's *Dau-apa*!"
"How did you get here?"

Dau-apa, getting down from the carriage, inquired:
"And you yourselves, are you alive and well?"

Gradually the men came up, they didn't dare look them in the eye, and looked away in embarrassment. The women went on chirping heedlessly.

"*Oybay*, and where is the *biy aga*?" one of them suddenly recalled. The *biy* was Pakhraddin.
"Was Balkiya found?"
"Eh, my dear ones, why do you ask?" *Dau-apa* sighed heavily, straightening her sash and drawing herself up to her full height. She frowned. "I have lived to 70, and it seems there is a lot I have not seen in the wide world! Eh? That bitch Balkiya...Pakhraddin went to look for her, then fell ill... He remained there, on the road. Whether he is alive or dead, I don't know. Syrga was with him. So with these two" – she pointed to the children – "we dragged ourselves here like dogs. God came to our help, and brought us to government people..."

Then, under the open sky, they lay out their rugs, *syrmaks*[200] and *koshmas*. *Dau-apa* and Khansulu were seated at the head of the *dastarkhan* as the guests of honor. The old men arranged themselves around them in a circle. Efficient women busied themselves with the *dastarkhan*. Kulzipa sprinkled some fried wheat grain on it. Katira nimbly chopped up the sugar.

Khansulu realized that among the people who had settled on the banks of the river, there were particular people whom she did not know. They were not at the *dastarkhan*. They had pitched their tents separately, built their hearths and led their own individual life. Along the way her, as Khansulu learned, Katira's old mother died of hunger, and four of her children, among them, three sons of the poor man Maylybay...

The aul-dwellers who had been here longer had already picked up strength. And their conversations were different and their voices louder. They talked about a ship – they called it a steamship – that would be coming soon. They had expected it today. Representatives from Kazakhstan on this steamship would take them to the station, so that they could then reach the city of Auliye-Ata. In Auliye-Ata, they would be taken to the surrounding kholkhozes. That was the news.

"Eh, just so we don't starve, let them take us there," the old people nodded in satisfaction.

After lunch, tired, *Dau-apa* lay down to rest. Khansulu went with the boys to the river. The bank was a cliff, the height of a person. The water below beat noisily against the rocks. The current was rapid; it was terrible to look at it, you got dizzy. The water swirled, and in some places whirled into funnels. The wood chips that the boys threw down twirled and twirled in place until they finally dove into the abyss. Khansulu was surprised, where had so much water come from? Far, far away, somewhere on the opposite shore, there was a boat, and the silhouette of two people in it. Looking at the boat and the couple, Khansulu broke into tears. She remembered her father and mother. What had happened to them? Were they alive? And perhaps they had

---

[200] A *syrmak* is a patterned Kazakh rug made of pieces of felt of contrasting colors, with a mosaic inlaid over the surface.

long ago become prey for ravens under some bush?! Oh, God preserve them, save them! Oh, God, what had happened to them?

Ohh, life, how cruel you are! You were sated, you had stuffed your throat, and you were happy…You forgot about everything at the *dastarkhan*, about the entire world, you had only thoughts of food. All that time you didn't once think about your unfortunate parents, left half-way on their journey. And only now, satiated, did you remember them. Oh, cruel life! Was your reason not clouded when you left them? You set off somewhere, leaving your father and mother in the unknown? How would she go to this Auliye-Ata without finding out what happened to them?!

"*Apa,* what should we do?" Khansulu asked, losing patience.

"Calm, child, calm." *Dau-apa* frowned, thinking her own thoughts. She looked at the sun. It was inclining toward the horizon. It seemed that the courageous, willful old woman, who had suffered everything in life, intended to find for Khansulu a way out of this situation.

The children, playing on the bank, suddenly shouted together:

"Steamship! Steamship!"

"*Alakay,*[201] steamship!

As if in reply to the children's joyful exclamations, from far away, the steamship gave a long toot of its horn. The delighted boys shouted all the harder.

The ship was rising from a lower current of the river, growing in size, wrapped in black clouds of smoke. It was not known whether *Dau-apa* had ever seen a steamship, but Khansulu was encountering one for the first time, and she didn't tear her eyes of it. The ship sailed against the current. Khansulu felt that if she were to leave, then she would never, ever see her parents or Shege again. It would be as if it carried her away to the very edge of the earth. Weren't Auiye-Ata and the edge of the earth the same thing?

"*Apa,* I won't go anywhere!" she announced.

"*Oybay*, child, I was just thinking the same thing!" said *Dau-apa.*

---

[201] *Alakay* is a Kazakh child's exclamation of amazement, delight.

8

The boarding began in the twilight. The real name of the ship was a barge, and it quietly rocked on the waves. The barge was so large that one aul after another could load on to it, even with their livestock, and there would still be space left.

First, Asylbek's Red Army soldiers went on it and checked everything. Evening set in during that time. People stood ready on the shore with their *tyuks* and bundles, awaiting the order. *Dau-apa* and Khansulu had also packed up, supposedly to go on the road. In fact, they were waiting for a convenient moment to go away in the thick bushes in the confusion. Finally, the moment came. Shouting over the noise of the people, the order thundered out:

"Begin boarding!"

Oh, what came next! People rushed headlong toward the gangplank, pushing one another aside, nobody let anyone else pass by. The Red Army soldier shouted something, but who would listen to him in such a crush? Another three soldiers came to his aid, in order to block people's way, but the crowd pushed on like a mindless herd.

"Order, keep order!" the soldiers' cried, barely audible among the splash of the waves and the roar of the crowd. As it turned out, the reason for the disorder was a rumor that those who did not find a place on this boat would be left on shore until the next boat. But the next barge would take people to cold territories. Who wanted to go in the cold? Therefore, despite the crush, people poured on board like lava.

"Child, there won't be a more convenient moment!" *Dau-apa* said in a low voice.

Both of them, moving backward, began to withdraw until in a flash they were in the thick bushes. They had hidden their white *jaulyks* in the *korzhun* even before the boarding, so as not to attract attention. The children were on their backs, holding the bundles. Directly through the rushes and flax they moved toward the crimson sun setting in the west. Out of fear, they imagined they were being pursued, so they weaved their way through the trackless thick bushes. They were silent. Yedyge began whining, "*Azhe*, but why aren't we going on the steamship?" but *Dau-apa* barked, "Shut up!" at him and gave him a sharp slap on his behind.

It was difficult fleeing with children, and bundles, and the women broke out in a sweat. *Dau-apa* was already breathing with a rasp, but they stopped only when they felt they had come out to a safe distance.

"Oh!" signed *Dau-apa*.

The flax, as high as a person, concealed them. Breathing heavily, wiping away the sweat, they looked around, but what could they see through the thick undergrowth? From the side of the shore from which they had run an incomprehensible roar carried; there was a hubbub and the muffled cries of people boarding the barge. Far, far away, rushed a wisp of scarlet.

"What do you know!" cried *Dau-apa* in alarm, looking at the lower current of the river from which clouds were crawling along dismally. "If it would only rain, dammit!"

As if in reply, the northern wind began to roar and a wave ran over the tips of the flax. Khansulu was still unable to catch her breath. Her heart burst out of her chest, knocking hard, and bitter sweat poured into her eyes. She kept wiping and wiping her face. She stroked Tugelkhan's head. He was funny, standing ahead of her, his little legs planted wide. The little boy had no cares when his mother was nearby. If only Shege were to know that now Khansulu and Tugelkhan were in the bushes, unfortunates, holed up like tramps. But Shege didn't know this. He didn't know that his wife and son were being carried away like a tumble-weed through life... Shege! Where are you? Far away, most likely. He would rush here if he could. It would be good if they were fated to meet again some time. But if they were not fated? If this separation would remain a separation – she at one end of the world and he at another? This horrible thought flew through her head like lighting. It raced through as if warning her of the danger of the transitory world, as if whispering of the troubles of harsh reality.

Now Khansulu and *Dau-apa* faced one task: to reach Konyrat, and find there a Karakalpak man named Shamurat, an old friend of Pakhraddin's.

The twilight thickened to total darkness. They could barely make out the earth under their feet, and the wind pushed at their backs. Beyond the horizon, a storm was already angrily thundering. It looked like it would rain. And suddenly, with a deafening thunder, the sky opened. Oh, how frightened they were!

"*Bismallah*!"
"*Bismallah*!"
"It's too bad we haven't reached the city and it's already starting to rain," Khansulu muttered, bending even more under the weight of the sack.

"Well, what can we do? It's a spring rain."

Rushes appeared in the salt marsh where they were walking, rustling and pushing against their legs, preventing them from walking.

"Child, your eyes are young, look ahead, what's that dark ahead?" asked *Dau-apa,* peering at the horizon.

The rain began to fall. Khansulu let down the sack and sat down and peered at where *Dau-apa* was pointing.

"It's a big tree and something next to it, perhaps a wall that has caved in, or something…"

"Even so," *Dau-apa* replied joyfully. "We can find cover under the tree. Or else the children will catch cold."

They headed toward the tree. *Dau-apa,* in order to make the walk go faster, began to talk about herself, about her poor life, when there were so many rainy nights, storms, with snow even, and many other torments… What hadn't she had to see in this life…

"Many times I have had to spend the night alone in the deserted steppe!" she said.
While *Dau-apa* was talking, it grew darker and they reached the gloomy shelter of the tree in total darkness.

It turned out to be a mulberry tree. Next to it was the wall of an adobe hut that had caved in. No sooner had they reached the tree, then the rain let go with all its might. The women covered themselves with blankets, wrapped the children in down vests and hugged them to themselves. Thunder shook the area around them a few more times, then quieted down. Then what a downpour was unleashed on them! Everything was in motion; the leaves of the mulberry tree rustled and whispered; bubbles danced in rain puddles. The wind brought a surprising aroma of freshness. They sat in silence for a time, minding the voices of the powerful elements. The downpour did not let up. The children began to whine, asking for something to eat. They ate supper under the blankets, chewing pieces of tasty wheat bread. Once full, the children began to doze off. No matter how thick the crown of the mulberry tree, raindrops sapping against the wet blankets began to bother them. The blankets were heavy and damp. Khansulu drew her little boy even closer to her.

"How are you there," asked *Dau-apa*?

She lay with her back to Khansulu. Yedyge, safely protected by her big body, didn't likely feel the bad weather.

"It's dripping," Khansulu replied.

"Be patient, my dear, what can we do? Let it get a little lighter. By then it may clear up. Try to fall asleep."

Helpless with exhaustion, Khansulu did not notice how she fell asleep. She awoke from the icy water falling down her collar. She jumped up, shaking the sodden blanket. Her hem, right shoulder and right shoulder blade had soaked through. The rain had quieted down. Wrapping her son more tightly, she once again lay down, what was to be done... Now she couldn't sleep. The damp seeping through her clothing made her body cold, and Khansulu began to shiver. *Dau-apa*, exclaiming briefly in her sleep, mumbled, "My little stallion! Oh!"

She sighed heavily, in exhaustion. Dear *Dau-apa*! It seems she bore all her sorrows inside herself... She was remembering Bulysh, her little stallion. Poor mother!

Khansulu lay quietly, let *Dau-apa* get some sleep. But now, *Dau-apa* was already getting up, tying her jaulyk on her head and wiping her eyes. And the rain, it seemed, had stopped. Coughing hoarsely, *Dau-apa* called to her.

"Khansulu!"
"Yes!" Khansulu turned toward her, raising her head.
"We have to go. It's dawn."
Tying up the bundles, half-asleep, hoisting the children on their backs, they started off. The mud on the ground, and the wet grass made it hard to walk. As the sun rose, a large ravine could be seen to block their path. The city could be glimpsed beyond it.

"Look, daughter, there is water flowing along the bottom!" *Dau-apa* came to a halt.

That was something! There was really a lot of water at the bottom of the ravine, as if a little river was rushing along.

"Well, curses, we'll have to go around it!"

What could Khansulu say? She couldn't complain that she had a fever and her head ached. Reaching the dirty, clouded water, they laid their things over the scutch grass, lay down the bundles and took off their boots. The little boys, awakened, looked around the ravine curiously. *Dau-apa* stepped into the water first, her grandson on her back, and the *korzhun* and her boots in her hand.

"*Bismallah!*"

The stream was about 15 steps' wide. *Dau-apa* had already reached the middle of the stream. Khansulu, holding her boots in one hand, sidled into the murk. The icy water penetrated through to her bones. The pebbles along the bottom stabbed her feet. Khansulu heroically endured this trial. Grimacing, her teeth clenched, she kept going. Finally, the stream ended. Her feet, when she had climbed out on the loam of the shore didn't feel anything, they were so cold. Sitting down on the *korzhun*, Khansulu wiped her feet dry, wrapped them in bindings and then stuck them in her boots. Only once they were in armth did they come back to life.

On this side of the stream, there was even more of a muddy mess. Just try to get out of it, climbing up the side of the ravine, with the children and the load! *Dau-apa* didn't care about the mud, cursing, she climbed straight upwards. Holding her grandson, sometimes slipping down, she would immediately lean on her hand on the ground and get up. And each time, she cursed angrily:

"Oh, damn you!" She was already at the edge of the ravine. With all her heart, she cursed the mud.

Tripping, nearly falling herself, Khansulu decided to look for another way. She had noticed a fresh gully, gong along the flow of the river and turning upwards. Trying to step on clumps of grass, she tried to crawl through it. The child was on her back. *Dau-apa* had already scrambled to the top and was shouting loudly from above:

"Child, where are you?"

Khansulu, poor thing, was hunched over the very ground – her feet, slipping on the clay bottom, slipped backwards as she kept stubbornly trying to crawl upwards. At times she had to get on all fours. Sweat poured into her eyes, she could barely make out the bath, and sometimes had to stop from dizziness.

"Apa! Look!" exclaimed Tugelkhan, sitting on her back. Suddenly a flock of ravens fluttered up from behind the hill and landed on the ground to the side.

"What, sonny?" said Khansulu, wiping her wet face with her sleeve. She stood, weakly rocking on her legs.
"Over there! Over there! Look!"

Khansulu looked toward where her sun was pointing and went cold: from out of the clay hill, heaped carelessly, there were legs sticking out – several pairs. Khansulu froze. The night's rain storm had washed away the earth and exposed these legs. The bare feet stood out clearly, a row of thin children's legs and full women's legs, their calves exposed. It looked like they had buried people who had died from hunger here. Khansulu suddenly saw a small child's head with his eyes stuck closed…

"They died," said Tugelkhan. Only then Khansulu came to her senses. She was seized with trembling, her legs grew heavy and wouldn't heed her. She crawled on all fours. Damp with sweat, barely alive, she crawled out of the ravine. Her temples were pounding. Her soul was on the tip of her nose and was about to fly from her body...

Among the mulberry trees before the city was the mud wall. An old man in a lamb's wool *papakha* was driving lambs and goats out to pasture. He was apparently a Turkman; a cloak hung from his shoulders.

"*Apa*, my head is breaking," said Khansulu, pale and damp with sweat, unable to hold out any longer.

Dau-apa felt her forehead.

"*Oybay*! You are burning up!"

Dau-apa, leaving behind the children and things, hurried toward the old man in the papakha and cloak. Leaning on a stick, he had frozen like a statue among his lambs. After a little while, the old man in the *papakha*, taking their bundles, led the women and children to his home. Khansulu was in a haze. If only she could find shelter, she would immediately fall on the floor.

There was another little house in the yard, smaller in size. That was the summer kitchen. The old man led them there. There was a mat on the ground, and a runner placed on top of it. An old lady in a red kerchief opened the door.

"Perhaps the stove could be lit?" *Dau-apa* offered.

"*Khava, khava*[202], it must be lit," the old man agreed.

After lighting the stove, the house grew warm. *Dau-apa* poured hot water into a basin and put it before Khansulu.

"Put your legs in!" she said.

Khansulu stock her feet in the hot water and closed her eyes. It seemed she was in a dream. The warmth from her legs spread through her whole body. They were talking about something nearby, some of it she heard, some of it not. The old man covered her with a big fur coat.

---

[202]*Khava* is an exclamation of approval in the Turkmen language.

The old woman brought her a mug of melted sheep fat. *Dau-apa* rubbed the fat on Khansulu's legs up to her knees. Ogultech-*azhe*, as their host was called, brought some hot milk with butter and forced her to drink a whole pitcher. Whether it was from the heat of the stove, or from the hot milk, Khansulu suddenly broke out into a sweat.

"Lay down and don't move!" ordered *Dau-apa,* covering her with a warm blanket. She piled her clothing on top. "Lie still for a little while. And I'll go look for Shamurat."

Khansulu nodded. *Dau*-apa left her things behind and took the children with her. Khansulu lay near the stove. The tiny room, like a chicken coop, had a low ceiling carefully daubed with clay. Soon it was hot inside. Khansulu sweated through her clothes. Ogultech-*azhe* appeared and inquired:

"How are you feeling, little daughter?"

Kakabay-*ata*, the old man, asked the old woman from time how the guest was doing. She didn't understand everything in the Turkmen language, but she didn't need to – she sensed the kindness of the old couple through her soul. Not only the milk and the stove helped her. No less curative than the milk and the heat from the stove was the sympathy of her hosts, the light of their kindness.

Dau-apa returned only toward evening.

"Eh, child, we're lucky!" she said in a deep voice coming through the door. The huge man-like woman had to bend over hard to get through the door.

"I found Shamurat. The merchants at the bazaar know him, and where is house is, and his work. The children and I went directly to see him. We found him in, thank God! He was sitting on the *tor* in his home. And how are you doing here?"

Khansulu told her about the chicken soup which the old people had served her, and about their kind hearts. *Dau-apa* meanwhile continued:
"Shamurat turns out to be a clever fellow. Smart. He immediately took me to the NKVD. They registered everyone –

Pakhraddin, Syrga, and Balkiya, their names and ages. They said they would inform us if they found them. So thanks to Shamurat, consider that we have taken care of that matter. Then Shamurat, can you imagine, setting about finding a place for me. He brought me to his boarding house. He's the boss there, they say. Orphans live there, the children of steppe Kazakhs. He offered me a job there as a dishwasher in the cafeteria, and said meals would come with it. He also found a corner in the wood shed for me and my grandson, thanks to him. Let there be happiness through your children, I said, let the good that you have done me return to you from God... So that's how it is, child, and I was busy until evening, there was so much to do! We got lucky there. There are dead people in the city – God forbid! Corpses lay right out on the streets...

"So my parents didn't make it, it seems," Khansulu sadly stared up at the dark clay ceiling of the home.

"Eh, what can we do?" A heavy silence hung in the cramped room. *Dau-apa* also thought about the fate of Pakhraddin and Syrga. The women mourned. The chicken clucked outside. The boys were frolicking outside, apparently.

9

A helpless, curled-up body lay motionless under the agave – it was Syrga. She opened her eyes, and Pakhraddin was sitting up next to her. Syrga moved a little and groaned. Her thin fingers, like spikes of saxaul, were shaking, and began to grasp at something in the air. She was looking for something to eat. How many days they had not had even a crumb of bread in their mouths.... How many – Syrga no longer could say. She had long ago lost count of the days and nights. Time stretched out like tar, and was full of suffering. All of her hope was on Pakhraddin. She shouldn't suffer so, as long as Pakhraddin was alive and was next to her. How could she believe that the master of her hearth, her benefactor, knowing about everything on the earth, an experienced person, had gotten lost to such a degree that they kept going round and round the same dune? The Pakhraddin she knew should not have lost himself for no reason. Was he no longer the Pakhraddin he was, whom people revered as a leader?! What had happened? Why couldn't he get out of this dead end?

Syrga looked at the broad shoulders of her husband, who was sitting with his back to her, dejected, in a shirt that had once been white and a black *tyubeteyka*. His hair and beard had turned more gray. What could she extract from him, he was already so dejected and helpless?

"My falcon," Syrga called, still lying down.

Pakhraddin didn't respond. The wind fluttered his hair and beard, his shirt billowed out from his back. It was quiet, only the insects could be heard. It was noon, and burning hot, taking their breath away. Whirlwinds rolled along the desert in the distance.

Syrga stretched out her thin, helpless hand to her husband's back and touched it.

"We're lost...Yes?"

Pakhraddin didn't reply, only his face wrinkled up. He gazed at the distant horizon. From their dune, they could see half the world. And half the world was a hot desert, covered in haze, without a single person, as if everything had died out all around.

"The sky is clear today, and we'll go by the stars tonight," he said after a little while, not turning around, wishing to calm his wife.

If by the stars, well, then, by the stars. A note of hope had sounded in her husband's voice, and she roused the faith in her starting to extinguish. There had never been a time when Syrga had doubted his words. If Pakhraddin had said they would go by the stars, then they would go by the stars. And perhaps they would get somewhere. Maybe not all was lost...

Hypnotized, Pakhraddin followed the whirlwinds, twisting up into a column in the very center of the desert; now it would head off to the side. Oh, oh, it was as if poison had penetrated his soul... Pakhraddin signed sorrowfully: life was like a desert whirlwind. Like a dream, it had passed and disappeared. As if it were only yesterday.

It was as if it were all only yesterday: as a little boy, there he was mounting an unbroken foal for the first time; there he was as a *jigit*, saddling a bucking horse; there he was riding around the auls at night, where there were beautiful girls. It was as if it were all yesterday. Then he grew up, got smarter, and began to think of people's needs. He fought for justice. He began to take part in disputes; he was called a *biy* for his wisdom. He had not sought fame or rank. He had sought unity for the people. Eh, those were the times. That was the life, the nomad's life of the steppe-dweller, with its unchanging felt yurt; that life was gone. Everything had disappeared somewhere. Out of many words, one thought stuck: having reaching 60 years, his hair white, Pakhraddin did not think that his life would end, crushed with the bony hand of hunger. He didn't think his body would not be buried and would become food for the vultures and ravens. Oh, Creator, for what sins was he doomed to this dog's life? At the very worst, at least before death, God would let him understand the reason for such misfortune. Oh, why?!

The bitterest thoughts tormented Pakhraddin, whose soul was teetering on the edge between life and death. From time to time, he raised his head, and with a tired look gazed over the empty desert, languishing under the sun. He was looking for a traveler passing by, and he found none. The thick grove of rana changed to spills of sagebrush, endlessly green, and in the distance, lines of dunes flowed into the white-foamed feathergrass. His gaze slipped from this expanse and focused on the east. And he saw a sloped hill, plunged in haze that looked like it was a blue lake. And suddenly on that long hill like a hunched back, oh, Creator – could he believe his eyes or not? – he saw a Yurt. An ordinary, Kazakh yurt, round, with a cupola. The haze half covered it, but it was there, a yurt, large, white, with a cupola!

His heart beat faster.
"Baybishe!" he called, not able to hide his joy.
"Yes!" Syrga replied, not opening her eyes.
"Baybishe, there's a yurt there!"
"What?" Syrga opened her eyes, with effort.
"There's a yurt there! Oh, God, it's our yurt!"

Syrga quietly turned her head away.

Pakhraddin had already got to his feet, and was standing, swaying in place. He stretched his hand out, like a mad man, not tearing his eye from the horizon.

He made a step, then another. Then he stopped.

"There, on the ridge, do you see it? Our yurt…"
"Where?"

Syrga, raising her hand to her forehead, peered at the long ridge. She didn't see anything. The whole world was in a blue haze. The horizon swam and melted… Straightening, Pakhraddin swayed in place. He tried to take a step. His legs were like cotton, dead…

"Where is the yurt?" whispered Syrga. Pakhraddin didn't hear her. The wind billowed out the shirt on his back, and he walked along, barefoot. He staggered along like a blind man, his hands outstretched, as if grabbing at the air, and his gait was uncertain. He seemed like a big child to Syrga at that moment, who had just barely learned how to walk on the ground.

"My God, he'll fall…"

Syrga's heart trembled. But Pakhraddin did not fall. She prayed to the spirits of their ancestors.

"Oh, Barak-*ata*! Oh, Beket-*ata*! Help us…Support us…"

Pakhraddin gathered all his remaining strength so as not to fall and descended the sandy incline to the hollow. His knees, curse them, did not hold out. From the weight of his own body, he was forced to lean first to the right, then to the left. However, Pakhraddin, while he was still alive, would not give up. Although he would fall, he would not go back. He must reach the yurt, it was his last hope, the last light twinkling in his eyes. He would reach it, and say that there, on the dune, was Syrga, that she had to be helped. He would tell this, and die. Save Syrga, and die.

The hollow into which he was descending had an abundance of growth – steppe acacia, agave and feather grass. On the smooth sand there were trails left by beetles and lizards, and there were the prints of Pakhraddin's own bare feet. The heavy stillness of the desert, hanging for ages was only disturbed by the beating of Pakhraddin's heart and his ragged breathing. Could he on such legs raise the impossible weight of his body from this hollow? Sweat poured into his eyes, and everything grew dark before his eyes. That was likely from hunger.

There was fog in his head, his consciousness was strangely detached, as if everything was happening in a dream. His mouth was dry and his tongue was swollen. But some unknown force dragged him forward, forcing him to forget about all these tortures.

At the edge of the hollow he dropped to his knees and on all fours, clambered up the ridge. Straightening, he wiped the sweat pouring into his eyes with his hand, and his gaze feverishly sought the white yurt, hidden by the haze. The mirage, as blue as can be, shimmered ahead of him like a lake, but the yurt…there was no yurt. It had disappeared without a trace. It was as if the earth had swallowed it up. *Astafiralla,* had he hallucinated it? No! Pakhraddin couldn't believe his eyes. Another step…yet another…his legs barely held up…he climbed up on the hill and looked around. Oh, Creator! Had he become deprived of reason on a clear day? Where was the yurt? Where was the white yurt?

The hot dry ground lay hushed, like his impending fate. Harsh fate… Pakhraddin had been fooled by a mirage, it seemed. The mirage had misled him. He had been deceived himself and had led Syrga, the poor thing, astray as well. Oh, crazy man!

Pakhraddin turned around and looked back. He didn't see his wife on the dune under the agave bush. But it seemed she had raised her head and looked at him. He saw she lay down again. His eyes grew dark, his head swam, and Pakhraddin swayed. What was next, he didn't remember, how much time had passed, he didn't know.

Coming to his senses, he opened his eyes, and noticed that the burning sun had let up noticeably, and the shadows of the bushes had lengthened. His face burned. It turned out he had fallen on an ant hill, and the little beasts had bit him, and not spared him. His lips were swollen. Pakhraddin collected his thoughts, and sat down. His insides burned no less than his face, and he was thirsty. Thirst tortured him more than hunger. His eyes concentrated on the greenery. Beyond the agave bushes, among the rana, he saw some onion. It was a clump of wild onion. There was just one. Could he rise and dig it up, but how could he? He didn't try. He crawled to the only sprout on all fours. He didn't tear his eye off it. He was afraid it would turn out to be a mirage as well.

No, the sprout wasn't a mirage, his hand reached it. He couldn't wait, he didn't start pulling it up, he fell on it and bit it down

The Lonely Yurt • Smagul Yelubay

to the root. Oh, Creator! The bitter juice of the onion seemed to him the taste of life itself. Pakhraddin crawled further, looking greedily for grass. He wanted more onion, more. His hungry eyes sought onion. Thus, on all fours, he crawled to the acacia, with its bountiful leaves. Underneath it, in a space equal to what a yurt usually took up – oh, God, how great is your might! – he discovered that next to the thick undergrowth of rana were sprouts of onions. There was a lot here – his eyes couldn't take it all in. Generous was the Creator, when he wishes to restore! Pakhraddin lay down in the onion patch, and didn't pull them up. He moved about on all fours, pulling at the roots with his teeth and chewing them. He forgot about everything on earth. He wanted one thing: onion, luscious, oozing juice. To tear it, to chew and swallow again and again... Thus he "mowed down" the whole meadow.

When he came to himself, he saw that he was not eating onion, but rana, grass, such as the herds ate. It turned out he was grazing like the last animal...

His mouth was full of the bitter grass, and he spit it out. He helplessly hung his head, tears rolled on to the sand in large drops. How had he angered God, that he refused him the death of a worthy man? How? How?! Why should he, like the last dog, expire here to the delight of the crawling worms and ants?

Oh, world! You are mute! You are brutal! You are traitorously changeable, oh world! First you turn your face toward us, then your back. You threw the honorable pieces from the *dastarkhan* of life to the dogs like Bukhabay and Kuren... You set them on him as well. Worse, you gave them up to the destruction of the people. Did you want this?! Eh, you exhausted mules. You drove away simple people like mad dogs, they flew off like sparrows and wandered away. They grew poor and lose themselves. Did you want that, hypocritical world?! Why are you silent? Is your anger sated? Full? Oh, time, mad time! What else can be asked of you, a drop of water poured in vain, they ask! People's blood doesn't stop you! Little children's tears don't stop you! You will answer for this! Not a single one of your crimes will remain without answer, not a single one, do you understand! You will answer for everything! For everything! For everything!!! Pakhraddin gasped and fell down. He fell forward, and his face plunged into the ground. He wanted to shout all this, let even the desert Iye hear his despair[203], but only a whisper escaped from his dry throat.

He lay for a long time unconscious, and when he woke up, he began little by little to come to his senses. First he smelled the scent of young grass. He wanted to open his eyes but then realized he was lying face down. Thirst tormented him, his insides burned, and his tongue seemed stuck to the roof of his mouth. He tore off a blade of grass with his teeth.

And then it was as if the voice of Labakh-*akhun* carried to him.

"Did my prophecy not come to pass? The mountains will clash with the mountains, the sea will escape from its shores, fires will appear, one in the West and one in the East. Isa[204] will descend from the sky and Madi[205] will come out of the earth. The time of the highest revelation will come…the face of God will be revealed to the people. The Last Judgement over humankind will be made in the presence of the Lord… Did I not speak of this, my brother? Did I not speak? I have seen the End with my own eyes… But you, I see, are reluctant to part with this sinful world. You are chewing green grass. You thirst to live? Think again, overcome your wish. Reconcile yourself and close your eyes, and you will see before you the light – the gates of another world. You will rise above this temporal, deceitful world to eternity… There I hastened to you. To save myself from this hellish fire, I have turned away all charms of existence. Don't torture yourself, subordinate your tongue to the *kalima*[206]. Pray for the light to be revealed to you. Pray for God for forgiveness…

Pakhraddin, moving his lips, began to recite the prayer. He thought he had grown angry in vain, he had reproached the Almighty in vain for the sins of people. Now he prayed to the Savior for forgiveness.

With great difficulty, Pakhraddin raised his chest. His shoulders hurt. Gathering his last strength, he sat up. His head swam. The sky tilted. The earth rocked and swam to the side. He didn't wipe out his mouth, spattered with sand.

---

[203] Iye is the spirit of the land.

[204] Isa is Jesus Christ.

[205] Madi is the Shiite messiah of the Last Times.

[206] The *kalima* is the main prayer in Islam.

"Akhun-*aga,* what became of the people who have gone away?"

"Eh, some died, and some are alive, my brother…"

"And those who remained on Ustyurt?"

"Oh, cursed be their affairs… The youth are corrupted, they encroach on the peace of graves and anger the *aruakhs.* They thoughtlessly destroy the mosques, and draw God's anger on them. Hunger has descended on your people, people have scattered, they catch mice in the steppes… The young people do not answer for their sins, so all the punishment has fallen on them…Terrible times have ensued…

"Eh," Pakhraddin signed in despair. His head dropped to his chest. In sorrow, he folded almost in half. He was muttering something under his breath, talking to himself.

"Eh…the pikes have swum higher than the trees…[207] the sparrows run into the falcons, the chicks peck the eagle…now it is coming. What could be expected from a people led by Kuren and Sur Jekey…Jdakhay and Kozbagar… People grow up without a worthy ruler… Men grow up without worthy comrades… Evil has put down deep roots. Oh, Creator, why should I see this, why should I not become ashes? Why, oh God, did you lead me to such a day so as to suffer doubly? Why not just once, but twice do you want to lead me through death? To burn me alive in the hell fire? And that means you withhold death from me? It was not enough that Pakhraddin for 60 years burned in the hell fire? For sixty years, fighting with the devils and the werewolves in the form of human ignorance and evil…it's not enough? Oh, God, you should take me from this transitory world, and at least not sadden the end…

After a little while, Pakhraddin realized that he was crawling somewhere, and mumbling something. He stopped – his head was clouded and he had forgotten where he was crawling. Suddenly Pakhraddin remembered where he was crawling. Syrga was there, after all, on the dune, alive still, he was crawling to her, he needed to get to her.

There is a time in the desert when the sun sets and the shadows all around begin to flow into one solid darkness. Pakhraddin

---

[207] Incantation of poetry of the *akun-jyraus* about the signs of the Last Times.

crawled toward the dune. He had two onions in his pocket. He tried to keep his thoughts concentrated on Syrga. Perhaps…perhaps…she had died? And he…he…he wasn't with her before the end! A dog's lot, a dog's fate…

The sun had almost set, a wide fan of red rays turned the whole world crimson. With incredible efforts, he clambered up the dune. Syrga was lying on her back. Under the agave. She was not rustling. She had on a crimson silk dress, her favorite, and her head and neck were bound by the *jaulyk*.

"Syrga!" he exclaimed, taking the slender, withered hand of his wife.

Syrga was alive, her eyelashes jerked. She opened her eyes, and sorrow, inexpressible sorrow drowned in her dimming eyes. Her gaze was tired, lifeless, and after slipping over Pakhraddin's face, crawled downward. She stopped at his pocket. He put the onions, both of them, in her hand. He held her head. Syrga was weightless, as light as a tumbleweed.

She held the onion with slender, helpless fingers, but couldn't raise it to her mouth. Pakhraddin himself stuffed the onion into her mouth. Slowly, moaning quietly, Syrga began to chew it. Two sad, two desolate people drowned in the night on the nameless dune in the waterless desert…

The blue-black sky with silver stars, spreading its wings wide, descended on the expanse of the steppe salt marsh, resting from the heat of the day. The squint of the far-off horizon grew dark, the hollows grew clouded and the shadows lengthened in the ravines. A great silence, depressing the spirit, covered the world. Like a wolf, carefully, without a single sound, hiding behind the bushes, creeping closer and closer, it came up to the couple.

Right nearby, behind their backs, disturbing the primal silence ringing in their ears, a night-jar cried pathetically. Syrga, resting on Pakhraddin's lap, started. And Pakhraddin sensed a chill running up his spine. Syrga, rolling herself into a ball like a rabbit, whispered something to him. He leaned over, trying to hear.

He leaned even lower. Syrga was raising her eyelashes with effort. She was already gazing from far away, from a remote distance. As is from another world. It seemed she was trying to say with her eyes what was in her soul, but was not able to express with words. She was tormented, realizing that she wasn't managing this. How to know, she was saying goodbye, likely... With tears welling up in his eyes, Pakhraddin's gaze was fastened on his wife's greatly withered, elongated face. And Syrga, hanging by a thread, was begging something with her look. Her silent, unyielding gaze. She didn't want to part from him. He began to stroke the withered face of his wife with his broad palms. Tears flowed from the corner of her eye. A hot drop burned Pakhraddin's hand.

The night-jar called without ceasing – he sat lonely on the branch on the branch of a dwarf acacia. The moans of the little bird filled the desert expanse, they increased the sense of fear. They summoned trouble...

They lay, embraced on the dune, he and she. Below, underneath them, was the ground covered in darkness; above was the cupola of the sky, stitched with stars. The world was a big yurt, the cupola of which blended with the sky.

The night bird, flapping its wings, broke away from the branch and flew into the unknown...

1982- 1985 г.г.

Line translation by Lina Kosmukhamedova
Literary editing by Aslan Jaksylykov
Editing by Vladimir Kartsev

Ethnographic Glossary for Readers

Abay – a great Kazakh poet of the 19th century.
Aga – a suffix that denotes respect.
Agata-au
Aguzzi billakhim – the beginning of the leading surah or chapter of the Koran.

Akhal-Teke – Turkmen breed of horse.

Akhun – a high-ranking Muslim clergyman.

Aksakal – an elder

Aksiyek – an ancient children's game with bones, in which white bones are thrown in the dark to see who can be the first to find them.

 Al-ayat – the Arabic sign prayer, said by Muslims during an eclipse or other omen.

Alakay! – Hooray! (children's exclamation).

Altybkan – cradle.

Apa – mother.

Apanas – the Kazakh name for Afanasy Grinin, a former exile in Western Kazakhstan.

Arba – wagon.

Artel – collective farm.

Aruakh – the spirit of an ancestor.

Aruana – a one-humped camel.

Asan-Kaygy – legendary wise man and martyr of the 15th century who searched for a promised land for nomads.

Asaul – legendary hero of the 18th century.

Ash-shadan la-ilakhi il-alla – the beginning of the daily namaz or prayer.

Assalaumagaleykum – "Greetings!"

Astafiralla – "Oh, God!"

Astapyralla – "Oh, God!"

Atan – a gelded camel.

Attan – on your horses!

Arystybay – a corrupted form of the Russian word *arestovanny* which means arrested.

Aruakh – the spirit of ancestors

Aytys – a traditional oral poetry contest of poet improvisers.

Aul – a nomad village consisting of at least 15 yurts.

Aulnay – the aul leader

Auliye-Ata – the modern city of Taraz in Kazakhstan.

Ayat – part of a surah or chapter of the Koran.

Ayran – kefir.

Azamat – dashing young fellow – a Central Asian term which originated from the Arabic term for "greatness".

Azhe – grandmother

Baige – long-distance race

Barakeldy! – Good for you!

Barsa-Kelmes – you will go away and never return; a remote area.

Basmachi – bands of armed resistance to the Soviet government.

Batrak – a hired hand or servant.

Batyr – an epic warrior

Baursak – a form of fried bread

Bay – a wealthy man.

Baybishe – senior wife.

Bayga – a race.

Beket-Ata – a great sufi of the 18th century in Mangystau in western Kazakhstan.

Beskala – old name for modern Karakalpakstan at the lower reaches of the Amu Darya River.

Binayat – distorted form of the Russian word *vinovat* or "guilty".

Bismillah – Arabic prayer; "In the name of God".

Biy – arbitration judge

Blind goat – a version of blind man's buff.

Borik – a round cap.

Borzhoi – a distorted form of the Russian word *burzhuy* or "bourgeois".

Bukha – 1) respectful form of the name Bukhabay; 2) a bull.

Buyrshyn – a two-year-old camel.

Chalma – Muslim headgear.

Chapan – a type of robe

Chu – an expression to goad a donkey.

Contra – a counterrevolution.

Daret – Muslim ritual of ablutions before *namaz* or prayer.

Dastan – heroic epic.

Dastarkhan – a tablecloth; a symbol of unity and peace for Kazakhs.

Dombra – two-stringed musical instrument.

Djent – ground millet with butter and sugar.

Dau-apa – 1) nick-name; 2) *Dau* – great; *apa* – mother.

Daut – name of sacred *batyr* or warrior of the 18th century.

Duval – Central Asian fence made of mud and clay.

Enkebe – distortion of NKVD, acronym for Soviet People's Commissariat of Internal Affairs.

Eskendr – Alexander of Macedonia

GPU – Russian aconymn for *Gosudarstvennoye politupravleniye* or state political directorate, the precursor of the KGB or Committee for State Security.

Irimshik – a type of cheese.

Isa – Jesus Christ

Ishan – a learned clergyman.

Iye – a spirit, protector.

Janazhol – 1) Name of village; 2) literally *jana jol*, "new path."

Jarbay – the worst breed of camels

Jaulyk – white kerchief worn by married women.

Jaylyau – summer meadow for pasturing livestock.

Jaynamaz – prayer rug.

Jdeke – diminuitive form of the name Jdakhay.

Jem – the River Embe in western Kazakhstan.

Jeneshe, jeneshetay – wife of elder brother or sister-in-law

Jezde – husband of elder sister or brother-in-law

Jigit – dashing young fellow; good man; used for any young men.

Joneyt Khan – head of the Turkmen resistance to the Soviet government.

Jylybulak – 1. Name of spring; 2. Literally "warm spring".

Jyr – heroic epic tale.

Jyrau – poet, bard.

Jyrsh – poet, singer, improviser

Jideli Baysyn – promised land.

Kafir – unbeliever.

Kalima – Islam's main prayer.

Kalyn – the bride's price, which the groom's father would pay the bride's father.

Kallektep – a distorted form of the Russian word *kollektiv* or collective.

Kamcha – whip

Kampeske – distorted form of the Russia word *konfiskatsiya* or confiscation.

Kamzol – cinched women's upper garment; vest.

Karagannik – *Caragana arborescens*, Siberian peashrub

Karakum – the great desert of Turkmenistan (literally "black sand").

Kaynaga – husband's elder brother.

Kazan – very large, round cast-iron kettle

KazTsIK – the Kazakh Central Executive Committee of the Soviet government.

Kebenmat – distorted form of Russian swear words.

Kebezh – large wooden trunk

Kebis – type of women's shoes

Kelin – sister-in-law

Kerege – latticed assembled framework for a yurt

Ketmen – peasant tool for earth works.

Khava – expression of approval in the Turkmen language

Khordzhun – horse-rider's saddle bag.

Khorezm – old name for the foothills of the Amu Darya River

Kibitka – nomad tent.

Kizyak – dried dung used for fuel.

Kogen – sheep pen for milking sheep.

Koke – father.

Kokpar – a form of sport like polo on horses played with the carcass of a goat.

Kolkhoz – Soviet collective farm.

Komones – a distorted form of Communist.

Komsomol – Russian acronym for the Communist Youth Union.

Kotek – women's exclamation of fright.

Korpe – blanket.

Kumgan – iron pitcher.

Kumys – special drink made of mare's milk.

Kurban-aut - Eid al-Adh is the Muslim "festival of the sacrifice," commemorating Abraham's willingness to sacrifice his son, when God intervened through his angel Gabriel to tell him his sacrifice was already accepted.

Kurt – dried, hard cheese or curd.

Kydyr ata – patron saint of the traveler.

Kulshe – a flat roll baked on a skillet.

Kybla – the direction toward Mecca

Komones – distorted form of Russian world *kommunist* (communist).

Mazar – a construction over graves.

Madi – messiah of the Last Days.

Malakhay – a type of fur hat with ear flaps.

Maysok – ground millet with butter.

Mekelay – distorted form of Russian name Nikolai, as in Tsar Nikolai II.

Myrza – a gentleman.

Mullah – spiritual teacher.

Neke kiyu – wedding ceremony.

Nar – one-humped male camel.

Namaz – Muslim prayer.

Nasybay – a type of Central Asian chewing tobacco.

Neke kiyu – wedding ceremony.

Neshaua – distorted form of Russian word *nichego* or "it's nothing".

NKVD – Russian acronym for People's Commissariat of Internal Affairs, the predecessor of the KGB or Committee for State Security.

Ochag – iron tripod for a kettle.

Oripek – the Karakalpak women's *oripek* was a high helmet-like headdress with hanging fabric decorated by beads

Otau-yurt – a yurt for newlyweds; *otau* is the new family of husband and wife who separate from their own families.

Oybay! – exclamation of fear.

Oykhoy – exclamation of admiration

Oysylkara – patron saint of camels

Peri – mystical maidens like fairies.

Piyala – a wide Central Asian drinking cup.

Prezdem – distortion of Russian word *prezidiym* or presidium; governing body or chairs of a meeting.

Oybay! – exclamation of fear.

Rayon – regional government in the early Soviet era.

Rebelsener is how Shege pronounces the Russian word revolyutsioner or "revolutionary."

RIK – Russian acronym for District Executive Committee, the local Soviet government.

Saba – a sheepskin bag.

Sabetski blasty – distorted form of Russian phrase *Sovyetskiye vlasti* or Soviet government.

Saiga – antelope.

Samsa – triangular folded meat pie.

Saxaul – large desert treet; saxaul

Shalwa– a type of Central Asian pantaloons.

Shanyrak – round wooden frame for the upper cupola of the yurt.

Sharovar – baggy pants or pantaloons.

Shaytan arba – bicycle; lit. "devil's wagon".

Shchezhire – Kazakh geneology or family tree.

Shekpen – camel-hair robe

Sheshen – orator.

Shok! – on your knees! A command to a camel.

Sholp – silver bell at the end of girls' braids.

Shubat – fermented camel's milk.

Shygyr – special construction to extract water from a well.

Som – *Som* is a Turkic word for currency meaning "pure," as in gold. It was used to describe currency in the Soviet era in Central Asia.

Sultan Suleimen – Ottoman ruler Suleiman I, known as Suleiman the Magnicifant in the West.

Sulutay – a nick-name for Khansulu.

Sunduk – wooden trunk

Sur Jekey – nickname for Jekey. Sur = gray.

Suyunshi! – literally "sweets," a word said to demand a present for good news, a Kazakh custom.

Syrmak – a patterned Kazakh rug made of pieces of felt of different colors, with a mosaic inlaid on the surface.

Tabarysh – a distorted form of the Russian word *tovarishch* or comrade.

Talak – Muslim form of divorce.

Tandyr – round, adobe oven on the ground where items such as bread are cooked by slapping them on the sides.

Tekemet – felt floor coverings.

Terme – a poetic song of edification.

Tokal – the junior wife.

Tor – place of honor in a yurt.

Torba – rucksack

Torsyk – goatskin bag.

Tostagan – wooden mug.

Toy – wedding or holiday.

Toybastar – a song prelude to a holiday.

Tulpar – a winged horse in Central Asian myths akin to Pegasus.

Tunduk – opening at the top of a yurt's cupola or dome.

Tushpara – *manty* or type of meat patty.

Tutovnik – massive tree that grows in Central Asia

Tyubeteyka – Central Asian skull cap.

Tymak – a fur hat.

Tyyrlyk – external felt covering of a yurt.

Ugly – an affix which means "son of".

Uyezd – the administrative unit in the Tsarist era.

Yurta – yurt, the nomads' moveable dwelling

Uran – nom de guerre or nickname in war.

Uyk – the upper poles of the cupola on the yurt

Ustyurt – great plateau between the Caspian and Aral Seas.

Uzunkulak – rumors. Literally "long ears" in Kazakh.

Volost' – a regional division or district in the Tsarist era.

Zimovka – winter home dug out of the side of a hill.

Zindan – underground prison.